Acknowled

First, let me start out with the all of the readers that voiced support for my first novel, *The Jakarta Pandemic*. Your encouragement and interaction has been genuinely welcomed, and I encourage readers of *Black Flagged Alpha* to reach out with the same enthusiasm.

So, here we go...

To my wife, the first reader, who devoured the novel without taking a break. I figured this was a good sign, especially since this is not her typical genre. She actually beat me to the end and demanded that I finish the last few chapters. If you don't like the ending, you can blame her for rushing me.

To my writing group, who warmly welcomed me into their world and endured *Black Flagged Alpha*'s opening chapter violence way better than I expected. After reading several other submissions within the group, I thought I might need to tone down my material for our gatherings. I couldn't have been more mistaken. I've gained valuable insight about my own book and have been exposed to the talents of new writers in a wide spectrum of genres. Joe, thank you for introducing me to this group...and for your continuous critiques and suggestions throughout the process of writing both books.

To my pre-readers...most of whom volunteered, some of whom I didn't know before writing *The Jakarta Pandemic*. Bill, for the valuable guidance regarding the structure of the entire series, and for some spot on advice about Daniel Petrovich, *Black Flagged*'s main character; Trent, for once again going above and beyond the call of duty. I couldn't ask for more...a marked up manuscript and plot pacing suggestions for the book's big twist. As a D.C. resident, he also helped me to structure some of the local scenes. Finally, Bruce, for catching some really elusive typos and keeping the Portland references accurate.

To Felicia A. Sullivan, editor extraordinaire. I'll just thank you in advance for the professionalism you put into expertly editing *Black Flagged Alpha*, and the enthusiasm you'll bring to promoting it.

Finally, to Jeroen ten Berge, for knocking it out of the park with his cover design. He really captured the essence of the *Black Flagged* series with his bold vision.

Dedication

To my wife and children, who are my constant motivation, and graciously put up with the time and energy that I devote to writing.

Cast of Characters

Serbian Paramilitary

Srecko Hadzic - Leader of the "Panthers," a quasi-organized crime network and Serbian ultra-nationalist paramilitary group serving Slobodan Milosevic's regime

Pavle Hadzic - Hadzic's handicapped brother

Radovan Grahovac - Hadzic's "right-hand" man and chief-of-security

Marko Resja (aka Daniel Petrovich) - Midlevel soldier and undercover U.S. operative

Mirko Jovic - Leader of "White Eagles," a rival paramilitary group

Goran Lujic - "White Eagles" enforcer

FBI

Benjamin Shelby - Director

Executive Assistant Director Fred Carroll - National Security Branch

Associate Director Sandra Delgado - National Security Branch

Special Agent-in-Charge Ryan Sharpe - Task Force HYDRA's investigative leader

Special Agent Frank Mendoza - Sharpe's second in command

Special Agent Heather Olson - Primary investigator, HYDRA murders

Special Agent Dana O'Reilly - Lead data analyst, HYDRA

Special Agent Justin Edwards - Lead investigator for Mohammed Ghani murder scene

Special Agent Keith Weber - Communications section-head, HYDRA

Special Agent Gregory Carlisle - Lead Interrogator, HYDRA murders

CIA
Audra Bauer - Director, Counterterrorism Center, National Clandestine Service

Karl Berg - Assistant director, Counterterrorism Center, National Clandestine Service

Randy Keller - CIA liaison to Task Force HYDRA

Black Flag Operatives
Daniel Petrovich - Former Black Flag operative

General Terrence Sanderson - Created original Black Flag program

James Parker - Sanderson's "right-hand" man

Colonel Richard Farrington - Compartmentalized Information Section (CIS), Pentagon

Jeffrey Munoz - Suspect in the shooting of Umar Salah

Others
Jessica Petrovich - Daniel Petrovich's wife

Julio Mendez - Janitorial custodian, Pentagon

Darryl Jackson - Executive, Brown River Security Corporation

Jeremy Cummings - Team leader, Brown River Security Corporation

Derren McKie - National Security Agency employee and former Black Flag operative

BLACK FLAGGED:

"Classification given to an agent or intelligence officer who is to be interrogated and summarily killed if apprehended."

BLACK OUT

2:35 p.m.
A few miles outside of Vizic, Serbia

Marko Resja peered cautiously over the top of the jagged stone wall, scanning the lodge's covered porch with powerful binoculars. Through the driving downpour, he counted four men. *Perfect.* With the entire external security team in one place, approaching unseen shouldn't be a problem.

He kneeled on the spongy, pine-needle-covered ground behind one of the sharp granite chunks that formed part of the estate's perimeter wall. Created by haphazardly dumping large uneven rocks around the lodge on all sides, the utilitarian border marked the divide between hastily cleared land and the impenetrable Fruska Gora National Forest.

Marko had arrived at the perimeter an hour earlier, hampered by the same relentless rainfall that had kept NATO aircraft at bay for more than a week. Concealed in the dense pine foliage behind the jagged rock barrier, the distant roar of high-altitude jets rumbled through the dark clouds. NATO pilots had started testing Belgrade's air defense network from a safe distance, impatient for the weather to clear over the northern Balkan Peninsula.

He stared at the wavering pine forest for a moment, before turning his full attention to the lodge. The two-story, modern, stone and beam structure looked sturdy enough to withstand an artillery attack. A similarly constructed, one-story garage stood between him and the house, partially obscuring his view of the main structure.

Srecko Hadzic, ruthless leader of the paramilitary Serbian Panther crime syndicate, had built the lodge for the sole purpose of hiding his brother, Pavle. Rumors of NATO commando teams operating within Serbian borders had taken root among upper-level leadership, raising paranoia to near panic levels, and Hadzic almost feared Pavle's capture more than his own at this point.

Marko took one more look over the top of the wall, just to make sure all four men were still on the porch. The bright orange glow of cigarettes and shifting of shadows under the roof confirmed his assessment. He didn't expect any of them to emerge from their cozy shelter, but he had to keep in mind that these men were all current or former Serbian Special Operations types. Despite the overindulgences often associated with paramilitary security details, all of these men had been hand-picked for their competence. Three more had accompanied Radovan Grahovac, Hadzic's chief of security, into the lodge to meet with Pavle.

They had arrived dressed in civilian clothes, which suggested that the crew might head north for a night of prostitutes and drinking along the banks of the Danube River in Novi Sad. Despite their casual dress, however, each man carried a compact assault rifle and a pistol. Under normal circumstances, this was not a crew he would mess with. Today, Marko was willing to make a notable exception.

Satisfied that all four men were still in the same place, he picked up a long, black duffel bag and ran to a position along the wall that was completely obscured from the porch by the garage. Based on his observations from two previous reconnaissance trips, he knew that Radovan didn't stay more than ten minutes. There was little time to waste.

From his new vantage point, he glanced over the wall and saw one of two dark blue Range Rovers that had arrived at Pavle's hideaway a few minutes ago, depositing Radovan and his heavily-armed security detail. The other Range Rover was parked several meters behind the first, hidden from his view by the garage.

Marko kneeled low and wrestled a Serbian-made assault rifle out of the waterproof bag, extending the weapon's foldable shoulder stock. Placing the weapon against the rocks, he reached back into the bag for one of two detachable ammunition drums and swiftly attached it to the weapon. The second seventy-five round drum disappeared in his hip satchel.

Beyond the high-capacity ammunition drums, he carried four thirty-round magazines in quick-access pouches on his combat vest—nestled among four stun grenades. He screwed a one-foot long suppressor to the rifle's threaded barrel and chambered a round—glancing over the wall to make sure Radovan hadn't emerged from the house. *Clear.* The final item he removed from the bag was a gray, aluminum, ice-climbing axe, which he attached low on the side of his vest. Marko was ready.

Gripping the rifle with his left hand, he pushed off one of the sturdier looking rocks with his other hand and vaulted the rock wall. Splashing down in ankle-high water Marko slogged through the thick mud to reach the left corner of the garage, where he could keep a closer eye on the security detail.

The rain intensified for a minute, pummeling him with sheets of rain. Despite having been exposed to the frigid early spring downpour for nearly two hours, he didn't feel cold. Under his paramilitary camouflage outfit, Marko wore an insulated, waterproof jumpsuit. Certainly not standard issue for elite Serbian commandos, or even the most pampered members of Hadzic's paramilitary forces. Nothing in Marko's equipment load-out was standard paramilitary issue. General Sanderson had no intention of taking any chances with spotty gear. Not today.

A car door slammed, and Marko peeked around the corner of the garage. One of the men threw a lit cigarette into the front yard, while another man talked excitedly into a small handheld radio. *Showtime.*

Marko released the weapon's safety and pulled a rain-soaked black ski mask over his face. Peering cautiously around the corner, he watched the men scramble off the porch. When they vanished from sight, he moved rapidly down the unobserved side of the garage to the front corner and risked another look. As expected, the lead SUV was already loaded with Radovan and the three men who had accompanied him into the lodge. The four commandos from the porch jogged toward the rear SUV.

Engaging a trance-like mindset, he stepped into the open and aimed at the last man in the group. With the weapon's reflex sight centered on the man's upper back, he pulled the trigger and discharged a short burst. The automatic rifle bucked hard against his shoulder, but he kept the muzzle rise under control and repeated the process to eliminate the remaining guards.

** **

Radovan sat impatiently in the front passenger seat of his Range Rover, listening to the rain hammering the truck's thick metal roof. He hated these trips and absolutely despised handing their hard-earned cash over to Hadzic's "gang-banger worshiping" brother, Pavle. Radovan was a committed ultra-nationalist and had no tolerance for the newly arrived

American "gangsta" music that had penetrated the Belgrade club scene. When Radovan hit the town, which he frequently did, Belgrade went hip-hop free. Nobody risked incurring the security chief's wrath.

"Why the fuck are we not out of here already?" he yelled at the rain-blurred windshield.

He turned his head and leaned over the center console to check on the rear security team. Through the wide back window of the Range Rover's gate, he noted a figure sliding down the right side of the rear SUV, but never had a chance to form much more of an impression about the situation. Several steel-jacketed bullets ripped through the commando seated behind him, showering the cabin in aerosolized gore.

Radovan was immediately hit by two of the bullets that passed unhindered through the guard's throat. One struck him in the upper left shoulder, where it stayed, and the other ricocheted off the metal headrest post and grazed the right side of his neck. The windshield in front of Radovan crumbled as he instinctively grabbed for the short-barreled assault rifle that rested between his right leg and the door. Before his hand completed the twelve-inch journey, the front passenger door erupted in a fusillade of torn plastic, metal fragments, and safety glass. His hand never touched the rifle.

**

Against all odds, the driver, Jorji, survived the seemingly endless hail of bullets. He was hit several times, but knew that he was not critically wounded. When the first bullets passed through the car, Jorji twisted his body to the right, pressing down on the center console, trying to present the lowest possible target to his attackers. This was not the first time he had been attacked in a vehicle, and his previous experience kept him alive a little longer than the rest of the Range Rover's occupants.

Several bullets pierced the back of his seat and tore into the top left side of his body, shredding muscle and tendon from his left hip all the way up to his shoulder. The extensive muscle damage along his entire left side kept him locked in place over the center console, with his face nearly buried in Radovan's lap. No matter how hard he tried, he could not sit up, which was another reason that he was still alive.

**

Marko dropped to the soaked gravel near the front left tire of the Range Rover and rolled over onto his left side, which gave him easy access to the hip satchel containing the second ammunition drum. The gun's barrel sizzled as the rain struck the dangerously overheated metal. A hundred thoughts and stimuli flashed through his brain, which were immediately prioritized and processed for his use. His trance reduced useless distractions like emotion, hesitation or fear, and enhanced his focus on the highly-specialized skills required to survive.

"Reload weapon" was at the very top of the list. His weapon wasn't empty, but he knew that seventy-five rounds didn't last very long at the rate he had fired. In the flash of a synapse, "driver still alive" was also broadcasted, and his eyes narrowed. He had fired long bursts into each passenger as he moved counterclockwise around the SUV. After targeting the rear right guard and Radovan, he fired a lengthy burst at the driver through the rear right door window. Marko knew the bullets had passed through the seat and connected with the driver, but the man's demise was not conclusive, and he knew it.

He detached the drum magazine and threw it out of the way. The second drum was out of the satchel and attached to the light machine gun in a blur of his hands. Marko raised his body into a low crouch, keeping well below the window, and fired a sustained burst through the center of the front driver door.

**

The silence felt like an eternity to Jorji, but he knew his lifespan was now measured in seconds, unless he could take the offensive. Jorji lifted his head up far enough out of Radovan's blood-soaked lap to catch sight of the assault rifle jammed against the door by Radovan's leg. Jorji knew this was his only hope. His only weapon, a small semi-automatic pistol, was jammed under his right armpit in a concealed holster, and he couldn't lift his body to free it. Not that it would have mattered if he could. Jorji was left handed, and a bullet had passed through the back of his left elbow, rendering his arm useless. He strained to slide his right arm free, and his hand managed to reach the rifle just as several bullets punctured the driver door and put an end to any hope that he might survive.

**

Peering through the shattered driver's side window, Marko saw a figure slumped over Radovan's lap. The man was shredded and bloodied, but his death was still far from conclusive. A quick trigger pull removed any doubt that Radovan's security team was finished.

He backed against the house and absorbed the scene. The carnage resembled a well-executed, coordinated ambush. Riddled by bullets on all four sides, most of the vehicle's safety glass lay shattered on the packed gravel. Since he'd fired from nearly every angle around the car, the pattern of 5.45mm shell casings suggested multiple attackers.

Even better, two of the guards from the rear SUV had fallen on top of each other. He'd stuff one of them into the trunk of the luxury Mercedes in the garage and dump the car into one of the lakes near Belgrade. The absence of a junior member of Radovan's inner sanctum would lead Hadzic to suspect that this was an inside job.

Marko decided to skip any further house surveillance. He had done a mixed job of keeping the noise level down, and didn't want to waste time if Pavle's bodyguards had been alerted.

The suppressor had performed as advertised, ensuring that the automatic weapon would not draw anyone's attention over the rainstorm, but the Range Rover had been a different story. He was not at all satisfied with the noise created by the bullets that struck the SUV's heavy steel frame. To Marko, it had sounded like multiple, low speed fender benders.

He tried the doorknob, hoping for a break, but it didn't turn. Wasting no time, Marko reached into his hip satchel and removed an object that resembled a small plastic explosive charge. He pressed it firmly between the doorknob and door trim, before pulling a small plastic device out of a pouch on his vest and sliding it upward along the door from the first small charge. The device's LED turned green about two feet above the doorknob, where he placed a second charge from his vest against the trim. With the two charges in place, Marko pulled a small cotter pin on each of the homemade devices and pressed himself flush against the stone side of the lodge.

In rapid succession, each device ignited and burned intensely for several seconds. The thermite packages created very little noise, but generated an incredible amount of smoke—usually on both sides of the door. He pushed firmly on the heavy oak door, which gave way now that the locks had melted. Holding his breath, Marko stepped into the house. The caustic smoke obscured his vision and burned his eyes momentarily, but he immediately recognized that he was on a small landing. Several stairs led up into the house through an enclosed stairwell that separated the entrance from the main house, keeping him out of sight.

A hardcore rap song thumped in the background, easing any fears that his attack had been compromised. A Serbian-accented "yeah, motherfucka!" confirmed they were too preoccupied to have noticed his entry.

He eased up the stairs and peeked around the corner. Floor to ceiling windows, split by a dark gray slate fireplace and chimney, rose into the timber-framed ceiling. Pavle's men gathered around a rustic, dark wooden coffee table, which was centered on the fireplace and littered with a pile mixed currency. A dimmed chandelier hung low over the coffee table, attached to the ceiling by a thick, black chain.

Marko spotted Pavle immediately. Paralyzed from the waist down, Hadzic's brother was confined to a wheelchair. Facing the fireplace, both of Pavle's outstretched arms embraced the deep hip-hop beat with a slow, synchronized wave—each hand holding a thick stack of American bills.

He assessed the bodyguards. A large, stocky man in a black turtleneck sweater and brown jacket stood in front of Pavle, bouncing up and down completely out of rhythm. The second bodyguard sat on a dark, rich leather couch to the left of the table, rolling what Marko assumed to be a joint. He didn't detect any obvious weapons.

Ready to make his move, he took the time to touch the razor-sharp edges on both the front and back of the climbing axe. The axe would provoke the final outrage. The inevitable civil war between two of Slobodan Milosevic's largest paramilitary groups would tear Belgrade apart from the inside, giving Marko the cover he needed to tie up the rest of his loose ends. For the first time in several years, he felt hopeful.

His time in this shithole of a region had reached an end, and he intended to walk away with a little more than just the satisfaction of a job well done. Pavle held the key to his brother's vast criminal fortune, which would soon belong to the United States government—minus a finder's fee.

BACK IN BLACK

May 25, 2005

Chapter One

Daniel sat at a brushed metal, modernist workstation in his expanded cubicle, staring blankly at a sleek flat-screen monitor. An MBA from Boston University's School of Management had earned him a little extra space in one of the outer cubicles and a partial view of the tall pine trees behind the building's rear parking lot. His one-hundred-square-foot home at Zenith Semiconductor was as close to the "corner office" as modern workplace design theory would allow, and he had fellow MBAs like himself to thank for it. At least his position entitled him to a frosted glass "privacy door," which he could slide shut to emphasize his desire to remain undisturbed.

The door had been closed for fifteen minutes, and he'd already counted at least five lingering shadows behind the translucent glass. Daniel continued to gaze at the market analysis presentation on the screen, unmotivated to continue. His indoor soccer team pulled the late slot last night, and he still hadn't recovered from the three-hour sleep deficit. The phone rang.

"I almost escaped," he muttered, donning his headset and pressing a button on the gray desk phone. "Daniel Petrovich."

"Daniel, it's Sandy. I have a call for you from Azore Market Solutions."

"Do you know who it is?" Daniel said, surprised to be hearing from Azore so soon.

"They didn't say," Sandy said, one of the junior assistants assigned to the marketing department. "Just that they needed to talk with you immediately."

He had contracted with Azore Market Solutions to provide raw data for an overseas regional marketing analysis, but didn't expect to hear from them for another month. Daniel usually conducted business with them via e-mail, so he was slightly concerned about the call. If Azore couldn't deliver the data, he'd have to start the process from scratch, which would put

Zenith's South American market expansion efforts behind schedule, and his job at risk.

"All right. Put whoever it is through. And Sandy…would you please ask who's on the line next time? I don't know if I'm talking to the CEO or a janitor," he lamented.

"I don't think it's the janitor, but I'm not sure. Do you want me to ask who it is before I put the call through?"

"No, don't worry about it this time," he said, pressing the button to connect the call.

"Daniel Petrovich."

"Oh, I'm sorry. I was hoping to reach Marko Resja," the male voice said, betraying no emotion.

His brain switched over to a long dormant mode of operation, and he ceased to function as Zenith Semiconductor's Emerging Markets' Analytical Lead. Daniel stood up slowly, glancing over the vast sea of cubicle tops.

"I'm not in the building, so you can sit back down," the voice said.

Daniel remained standing and opened his cubicle door.

"Are you sitting?"

"I am," Petrovich replied.

"That's better. Do I have your attention?" the voice said, confirming that Daniel was not under direct surveillance.

"You never lost it," he said, activating the "wander" function of his headset.

As long as he remained on the third floor of Building A, his headset would function without a hard-wire connection, which might give him a slight head start against whatever was coming his way. He opened the top drawer of his desk, pocketed his keys and cell phone, and started to walk toward the nearest staircase.

"The general has a proposal for you," the voice said.

"I'll be sure to look him up the next time I'm the D.C. area," Daniel said, approaching the door to the stairwell.

"This proposal is extremely time sensitive."

He wrapped his hands around the staircase door handle. "I don't really care."

"He thought you might say that. He told me to tell you that 'he knows everything.'"

"I'm still not impressed," Petrovich said.

"Zorana Zekulic," the voice uttered.

Daniel paused for a few seconds. Sanderson hadn't bothered him much since they parted ways. A Christmas card one year, a birthday card the next. Just a friendly reminder that the general was still out there. Using Zorana's name was more than a nudge. It was more like poking him with a knife.

"Where do we meet?"

"Starbucks. A few blocks from your building. Five minutes."

"No good. I'm a regular there. I'll meet you in Designer Grinds at Northgate Plaza," Daniel countered.

"Where is that?" the voice said.

"Figure it out," Daniel said and disconnected the call.

He stuffed the headset in a trash bin by the door and sprinted down three flights of stairs, opening the door to the lobby and walking briskly toward the rear security station.

"No need to get up, Harry. I'm just running a quick errand at Target before I forget. I have a pick-up soccer game after work, and if I don't do this now, it'll never get done."

The guard eased back into his chair, barely turning his head far enough to watch Daniel move swiftly through the sliding door. Daniel strained to keep from breaking into a full sprint toward his BMW 545i sedan, which sat three rows deep in the lot. Though he was out of the security guard's sight line, five levels of windows faced the back lot, and the sight of anyone sprinting in the parking lot was sure to attract the wrong kind of attention—especially in the middle of the afternoon.

He fished a ring of keys out of his front pocket and pressed the ignition button on his key fob. The sedan's powerful 325 HP engine roared to life and settled into a low hum. Seconds later, Daniel screeched out of the parking lot, headed for the Turnpike entrance.

**

James Parker tossed the burner cell phone onto the passenger seat and began to program the dashboard-mounted GPS system as if his life depended on it—which it did. After pushing several buttons, he located the Designer Grinds store in Northgate and activated the navigator, which displayed the shortest, but not the quickest, route to the coffee shop. He pulled his Grand Cherokee out of the parking lot and wove through traffic on his way to Congress Street.

Roughly one minute after speeding out of the parking lot, his SUV passed the entrance to the Zenith Semiconductor Industrial Complex. A few weeks earlier he might have spotted Daniel in the building's parking lot, but May had unleashed thick rows of brilliant yellow Forsythia bushes, which completely obscured his view of the complex's ground level. He pressed on the accelerator and shot toward Maine Mall Road. The GPS unit announced he would "arrive at his destination in thirteen minutes."

**

Daniel arrived at the Northgate center ten minutes later and parked his car in the middle of a crowded parking lot to the far right of the grocery store that anchored the shopping complex. Scanning every direction, he couldn't conceptualize any way for his adversary to spot the car from the three approaches to Designer Grinds. Reaching into the back seat, he grabbed a dark blue, zippered, nylon jacket and a dirty Red Sox ball cap. A compact Sig Sauer pistol materialized from a concealed holster under the driver's seat and disappeared into the rear belt line of his dark brown wool pants. Before jogging across the parking lot, he donned the jacket to completely conceal the pistol.

He passed the grocery store's automated entrance and glanced around, spotting three open parking spaces in front the coffee shop. A dozen additional spaces sat unoccupied among the three rows of parking available further back from the storefronts. Daniel didn't have much time to position himself, so he trusted his instincts and walked briskly into the field of cars directly across from Designer Grinds.

Thousands of possibilities, variables, and scenarios raced through his head, as he searched for an unlocked car in the third row away from Designer Grinds. After checking several vehicles, he found an unlocked sedan and slipped into the back seat.

**

Parker veered his SUV left at the split of Auburn Street and Washington Avenue, and spotted the traffic signal that marked the front entrance to the Northgate shopping center. His stomach was knotted, and he tried for the hundredth time since arriving in Portland to stop grinding his teeth. He'd seen enough of the Petrovich file to warrant an ulcer.

He arrived at the red light and scanned the parking lot in front of the coffee shop for a BMW, though he was reasonably certain that he'd beaten Petrovich to the shopping center. His only goal had been to get into Designer Grinds alive, where, in front of witnesses, Parker would at least have a brief opportunity to explain that he knew nothing about Zorana Zekulic. The general had made it clear that this would be the most pressing business on the table, and that his survival would depend on it.

The light turned green, and Parker sat for a few seconds, momentarily paralyzed. A horn jarred him back to reality, and he pulled into the plaza, cruising slowly while he searched for the BMW.

**

Daniel spotted the Cherokee immediately thanks to an impatient Mainer. Three short horn blasts drew his attention to the front entrance of the parking lot, where even the most unobservant field agent could spot Parker craning his neck in every direction as he cruised past the grocery store entrance.

He peeked through the Accord's headrest and watched the Cherokee drive past the coffee shop and turn into the second row of cars. As the SUV headed in his direction, one row away, Daniel slid himself across the back seat and unlocked the passenger door. Hand on the door handle; he waited for the Cherokee to park.

The driver guided the SUV into a parking space two rows back from the entrance to Designer Grinds, and Daniel slid out of the back seat of the sedan. Staying low, he sprinted from one row of cars to the next, centering on the back of the Cherokee to avoid detection in either of the Cherokee's side mirrors. When the doors unlocked, Daniel opened the door and pressed the barrel of his pistol to the back of the man's head.

"Hands up on the dashboard above the radio. Do not turn your head. Understood?"

Daniel closed the rear driver car door, settling into the back seat and easing the pistol back from his head. The man nodded once and carefully placed his hands palms down on the dashboard.

"I'll ask you some questions. If I don't like the answers, all the general's horses and all the general's men, won't be able put you back together again. Understood?" Daniel said, and the man nodded once more.

"I assume you've read some kind of file regarding my previous line of work?"

"Yes, but I don't know anything about the name I mentioned earlier."

"Which name?" Daniel said, curious if he'd repeat it.

"Zorana. The general told me to use this name if I didn't think you would meet with me."

"Well, the general must not like you very much, because he knows damn well I won't entertain any of his proposals…and giving you that name was a potential death sentence. How well do you know General Sanderson?"

"I've been working directly under General Sanderson for two years."

"He's not a general any more. Pissed on too many people. Important people. How did you get stuck with him?"

"We met in Afghanistan before he retired," he said.

"Retired? Doesn't sound like he retired."

"He didn't. That's why I'm here."

"What do you know about Zorana Zekulic?" Daniel whispered and pushed the pistol into the base of his skull.

The man cleared his throat. "Absolutely nothing beyond the name. The general stressed to me that the first thing I needed to clear up with you is the fact that I know nothing about Zorana. He said my life depended on it."

"And you still showed up?" Daniel said, pulling the pistol back, but keeping it aimed at the back of Parker's seat.

"I didn't really have much of a choice."

"That's the problem with General Sanderson. He doesn't like for any of his people to get comfortable with the concept of free will, which is why we parted ways long ago. I'm done with your general, Mr…?"

"Parker. James Parker. Can we talk about this over some coffee? The mission is critically important to our work and national security. You might change your mind."

"I'll listen, but I need you to know that I won't hesitate to add your brains to the artwork on the walls. Are you armed?"

"I have a small folding knife in my right front pocket."

"I expect to hear that knife clatter on the pavement as soon as we start walking. You can pick it up later, if it's still there. Coffee's on you. Fair?"

"Fair," Parker said, clearly relieved.

A few minutes later, Parker placed two coffees on the table and took a seat across from Daniel, who sat against the back wall, one hand hidden under the table. Daniel examined him for a few seconds as he reached out for his drink. Parker had deep blue eyes and thick, black hair, closely cropped for a neat, trimmed impression. Not short enough to immediately betray a military background, but clearly the preferred look for someone not completely comfortable with civilian life. His outfit matched the haircut: khakis, casual blue dress shirt with no tie, and a dark blue blazer. Business casual for the ex-military officer. Petrovich suspected that he had been a senior army captain or possibly a major. He looked lean and slightly muscular.

"Special Forces in Afghanistan?" Daniel said and took a sip of steaming hot cappuccino.

"Navy SEAL platoon commander. I met General Sanderson at Forward Operating Base (FOB) Anaconda in 2004. He showed a lot of interest in the spec ops guys operating out of the Korangal Valley. That was before we started sticking outposts up there. Fucking Wild West. We stayed in touch, and he offered me a job as a security consultant when I got out."

"So what's in the bag, Mr. Navy SEAL?"

"Mission specifics. Untraceable weapon," he responded, glancing around secretively as he spoke.

Daniel kept control of the tension evoked by the sudden realization that Parker had lied about being armed, and only slightly tightened his grip on the pistol hidden under the table.

"I thought I said no weapons," Petrovich said.

"The case is locked, and I don't have the combination. I have a phone number for you to call, which is programmed to respond to your cell phone number. You get the combo from a recording. I know who the target is and all of the mission details, but Sanderson did not want me to have access to the contents of the briefcase. I don't ask questions."

"What's the phone number?" Petrovich said, removing his cell phone from one of the inside pockets of his jacket.

"You're going to open the case here?" Parker asked.

Petrovich leaned across and whispered, "You're goddamn right I am. I don't need this case exploding inside my car...and if I don't like the contents, I don't want to make another trip to return it. The number, please."

Parker recited the number as Daniel dialed. The call lasted less than thirty seconds before Daniel abruptly snapped the phone closed. He leaned over the left side of the table to look at the nylon case.

"May I?" Daniel said.

"The case is yours."

Daniel lifted the case off the floor and placed it in his lap, backing his chair up flush against the wall. He still wanted some room to maneuver, just in case this elaborate set-up was a trap, though he felt comfortable enough about Parker. The guy was far from a trained agent or contract killer. Daniel suspected that he was exactly what he claimed to be.

He dialed the four-digit combination and flipped open the top of the case, finding a Ziploc bag enclosed pistol in the padded compartment normally reserved for a laptop computer. He found two sealed documents in the other side of the case and removed them. One was a thick packet, and the other was a small envelope.

"Do you have to look at this here?" Parker said, glancing nervously over his shoulder at two women who occupied brown leather chairs several tables away.

"You need to relax. I didn't drag the gun out, did I?"

Parker didn't look relieved by his response and continued to look over his shoulder while Daniel unsealed the packet. Daniel extracted the contents and placed them on the table next to his coffee. The top item was a picture.

Petrovich opened and read the contents of the envelope and replaced the letter. He put the envelope back into the briefcase and took the picture off the table. Staring at the picture, he asked, "I suppose this gentleman needs to take a permanent vacation?"

"Something like that. His name is…"

"I don't need to know his name. I assume this packet contains all of the information I'll need? Places of business, hours of work, gym, favorite bars…though I get the feeling this guy might not partake in the consumption of alcohol or bacon."

For the first time since Daniel placed a gun against his head, Parker cracked a smile.

"Ah, a sense of humor. I don't think the general likes those either," Daniel said.

"So, I'll track this guy down and find an opportunity, but I need to talk to your general personally, right now, or this whole thing is off."

"The general isn't available to talk right now. He went offline right before I arrived in Portland."

"Get him on the phone, or you're going to have to kill this guy yourself. I don't think this kind of work would suit you."

"I'll try, but I'm serious about…"

Daniel's cell phone interrupted Parker's sentence. *Unknown number.*

"Daniel Petrovich," he answered dryly, now pretty sure he was under surveillance. *Another deception by Parker.*

"Danny! It's been a while. Great to hear your voice."

"Well, you can play it back all day and night, I suppose," Daniel said.

"Newest technology on the streets. Turned Parker's cell phone into a bug without him knowing," General Sanderson said.

"Congratulations. I'm glad to know you didn't spend the Hadzic trust fund all in one place," Daniel said.

"I need you in on this operation, Daniel. We're sending a strong message to the Muslim fundamentalist movement here at home…"

"Are you fucking kidding me? Save that bullshit for the rest of your zealots. I'll take a look at the file. If I agree to do this…I don't want to hear from you again. Ever. Is that clear?"

"If that's what you want."

"It's what I always wanted, but here we are. I'll need a few days for reconnaissance…"

"I need this done tonight. Our timeline is set in stone," the general said.

Parker shifted in his seat uncomfortably, as if he sensed an immediate threat to his existence, which couldn't have been further from the truth. Daniel's brain worked like a perfect machine when under pressure, and his processors analyzed hundreds of solutions to his current dilemma within seconds. Killing Parker in a suburban Designer Grinds never passed through Daniel's neural connections. Petrovich knew that the general had the upper hand and that all paths led to the completion of the task outlined in the briefcase. It had been no accident that Parker arrived only hours before the mission's deadline.

"I'm done after this. You understand that, right?"

"I understand. I apologize for pulling out the trump card—"

"Apologies never suited you, General, and I don't believe it for one fucking second," Daniel said, shaking his head slowly.

"Whether you believe it or not, your actions will make a huge contribution to the war on terror, and—"

"Save the elevator speech for Parker. I have a long afternoon ahead of me. My slate is clean."

"Clean," General Sanderson said.

"I'm curious, how long have you known about her?"

"Do you remember one of the first things I told your training class? There's no such thing as a coincidence," Sanderson said and disconnected the call.

Petrovich set the phone down on the target dossier and glanced up at Parker. The former special operations soldier looked tense and ready to make a bad decision.

"Parker, chill out and drink your coffee. You're making me nervous. I need a contact number in case I run into unforeseen circumstances," he said.

"You'll find instructions for that in the file. I'll need to collect the dossier and the gun when you're finished," he replied.

"I'll leave it all at the scene for you," Daniel said and slipped the file into the briefcase alongside the table. He collected his cell phone and picked up his coffee. "Don't bother getting up. Thanks for the coffee, by the way."

"My pleasure," Parker said.

Daniel left with the briefcase, checking over his shoulder once to make sure Parker stayed seated. As soon as he walked out the door, he was hit in the face by a cloud of cigarette smoke from a homeless man sitting at one of the coffee house's outdoor wrought iron tables. The tobacco smoke reminded him of a past he apparently couldn't escape.

He walked back to his car, sipping coffee and firmly clutching the briefcase. Sanderson was a careful and thorough operator, so he felt considerably secure that he would not have to play the counter-surveillance game this afternoon. If Sanderson suspected his plot had been compromised, he would have given Daniel some warning. Not for Daniel's safety or wellbeing, but to give Daniel the best possible shot at accomplishing the mission.

The outcome had always been the general's only true concern. He could be unfailingly loyal, as long as your usefulness outweighed your burden. Daniel had learned this early and leveraged it throughout his "stay" overseas. Unmarked graves scattered across the continents covered the remains of "graduates" that never quite grasped this concept.

Daniel reached his car and deactivated the alarm system, which emitted two sharp chirps. Three low chirps would have indicated that someone or something had made contact with the car in his absence. The vibrational sensitivity of the system could detect someone leaning against the car, or even the slightest bump of an opening door. The alarm would only sound if someone tried to open one of the doors or forcefully hit the car.

He started the car and moved it to an empty row in the back of the parking lot, where he opened the case and pulled out the file. He quickly thumbed through the documents, taking in all of the salient points. The general's operational files hadn't changed in years. Functional and easy to navigate, Daniel had a solid assessment of the job within minutes. A rough plan developed before he could shift gears and speed out of the parking lot. He had a lot to accomplish before soccer practice tonight.

Chapter Two

Daniel checked his watch before opening the door to the house, determining that he was well within the range of returning from soccer practice. He pressed the garage door button and stepped inside as the door motor hummed behind him.

"That you, Danny?" he heard from deep inside the house.

"Were you expecting someone else?" he yelled back, kicking off his running shoes onto the gray tile floor.

Daniel placed a dark blue gym bag down on a small white bench in the crowded mudroom.

Jessica appeared under the soft glow of the kitchen's pendant lighting and placed a book on the butcher-block island.

"Yeah, I keep bringing Thai food home for Antonio Banderas, but to no avail. You want some Thai food?" she said and ran both hands through long, dark brown hair, tying it with a black scrunchie she had kept hidden on one of her wrists.

"How do you think that makes me feel?" he said, stepping into the kitchen.

"You don't like Thai food anymore?" she asked, closing the distance between them.

Daniel took her hand and pulled her in tight, giving her a passionate kiss. Her arms wrapped around him, and she pressed her body against his. They kissed for several moments before Jess untangled herself.

"You…need a shower. How was soccer?" she asked.

"Not bad. We needed this practice badly. We got our asses handed to us last night. Did you eat?" he asked and opened the refrigerator.

"I was waiting for you. It's still bagged up in the fridge," she said.

He saw one large brown take-out bag and reached for it, but his hand swerved toward a corked bottle of white wine in the door.

"How about we both take a shower and bring this bottle along with us?" he asked, pulling the bottle out and shutting the door.

"Sure you're not biting off more than you can chew? Late game last night, extra practice today, late dinner. Can you handle it?" she teased and turned to walk toward the staircase.

"I can handle it," he said.

**

Sitting on the floor in front of the couch, Jess and Daniel finished the last of the Thai dinner and Riesling about an hour later. Two pillar candles burned low on the round coffee table, casting a flickering orange glow over plastic take-out containers and empty plates.

"That was great," Daniel said, leaning back into the couch. "This turned out to be the perfect night. Surprise take out, good wine, great sex. What's next? A massage for these sore legs?"

"Dream on, lover boy. This girl is done for the evening. I'll let you clean up down here while I get ready for bed. It's been a long day," she said, getting up.

Daniel didn't budge. "Long day is right," he whispered.

"Hey, do you have anything in your gym bag that needs washing? I can grab it on the way up," she said, heading toward the kitchen with her plate and wine glass.

Daniel popped up and rushed behind her into the kitchen. "No, I'll take care of it. Some two-week-old shorts in there. Not the kind of thing you want to deal with, trust me."

"Thanks for the warning. I'll be upstairs," Jess said.

Daniel walked over to the mudroom and listened for her footsteps on the creaky stairs. Once the bathroom door shut and the water started to run, he opened the gym bag and removed the briefcase. He needed to find a secure location to hide the briefcase until he had the time to properly dispose of its contents. The cellar door caught his attention.

PAINTED BLACK

May 26, 2005

Chapter Three

Special Agent-in-Charge Ryan Sharpe replaced the handset of his desk phone and lowered his head all the way to the surface of his cluttered desk. He exhaled deeply and ran his hands through his thinning brown hair, keeping his head down for a few moments.

Sharpe turned his head slightly and glanced out of his window onto 9th Street. The traffic had already thickened. A long ribbon of light blue stretched over the vast sea of buildings. The chaos in D.C. started too damn early. He could use just a little more time today to figure out exactly what had destroyed his three-year-long investigation.

A few minutes after one in the morning, Sharpe had received a call from Operation Support's duty section head with news that one of his red-flagged profiles had been murdered. When his cell phone rang again before he had even reached the bathroom, he knew this might be the shittiest day of his career. The second phone call confirmed his suspicions. Two of eight key targets in his ongoing investigation had been murdered within the span of a few hours. By the time his car passed through the security station at the J. Edgar Hoover Building, he had received six more calls. Task Force HYDRA was finished.

The damage done to his investigation permanent and unrecoverable. All eight heads had been cut off at the same time, and he needed to quickly determine what had happened. He had solid evidence linking all of them to Al Qaeda's financing arm, and their sudden termination sounded an earth-shattering alarm. Sharp didn't have long to come up with answers. He heard a knock and barked at the door. His immediate assistant, Supervisory Special Agent Frank Mendoza, stepped into the doorway of the office and nodded.

"Everyone's ready. Need any coffee?" he said, walking all the way into the office.

"I've already had three cups. I just got off the phone with Delgado," Sharpe said grimly.

"Shit. How high has the news gone?" Mendoza said, wincing, waiting for the answer.

"All the way to the president. Homeland raised the threat level to Orange until we can provide solid evidence that we're not on the brink of another 9/11. Obviously, the director is hot on this, so I wouldn't expect much breathing room today. We've been given top priority for resources."

He decided against mentioning the director's immediate concern that Task Force HYDRA had been compromised by a traitor. Sandra Delgado, his immediate superior, had kindly informed him that the Internal Affairs Department would quietly pursue this possibility from the sidelines, for now.

"I think we already commandeered half of the building," Mendoza said.

"Stand by to grab the other half. We'll be in the frying pan until we figure out what happened last night. Let's go."

He stood up from the desk and walked out of the office, pulling the door closed. Mendoza fell in behind him as they approached the door to his task force's operations center. He heard considerable chatter behind the door and paused for a second before opening it. The room fell silent when the door swung open, and Sharpe walked to a desk that had been reconfigured to serve as a makeshift podium. The air quality in the room had deteriorated significantly. Rank and humid, the room reeked of bad coffee and faint cologne. The building's air circulation system was unable to compete with a room stuffed to nearly four times its intended capacity.

He glanced behind him and saw that one of three enormous, side-by-side-mounted plasma-screen monitors showed a map of the East Coast. The map stretched from South Carolina to Maine and contained markers that indicated the location of each murder. Charleston, South Carolina; Virginia Beach, Virginia; Annapolis, Maryland; Long Island, New York; Manhattan, New York; Rye, New York; Newport, Rhode Island; Cape Elizabeth, Maine. Sharpe turned to face nearly sixty agents, hastily assembled hours ago to start unscrambling the mess."All right, so what do we have?"

A young special agent stepped forward with a few sheets of paper in his hands. "Sir, as you can see, we're dealing with what appears to be a coordinated strike on all eight of our key surveillance targets. Most of the murders appear—"

"Rob, are you going to tell me anything I don't already know?" Sharpe interrupted.

The young agent looked to his supervisory agent for support.

"I'm not trying to be an ass here, agent," Sharpe explained.

"I just don't have time for a recap of events. We need to move this investigation forward at a record pace, and I don't need to remind everyone here of the implications surrounding these murders.

"These guys," he continued, pointing behind him at the screen, "were conduits of financing for dangerous people. We need to figure out exactly why this coordinated attack occurred. The director is under increasing pressure from the White House, so you can imagine what it's going to be like for the task force as the day progresses. The primary concern is that we have another 9/11 imminent, and that Al Qaeda is cleaning house and cutting ties. This is our focus. Investigations, where do we stand at the different sites?"

A female agent sitting on the edge of one of the closest desks stood up. Her suit looked crisp, and her face appeared unaffected by the early wake up. She stood in stark contrast to several of the agents clustered near her as she spoke. "Sir, Supervisory Special Agent Olson. Agents from the closest field offices were dispatched a few hours ago to each site to assist local law enforcement in their initial assessment of the scene. I've taken reports from each site's lead agent. So far, we don't have any witnesses, and evidence appears scant. I think we'll start piecing this together once the sun is up, and we can take a hard look at each site. Start knocking on doors. We'll get this moving fast. I've also requested additional agents from other field offices within each region. I want to establish a second tier of FBI support at each site."

"Let's get a third tier in the works. I want to send a headquarters team to each site. Four agents minimum. Let's make sure we have one member from Terror Financing in each group, then a good mix of agents from Investigative and Counterterror. We need our own agents on scene ASAP. We can't afford to miss anything," Sharpe said.

"I'll work with Agent Mendoza to get the teams assigned and out the door with the necessary field support," Olson responded immediately.

"Great. I want those teams on site by mid-morning," he added, and both Mendoza and Olson nodded vigorously.

"Next. Comms. Anything?"

Special Agent Keith Weber walked forward a few steps from a position against the left wall of the room. He flipped open a battered pea-green government-issued logbook, which barely looked more weathered than he did. Sharpe saw that he had a sizable coffee stain on his light blue oxford shirt, which could not be hidden by fully buttoning his rumpled suit jacket. Weber pushed up a pair of wire rim glasses to squint at the logbook through puffy, red eyes.

"I've been on with Fort Meade all night. Nothing unusual prior to the murders. We've been poring over this for hours, and we don't see any chatter or patterns that I would classify as suspicious, or even remotely interesting."

"It didn't go dead before the killings?" Sharpe interrupted.

"Not that we could tell. We traced the patterns back a month, and we're seeing the same level of activity," he said.

"And this morning?"

"We've seen a growing increase in communications, both national and overseas. In my opinion, news of the murders is starting to spread through these networks. We're doing everything we can to scan for more meaningful information or patterns, but so far, we haven't detected any direct previous link between our targeted communications and the coordinated attack. There is clearly a growing response after the event," Weber stated and moved back to the wall.

"I can't stress enough the importance of figuring this out. If Al Qaeda pulled the plug on these guys, we could be looking at an attack on our country or U.S. interests abroad. Until we figure it out, we need to treat this like an imminent threat."

He looked over at Supervisory Special Agent Olson and added, "Get those teams out the door before this investigation is hijacked by National Security. Our liaisons will have the best chance of uncovering something useful."

Sharpe was interrupted by Agent Mendoza, "Sir, I just took a call from the lead agent in Newport. They're pretty sure they just captured the shooter alive. He apparently slipped on some rocks and knocked himself unconscious trying to climb down the seawall behind Umar Salah's mansion. They think he's been lying among the rocks all night. They're moving him to the Newport police station."

"Get back on the phone and tell him that I want the suspect transported to the Boston field office. Just make sure they don't piss off local law enforcement. We'll still need their cooperation on scene at the house. And tell him I want that guy in an armored personnel carrier."

"I'm not sure they'll be able to—"

"I'm just trying to underscore the importance of his safe delivery. Did they say whether the suspect was Arab?" Sharpe interrupted.

"Dark-skinned. That's all I got. I'll get more details," he said and stepped out of the room to make the call.

"Agent Olson, I want you to oversee this personally. Call Gregory Carlisle in Counterterror, and tell him to bring his special interrogation team with you to Boston. He'll know what I'm talking about. I want this guy talking."

"Yes sir," she said and pulled out her cell phone, sitting back down on the desk.

"All right, that's it, let's get the teams organized and out of here. Support, I want full links set up to each site. Mobile links for the teams. Data, voice, video…the works. I want to be able to process everything as quickly as possible," Sharpe yelled, as the room erupted into a chaos of multi-tasking FBI agents.

"You got it, boss," yelled a dark-haired, slender, male agent from the back of the room.

"Agent Weber," he yelled.

Weber barreled through the gaggle of agents breaking for the door. "Sir?"

"How long have you been up?" he asked.

"I never went home yesterday. I took the duty section's first shift last night. I was on my way home when I got recalled at about one forty."

"I wish I could tell you that sleep was in your near future, but it doesn't look that way. First thing I need you to do is prepare a media-withhold request for immediate distribution to local law enforcement. I need this in ten minutes. I want to shut down all publicly available information until we have a handle on what we're dealing with."

"I'll have it for you ASAP," he said and turned to leave.

"And, Keith, the coffee works better when you drink it," Sharpe said, touching the coffee stain on Agent Weber's shirt.

Special Agent Weber smirked and bolted out of the room.

Sharpe turned and approached Heather Olson, who had started to dial her phone to contact Counterterror's duty section-lead.

"Heather, I want you to lean on this guy. Tell Gregory to give me a call immediately. I don't want him to hold back on this one. The stakes are too high. We might have to push the envelope here. I hope that doesn't bother you."

"I'd hate to think I've developed a reputation for being squeamish," she replied with a grin.

"On the contrary. That's why I woke you up at one thirty in the morning instead of your boss. Keep me updated. Frequently. Good luck."

"Understood, sir. Thank you," she said and turned back to her phone again.

Chapter Four

Daniel stepped out of the shower and dried himself in front of a full-length mirror hanging from the back of the closed bathroom door. The steam-obscured image of his body gradually clarified as he wrapped a towel around his waist. His body was well toned from a regular routine of calisthenics, running and soccer. He carried very little body fat, which gave him a slightly gaunt appearance, which Jess said could be fixed by adding about five pounds to his frame. He'd have to stop exercising to gain any weight, and sometimes a ten-mile run was the only thing that kept his head clear.

His torso was covered by numerous scars, some short and deep, others long and shallow. Two particularly nasty scars crisscrossed his chest, evidence of a knife fight that had ended badly for Daniel, and worse for the young Kosovar militant that had stumbled upon his sniper position. Most of the scars were reminders of his fickle luck; shrapnel and bullet fragments that hadn't found a lethal home in Daniel's body. A few of the scars were self-inflicted, part of his indoctrination at the "Ranch." The most notable mark on his body sat high on his right arm. A faded panther tattoo.

He opened the bathroom door and saw Jess standing at the foot of their bed. She looked stunning, as usual. Her dark brown hair, cut and styled straight, rested just below the shoulders of a navy blue blazer. Collar points of a crisp white blouse lay over the blazer's lapels, brightly contrasting the dark jacket. She had chosen to wear matching suit pants instead of a skirt, which slightly disappointed Daniel. He thought she looked killer in a fitted skirt. Her eyes were fixed to a television hidden inside of the dark red armoire that sat against the wall, in front of their bed. She pulled a black belt through several loops of her pants while staring at the television.

"You missed a loop," he said.

Jess took her eyes off the television to face him. "Quit staring," she said jokingly.

"I really can't help myself," he said.

He examined her face, still amazed by how similar, yet different she looked since they had first met at school. Her seductive light brown eyes added a soft, exotic dimension to her dark complexion. She was more stunning now than ever before, and his love burned stronger than ever. He was convinced it would never burn out. It was a love forged by a fire few could possibly imagine.

"Check this out," she said and nodded at the television.

Daniel walked over to help her with the loop she missed, and stared at the screen. A local reporter stood in front of two Cape Elizabeth police cars, which blocked the entrance to a long driveway. The driveway extended through a stone archway with dark iron light fixtures on each side, and led to a partially obscured luxury home settled behind mature pine trees. The archway connected to a three-foot-tall sandstone wall that extended the entire length of the property's road frontage. A local police officer leaned against the left side of the arch with his arms folded, keeping a close eye on the media crowd. Daniel caught a sparkling glimpse of Casco Bay through the archway, just past the house.

The reporter identified the deceased as Mohammed Ghani, an importer with offices in Portland and Boston. Police were withholding details, but an anonymous source reported that Ghani had been stabbed to death outside of his home. Another source confirmed the presence of federal agents at the crime scene, but Portland's FBI office had refused to comment. Daniel decided to change the subject.

"Hey, are you going out for drinks with the ladies tonight? I could meet you for dinner after."

"That would be nice. We can grab sushi at Sakura's. It's right across the street from The Lounge," she said, turning to face him.

"Ah…The Lounge. Where all the young ladies gather to sip cosmos…"

"And all the men stand around watching them," she added.

"I can't wait to pluck you out of there, right in front of all those desperate guys. Can we pretend we don't know each other?"

"I can't guarantee the behavior of the women in my office, so it's probably not a good idea. Sounds fun though," she said and kissed him.

"The betrothed members of the crew usually start heading home around eight, so meet me any time after that."

"I can't wait," he whispered and kissed her passionately.

Chapter Five

Randy Keller strode casually down a crowded corridor in the National Clandestine Service's wing of the Central Intelligence Agency's headquarters building. At seven in the morning, the Counterterrorism Center's section was quiet; most of the analysts and staff were sitting in sluggish traffic, still thirty to sixty minutes away from the CIA's sprawling McLean, Virginia, campus. In about thirty minutes, the place would explode, and he prefered to be back on the road when it did.

He reached the end of the corridor and paused at a door that read *Karl Berg, Assistant Director, Counterterrorism,* before knocking.

"Come in," he heard someone yell.

Keller scanned the room as he stepped inside, surprised to find both Berg and Audra Bauer, director of the Counterterrorism Center (CTC), huddled around a computer workstation next to Berg's desk. Neither of them looked up as he hesitantly entered. He hadn't expected to make a report directly to the CTC's director.

"Grab a seat, Randy. The director and I just finished with the latest feed from the FBI. This link is fantastic work."

"Thank you. You're seeing what they feed out to their on-scene agents and key section heads. They add agents to the feed as they are brought into the investigation. It keeps everyone in the loop and on the same page, but it's not always the fullest picture," said Keller.

"And that's exactly why we have you over there. I've read your summaries of this morning's events. I agree that the FBI had been compromised. Please have a seat," said Bauer.

Keller turned a chair to face them and sat down. He glanced at the window and wondered if they were really designed to resist electronic listening devices. In over fifteen years at the CIA, this had never been a concern for Keller, since he had never sat behind a desk in a room with a window. His office at the FBI was the closest he'd ever achieved, located across the hall from the coveted window offices.

"Do you have any ideas about where to start looking?" said Bauer.

"Ma'am, it's difficult to say. They don't compartmentalize their operations like we do here. This is one of their highest priority investigative task forces, but they still have no organic support assets. The core team is permanently assigned to HYDRA and is comprised of mostly Terror Financing personnel, but they rely on key players in nearly every other section for critical, daily support. These key personnel probably spend most of their time working for the task force, but they also support other investigations within the entire Counterterrorism Division. I see new names and new faces on a weekly, if not daily basis. I've managed to compile a list of everyone that I've seen, but I guarantee this is not a complete list. Just too many people involved to count. You should've seen how many people they assembled this morning. Lots of fresh faces," he said and handed a flash drive over to Berg.

"Nice work. We'll start looking at financial records, communications trails…get the groundwork rolling on this. I'll walk this over to Counter-Intel," said Berg.

"Take it to HUMINT, too. They need to know what to start looking for immediately. Have them look back at least one year. Eight simultaneous murders? I guarantee this has been in the works for months, if not years," said Bauer.

"No mention by Sharpe of a possible leak?" said Berg.

"Not to the group…or to me."

"That's not much of a surprise. Sharpe doesn't completely trust you, and he needs the task force to focus on evidentiary procedure. Any mention of a leak this early would undermine the investigation," said Bauer flatly, then added, "We need to let them focus on what they do well, while we start digging into all the possibilities."

They all nodded, and the director stood up. Berg and Keller joined her.

"All right, I'm going to brief the deputy. Keep me directly in the loop on everything. I'm not sure what we'll get from our in-house FBI liaison. He's back in D.C. doing the same thing you're doing. Randy, I need you to figure out a way to get us inside their interrogation efforts. I'm tempted to send someone out to Boston," she said from the door.

"I don't think it will be necessary. Sharpe made it clear that he wanted a live interrogation feed, and I don't plan to stray very far from Sharpe's side, unless something interesting pops up," said Keller.

"Stay close. I don't think Sharpe has thought this through all the way. He's sending a special team up to Boston with special orders that may not play out too well over a live feed. He'll shut it down pretty quickly if Mr. Carlisle pushes the envelope," she said and left the room.

"Back to DC with you. Good work on this. Let me know what you need, and it's yours," said Berg.

"I think I'm going to need a cot for my office."

"For what? I can't imagine any upcoming scenario in which you sleep."

"Good point. I'll see if we can get in on the feed from Boston. One way or another," said Keller.

"Now that would be an epic score on your part."

"That's why you have me over in FBI land."

"Among other reasons. Make sure to grab whatever you need on the way out. I'll call tech support as soon as you leave my office, which should be in a few seconds," said Berg.

"I'm gone," he said and closed the door behind him.

Keller weaved his way through the growing crowd of analysts, displaying a combination of strained smiles and harried expressions that effectively discouraged anyone from engaging his attention. Reaching the elevator bank unmolested, he jabbed the down button several times. He needed to get back to FBI headquarters before the Boston interrogation began.

Chapter Six

Daniel stared intensely at the flat-screen monitor in his office. His door was closed, and he hadn't been interrupted since arriving at 7:45, nearly thirty minutes earlier. This came as no surprise, since everyone was busy poring over their reports and preparing their speeches. The overseas marketing division had a meeting at 9:00, followed by a general marketing department meeting at 10:00. It was that time of the month for mother Zenith.

Sitting in his cubicle, Daniel felt sick to his stomach. He didn't like what he had uncovered on the Internet. A simple Google search yielded seven overnight murders similar to the one in Cape Elizabeth. Wealthy Muslims, all murdered last night. Details remained sketchy in most cases, almost as if they had been withheld. In one case, the Google link had been deactivated. The story had been filed in the *Providence Journal*, and its tag line had piqued Daniel's interest the most:

"In Newport, a prominent businessman was found shot to death on his patio…local authorities report suspect in custody."

He didn't like the idea of a suspect in custody, and was pretty sure Sanderson wouldn't like it either. Daniel sifted through the favorites links again and examined the information.

"Muslim art trader slain outside of Mount Pleasant Home. Apparent close range shooting…"

"Couple killed in bizarre drive-by shooting, while walking at night in the Eastport subdivision of Annapolis. Killings shock neighbors, who describe Sa'id and Adia Faris as generous, peaceful members of their small community. No suspects in shooting…"

"Jibran Nazir's body was found by his wife outside of the entrance gate to their Hampton estate. The passenger side of Nazir's car was riddled with bullets, leaving him dead on the scene..."

Daniel clicked the mouse button on the next link. *"The link you have requested is inactive or no longer exists."*

Someone is shutting this down quick.

He quickly shuffled through two more links. Two more shootings, one a break-in at a Rye waterfront townhouse, husband and wife murdered; another in the upper west side of Manhattan, doorman and Asim Shareef executed just inside the lobby of an exclusive apartment building. Three out of the eight articles mentioned federal law enforcement involvement, which included the stabbing of Mohammed Ghani, on the driveway of his Shore Road residence in Cape Elizabeth, Maine. *Only one stabbing?* Interesting.

He entered several different search strings for the murder that concerned him the most. Nothing. The murder in Newport, Rhode Island, had been erased from the public's eye, which was an unsettling development. If the feds actually caught the killer, Daniel's life could unravel quickly. He softly pounded the keyboard tray with a closed fist.

He should have known better than to take the assignment. Daniel had enjoyed five great years with Jessica, finally settling into a pleasantly tolerable "normal" life. He didn't take much pleasure in his job, but who did? Daniel didn't want to start over again, so he took the job, thinking that Sanderson would go away. He'd been kidding himself. Not that it mattered. If he'd refused, vanishing to rebuild with Jessica somewhere else, it looked like the result would have been the same. Sanderson was up to something big, and it would have swallowed them either way.

Daniel closed the Internet browser and turned his attention to the files stacked up on his desk. He needed to maintain appearances for at least a few more hours, despite how very little he now cared about Zenith's overseas emerging markets.

Chapter Seven

Special Agent-in-Charge Sharpe stared up at the plasma-screen monitors in the task force operations center. The screens had changed little over the course of the morning. Eight separate crime scenes, and Sharpe had very little to show for their investigative progress. A few sets of partial footprints, scattered witness statements and a flurry of ballistics reports, which had so far told them nothing they couldn't determine with their own eyes. The victims were either knifed, shot in the face with a pistol at close range, or shot in the head with a sniper rifle from a longer range. It was pretty easy to tell the difference between the pistol and sniper kills; the pistol rounds left the heads intact. No forensics required.

"We don't have shit," he stated to Special Agent Mendoza, who had just entered the room with a stack of papers.

"We have one of the shooters," Mendoza said, joining Sharpe at the screens.

"And he hasn't said shit. We don't even know who he is, and we still haven't found his car. All we know about this guy is that he's pretty handy with a scoped Remington 700 rifle. I'm not even sure that advanced interrogation techniques would be effective with this guy," Sharpe said.

"Have you forwarded the request?" Mendoza said in a weak tone that betrayed the fact that he knew the answer already.

"That, my friend, is a slippery slope for someone at my pay grade. Carlisle is our best interrogator. He'll take the interrogation as far as he can. After that, someone else will have to decide how to proceed. I'm about to authorize Carlisle and Olson to suggest the possibility of a deal. Based on the lack of evidence we pulled from the other crime scenes, I have a feeling he didn't expect this little side trip. The mention of an immunity deal might soften him up a bit."

"It's all we have left at this point," Mendoza confirmed, placing the stack of papers on Sharpe's temporary workstation.

Sharpe nodded at the pile of papers. "More personnel requisition forms?"

"Yep. This should be the last of them. We now have most of the building working for us," he said, in hopes of eliciting a laugh, or at least a smile.

"We'll lose these agents just as quickly if we don't start to produce more than phantom footprints and muddled witness statements. I need to make some calls from my office," he said, grabbing the stack of papers.

The calls would be placed to the lead investigative agents at each crime scene, and he would condense their verbal reports for his final call to his immediate superior within the Terror Financing Operations Section, Associate Director Sandra Delgado. He imagined Agent Delgado would turn right around and call the Executive Assistant Director Fred Carroll, who had overall responsibility for the FBI's Counterterrorism Division. On and on the calls would go, rising up the chain of command, until Sharpe started the cycle over again less than an hour later. It was part of his job as special agent-in-charge of Task Force HYDRA.

Chapter Eight

Special Agent Justin Edwards stood several feet away from Mohammed Ghani's body, staring out at a multi-million-dollar view of the Atlantic Ocean. An endless stretch of shimmering water, interrupted by an occasional lobster boat and a sparsely inhabited island across Portland's shipping channel. He tried to imagine what the view would be like on the island, but a cool, salty breeze that threatened his perfectly-coiffed hair, interrupting his thoughts. Special Agent Margaret D'Angelo stood with an impatient look on her face.

"I'm sorry, I just can't get over this view," he said.

Edwards finally brought his attention back to Portland's resident FBI agent, the only agent permanently assigned to the local satellite office. He wondered whom she had pissed off to get stuck here, though he could get used to sipping cocktails with the views like this in the backdrop.

He tried to focus on D'Angelo, but found her uninteresting. She was attractive, in a middle-aged, married female kind of way, but certainly not Justin's type. Like most female agents, she dressed conservatively and put little effort, or money, into her hair. D'Angelo apparently hadn't even bothered to try this morning. Her hair was pulled back into some kind of "who gives a shit" bun, reserved for women who have simply given up.

"Please continue. Sorry," he said.

"Mr. Ghani's body was discovered last night at about ten thirty by a private security guard, who had been dispatched by a technician at the security company's centralized headquarters in Omaha, Nebraska," she said.

"Anything out of the ordinary with the security guard or the company?"

"Everything checks out so far. The company is one of the largest in the country, and the guard has been an employee of the company for twelve years. We still have him down at the Cape Elizabeth police station. The company dispatched him at the request of Mr. Ghani's wife, who hadn't heard from her husband that night."

"She's obviously not here?"

"No. She's been in Pakistan for the past few weeks, scheduled to return in early June. Apparently, he always takes her calls, and she got worried when he didn't answer last night," she said.

"No security camera?"

"Wishful thinking," she added.

He squatted down near the body, which was covered with a gray tarp, stenciled in black with "CE Police Dept." The covered body lay several feet from the driver's side of a previously sparkling white Mercedes convertible sedan. The convertible's tan ragtop was down, and the side of the white sedan was covered with thick, dark maroon stains, indicating a strong arterial spray pattern. Edwards could see similar dark splotches on the light tan driver's headrest and could imagine that the rest of the light-colored interior had been ruined by Mr. Ghani's blood.

A large pool of dried blood extended around the body in an oval shape, stretching toward the end of the small driveway that joined the circular drive. This small section of asphalt serviced the four-bay garage, and the Mercedes was in a position where it had either been purposely parked outside of the garage or had been stopped before making the turn into one of the bays. The far garage bay door was open, and he glanced back at the circular driveway, which was crammed with police vans, squad cars and SUVs.

He saw a few of the ever-present SWAT officers standing near one of the oversized SUVs, cradling assault rifles. They were always looking for an excuse to dress up and parade around in their gear. At least they had their helmets off, though he could think of no conceivable reason why they would need to be carrying military-style weaponry on this estate.

Edwards returned his attention to the garage bay door. "Anything out of order inside?"

"Not that anyone could tell. So far, the crime scene techs haven't found anything useful. Right now, they're focusing on the outside, looking for anything the killer might have left us while breaching the perimeter," said D'Angelo.

"Have they checked the seaside approach? You heard about Rhode Island, right?"

"Just that the guy there had been shot from a distance. Did they find a boat or something?" she said.

She obviously hadn't been brought into the circle on this one, and that was fine with Edwards. Sharpe didn't want to alert the rest of the terrorist network responsible for last night's murderfest and had imposed a media blackout. So far, only one Internet article had been written about the suspect in custody, posted by a local Newport publication, and they had graciously agreed to remove it while the investigation proceeded. Edwards hadn't realized that the same information blackout applied to the rest of the FBI. This was exactly why he would never accept a posting like D'Angelo's. He couldn't stomach the concept of being an outsider.

"They need to give the seaside approaches the same attention as the perimeter fence. That's all I can say for now. What about the body and the car? Do they need to process this?" he said.

"No, they're finished here and in the house unless we get specific information regarding the residence," she said.

"Do you trust them? I have a team showing up in an hour."

"I have a close working relationship with the lead investigator and his team. They're competent, thorough, and I've used them before when other assets weren't available. This isn't the most complicated murder, but I understand the importance of this case," she said, and Edwards highly doubted she truly understood the implications.

"We'll have our own team talk to the locals that processed the body, then they'll take a quick look together. Looks pretty straightforward. The key here will be finding something to lead us back to the killer. Frankly, I'm not very hopeful."

"Aside from massive blood loss," he continued, tracing the wide swath of dried blood back to the circular drive, "what is the initial assessment for cause of death?"

"Mr. Ghani has a deep penetration wound at the front of his neck, slightly to the right, which severed his carotid artery. Anthony Boudreau, the forensics chief, said the wound indicated the work of a professional...possibly a sick one," she said.

"What did he mean by that?" Edwards said.

"Boudreau said the killer held the knife deep inside Ghani and scrambled things up pretty bad. He couldn't tell how big of a blade, but based on the tearing around the neck, he's pretty sure the killer fished it around for a while, which he thought was unusual," D'Angelo said.

"Boudreau has a lot of experience with cuts like this?" he said, not convinced that a Portland, Maine, based forensics guy would have the extensive experience to make this kind of assessment.

"He worked forensics in New York City for twenty-three years," she commented and paused. "Said the knife attack resembled one of several used by commandos or special forces to instantly disable sentries, but that this particular method was not typically their first choice. He said the most common surprise knife attack put the blade through the back of the victim's neck, high up near the skull, which instantly severed the spinal cord at its highest point. Instant shutdown. Scrambled the brain, too, if the knife passed into the skull."

"Sounds wonderful. What's wrong with Mr. Ghani's wound?"

"Nothing, really. This cut kills just as effectively, but doesn't always sever the spinal cord. If it does, the cord is cut below the entry wound. It's an extremely painful death, if the shock doesn't kill you instantly. Boudreau said the Russian Spetsnaz specialized in this one. He also thinks this one twisted the knife around more than necessary. I wouldn't want to run into the person that pulled this off," she finished.

"Unfortunately, that's exactly what we need to do," he said.

"I'm going to familiarize myself with the grounds. If you could have the forensics teams start to look at potential seaside approaches, I can send a comprehensive initial report as soon as my team takes a quick look around," he said.

"Do you want me to introduce you to some of the key players on the local force?" she asked.

"That's all right. I'd rather you handled them. If I need anything, I'll go through you," he said, hoping she didn't press the issue.

He hated dealing with the local cops. Absently shaking hands with everyone who had a horse in the race, even if their horse had no chance of winning. He'd have to make pleasantries with Cape Elizabeth's police chief, and hear about how officer "whoever" responded to the call and made sure to preserve the scene. He'd then commit his entire police force of ten officers to help Edwards in any way possible. Same thing for several other towns and two counties, finally graduating to the Portland Police Department, the only people he slightly cared to interact with. Edwards preferred to remain aloof, which would generate more respect in the long run. Plus, he could make D'Angelo feel important, and foster her relationship with the people she'd need to work with long after he departed.

"Okay...let me know if you need anything. I'll be talking with

Boudreau," she said and stepped away.

He watched her walk away, and his eyes were drawn to the front gate of the estate. Two women jog by the entrance along Shore Road, slowing as they passed to get a look at the commotion. They were both dressed in skintight athletic gear, sporting long, thin athletic bodies. He started to fantasize about having a threesome with these women on the patio of a house like Mr. Ghani's, but a sudden idea interrupted his daydream— a rarity for Edwards. The thought was work related, oddly connected to the women he just witnessed running by the house. Maybe the killer simply jogged onto the grounds as Ghani's car passed through the gate.

"D'Angelo!" he yelled.

She turned around, already halfway to the forensics van and several officers drinking Dunkin' Donuts coffee. He could use some coffee, he thought, but not that stuff. The officer that D'Angelo had sent to pick him up at Portland's Jetport didn't seem to know where to find coffee other than at Dunkin' Donuts and was of no help to Edwards in his search for a proper cappuccino. He should have grabbed one in Portland's sad excuse for an airport, but the line at the small Starbucks kiosk was eight deep, and the workers behind the counter didn't look like the A-team, so he'd passed.

"What?"

"What was Boudreau's estimation for Ghani's time of death?" he yelled.

"6 p.m., roughly," she yelled back.

"Thanks," he said.

A broad daylight killing took some nerve. He glanced at the gate again and wondered if the killer hadn't just jogged in behind the Mercedes and stabbed him. He'd counted six joggers already, and that was in the morning, during the workday. There would be twice as many in the evening, after work. Not a bad cover to slip onto the estate. He turned back to the body, wondering if Ghani had an espresso machine.

Chapter Nine

Petrovich steered his BMW over Woodford Street's faded median line and onto Lawn Avenue. His speed drew disapproving stares from a pair of perfectly-manicured stroller pushers, causing him to ease off the gas and nod an apology in their direction. Still pushing the speed limit of his neighborhood, he rolled cautiously through two stop signs before arriving at his house. The top of his sedan barely cleared the rising garage door as it lurched into the darkness.

He wasted little time inside the house. Upon returning to his office, after what seemed like an interminable amount of time spent watching Power Point presentations, Daniel found a message, handwritten by one of his assistants on a Zenith memo pad.

"From Jeff Hill, VP, Sanderson Resources: Have further business proposition. Would like to meet and discuss recent government acquisition of Newport based assets. Acquisition of Portland assets likely in very near future. My schedule is clear to meet tonight or early tomorrow."

The message was clear. Somehow the feds had nabbed Sanderson's Newport shooter, and the general wanted him out of town immediately. He had stared at the handwritten note, trying to rationalize any way he could stay, but it served no purpose. Daniel had known since yesterday that their time in Portland was drawing to an immediate end.

While sipping coffee and making small talk with Jessica this morning, he formulated a rough plan for their disappearance. Unfortunately, Jess would have to stay in Portland for a few days. If the FBI actually found a link to Daniel, he needed her in Portland to buy him some time. Vanishing required more than a few plane tickets and a passport.

He passed through the kitchen and entered the basement, fumbling to turn on the lights. Cool, moist air entered his lungs at the bottom of the stairs, as he turned into the center of the dimly lit subterranean storage area. A few cardboard boxes sat against the closest wall, next to a dozen evenly stacked plastic bins. The labels on the bins indicated that they were filled with seasonal clothing, professional books, and camping supplies.

He continued to the furthest reaches of the basement, approaching the heating oil tank. Several cardboard boxes sat on the floor in front of the tank. Daniel opened one in the center of the pile and removed the briefcase given to him yesterday, examining its contents again. A file he needed to permanently destroy, and a Heckler and Koch USP 9mm pistol with suppressor. He'd hold onto the pistol for as long as possible.

Daniel headed toward the rows of large plastic bins, removing the two top-most plastic containers from a stack in the middle. A bin labeled "Old Clothes" remained. He ripped the duct tape from the sides of the plastic storage container, which hadn't been disturbed in a few years, and lifted the cover. The musty bin was stuffed with dated sweaters and oversized sweatshirts. Daniel buried his arms in the clothing and removed two black nylon gym bags, spilling sweaters onto the basement floor.

He slid the bags behind him, along with the briefcase, and recreated the orderly scene he encountered upon first descending the basement stairs. Five minutes later, after packing a small carry-on bag, Daniel backed the BMW out of the garage and onto the street. He pulled forward and stopped to stare at his house through the passenger window, leaning over the center console to get a better view.

A low, white picket fence outlined the front yard of the yellow Cape Cod style home, extending along the driveway to the attached garage. Dark green shutters accented the white windowpanes, competing with the neatly trimmed evergreen bushes reaching upward toward the bottom of the window trim. Just beyond the picket fence, two large maple trees flanked a red brick walkway that ended at an oversized granite stoop.

"We almost did it," he muttered, taking his foot off the brake.

He doubted he would ever see the house again, or any of the memories contained within it. He knew it didn't really matter, but it was hard to conceptualize abandoning the physical remnants of their life together. Nothing could go with them. There simply hadn't been enough time. This house, their friends, his office—all of it. He had simply walked out of Zenith Semiconductor without a word and would never return. He didn't really have a choice. It was a simple matter of survival.

Chapter Ten

12:45 p.m.
FBI Field Office, Boston, Massachusetts

Agent Olson stepped out of the interrogation room into the darkened observation deck, closing the door tightly behind her. She stopped in front of the one-way mirror and stared at Jeffrey Munoz, who was attached to several electronic monitoring leads. Gregory Carlisle sat across the desk from Munoz, with his hands crossed. Inside the observation room, three agents studied the biometric feedback displayed on several laptop screens. One of the agents, a young, sharp-faced woman with short hair, focused on a large flat-screen display of various vital signs.

"What do you think?" Olson uttered, without taking her gaze off Munoz.

"Bio says he's nervous as hell, but I'm not getting any of the traditional markers associated with deception. If this was a standard observation, I'd say the suspect was telling the truth…but given the circumstances, I think it would be prudent to change the interrogation parameters. See how he responds. His base stress level hasn't changed much since we started taking readings. It's high, but I haven't seen any significant spikes," the agent said, turning her head toward Olson.

"It doesn't surprise me, given what he's said so far. Tell Greg to walk out of the room, and let Munoz sit there for a few minutes. When he returns, have Greg tell Munoz that there is no way he'll be given any deal. I want Greg to mention that he'll be transferred within the hour to Logan Airport for further transport. He should hint that Munoz might be a little warm in the clothes he's wearing. I want this guy to think he's being rendered to a location outside of the country. We'll see if his story holds together."

"You got it," the agent said, with a smirk of approval hidden by the dark.

Chapter Eleven

Retired Brigadier General Terrence Sanderson leaned back into the leather comfort of the Suburban's rear seat and dialed one of several disposable cell phones available to him in his briefcase. He had dozens more stashed in several locations around the D.C. Metro Area, and hundreds placed in other likely areas of operation along the Mid-Atlantic seacoast. He had gone "dark" several days ago, moving back and forth from several untraceable locations.

He had plotted and planned this day's events for over a year. Some of the key links in the chain had been initiated more than two years earlier. Sanderson was a careful, patient soldier, leaving little to chance, except for Petrovich. He hadn't counted on using Petrovich for one of the assassinations, but unexpected circumstances had left him with little choice.

"You did an excellent job with Petrovich. From what I can tell, he did the job…maybe a little too well. Knife work was never one of his loves," said Sanderson.

"Maybe sending us a message? He didn't look pleased to have been dragged back into this," said Parker from the driver's seat.

"Truthfully, I wouldn't have been surprised if Mr. Ghani had woken up to a glorious sunrise over the Atlantic. I gave the entire situation a fifty percent chance. It wouldn't have mattered anyway. Seven, six…even five murders would have been enough to cause a panic in the Hoover building. All eight? Icing on the cake. Is he headed our way?"

"Yeah, he should arrive on the ground by four at the latest. Should we be worried?" said Parker.

"With Petrovich, you should always be worried, though I'm pretty sure he still need us to get out of the country safely. He's one of the best we ever graduated…and by far the most productive in the field. Who knows, we might get him back, or..." he trailed off.

"Or what?"

"Or we could have a war on our hands. Unlikely though. He's one of the most practical individuals I have ever dealt with. Hold that thought, I need to check in with someone," he said and dialed the phone he had been holding near his ear.

The call was answered on the second ring.

"Colonel Farrington, Special Information Division. How can I help you?"

"Hello, Colonel. Major General Smith here. Just checking to see how my information requests are proceeding?"

Without hesitation, Colonel Farrington replied, "Sorry, General, no progress has been made so far, though I'm keeping a close eye on the requests myself. You'll be the first to know when the ball starts rolling."

"Sounds good, Colonel. Keep me in the loop," said General Sanderson.

"Roger that, sir. I would expect an update within the hour."

Sanderson hung up.

"Still nothing. Shit, the FBI is moving slow. I expected them to be down there already. This is the kind of shit I've always been railing about. Bureaucracy, government red tape, rules of engagement...they all have their right place and purpose, but not if you need results, and fast. I wish we had someone inside the FBI headquarters," he said to Parker.

"It's just a matter of time, sir," said Parker, as he pulled the Suburban off the Beltway at exit 177B, heading toward one of the general's "safe houses" in Alexandria, Virginia.

**

Less than ten miles away, Colonel Richard Farrington, United States Army, leaned back in his shitty, worn government chair and placed the cell phone in a black nylon briefcase tucked away under his desk. Cell phones were technically off limits in his section, and if anyone saw him using it, he'd just say that he'd forgotten to leave it in the car and received a call. No big deal, especially since he was careful to select a phone without a camera. He wasn't really worried either way, his bag received a cursory inspection upon entry and exit, and not very many people at the Pentagon were cleared for his section.

He'd been at this posting for nearly two years, biding his time, even extending his tour for another six months to give Sanderson some leeway in planning. He wouldn't need it. Either today or tomorrow, Farrington would walk out of here for the last time and join his old battalion commander in exile.

***

Julio Mendez peeked through a one-inch crack between his office door and the doorframe. Calling the room his office was a stretch, since it was really a janitorial supply closet, but Julio didn't care. Even the highest-ranking officers and civilians sat in cubicles within the Information and Data Section. Everything was transparent, and the only true privacy came in the form of a bathroom stall, where someone could still see your shoes and hear your daily contribution to the D.C. sewer system. He may just be the janitor, but he had what nobody around here had—a private room.

He'd been spying on Colonel Farrington for two days, after seeing the colonel hide something when he passed his cubicle. Julio had pretended not to notice, singing a few lines of a song, as soon as the colonel looked up at him. Julio had caught him using the phone on four separate occasions over the past few days, which seemed out of place for the colonel. He'd peeked out of his door before to spy on several nearby staff members, including the colonel, and had never seen anyone using a cell phone. He thought the Colonel might be going through a divorce, but remembered that he'd never seen any pictures indicating a relationship on his desk or cubicle walls. No pictures of kids or a wife, just a few photos of the colonel and other soldiers taken in various Godforsaken parts of the world. A few military plaques commemorated distinguished service with different units, but nothing beyond that.

Julio always trusted his instincts, and they were whispering bad things about Colonel Farrington. If something was wrong, he could be the nation's first line of defense. He wasn't a military hero, but Julio knew a thing or two about bravery. He had burn scarring over half of his torso to prove it. He'd worked in the West Block, when American Airlines Flight 77 hit the Pentagon and sprayed burning jet fuel through a corridor he'd been sweeping.

The initial blast knocked him through an open office door, into the lap of a startled navy captain, saving him from the aerosolized fuel explosion that vaporized anyone still in the hallway. After extinguishing their own personal clothing fires, Julio and Captain Reynolds rushed into the hellish inferno to look for survivors. Julio was a true hero, well respected at the Pentagon, but his service to country didn't end on September 11, 2001. He kept a close eye on the place, because he had always suspected that the next attack would come from the inside.

"I got my eyes on you, Colonel Sanders," he muttered with a sarcastic grin, wishing he had packed some fried chicken for lunch, instead of a ham sandwich.

Chapter Twelve

Sharpe stopped writing on the yellow legal pad and glanced up at Agent Mendoza, nodding enthusiastically.

"How confident are you about Munoz's statement? If we start pushing Pentagon buttons, we need to be rock solid on our assessment. This could get ugly...real quick," said Sharpe.

"Carlisle's assessment is definitive. He walked me through the biofeedback. Either Munoz is telling the truth—or he's the perfect liar. He's a tough book to read on the outside. Impassive. No apparent signs of being rattled. But bio showed a different story when we hinted that we might render him out of the country. His vitals spiked, but he kept himself under control. This guy is a cool customer. Highly trained, somewhere, and not the kind of training his army service record would indicate. Four years as a field artillery officer? We might have stumbled onto something huge here," said Agent Olson.

"I think I agree. Have Carlisle put together a package with his assessment...and yours. I want to walk through the director's door with everything I need to make a case for a deal. Once the deal is signed, we need to move fast. What do you know about General Terrence Sanderson?"

"I've never heard of him before today. I did a quick Internet search. Special Ops for most of his career. Details are sketchy, but it appears that his boots touched Iranian soil during Operation Eagle Claw. Plank owner in the Delta Force community. Meteoric rise through the ranks, then a flat line. Didn't make a lot of friends on the Hill from what I could tell. He retired, or was put out to pasture in 2001. Pretty much fell off the radar. Munoz is ready to connect the dots once the deal is in place," Olson said.

"Looks like Sanderson just popped back up on the radar scope, in a big way. Keep pressing Munoz for more details. I don't know if I have enough for a blanket immunity deal. He'll probably have to sign a contingency deal, which means he'll have to show us his cards before we go to the Pentagon. If the Pentagon refuses to share, no deal," Sharpe said.

"I think he'll take the risk. The threat of being moved to a facility out of the country scared him. He really wants a deal," Olson said.

"So do I. This could be a huge break. Eight coordinated murders on the same night. I'm willing to let this guy walk if he leads us to the jackpot. Tell him we need more information to make the deal stick. I'm gonna get things rolling on my end. Good work, Heather."

"Thank you, sir," she said, and Sharpe replaced the receiver on the desk phone.

"Sounds like Olson was the right agent to send to Boston," Mendoza piped in from his chair.

"She's one of the best investigators in the FBI. She was my first phone call after waking you up this morning. So, do we know anything else about Mr. Munoz?"

"Average Joe, more or less. Lives outside of Hartford, in Windsor."

"How far is that from Newport?" Sharpe asked.

"Just under a hundred miles," Mendoza said.

"Did they find his car yet?"

"Nothing on the streets near the mansion. They're searching a nearby college. The campus has waterfront acreage that connects to the cliff walk, which is a well-trafficked path this time of the year. Munoz was found sprawled on the rocks a few hundred yards north of the mansion, just off this path. He might have been trying to duck a few nighttime strollers and slipped in the dark."

"We need to figure out how he got there, and how long he's been casing the residence. Start piecing this all together. He'd have to pay a toll somehow to get into Newport, unless he hitchhiked. We might find a file in the car, especially if these attacks were coordinated by an ex-special forces type. The car is important," Sharpe said.

"We pressed him on the car, and he wouldn't budge. I'm sure he'll tell us about the car once he has a deal."

"I'm not counting on a deal, Frank. He's not giving us enough up front."

"He's walking a fine line," Mendoza said.

"Well, it's not good enough. I need some corroborating evidence to push this through. I think Munoz is worried about the car. We just might not need him once we find it."

"I'll make sure finding the car is Newport's top priority," Mendoza said and stood up to leave the office.

Chapter Thirteen

Daniel parked a dark blue, late model Toyota Camry between two other nondescript sedans in Logan Airport's central parking lot; the car's Massachusetts plates blending in with nearly every other car in the row. He had exchanged his BMW for the pre-staged Camry in Portsmouth, at the largest self-storage facility in seacoast New Hampshire.

Before driving out of the storage facility, he made a point of talking to the desk clerk long enough to create a lasting memory. If investigators got this far, he wanted them to know that he was now driving one of the most common automobile models on the road in the U.S.; one of thousands registered in Massachusetts alone. To make matters worse for the FBI, he left the 95 Interstate at Newburyport and found a secluded spot to change the license plates. The storage facility had cameras, and he needed this car to stay hidden.

He put the parking lot ticket on the passenger seat and wasted no time retrieving one of the two black nylon duffel bags from the trunk, along with a small black carry-on bag. After slamming the trunk shut, Daniel noted the car's location and searched for signs that would lead him into Terminal C. He had about twenty-five minutes to catch a Jet Blue flight to Baltimore/Washington International airport—making a clean break from New England.

Eight minutes later, he rushed up to the airline counter and handed his driver's license to a slim, brown-haired woman in a blue uniform. She compared the picture on the license to Daniel, squinting briefly before scribbling something illegible on his boarding pass with a red marker.

"Any bags to check?"

"Not this time. I think these should fit onboard," he said, lifting his two bags a few inches off the ground where she could see.

"That should be fine. You're all set, Mr. Harrell. The gate number is printed on your ticket," she said and smiled.

Daniel nodded and briskly moved toward the security checkpoint.

Chapter Fourteen

Agent Olson stepped into the interrogation room with a brown file folder. She slapped it down on the white Formica tabletop and stared at Munoz. The right side of his face was scraped and bruised from his fall onto the rocks. Dried blood covering most of his ear. He sported a nondescript, medium-length haircut, faded lightly on the sides. A horizontal scar grazed the hair above his left ear, and another visible scar showed through the stubble on the right side of his chin. Dark-skinned, with deep brown eyes and an angular face, he was a handsome man despite his rough condition.

Munoz looked up at Olson, his face remaining expressionless.

"Do we have a deal?" he uttered.

"We do, but it's contingent..."

"Good luck with your investigation. I'm ready for a vacation. Somewhere warm, I hope," Munoz said, leaning back in his chair.

"Contingent on proving this conspiracy. Black Flag better be real. Do you have any idea what happened today?" she asked, taking a seat across the table.

"Don't worry, it's real. Has my attorney seen the deal?"

"We have her standing by for a videoconference. She'll verify the details of your deal, but I'll tell you something..." Agent Olson leaned forward, her face several inches from Munoz. "You're not going anywhere until we figure out what happened today."

"I can go wherever I want. Whenever I want," he stated with a suppressed grin, placing his hands on the table in front of him.

Agent Olson reeled backward. Munoz had somehow managed to free his hands from the handcuffs that had been secured behind his back to the chair. Agent Carlisle reacted swiftly, charging around the side of the table, but stopped as Munoz placed both hands on the top of his head. Both agents moved backward from the table, weapons drawn and pointed at the suspect.

"None of you have any idea what you're dealing with here," said Munoz.

"Keep your hands on your head! Back away from the table and get on your knees. You will not be warned again," Olson yelled.

The door opened, disgorging three agents who approached Munoz. One of them held a Taser, the other two carried MP-5 submachine guns. Five agents stood well outside of Munoz's lunge radius, aiming weapons in his direction. One false move would erase Munoz from existence and eliminate any chance the FBI had to make sense of the day.

Munoz had told them that a link existed between General Terrence Sanderson and today's events, and that he would trade information about Sanderson for full immunity. Without more information, they couldn't move on Sanderson. Since the FBI still had no idea who had masterminded the string of murders; they needed every bit of help available. Munoz represented the only break in their investigation. The Department of Justice, with the full backing of the White House, agreed with this assessment.

"Patch me through to my lawyer. We're wasting time. As soon as you get what you need, I walk out of the door. If you fuck with me on this deal, they'll carry you out the back door with a tag on your big toe," he said, lowering his body to his knees.

Munoz closed his eyes as two of the agents grappled him, tightly affixing with zip ties and handcuffs. Agent Olson kept her weapon drawn while the agents lifted Munoz to his feet. As he passed Olson, she grabbed the collar of his dark blue hooded sweatshirt and pulled him close.

"Your information better be worth this deal. I have a feeling you wouldn't last very long on the streets if we publicized the time and location of your release," she whispered.

"Don't worry. This information is worth a thousand deals. And just for the record, I wouldn't worry too much about my survivability on the streets. If the Pentagon coughs up my real file...you'll spend the next few days wondering why you're still alive," he said and pulled away from Agent Olson.

"Maximum security. No contact...just the videoconference with his attorney," she said.

Chapter Fifteen

The raucous din from Task Force HYDRA's operations room could be heard fifty feet down the hallway in either direction. Like a dying star, the Terrorist Financing Operations Section had imploded that morning, sending a dense, pulsing gravity throughout the building; a black hole that sucked agents in and wouldn't let them go. Agents wishing to go home that night steered clear of the noise inside the Counterterrorism Division.

Special Agent-in-Charge Sharpe listened intently to the silence on the phone. He stood in front of the large display screen, staring at information assembled regarding Jeffrey Munoz. There was nothing in his military service record or civilian records to suggest his possible involvement in today's fiasco. Munoz owned a successful chain of five coffee shops in Hartford, Connecticut, leaving the day-to-day operations of the entire business to one of the shop managers he had promoted two years ago. David Stebbens.

Agents interviewed Stebbens and several other employees. Their stories were the same. Munoz loved his work. He spent most of his days and evenings in the coffee shops, chatting with patrons and suppliers, between day trading on his laptop. Financials for The Toasted Bean were solid, and Stebbens confirmed that he and Munoz had just run the numbers for opening a new shop. No red flags. Nothing to suggest Munoz would drive over a hundred miles to put a bullet through Umar Salah's head.

Sharpe waited patiently for the associate director for National Security to take the line. The FBI's request to the Pentagon for access to the Black Flag files had been formally submitted over an hour ago, followed by a few high-level personal calls. It was rumored that the director of the FBI would contact the secretary of defense personally to express the urgency of the situation. The line suddenly went live.

"Mr. Sharpe, I have the executive director for you now," a male voice said, followed by a click.

Sharpe stiffened. He had expected to speak with the associate director, Sandra Delgado, who he knew on a personal level. Delgado and Sharpe had attended The Academy at the same time, one class apart, and had stayed cordially in touch over the years. Sandra and her husband had dined with Ryan and his wife several times over the past year. Sharpe didn't know what to expect from the director, and he didn't like surprises.

"Ryan, its Fred Carroll. Sorry to ambush you like this, but the situation has changed slightly, and Sandra will no longer be included in the communication chain between the Pentagon and the bureau."

"I hope nothing is wrong, sir," Sharpe risked.

"Nothing wrong with Agent Delgado. Apparently, there is something very wrong with the Black Flag files. We need to maintain a minimal chain of information custody with regard to Black Flag," Carroll said.

"So Munoz wasn't lying?"

"Apparently not, and whatever is in those files is protected by the Department of Defense's strictest compartmentalized protocols. The Pentagon has agreed to grant us limited access. We will be allowed to use the information to unravel today's events and determine if an immediate threat to the U.S. exists. My assistant will pass the protocols to you immediately. Don't mess around with this information. The director himself convinced the White House that access to Black Flag was critical, but I have a feeling that the doors to this vault could slam shut at any time. Black Flag is a ticking time bomb that nobody wants aired in public. Contact me directly with updates. Instructions for direct contact will be contained in an email you should have just received. Let's get to the bottom of this ASAP, without pissing off the Pentagon."

"Understood, sir. I have the best agents working every angle of this case," Sharpe said.

"If you need more than that, don't hesitate to ask," Executive Director Carroll said, and the line went dead.

Sharpe waved to Mendoza, who pushed his way through several agents huddled over a bank of computer screens in the middle of the operations center. By the time he arrived a few seconds later, Sharpe had read the director's email.

"Frank, take two agents from Counterintelligence and report to the Information/Data bureau of the Pentagon. Your point of contact there will be Colonel Richard Farrington. I'll need you there long enough to thoroughly assess pertinent information in the Black Flag files. From what I've been told, the files are explosive and could be yanked out from under us without warning. Focus on information regarding Black Flag personnel.

"Munoz lived close enough to his assigned target to imply a geographic-based assignment, so let's get names and start mapping out last known locations of all Black Flag operatives. We might find a trend. If we can nab another one of these murderers, we'll have our best chance at nailing this to the wall by the end of the day. I don't know what kind of information they will be willing to release, but I'd like to know about capabilities. If we need to take one of these guys down, I want to know exactly what kind of training they received. We need to know what we're up against."

"All right, I'm on it. Does Counterintel know I'm coming to grab more of their talent?" Mendoza asked.

"They will in a few moments. And, Frank, you and the two agents will have to sign Category One, Compartmentalized Information Security agreements prior to viewing any of the Black Flag documents. Any agents who hear the words Black Flag will be required to sign a Category Two," Sharpe said.

"Christ. We better get word to Boston. The fewer agents exposed to this the better," Mendoza said.

"Once you arrive at the Pentagon, you will see a list of approved Category One personnel. You are entitled to share any information you see with these individuals personally on a face-to-face contact basis. That should be a very short list. Myself, the two counterintelligence agents and Executive Assistant Director Carroll. That's it. I expect that you'll be running back and forth all day to report to me. The two agents will be required to stay inside the Sanctum during the active investigation or until the Pentagon shuts us down. Let's nail this down quickly, Frank."

"We'll be thorough and get everything we need as quickly as possible," Frank assured him, exhaling deeply.

"The Pentagon will approve and classify all information to be shared, so be aggressive and fight for anything that might help us figure out what happened today. They have a protocol for this. Start with the names. I think this is our best starting point. Remember, you can share anything with me personally, but if it's not approved by the Pentagon, it's not going onto these screens. If they won't approve something you feel is critical to the investigation, you need to get your ass back here as fast as possible, so we can press the director for more cooperation," Sharpe said and picked up one of the nearby phones.

"I'll be in touch," Mendoza said and made to bolt out of the room.

"Frank!"

Agent Mendoza looked over his shoulder.

"You better take Keller with you. I'll see if I can get him full access," Sharpe said.

Chapter Sixteen

Colonel Farrington watched the group approach from the direction of the Information Section's only access point: four men, escorted by a navy lieutenant commander wearing the summer white uniform. The navy had recently shifted uniforms, trading service dress blues, which resembled a dark blue suit, for a white, short-sleeved uniform that reminded Farrington of the old fashioned Good Humor Ice Cream man.

"Thank you, Commander, I have them from here. Gentlemen, welcome to the Compartmentalized Information Section. Let's take a seat in the briefing room and get the formalities out of the way so you can go to work," he said and led them to a room adjacent to his cubicle.

He fished a pair of keys out of the front right pocket of his crisply pressed dark green uniform trousers and opened both of the locks to the room. The briefing room was sparse, decorated with a heavily varnished, rectangular conference table that could seat twelve. Harsh fluorescent lights recessed behind large opaque plastic ceiling tiles illuminated the room. No pictures adorned the ugly off-white walls, and Separate stacks of paperwork sat neatly arranged on each long side of the table. Each stack was topped with a face sheet that displayed one of the agents' names. There were no chairs in the room.

Colonel Farrington walked to the far end of the table and waited for everyone to find his or her stack. Before anyone uttered a word, three more people filed into the room and stood against the wall facing the colonel, on the opposite side of the room. The last one in, a female marine staff sergeant, closed the door behind her. Farrington registered a look of discomfort on one of the FBI agent's faces, which gave him some satisfaction.

Prior to Farrington's arrival at the Pentagon, the room had been used as a staff member hangout, featuring comfortable chairs, pleasant lighting from several dimmable standing lamps, wall hangings and a fully stocked coffee station.

One of his first acts was to strip the room bare. He didn't want any sense of comfort to exist here. In fact, he preferred that the room make everyone feel on edge. Only clear plastic sheets covering the walls and floor would make him happier about the room. His job was to enforce the Department of Defense's strictest information-sharing protocols. Penalties for leaking information in the Sanctum ranged from a simple career-damaging letter of censure to life imprisonment without the possibility of parole—on charges of treason. He liked to set the right tone from the beginning.

"All right, let's get started. There are four documents that each of you must sign to enter the Sanctum. First, an explanation of the CIS categories and specific instructions regarding the management of sensitive information under each category. CIS stands for Compartmentalized Information Security. You will all need to read and sign the acknowledgement under CIS Category One, which I'm sure you are all aware, is the highest level of information security, carrying the highest levels of penalty for any accidental or purposeful unauthorized breach. Category One is the easiest to remember. You can only share information with the individuals listed on your agreement, and only in person. In person means physically face-to-face in a secure environment, taking all reasonable precautions from eavesdropping, purposeful or accidental. Videoconferencing doesn't count."

Agent Mendoza opened his mouth to speak, but was cut off by the colonel.

"Before any of you lays the proverbial egg, there is a procedure for disseminating information pertinent to your investigation. My staff, and Mr. McKie from the Defense Intelligence Agency, will assist you in this process. Our charge is to protect sensitive, classified information, while at the same time helping your investigation. I'm sure we will all butt heads today, but I assure you we are in no way trying to hinder your progress. Anything cleared by Mr. McKie will be retyped by one of my staff, either Staff Sergeant Brodin or Technical Sergeant D'Onofrie, and faxed directly to your operations center with a CIS Category Two classification. Mr. McKie will make the ultimate call on what is Category One or Two, and what can be transmitted or communicated.

"If you see something in the files that Mr. McKie won't release via fax, then you'll need to personally carry the information in your head to your immediate director, Agent Sharpe, who will not be able to share it with anyone outside of the list. Are your heads ringing yet? It's a lot to process, but we'll try to make this as easy as possible for your organizations.

"As representatives of their respective organizations, Agent Mendoza and Mr. Keller are free to leave and reenter as they wish; however, we do require that Agents Harris and Calhoun stay within the Sanctum until the file is resealed. My staff will be required to make the same sacrifice. The Sanctum has full bathroom and shower facilities, cots, coffee, and you can order whatever you'd like from the canteen to be delivered at any time. We'll send the bill to your agencies. Spare toiletry kits can be found in the bathrooms."

He paused and looked directly at Mendoza and Keller. "As for the two of you, anyone moving in or out of the section must do so with an escort, and you'll be subjected to our strictest security protocols on the way in and out of the building. No rubber gloves, gentlemen, but you will be scanned and frisked. Cell phones must be surrendered to security personnel; they are strictly prohibited in this section. Wear your security badges at all times. If there are no further questions, please read through the documents and sign them. Once you're done, we'll get you situated in the Sanctum. Entry and exit from the Sanctum is strictly controlled by me, and I will be available at all times to facilitate your comings and goings. I'm here as long as you're here."

"Will you be stationed inside of the Sanctum with us?" Agent Harris asked, shuffling through his paperwork.

"No. I unlock and release the file to Mr. McKie. Once he has confirmed that the contents of the file match the contents requested, you won't see me again inside the Sanctum until it is time to lock the file back up for good. I simply serve as the gatekeeper and document custodian. I have no idea what you've requested, only that the strictest of security protocols has been assigned to the handling of the information contained in the file. Take a few minutes to finish the paperwork, and I'll get you situated."

Ten minutes later, Colonel Farrington walked out of the Sanctum, satisfied that everything was in good order. McKie had enthusiastically confirmed that the contents of the vacuum-sealed, pressure-activated storage locker matched what the FBI had requested. Project Black Flag. As usual, General Sanderson's intelligence was right on the money. The files were stored in a single oversized, modern briefcase, which surprised

Farrington. Most of the files in the Sanctum had been converted to thumb drives, hard drives, or even full laptop computers. The briefcase contained all of the known surviving documents pertaining to Sanderson's notoriously successful covert operations program, and judging by a glimpse of the contents from across the table, the documents were originals.

Farrington sat down in his cubicle and glanced around the section. All clear. He dialed one of fifteen phone numbers that he had committed to memory over the past year, in preparation for this day.

"Are we in business?" General Sanderson's voice asked immediately.

"Yes, sir. The files looked to be in an original form."

"Do you have a timeline for extraction?" Sanderson's voice replied.

"I have seven in the Sanctum right now, but I expect the herd to thin as they wade through the file. Two of them will likely depart within the hour. I'm looking at an early evening, possibly a late afternoon timeline."

"Take your time, Rich. The file will be open for at least twenty-four hours, if not longer."

"I understand, sir. But once these files are secured, we won't have another chance to retrieve them," Farrington uttered.

"You'll have ample opportunity, I'm sure of it. Even if they suddenly shut down access to the file, you'll be the first to know. I trust your skills, Colonel. We've known each other for a long time."

Colonel Farrington's beeper vibrated, and he checked the number. "I have to go, sir. Looks like a few of our guests might be leaving earlier than I expected."

"Understood. Keep me posted," the general said, and the line went dead.

Farrington ensured the cell phone was placed in meeting mode, to keep it silent, and grabbed his desk phone. He pressed one of the conference call buttons and was immediately connected to Staff Sergeant Brodin within the Sanctum.

"Sir, Mr. Keller wishes to depart the Sanctum," she informed him.

"That was fast. I'll be right there," he replied and glanced at the Sanctum's security door adjacent to his cubicle.

"And sir?" she whispered.

Colonel Farrington continued to listen without responding. Sergeant Brodin lowered her voice even further.

"I think Keller might be eidetic."

"Interesting. How long did he look through the files?"

"Six minutes. He didn't appear to do much more than glance at the sheets, like he wasn't really paying attention. McKie didn't appear to be bothered by it. I just thought you should know, sir."

"That's why I have you in there, Staff Sergeant. I'll be right over," he said and hung up the phone.

A photographic memory. Very interesting.

Chapter Seventeen

General Sanderson sat at a dark brown Shaker-style table in an apartment on the outskirts of Alexandria, Virginia. He had recently acquired the unit through a real estate holding company owned by a loyal, longtime friend. A powerful friend who had more to do with the day's events than providing an untraceable real estate purchase.

Sitting at the rectangular table, he faced a sliding glass door that led to a modest balcony two stories above a lush garden and small, undisturbed pool. Thick curtains gave him privacy from prying eyes on other balconies and reduced the glare from a bright, declining sun. A stainless steel refrigerator hummed behind him and marked the beginning of a granite and cherry cabinet appointed kitchen that filled the space to his immediate left. A sizable, sparsely furnished media room loomed to his right, containing a simple dark leather couch, coffee table and wall-mounted flat-screen television. Empty built-in bookshelves flanked the television.

The general alternated his attention among three laptop computers situated in a semi-circle on the table. A tangle of wires extended over the back of the table, split between a massive power strip and a broadband modem jammed at odd angles on one of the chairs. He confirmed Petrovich's flight schedule and picked up one of five cell phones sitting on the table next to the computers. Each one was plugged into a charger connected to the same power strip as the computers.

He dialed Parker.

"Sir?"

"Our guest should be arriving shortly. I want you to pick him up and find a rental car agency well away from the airport. Rent a car in your name and give him your SUV. I don't expect our friends to piece things together this quickly, but we can't take any chances. Take him to my place north of the city, and wait for instructions. Make sure to outfit our friend well. I may need him at a moment's notice."

"Understood, sir. I'm a few minutes away from the airport. Any word from Farrington?"

"Everything is in place. We're just waiting for the right moment. Let me know when the two of you have arrived safely," the general said and ended the call.

Chapter Eighteen

The first encrypted fax from the Pentagon arrived thirty-two minutes after Special Agent Frank Mendoza and his team entered the Sanctum. Sharpe took custody of the sealed folder from Special Agent Keith Weber.

Weber's face appeared even more exhausted than this morning, though he had managed to find a new dress shirt to replace the crumpled mess he had presented to the task force. Since then, the pale, lanky agent had never been seen without a cup of coffee in his hands. As tired as Weber might be, Sharpe was relieved to see him still functioning at full capacity. As chief communications officer for the task force, Weber was unlikely to find a moment's rest in the next twenty-four hours, especially with CIS Category Two protocols blanketed over the entire task force. Any breach of information security would fall squarely on his shoulders...and Sharpe's.

All eyes in the task force's operations center drifted toward Sharpe as he broke the packet's security seal. Aware of his audience, Sharpe motioned for Special Agent Dana O'Reilly, from the criminal investigation section, to join him at the front of the room. As she navigated the workstations, Sharpe removed the two-page document and began to read, his face betraying no initial response to the information as he processed what Mendoza had been able to push past the Pentagon gatekeepers. It was more than he had expected. He handed the first sheet over to Agent O'Reilly.

O'Reilly was another rising star within the FBI. Graduating number one in her class at the Academy, she had reported to the Los Angeles field office in 1999 and made a positive, lasting impression on Special Agent Olson, who personally requested her assignment to headquarters in 2004, several years ahead of schedule on a typical agent's career-ladder climb. As usual, Olson's instincts had been dead-on, and Agent O'Reilly didn't disappoint. Her investigative skill and efficiency matched her sharp, angular face and short brown hair.

"Agent O'Reilly, I want full workups on each of these names. Start with their most current known locations and move outward. I'm looking for a possible geographic pattern. Munoz lived within easy driving distance of Newport. Focus on the East Coast. If their last known address isn't on the East Coast, or close, move on to the next name. I want to start shaping this investigation in twenty minutes."

"We'll process all of the names at once, with an appropriate geographic priority filter. Give me ten minutes to get this up on the screens," she said and rushed away before Sharpe could respond.

"And I want these names, with pictures, to go out highest priority, everywhere. Classify them as suspected terrorists."

He sat down at his temporary workstation near the front of the chaotic room and watched as several agents and technical support staff moved about in a flurry of activity, reenergized with the new information. Agent O'Reilly rolled a chair up to one of the occupied workstations and handed the list over to one of the task force's tech staff. She gestured toward several other workstations, then the large screens above Sharpe's head.

Satisfied that O'Reilly had this under control, he turned his attention to the second sheet. He thought Mendoza must have fought the Pentagon to get this sheet released. Although he could drop this sheet on the subway, and nobody could make sense of it, he was seasoned enough to understand the sinister implications. The notes provided by Munoz gave him a unique frame of reference to analyze the sheet.

Confirmed that General Terrence Sanderson founded program. Seeking additional details.

Areas of focus for investigative cross-reference: Serbia (1990s), Colombia (1990s), Russia (1990s), Mexico (1990s), Afghanistan (1990s).

All subjects trained extensively in following skill areas: hand to hand combat, edged weapons, urban combat, undercover operations, sabotage, field espionage, improvised combat, deception and disguise, marksmanship, explosives, forgery, extreme conditions survival. Each subject given custom specialized training in skill areas deemed most appropriate to assigned areas of operation. Most common specialized skills include: sniper operations, electronic surveillance, computer networking, advanced urban combat, improvised explosives, security systems manipulation, narcotics manufacturing.

Consider subjects highly dangerous and unusually capable of escape or evasion. Recommend use of highly-trained, tactical law enforcement teams for apprehension or pursuit. Do not underestimate subjects' capabilities.

Subjects sent to operate undercover without support for extensive periods of time (2-3 years). Fatality rate for program graduates in operational assignments: 30% first year, 40% second year. No graduates are known to have survived third year.

Sharpe leaned back in his chair and processed the information. Everything squared with Munoz's description of Sanderson's covert operations program, but the implication burrowed much deeper, and Sharpe wasn't sure he wanted to turn over any additional rocks. The information contained on these two sheets might be enough to shed the appropriate amount of light on today's events and allow him to figure out if a further danger existed.

His own task force's investigation was permanently destroyed, but he might still have a chance to turn this into an opportunity. If a deeper conspiracy lurked beneath the surface, his team might possibly be able to stand at the vanguard of a new, permanent investigation. But first, he needed to convince the director that the week wouldn't end in a spectacular, mass-casualty attack on the United States. To do this, he needed to capture another Black Flag operative. Munoz had a deal, although Sharpe had no intention of releasing him yet.

Special Agent O'Reilly yelled across the room. "Sir, we have a preliminary picture coming up in a few seconds," she said and leaned into a screen between two busy data techs.

Sharpe stood up and took a few steps back from the bank of plasma screen monitors.

"We're linking it to the map, sir. A few more seconds," O'Reilly said.

The center screen still displayed the same map of the East Coast, with each murder site identified by an icon and a few lines of information. The screens flanking the map contained investigative information linked to each scene. So far, very little physical evidence had been recovered at any of the sites, emphasizing the sheer luck surrounding the capture of Munoz in Newport. The assassins had vanished like ghosts, leaving nothing behind. If Munoz had stepped on a different rock in the darkness, Sharpe would have very likely spent the next several days staring up at an unchanging screen, watching his career crumble.

The display blinked, and Sharpe watched new icons begin to populate the screen from north to south. He counted eleven new icons and immediately saw a pattern. One icon riveted his attention.

"Can you zoom in on the area surrounding Cape Elizabeth, Maine? Send it to one of the other screens. O'Reilly?" he said, waving for her to join him.

The same map appeared on the screen to the right and zoomed into New England, continuing to a small coastal area in southern Maine.

"There!" Sharpe said, and the map stopped moving.

O'Reilly stood a few feet behind Sharpe, to his left.

"Jesus," she whispered, and Sharpe nodded in agreement.

The map showed two icons, each on the opposite side of the screen, but within the same metropolitan area. The icon on the far right, at the water's edge, was one of their murder scenes. The other, buried within Portland, Maine, contained a name. Daniel Petrovich.

"What's the distance between the two?" he said.

Before he finished the sentence, the techs answered on the screen with a line connecting the two icons. 5.9 miles. He turned to O'Reilly and spoke softly.

"I want to know everything there is to know about Daniel Petrovich. Notify our Maine team, and start the ball rolling for a coordinated, local law enforcement effort to find Petrovich. Our Boston-based SWAT team is occupied with Munoz and won't be available to assist. We'll have to rely on local and state SWAT. Based on Petrovich's profile, make sure they understand that this is a high-risk apprehension and that the teams need to focus on nonlethal methods. This is critical to national security. I'll work on the warrant."

"Understood, sir," she said and disappeared again.

Sharpe returned his focus to the center screen, counting at least eleven former Black Flag operatives, including Munoz, within reasonable driving distance of the crime scenes. He suddenly had doubts about Daniel Petrovich. Why would General Sanderson use someone so close to one of the targets? All of the other operatives lived at least an hour or more away, which would make them less obvious suspects. For the Maine assassination, Sanderson had the option of using an operative living in Concord, New Hampshire, about two hours away.

Then again, Sharpe wondered why the general would use anyone near the East Coast at all. If Munoz lived in Denver, Colorado, his task force would be forced to consider every Black Flag operative within the U.S. Munoz's proximity to the target suggested otherwise. Sanderson may have called others in from around the country, but it was clear that this was not the rule. Sharpe's best chance lay with the eleven operatives listed on the screen. Before he could finish his thought, six more Black Flag operatives appeared throughout the Midwest.

"That's it, sir. That's the list," Agent O'Reilly said.

"What do you mean that's it?" he said, walking toward her workstation.

"Half of the names on the list turned up with last known addresses dating back into the early nineties. I'll still work up full packages on them, but I thought it would confuse the overall picture on the screen right now," she said.

"Good call. None of these names extend past the Mississippi. What about the rest of the country?" Sharpe asked.

"If you want my guess, I'd say we didn't get the entire list."

"Damn it. Weber," he yelled across the room, "request more detailed information on each of these names. Priority goes to the ones on the East Coast. Also, request the full list of names. This can't be all of them."

Weber gave him a "thumbs up" from across the room and went to work at his computer station, as Sharpe glanced back at the screen and grimaced. They would have to coordinate a simultaneous strike on all ten remaining locations. He had no idea if any of the operatives were in communication with each other, but he couldn't risk raising a general alarm among General Sanderson's co-conspirators. They only needed to catch one of them to move the investigation forward. The more the better, obviously, but Sharpe wasn't greedy.

He also needed to talk with Mendoza immediately. They needed more details about the operative in Portland, Maine. Daniel Petrovich. If Sanderson used Petrovich for the Cape Elizabeth hit, like Sharpe suspected, it would prove to be a big mistake.

Chapter Nineteen

4:14 p.m.
Baltimore/Washington International Airport, Baltimore, Maryland

Daniel Petrovich waited patiently in his seat while the 747 taxied up to the gate at BWI airport. He had carefully, but surreptitiously watched the flight crew since about halfway through the two-hour flight. Boarding a flight this late in the afternoon had been a calculated risk, but he had been assured by General Sanderson that the net wouldn't fall on him until the early evening. Daniel's previous experience with the general had taught him that the man was rarely wrong, which is why Petrovich sensed that something was off about the day's events.

He glanced at the senior flight attendant, Elaine, a dark-haired, middle-aged woman who had seemed friendly enough throughout the flight. If the authorities knew he was on board, he had to assume at least one member of the flight crew had been notified, and his bet was on Elaine. So far, she'd only locked eyes with him twice, which was normal in Daniel's experience. She didn't look away quickly, or stare at him too long. Her behavior fell well within the normal parameters defined by an instinct he had sharpened to a razor's edge. He survived undercover for two years among the most dangerous, unpredictable men in the world, where the slightest change in expression was often the only warning that preceded a rusty buck knife across your throat.

The aircraft rolled gently to a stop at the gate, and the fasten seatbelt sign was deactivated, releasing passengers to crowd the aisles. He was pretty sure that the pilot would have kept the passengers in their seats if a tense, heavily armed SWAT team waited in the jetway.

Ten minutes later, Daniel walked through a non-automated door next to a large swivel exit. He thought about how easy it would be to trap someone inside one of those large aquarium-like rotating doors, which is why he avoided them. His transformation back into Marko Resja had accelerated.

Glancing up and down the pickup zone, he spotted Parker's green Grand Cherokee five cars down to his right. He tossed the cell phone he had used to contact Parker—and its separated battery—into a tall, gray trash receptacle next to a concrete pillar behind the SUV.

Daniel threw the black nylon duffel bag into the back seat and opened the front passenger door, barely nodding at Parker, who actively scanned the mirrors. He buckled his seatbelt, still half expecting to be rushed by federal agents from all sides, before Parker put the car into gear and cruised forward past an unoccupied, parked police car.

Once out of the airport, Parker started to navigate them toward the Baltimore Washington Parkway, which would intersect with the 495 Beltway north of Washington, D.C. Daniel had no idea where Parker intended to take him once they were inside the Beltway, but he had his own plans for staying quiet until the general needed him.

Parker finally broke the silence. "General Sanderson wants me to take you to a rental car agency. I'll rent another car, and you'll take mine."

"So he can keep track of me? No, thanks."

"He doesn't want any chance of a rental car transaction being traced to you."

"Does he think I'm going to use my driver's license?" Daniel asked as Parker turned the Cherokee onto the Parkway.

"If the feds think you're headed to D.C., they'll be able to figure it out, even if you use a fake ID."

"Why would they assume I'm headed here? I'd think this is the last place they would expect me to materialize."

"The general doesn't like surprises," Parker said.

"Then losing a man to the feds must have ruined his entire year."

Parker looked over at Daniel with a concerned expression. "The mission was a success, but the general's come too far to take any further chances."

"I'll bet," Daniel said and found himself lost in thought, staring into the thick traffic headed out of D.C.

"Once we get you a car, we'll head to a safe house in Silver Spring and wait for further developments."

Daniel didn't like the sound of this at all. With one of Sanderson's men in custody, he wasn't sure how fast the entire situation would unravel, if it hadn't already spiraled out of the general's control. Clearly, the general shared the same concerns, or he wouldn't have taken steps to get Daniel out of Maine so quickly.

Something kept bothering him, but he couldn't bring it to the surface. Parker suddenly showing up yesterday with Sanderson's barely-veiled ultimatum never sat right with Daniel. The Ghani killing was simple work, which didn't require his level of expertise, or exposure, and Sanderson had played a serious card to push him back into the fold. Mentioning Zorana Zekulic reeked of desperation and only served to underscore the insidious link bonding Petrovich to Sanderson.

The SUV slowed as they joined traffic headed into the capital, and Petrovich decided that it was in his best interest to maintain a safe distance from the general until a better picture of the situation developed. Given the nature of the Black Flag program, Daniel guessed that he wasn't the only program graduate with secrets that the general would rather see buried in an unmarked grave. Secrets that would ruin the general's reputation permanently and possibly land him in front of a firing squad…right next to Daniel. He glanced around at the standstill traffic and the area surrounding the Parkway. He needed to get out of this car and disappear.

Chapter Twenty

Keller walked down a dense, tree-lined street of brownstones deep in the heart of Georgetown, until he arrived at the waist-level wrought iron gate that marked the entrance to the law offices of Hopkins, Frederick and McDonough. He turned the thick brass knob imbedded into the gate, finding it unlocked. Pushing lightly, the gate swung inward and uttered a long squeak at the end of its swing radius.

He mounted the weathered, granite stairs, ascending several steep, narrow steps to arrive at a small, covered porch. Keller pressed the worn black button located under the law firm's shiny brass embossed business placard and heard a bell ring beyond the door.

Seconds later, the door buzzed, followed by a loud click. He pushed the thick wooden door inward and stepped into the building's cramped vestibule, turning his body sideways in order to close the outer door. Keller now faced a windowless door, which buzzed and opened slightly inward. He gripped the door's handle and leaned into the door, which opened slowly. Despite its similar appearance to the outer door, this door was constructed of reinforced steel core. Once he was through, the door closed on its own, a feature that always left Keller with the impression that it could open all of the way—if the person controlling it liked you.

Keller scanned the reception room when he entered. Ceiling to floor bookcases covered the entire wall to his right, filled with books that hadn't been touched for decades, or at least for the two years he'd been assigned to the FBI. If he turned around, he would see two uncomfortable, light brown upholstered armchairs under the larger front window, separated by an equally ugly brown pedestal table. Several coasters sat stacked in a holder on the table, implying that a beverage might be produced for someone sitting in these chairs. Not likely—especially for him.

He returned to the bookcase, focusing on a row of encyclopedias near the floor. A thin, genuine smile formed on his tight lips as he turned his attention back to the receptionist. Claire, an exceptionally stoic woman, continued to stare at a flat-screen monitor like he didn't exist. She was partially obscured by a green-glass-shaded banker's lamp, which lit the top of her desk, but did little to illuminate the rest of the room. He kept smiling at Claire, who finally looked up at him.

Dressed in a light blue blazer, which covered an ivory blouse, she wore a single strand of pearls, which hung just above the top button. Her gray hair was pulled back in a bun, leaving a few wisps of hair to flow freely down her high cheeks. She looked like old money to Keller, and acted like it too. Ice blue eyes pierced him as she spoke.

"Mr. Berg will see you upstairs," she said, moving her right hand below the top of the desk to press a hidden button—smiling the entire time.

Keller imagined she had a pistol strapped to the underside of the desk, or maybe a shotgun. Certainly she had a bank of buttons, each serving a function in the building. Maybe one of them activated a trapdoor leading to an incinerator.

"Thank you, Claire." He turned toward the ornate staircase on the wall opposite to the bookshelves.

He'd started up the stairs when he heard her say, "Good to see you again, Mr. Keller."

"You too, Claire," he said somberly. He stopped before disappearing up the stairs. "Oh, the encyclopedias are out of order. Number fifteen is in front of fourteen," he said, waiting for a response.

"I never noticed. Thank you, Mr. Keller," she said, looking up from the computer screen with a forced smile.

Keller continued up the stairs, wondering about Claire's exact role within the agency. She'd have to be highly trusted if she knew about his photographic memory. This was not common knowledge within the CIA, for several reasons. Most importantly, he would become a fought-over asset that not everyone could possess, and those who lost the fight to bring him into their fold would never trust him.

There was too much infighting, petty jealousy, and paranoia inside the CIA. Widespread knowledge of his eidetic memory would be a career killer. Berg knew about his memory, but Berg had recruited him, keeping him close. Keller's skill could be a limitless treasure if used under the right circumstances, and he found himself assigned to one liaison position after another, mostly reporting to Berg. Not exactly the exotic CIA career he had imagined when first reporting to Langley, but unlike most CIA recruits, Keller was still a spy.

He opened the door at the top of the stairs and stepped into a different world. Classical music drifted into the brightly lit hallway, which contained five doors and ended with a frosted privacy window. Keller knew that the open door to his immediate right was a modern conference room that extended to the front of the building, taking up at least a third of the second floor's square footage. He wouldn't find Berg here. He would be seated comfortably in the lounge at the end of the hallway, sipping a drink.

To his left, a closed door secured by a fingerprint access terminal reminded him where he stood. In the CIA, there was always another layer of secrecy, and he didn't have access to this room. He walked down the hallway and glanced into the open doors. One room contained a full kitchen, which was connected to the other room, a dining room with one large rectangular table. A crystal chandelier hovered precariously low over the table. He counted place settings for eight.

Keller arrived at the lounge and knocked on the doorframe before poking his head inside. Berg sat in a dark leather chair in the corner of the room.

"Randy, please. You always knock on the door. I find it so peculiar," he said.

"I always feel like I'm walking into someone's private den," he said.

Keller loved this room. It had to be the most exclusive lounge in Washington, and no expense had been spared to make it feel that way. Two brown leather chairs flanked an ornately carved, darkly-stained pedestal table, which held a bronze lamp with a deep red lamp shade. The lamp's soft glow drifted down onto a small tumbler filled with a finger of amber liquid. He stepped inside and inhaled deeply the comforting smell of expensive leather furniture and antique books. Three of the room's four walls were covered in bookshelves that contained real books, unlike Claire's faux reading collection. Classics, rare books, modern thrillers, curios. The shelves here were a treasury of gifts from dignitaries, world leaders, agency patrons, well-connected politicians and thieves. He cherished receiving permission to spend the night here.

Staring awestruck at the collection, he almost stumbled over the leather couch that dissected the room, separating Berg and the deep leather reading chairs from a fully stocked bar immediately to Keller's left. He saw two laptop computers on the oval coffee table in front of the couch. He'd use one of these to type his report, and Berg would use the other to simultaneously read and securely transmit his report to Audra Bauer, their director. His eyes caught a bottle of Chivas Regal standing guard over an empty tumbler on the shiny bar top.

"Pour yourself a drink," Berg offered.

"Thank you. Only a small one, though. I need to start typing this out while it's fresh," he said and moved toward the bottle of outrageously expensive scotch.

"It's always fresh. I bet you could type out the first psychological exam we gave you with ninety-nine percent accuracy." Berg laughed.

"One hundred percent. I dip into the ninety-nine range when I try to tap into the middle school years. I hope you're the one who moved the encyclopedias," he said, walking over to his favorite chair with a splash of Chivas.

"Simply amazing. I moved them a few weeks ago. I don't even think Claire has noticed. Salud," Berg said, raising his glass.

"Salud," Keller replied and clinked Berg's glass.

Berg took a long sip, relishing the drink. He leaned toward Keller like he was sharing a secret.

"I'm not going to bullshit you here, Randy. The CIA has very little on this Black Flag program. We know it was created and run by General Sanderson, with very little oversight. We are pretty sure it fell under Defense Intelligence Agency purview, and that it was abruptly shut down in 2001. It may have started in the late eighties, but details have been nearly non-existent. This was a word of mouth program, and we couldn't find any loose mouths willing to talk about it. General William Tierney, apparently one of Sanderson's many close rivals and enemies within the army, brought the program's activities to the attention of Congress in late 1999. Tierney quietly retired a few months later, and Sanderson followed suit shortly after that. The matter was quickly sealed and has remained that way until today. So, what is your impression of the file?"

"They need to burn this file as soon as they're done with it, and pray to God that these are the last remaining documents pertaining to this program," Keller said and emptied his glass in one swallow.

Chapter Twenty-One

General Sanderson picked up the buzzing cell phone on the table and answered it. "Good timing. I hope you've put some distance between yourself and the airport. An APB just went out with a dozen names. The FBI isn't wasting any time with this. We cut it really close flying him in," Sanderson said.

"Sir, I lost him. We were sitting in traffic, and he jumped out of the car just past the Laurel exit. I'm still stuck in bumper-to-bumper traffic and can't get this fucking thing off the Parkway. Are you sure bringing him here was a good idea?" Parker said.

An uncomfortable pause lingered, while he processed what this might mean for his plan. Nothing, really. He could never fully control Daniel. Extensive psychological testing had predicted that he'd be a volatile candidate for the program. Petrovich had a pathologic aversion to authority, balanced by a conflicting need to operate loosely within a structure. He caused considerable difficulty for the instructors at The Ranch, while excelling within the program. Sanderson had seen the unlimited potential in Petrovich. He still did.

"I'm not surprised. Trust me, there was nothing you could do to stop him. Remember what I told you. Don't ever stand in his way. He knows how to get in touch with us and will surface when he's ready. His world was turned upside down yesterday. Frankly, I'm just happy we managed to get him to D.C. We still need him. Continue to your destination and wait. He'll pop up once he's established a safe base of operations. He might be better off on his own."

"I'll be ready to roll, sir. Sounds like our man in Boston talked?"

"Things are moving quickly. The feds have connected some dots from the Pentagon file, so we need to proceed cautiously," he said.

"Understood, sir."

"Sit tight and wait. That's about all we can do at this point," he said and ended the call.

Sanderson leaned back in his chair and contemplated another possible snag in the plan. If the CIA liaison to the FBI could recite large portions of the Black Flag file, they faced a problem down the road. He had grave concerns about the CIA discovering Petrovich's Serbian alias, Marko Resja. In the wrong hands, this information could ignite a powder keg, drawing the wrong kind of attention to his plan.

Chapter Twenty-Two

Berg sat buried in the leather chair with an open laptop perched on one of the chair's oversized arms. The light emanating downward from the decorative lamp competed with the illumination cast from the laptop screen, casting a pale, ugly glow on his impassive face. His eyes scanned the laptop screen, oblivious to Keller, who typed away furiously on the couch. Keller was recreating the documents he had memorized at an unbelievable pace. He had typed twenty pages in less than thirty minutes, and his pace was quickening. According to Keller, he had memorized over a hundred pages of material, but was unable to adequately peruse over half of the file under McKie's watchful eye.

His eyes narrowed and froze on the screen, as he lifted the tumbler off the table and drained the remains of his Chivas refill in one long gulp. "Randy? Page twenty-one is another partial, right?"

"Yes. McKie had removed this page from the first stack he cleared for our group to examine, but I got a close enough look to make a partial imprint. I'm typing these out in the order that I saw them. It's easier for me that way."

"I understand. Can you remember if you saw the name Marko Resja anywhere else in the file?"

Keller closed his eyes for a moment, scanning his memory. He opened them when the answer came to him. "No. McKie withheld a sizable portion of the file from us. I assumed these were operational aspects of Black Flag, so I tried to imprint what I could see. I didn't want to push it. The name appeared at the top of what looked like an after-action report. Serbian operation."

"Yeah…the name jumped out at me, but I can't place it," Berg said absently, still staring at the name on the screen.

"Do you think it's an undercover name used by one of the operatives?"

"Possibly. Might be an active contact. I'm going to run this on the computer in the communications room, try and link the name to an active file. Keep plugging away at those files. The FBI expects you to make a report, but they might become suspicious if you're gone for too long. We probably have another hour. Focus on more names," Berg said.

"Right," Keller said, his fingers flying over the laptop's keyboard.

Berg closed his laptop and started to walk out of the room. He gave the bottle of Chivas a wishful glance, but decided that the last thing he needed to do was stoke the raging fire that burned inside of him. Pausing in the hallway just outside of the room, he took a few moments to gather his thoughts before continuing to the communications room.

After entering a six-digit code on the touch pad, a thin fingerprint reader lowered. A deep blue light pulsed on the device, as Berg pressed his thumb down on the glass. A few seconds passed, and the light turned bright green, followed by a faint pneumatic hissing sound from the door. He grabbed the doorknob, but didn't bother to turn it. Instead, he just pushed the door open and quickly walked in. The door closed and he once again heard the pneumatic hiss, which was always louder on this side.

Berg turned and faced the room, which left a lot to be desired compared to the lounge. The lighting was harsh, provided by overhead fluorescent ceiling lights that were activated upon entry. Specifications for all of the CIA's secure communications rooms were strictly uniform, and he'd learned years ago that there was little chance of receiving authorization to change anything. Adding to the misery of the lighting, the walls were unceremoniously painted white, which, combined with the pneumatic hiss of the door, always made him feel like he had just stepped into a mental rehabilitation room. He figured that the effect was intentional, designed to create a feeling of immediate discomfort. Berg understood why.

From this room, he could directly access the CIA's secure data banks. Two computer stations sat against opposite walls of the narrow room, each containing a keyboard and two flat-screen monitors. The CPU's were locked below each station in a tamper-proof casement. A black business phone sat next to each computer. Each phone contained the newest STU-III encryption software, designed to garble any attempts to intercept a conversation. There were no printers and no paper for taking notes. Several folding chairs sat stacked against the windowless outer wall of the room, further emphasizing the fact that the CIA didn't want anyone spending too much time in this room.

Unknown to Berg, his entrance to the room had been noted and ultimately approved by a duty technician at Langley. The access code and fingerprint device had confirmed his identity for the technician, who ultimately made the decision to grant him access. A small note electronically sent by Claire gave the technician an added level of confidence that it was indeed Karl Berg, Assistant Director for Counterterrorism, who stood in front of the door.

The technicians liked this additional confirmation because once inside the communications room, Berg had open access to all CIA files appropriate to his security clearance. A detailed record of his activity would be electronically filed for future reference and random audits, but beyond that, there was no way to actively manage the content Berg could access. The stand-alone communications rooms always presented the greatest risks to classified information.

Berg unfolded one of the gray chairs and placed it in front of the computer station on the right side of the room. He turned on both monitors and nudged the mouse, which activated the sleeping CPU. Within seconds, he stared at a warning screen with the standard CIA disclosures about classified information. He clicked "acknowledge," and was directed to a screen that required a six-digit numeric access code and ten character password, which were both changed monthly. After typing both codes, the computer took a few moments to launch the CIA data interface. He immediately transferred the data interface to both screens, which would give him the ability to conduct two separate searches. He typed "Marko Resja Serbian Paramilitary" into one of the interfaces, and the system began processing the request.

While the CIA database searched away, Berg opened his own laptop and placed it on the workstation, pushing the phone unit out of the way. Keller's typed pages flashed up onto the laptop screen, and he could see that Keller was still furiously adding to the report. The wireless signal connecting the two laptops was still intact, even inside of the communications room, which surprised Berg.

He wasted no time searching through the list of Black Flag operatives for characteristics that would narrow his search. He narrowed the list of eighty names in half by eliminating the obvious. Keller had identified five areas of operation served by the Black Flag program: Serbia, Colombia, Russia, Mexico and Afghanistan, so Berg discarded any Latino or Arabic names. He sorted the remaining list for Serbian names, which would serve as a starting point for comparison to Marko Resja. Six names jumped out at him, but about a dozen more could fit. He eliminated the obvious Russian names.

He chose a different interface imbedded within the CIA database for this search and was directed to the FBI's nationwide database, which contained publicly available information, giving him access to criminal records information. He started a multiple search string with three of six Serbian names, which was the system's limit, and waited. An image flashed on the first screen, and Berg found himself staring at a face he had tried to push out of his memory for the past several years. Marko Resja.

He didn't need to familiarize himself with Resja's file, he just needed the picture for comparison. Files for the first three names appeared on the second screen, each headed by a picture presumably taken for a driver's license. The FBI's sophisticated system would display any confirmed pictures associated with the name, and in most cases, this would be a state license photograph. Berg immediately compared the three images to the picture of Resja. He didn't see any resemblance, so he entered the next three names and waited.

The results appeared within seconds, hitting him with an adrenaline rush. One of the pictures was a possible match. Daniel Petrovich. He opened the file to look at the rest of the pictures, drawing in a deep breath as eight photos filled the screen. Three of the pictures showed Petrovich in various naval uniforms. The highest rank evident in the pictures was ensign, denoted by single gold bar or stripe on his uniforms.. The earliest photograph pictured Petrovich in the navy's summer white uniform, and had likely been taken immediately after receiving his commission as an officer in the United States Navy. Petrovich looked young and optimistic, very different from the malevolent image staring back at him from the single photograph displayed on the CIA database screen.

Three additional photos had been provided from different state driver's licenses in Illinois, Massachusetts and California, but evoked no response from Berg. The most recent picture showed Petrovich in a blue oxford dress shirt. There was very little trace of Marko Resja in the last image, though it was clear that they were pictures of the same man.

Berg's attention was drawn to one of the photos showing Petrovich in a khaki uniform, standing with his arms crossed, on the steel deck of a warship. Industrial buildings loomed in the background, indicating that the picture had been taken while the ship was docked. Petrovich's dark wavy hair was long and unkempt, pushing the limits of the navy's loose grooming standards. His face looked weathered and exhausted, staring with hatred at an object out of the camera's view. The expression matched the face of Marko Resja on the other screen. Berg couldn't believe he had stumbled upon this coincidence.

He had dreamed about this moment since March 24th, 2003, when Dejan Kavich testified in the trial of Srecko Hadzic, leader of the Serbian Radical Party and infamous commander of "The Panthers." The International Criminal Tribunal for the Former Yugoslavia (ICTY) had already spent two weeks presenting evidence against Hadzic and would soon convict him of running an organized campaign of genocide in the Kosovar border territories.

Berg had a very personal interest in Hadzic's trial. One of the CIA's long established undercover agents in Serbia had vanished without a trace toward the middle of April in 1999, leaving Berg and the CIA stunned. The disappearance was especially difficult for Berg. He had been assigned to groom the agent for the Serbian assignment in 1991, when she was first assigned to the National Clandestine Service.

A recent graduate from Loyola University in Chicago, Nicole Erak had scored perfect on every aptitude test used to measure a candidate's suitability for clandestine field assignment, and she spoke flawless Serbian. As a first generation Serbian-American, raised in a predominately Serbian suburb of Chicago, near Palos Hill, Illinois, her recruitment was no coincidence. The CIA had a critical shortage of reliable human intelligence flowing from the Balkans, and she was fast-tracked for deployment to the rapidly deteriorating region.

Two years after her recruitment by a low-profile history professor at Loyola University, Nicole was absorbed into Belgrade's gritty underworld as Zorana Zekulic, where she would emerge hanging on the arms of some of the most notorious men in Europe.

Ten years after seeing Nicole for the last time, Berg was reading transcripts of the trial, still searching for any possible clues about her disappearance, when he came across the testimony of Dejan Kavich, a low-level enforcer within Hadzic's Panther organization. Kavich recounted dozens of instances where Hadzic had personally ordered the murder of civilians and suspected Kosovar militants, which was nothing new coming from the long string of witnesses that had turned on Hadzic in exchange for Tribunal leniency. However, the Tribunal prosecutors asked Kavich to repeat the details of an incident that they thought would demonstrate Hadzic's ruthless nature, and this is where Berg's interest piqued.

Kavich described a bloody and hectic week in Belgrade at the beginning of April in 1999, which was nearly the same timeframe associated with Nicole's disappearance. Though NATO jets were still hampered by thick overcast skies, blood flowed on the streets of Belgrade. At the time, Kavich thought that the sudden civil war between two of Serbia's most powerful paramilitary groups was a simple blood feud sparked by the unprovoked murder and mutilation of Hadzic's handicapped brother. His security chief, Radovan Grahovac, had also been killed in the bizarre attack, along with his entire personal security entourage, which suggested that there was more to the event than a simple blood feud.

After years of investigative research, the Tribunal now understood why Hadzic had initiated a self-destructive war against rival paramilitary leader Mirko Jovic's "White Eagles." He not only suffered the loss of his brother and trusted security chief in the brazenly twisted attack, but more importantly to Hadzic, he had been robbed of his entire criminal fortune. Confiscated bank records showed a sudden, systematic transfer of his wealth out of long-held European bank accounts to new accounts scattered throughout the Caribbean and South America. From there, the money vanished along an untraceable trail of wire transfers. Some of the money had been transferred by Hadzic himself at the outset of NATO hostilities, but one hundred and thirty million dollars suddenly left Europe on April 23, 1999, and it all had previously belonged to Hadzic. The result was predictable for a man already considered to be one of the most ruthless and fickle psychopaths in Europe.

Hadzic dispatched his most trusted Panthers to take immediate revenge, and he particularly wanted to avenge his brother's death. Pavle Hadzic had been found hacked to death in his wheelchair, the obvious victim of an infamous White Eagle enforcer, Goran Lujic, who had used an ice-climbing axe as his personal calling card for over a decade on the Belgrade organized crime scene. Kavich had participated in two ambushes in Belgrade on the first day of hostilities and was almost killed the next day in a retaliatory raid by White Eagle commandos on a Panther safe house in Zemun, but the Tribunal wasn't interested in the back and forth fighting between paramilitary groups. The Hague wanted to pin as many civilian murders on Hadzic as the Tribunal jury could tolerate, and Kavich knew of a particularly gruesome murder.

On one of the deadlier nights of fighting, Kavich witnessed a bizarre exchange between Hadzic and a trusted Panther sniper, Marko Resja, in the basement of a safe house hidden deep inside a run-down suburb of Belgrade. Resja had arrived by himself, wearing a bloodstained, mud-caked camouflage uniform devoid of any insignia. A black watch cap was pulled tight over his head to merge with a face smeared black and brown with grease. He walked into the basement carrying a Dragunov sniper rifle in one hand and a large blue nylon duffel bag in the other. Kavich was located at the bottom of the basement stairs when Resja was searched in the landing off the kitchen. He heard one of the guards utter, "Oh fuck," and became momentarily alarmed, but the guard called down, "All clear," and he heard Resja descend the stairs.

Resja gave Kavich a barely discernible nod as he passed by, which wasn't unusual. Resja was all business and didn't fraternize with many of the Panthers. He spent most of his time in the field stalking Kosovar militia. On that particular night, Resja walked into the room and slung the rifle over his shoulder, freeing one of his hands. He was immediately greeted by Hadzic, who shook his hand enthusiastically and slapped him on the shoulder. Resja responded with a rare display of friendliness and banter, before he tossed the duffel bag onto the floor and declared that "he had gotten to the bottom of their problem."

Hadzic told the nearest Panther to show him what was in the bag, and the burly guard standing next to Resja kneeled down on the floor and opened the zipper. The unmistakable stench of rotting flesh filled the room immediately, and the burly guard gagged, mumbling protests against touching the contents. Hadzic ordered him to remove the contents, and the guard took in a deep breath before turning back to the bag. Resja softly told him to, "Take out Lujic first," and this caused some confusion for the guard. Resja added, "He's the one with the short hair." At this point, everyone in the room was deathly quiet, waiting for the guard to reach into the bag, which he did reluctantly, using both hands to remove the severed head of Goran Lujic, Pavle Hadzic's presumed murderer.

Goran's face had been brutally beaten, showing extensive bruising and pulverized eye sockets. One of his ears was missing, which Kavich learned was the result of Resja's extensively thorough torture routine. Resja announced that Lujic had confessed to torturing Pavle, for access information to Hadzic's accounts, and eventually killing him. The money was promptly transferred to accounts owned by Lujic's boss, Mirko Jovic, leader of "The White Eagles." Resja added that he had hacked off Lujic's head with the same axe used against Pavle. Hadzic nodded with stunned approval and looked down at the bag, which contained still another surprise.

While squirming under the knife, Lujic had implicated someone close to the Panther organization. He told Resja that they had learned of Pavle's access to the money through a woman that frequented the company of Radovan Grahovac's men in Belgrade. Apparently Radovan, or one of his close associates, suffered from loose lips while under the spell of liquor and beautiful women. One of the nightclub regulars had learned that Pavle actively managed his brother's vast monetary fortune, and the rest was history. Marko had found her hiding in a small White Eagle safe house on the outskirts of Belgrade and used the same axe on her.

Hadzic grew impatient while Resja explained and demanded to see the other head, but it was obvious that the guard still holding Lujic's head was in no condition to pull another one out of the bag. He was barely holding onto the first. On Resja's cue, he dropped the head back into the bag, which made an awful thunk against the concrete floor. Resja impassively pulled the other severed head out of the bag, his hand wrapped tightly around a long, thick spread of filthy, matted black hair.

He announced, "Zorana Zekulic," and "held the head up high, like Perseus is often pictured holding the Gorgon Medusa's severed head." Zekulic had been beaten worse than Lujic, bruises and contusions covering nearly every square centimeter of her once beautiful, angular face. Both eyes had been gouged out, and she was only identifiable by her long hair and a single diamond stud nose ring, which was miraculously still visible on her battered nose.

A few members of the Tribunal had chuckled at Kavich's obviously coached reference to Greek mythology, even admonishing the prosecution to cut the theatrics, but according to Kavich, nobody had laughed in that putrid, candlelit basement of the safe house. Everybody in that room knew Zorana, and everybody in that room had partied in the clubs with her at some point very recently. Hadzic had probably seen every one of them alone in her company within the past month, and the implications of her treachery were apparent to even the dimmest of henchmen huddled in that basement. They all wanted to run for the staircase because Hadzic looked like he had reached the point of critical mass.

"I hope you fucked her corpse," Kavich remembered him saying to Resja, before demanding to see the head of Mirko Jovic in the same bag. Resja told Hadzic, "I'll see what I can do," and walked out of the basement. When asked what happened to Resja, Kavich commented that nobody ever saw him again. They all assumed he had been killed trying to find Jovic and ended up in one of dozens of unmarked mass graves found in the fields surrounding Belgrade.

Berg remembered reading the transcript of Kavich's testimony with a strange sense of detachment. He had finally uncovered Nicole Erak's fate and the name of the man who had brutally killed her, but he felt no closure. Hadzic was eventually convicted of Lujic's murder, but no formal charges were filed against Hadzic pertaining to the brutal murder of Zorana Zekulic. The Hague issued a warrant and summons for Marko Resja, adding another name to the already impossibly long list of thugs and murderers associated with the paramilitary groups that flourished under Slobodan Milosevic's regime. Nobody cared about finding Marko Resja except the CIA, and Berg knew that even the CIA's interest had a limited half-life.

Agency attempts to locate information regarding Marko Resja led nowhere. Berg and other members of the CIA wanted to find Resja and make him pay horribly for Nicole's death, but Resja had indeed disappeared shortly after Nicole's murder. Belgrade in the spring of 1999 had a way of eating people up and spitting them out.

The memory of Nicole Erak's murder faded quickly at Langley. One year after Berg read Kavich's testimony, a star was added to The Memorial Wall in the Original Headquarters Building in honor of Nicole's sacrifice, but no name was added to the Book of Honor below it. The nature and fact of Nicole Erak's service to the United States would remain a guarded secret for eternity. Berg had attended the ceremony, which always drew a smaller crowd when the name was unknown. He shared a few knowing glances and returned to his office to move on. With the War on Terror in full swing throughout the Middle East, turmoil in the Balkans was the least of the CIA's worries. The Counterterrorism Center demanded his full attention, which he'd delivered uninterrupted, until about five minutes ago.

Reading the name Marko Resja on Keller's report hit Berg like a sledgehammer, bringing him right back to the moment he read Kavich's testimony. His mind flashed to the details of Nicole's mutilation and murder, and he jumped into action, immediately deciding that if Resja's face matched one of the operatives listed on the Black Flag roster, he wouldn't stop until Resja was dead.

Berg tapped a few more keys, and a new screen replaced Resja's file. He entered a separate access code and found himself staring at a new file matrix. He searched the list for Nicole's code name, Seraph, and opened the file. The words "deceased" filled the top of the screen, just above a searchable image gallery. He stared at the images displayed by the system.

The first picture was taken by CIA interviewers outside of Loyola University in Chicago and showed a classically beautiful young woman. She had soft, light brown eyes and jet-black hair. Typical of mixed Balkan descent, her skin carried an olive complexion, giving her a unique exotic quality among descendants of northern Serbs, but not enough to draw the wrong kind of nationalist attention in Belgrade. She wore an optimistic, yet guarded smile in the picture, appropriate for a sharp, observant young woman being photographed by complete strangers in a rented apartment on the north side of Chicago.

The second picture was taken during an early phase of CIA training and showed much less of the idealistic young college graduate. Taken in one of the classrooms at headquarters, it showed a close-up of Nicole seated behind a desk, staring skeptically at one of the instructors. By this point, she probably understood that she was not being trained to sit behind a desk in McLean, Virginia. Lying to family and friends about the nature of her employment had become second nature, and she might have strongly suspected, by the intensity and subject matter of her training, that her role within the National Clandestine Service would be atypical. She wasn't receiving the same diplomatic role-play training given to field agents assigned to cover positions at U.S. embassies around the world.

The third image barely resembled the young woman who had reported to Langley a mere two years earlier. Several close-up shots had been snapped by an embassy "employee" in Belgrade and caught her exiting a popular café on Knez Mihailova Street, near the Serbian Academy of Sciences and Art. She wore a gray turtleneck sweater under a tight black leather jacket. Black, knee-high leather boots rose up to meet a tight, dark maroon half skirt, leaving several inches of skin along her legs exposed to the cold Balkan winter. Her black hair was pulled back into a tight bun, accentuating her exotic face. From a distance, she looked like any well-dressed, cosmopolitan woman on the streets of Manhattan, but the next image showed a different story.

He clicked on a close-up of her face, and it showed signs of weariness. Heavy eye shadow outlined her eyes, but couldn't hide the exhaustion. A small diamond nose ring poked out of her left nostril. This had been recommended by members of Clandestine Branch responsible for creating her cover "legend," since it was a trend popular among women on the "professional" nightclub scene in Europe, especially Paris, where Zorana Zekulic had spent the last five years studying art and partying. Berg studied the photo closely. She looked hard. Attractive, sexy, an object to behold in Belgrade. But very little trace of Nicole broke through the icy exterior shell she had formed after a year in Belgrade.

He felt terrible for what had happened to her. She had spent six years in the company of some of the worst monsters in recent human history, spying on them, coaxing information out of them using methods he refused to contemplate. All to be murdered and only God knew what else at the very end of her assignment. The entire Milosevic regime had been about to collapse, and the CIA wanted her out of Belgrade before the NATO bombing started. All she had to do was drive over the border into Hungary or Romania. Less than a two-hour drive in either direction, and she could have put it all behind her.

She refused to leave. Her handler, another deep-cover operative assigned to Serbia, had stressed that she was no longer mentally stable enough to remain in place, and that she had begun to show signs of severe schizophrenia. According to his report, she believed she was Zorana Zekulic and had lost the ability to fully understand her reality. Based on his report and the rapidly deteriorating situation in Serbia, the CIA authorized a forced extraction. A plan was formed by special operators to kidnap her from the streets of Belgrade, but Nicole vanished before the plan could be executed.

A fourth picture showed Zorana Zekulic five years into her assignment. Every trace of Nicole Erak's essence had been erased. They had kept her in place too long, and it had killed her long before Marko Resja came along with Lujic's axe. He wondered if death hadn't been the best thing for her in the long run. Nicole had drawn some bad cards in life. She was raised by abusive parents, in a household that survived from week to week, never rising far above the poverty line. CIA psychological interviews and polygraph results suggested sexual abuse, which she successfully refuted on further polygraphs, but Berg never believed the results. He was convinced that she had either beaten the machine, or that the memories had been buried.

Winning a full scholarship to Loyola was one of the first good cards she pulled from the deck. Attracting the attention of a CIA recruiter was another ace, and by the time the CIA asked her to report to Langley, she held a royal flush. Unfortunately, she had to draw new cards at the CIA, and she drew the worst cards possible. The CIA was desperate to unravel the mess developing in the Balkans, and Nicole's skill sets made her the perfect match for the job.

Based on the inconsistencies with her psych profile, they should have known better than to send her at these men and then keep her there for six years. But what choice did the CIA have? Her situation was unique, and it provided the most useful information to come out of Serbia in decades. Nobody at Langley was willing to admit it, but they would have kept her there indefinitely if the situation hadn't imploded with NATO's involvement.

He closed Nicole's file, perfectly aware that opening it might have triggered an alert in someone's email box back in Langley. It didn't matter. He had no intention of using official channels to take care of things. Plenty of people owed Berg serious favors in this town, and he planned to cash in on a few of them. He navigated to the CIA's file on General Sanderson, scanning it for a piece of information he had come across earlier. He found the name, James Parker, quickly, and memorized several pieces of information that would give his friends a head start on finding Daniel Petrovich. He quickly closed down the computer, leaving the room as he found it.

Standing in the hallway, he pulled out his cell phone and placed a call to the National Security Agency. The call didn't last very long, but it set in motion a series of highly illegal surveillance protocols designed to find and track Parker. The second call would have to wait, but not for very long.

He had plans for Daniel Petrovich, or whoever he currently claimed to be. Berg would make sure he didn't live for very long. If possible, he'd be there to kill Resja himself. He had no idea how Petrovich had become Marko Resja, and he didn't really care. It had something to do with Black Flag, but that wasn't his problem. He had searched the CIA's files on Sanderson and found not a single mention of the general's secret program. He'd let the FBI decipher Black Flag, while he focused on Petrovich. Under the right circumstances, he might learn more about the clandestine program than Keller or the FBI combined. He was pretty sure the right circumstances would involve the purchase of a climbing axe from a sporting goods store in Bailey's Crossing, Virginia.

Chapter Twenty-Three

Darryl Jackson hung up the phone and contemplated his situation. He didn't like it, but he owed Karl Berg more than a weekend favor. He owed Berg his life. Four years earlier, Jackson and a small crew of Brown River paramilitary contractors found themselves fighting for their lives in a small wadi outside of Sorubi, Afghanistan, when Berg reached down from the sky to save him.

While conducting a site reconnaissance along highway A1, on behalf of the newly arrived U.S. Central Command forces, his convoy of two Land Rovers stumbled into a platoon-sized group of Taliban militants, who had just broken camp to move further south toward the safety of the Taliban-controlled mountains near Khowst. Within minutes, Jackson had lost both vehicles and half of his eight-man contingent. With his satellite phone destroyed in one of the mangled SUVs, Jackson was on his own until someone at Brown River's operations center back in Kabul declared them missing.

Jackson's team retreated to the cover of a dried up river bed and set up a perimeter to hold the Taliban at bay. Jackson's highly trained team had already inflicted serious casualties on the Taliban force, and he hoped that the Taliban leadership in the group would decide against suffering further unnecessary losses. Minutes later, a suicide attack on his position scrapped any hopes that the enraged hornet's nest of Muslim extremists would abandon their quarry.

The attack broke through his perimeter, killing an additional member of his team, but the wave of militants suffered enough casualties to cause a temporary withdrawal to the cover of Jackson's disabled Land Rovers. He counted at least twenty Taliban in the vicinity of the trucks, who started an organized volley of rocket propelled grenades, while a smaller group moved

110

along Jackson's left flank. A familiar buzzing sound momentarily drew his attention away from the crescendo of automatic fire.

He could barely lift his head high enough to scan the expanse of blue sky above, as bullets snapped past his head. In his peripheral vision, Jackson caught a glimpse of something moving in the sky. A Predator drone. One of his men yelled something encouraging and pointed to the drone, but Jackson wasn't optimistic. To him, the Predator drone simply meant that a crew in Nevada would watch their deaths live on camera.

Jackson wasn't completely correct about the location of the crew. The RQ-1 Predator drone circling overhead was indeed controlled by an air force officer at an undisclosed location in Nevada, but the video feed had the undivided attention of CIA officers in the Counterterrorism Center at Langley, who had requisitioned the flight to assess reports of an Al Qaeda way station operating outside of Sorubi. Osama Bin Laden's location remained a mystery, though there was little doubt that he would seek refuge in the mountains near Khowst. Electronic intercepts suggested that he had not reached this destination, and the CIA was very interested in any possible points of refuge along his projected escape route.

Berg watched the attack unfold from the drone's cameras, and an argument developed within the operations center about whether to render assistance to the civilian team on the ground. The drone carried two Hellfire air-to-ground missiles, which could easily turn the tide against the militants, but several of the officers within the center wanted to save the missiles for high-value targets at the suspected Al Qaeda rest stop. Berg quickly ended the argument. As deputy assistant of the Counterterrorism Center, the Predator flight was under his control, and he had no intention of abandoning the men on the ground. He relayed orders to the controllers in Nevada.

Thousands of miles away, Jackson took a grazing hit to his right shoulder, which caused him to hug the ground at a time they couldn't afford. Three guns barely kept the Taliban from organizing another rush of the shallow wadi. Just as Jackson said a prayer and lifted his body up to continue firing, he was hit with a concussion that snapped his head backward and slid him down the side of the river bed. A second shockwave fired through his small group, rolling Jackson onto his back. Jackson still held his rifle tight and waited for bearded heads to appear over the riverbank's edge to finish them—but nothing materialized.

He painfully scooted through the loose gravel to continue firing at the

Taliban positions, but the scene in front of him had been altered by forty pounds of high explosive charge. The shattered Land Rover hulks now sat thirty feet closer to Jackson, completely engulfed in flames. To his left, the Taliban flanking movement had been obliterated by another strike, which left a charred dead zone among the low rocks.

Nothing moved. Jackson scanned the sky above, but couldn't find their savior. He swore an oath to find the man responsible for diverting the Predator drone, knowing that the defense of paramilitary contractors was a low priority on the military's list of uses for expensive Hellfire missiles. He finally met Berg two years later at Brown River's headquarters in Fredericksburg, Virginia, and they had since become inseparable.

Darryl Jackson spun his chair around and opened a file cabinet drawer. He thumbed through the red files, pulling the one with the appropriate rosters. He needed to assemble a uniquely loyal team of highly capable special operators and get them inside of D.C. within two hours.

Their target was Daniel Petrovich, a rogue freelance operative that posed a significant threat to U.S. security, and Berg felt certain that this operative would arrive in the D.C. area tonight. He wanted the Brown River team to capture or kill the operative as soon as he surfaced. It was clear that Berg didn't want the team to attract any attention, and Jackson didn't even bother to ask if the mission was authorized. Berg said the rogue agent was "black flagged," and that was all Jackson needed to hear. He turned back to his desk and picked up the phone to start making calls.

Chapter Twenty-Four

Daniel threw his duffel bag on the floor of the hotel room and emptied the contents of two retail bags onto the foot of the bed. A dark green backpack, several pre-paid cell phones, a GPS receiver, hair dye, power bars, two knives, and three local maps—all purchased with cash—formed a pile on the thick down-feather comforter. He worked for several minutes to activate the untraceable phones and the GPS receiver, placing all of the product packaging back in the large bag for disposal in another location.

He grabbed one of the spring-loaded Gerber knives and effortlessly flicked open the black stainless steel serrated blade. The four-inch blade had a dual edge, perfect for close quarters combat. He moved the knife back and forth, trying several grips before returning the blade back into the aluminum handle. Satisfied, he slipped the blade into the back left pocket of his brown khaki pants.

The second knife had a smaller, one-sided blade and had been designed for concealment. A much thinner knife, he hid this in his front pocket after he repeated the same grip and slice test. Both knives were well balanced and would serve him well, if the need arose. He genuinely hoped it didn't because he hated the dynamics of edged combat.

A knife fight meant one thing: everyone involved gets cut. The trick? At the end of the fight, you wanted to be the one with the smallest cuts. Daniel would feel infinitely more comfortable with a pistol and hoped that Parker intended to equip him with one—whenever he decided to reconnect with General Sanderson.

His escape from Parker had been easy enough, and gave him the breathing room he needed to fully assess his situation. Parker had stared at him with disbelief as he opened the back door and retrieved his duffel bag. Daniel expected a fight, but Parker was clearly stunned at the unexpected audacity. He looked dumbstruck as Daniel sprinted through traffic on the Baltimore Washington Parkway. Parker tried to force his way over, but must have thought better of it. He really had no options to pursue. The next exit sat at least thirty minutes away in the heavy traffic, and Parker couldn't afford to attract the wrong kind of attention. He imagined that ex-SEAL's next phone call had been a tough one.

It took Petrovich about fifteen minutes to navigate his way to a rental car agency in Laurel, Maryland, and another ten minutes to drive away under one of his three remaining false identities. He disposed of two sets of driver's licenses, passports and canceled credit cards at a Starbucks just off Route One in College Park. Christopher Stevens, owner of a nondescript Toyota Camry previously stored in New Hampshire, and David Harrell, Massachusetts resident, simply ceased to exist soon after Daniel took a test sip of a steaming hot, grande cappuccino—with an extra espresso shot.

He rented the car and took the hotel room under the name Scott Barber, an untraceable New Jersey resident, leaving him with two more clean ID packages. Once he left the hotel room tonight, he was unlikely to return, and would be forced to dispose of Barber's ID pack. He was running out of identities, but suspected that General Sanderson could help him with this problem. General Sanderson assured him that his role wouldn't extend past tomorrow evening, so he shouldn't need another hotel room.

Daniel turned his attention to the maps and started to unfold them. He needed to quickly absorb the details of D.C.'s mass transit system, identifying locations that offered him rapid escape options beyond the rental car. He'd start with the Metro rail map, familiarizing himself with the different lines and timetables. With trains running frequently in both directions at every station, this would be his most likely primary emergency escape system. This system would attract the least attention and provided the most anonymous method of travel. He made a mental note to drive over to the Metro station near the University to buy a pass that would allow him unhindered access to the railway.

He opened a large road map of the greater D.C. Metro Area and placed it on the surface of the oversized desk. The smaller Metro map followed, smoothed over the road map. He would study both maps simultaneously, doing his best to orient the locations of major roads, Beltway exits and Metro stops. He didn't have as much time as he would like for the task, but it would be enough.

Before he began, he needed to make a long overdue phone call to Jess.

He had left a brief message on her office voicemail, which outlined his need to take a last minute business trip to meet with a representative from one of Zenith Semiconductors' largest overseas clients. He left few details beyond that. The less she knew the better. Still, he needed to contact her soon.

Chapter Twenty-Five

Berg sat impatiently inside his office at Langley, waiting for word from his contact at Fort Meade. Cell phone intercepts and electronic cross references had provided enough information to direct the Brown River team to Silver Spring, Maryland, but this was the narrowest geographic corridor the NSA intercept protocols could provide, given the limited amount of cell phone traffic generated by Sanderson's crew.

Sanderson's people were on the move, and it would take some luck to find them. For Berg, luck came in the form of a highly-placed friend at the National Security Agency, with just enough salt and authority to illegally co-opt one of the nation's most sensitive electronic eavesdropping systems. So sensitive, that the mere mention of the name "Munoz" and "safe house" in the same conversation, on the same phone, triggered a "high probable" alert and gave Berg the confidence to move the Brown River team to Silver Spring.

His cell phone rang, and he answered it immediately, recognizing the Fort Meade number.

"Berg."

"I have a confirmed location of interest. Marriott Inn and Conference Center, College Park."

"College Park? What happened to Silver Spring?" Berg said.

"Different cell phones. This is the one you're looking for. Call to a hardline in Portland, Maine. Listen to the tag words. Zenith, Jessica, Danny, Sanderson. We got lucky with the location. He used the words hotel and conference center. Fucked up big time. Cell node for the call is right next to the Marriott Inn and Conference Center in College Park. Do you need the address?"

"No. I have it up on the computer already."

"Karl, I need to pull the plug on this thing. I'm working well past my usual hour, and I'm going to start drawing attention from the nighttime duty section. It's a lot easier to pull this kind of shit during the day. They've got nothing better to do than keep an eye on the system right now."

"I know, Pete. Just a little longer. I promise."

"I can't be in here past eight."

"Thanks, Pete. I owe you big time."

"You said it. Not me."

Berg immediately placed a call to the leader of the Brown River team, who detached one of the two vehicles to the hotel in College Park. The team had everything they could need to identify Petrovich, but it would still prove difficult. He hoped to narrow things down for them before they arrived at the hotel, which was no more than a ten-minute drive from Silver Spring.

Fifteen minutes later, Berg was ready to drive out to the Marriott himself to strangle the night manager, who had been extremely uncooperative. Of course, Berg had absolutely no legal authority to compel any information from the woman, but the fact that she had thoroughly dismissed him and threatened to call the police didn't sit well with the senior CIA officer. He felt helpless sitting at his desk. Fortunately, the hotel parking lot had a single point of access from the hotel, and the Brown River team was already busy scouring hotel guests heading to the lot. Two minutes after his NSA friend's 8 p.m. deadline, Berg's phone rang. He snatched it off the desk.

"Tell me you have something, Pete?" he said.

"This must be your lucky day. I just got a nice intercept. Your target at the hotel just received directions to a Silver Spring address. One minute ago. 8800 Lanier Drive, Apartment 4B. Good luck, Karl."

"I can't tell you how much this helps. Thanks for hanging in a little longer. Drinks are on me," Berg said.

"For the whole month," Pete said, and the line went dead.

Berg immediately relayed the information to the team leader at the hotel. His next call went to Keller, hoping to catch him outside of the Sanctum. He needed to know how much progress the FBI had made since accessing the Black Flag file.

Chapter Twenty-Six

Daniel Petrovich walked out of the elevator into the Marriott lobby and studied his surroundings. The hotel's decor was modernistic. Shiny off-white marble floors contrasted with dark, mahogany walls, which were sporadically adorned with bright impressionist art. The lobby of the 226-room hotel was deserted except for the hotel staff at the desk to his left and a small party of adults laughing inside the bar located down the hallway in the opposite direction of the reception area. Nothing appeared out of the ordinary as he turned toward the main door that led into the courtyard adjoining the hotel with the conference center.

He was dressed in a simple, business casual outfit that wouldn't have garnered a second glance in the Capitol, or any street in America: dark leather shoes, wheat brown pleated pants, and a blue oxford shirt covered by a lightweight, dark blue golfing jacket. The black duffel bag in his right hand was the only part of his outfit that might warrant a second pass from a security guard or police officer, but he didn't have to worry about that here.

He scanned the remaining lobby space as he passed the desk, paying close attention to the faces of the hotel employees manning the reception area. He didn't register any response other than a smile and a nod from the young man talking on one of the hotel phones. The other hotel employee, a middle-aged woman with heavy makeup and bleached hair never looked up from whatever she was reading under the counter.

He didn't expect anyone to have found him at this point, but there was no reason to let his guard down. He wasn't completely sure of Sanderson's intentions, or the extent of his resources, so he would have to assume the worst. Even if he was completely safe for the moment, treating the situation as extremely hazardous would help him transition back into the mindset that had been drilled into him for close to four years in the Black Flag training program.

Although it still felt like second nature to him, he accepted the reality that his skills and capabilities had degraded over the six years since he escaped Serbia. He still kept in top physical condition, practiced martial arts, and maintained his marksmanship skills, but nothing could replace continuously sharpening all of these skills in an environment where the slightest advantage gained over an adversary or situation could spell the difference between life and death. Two years in Serbia had sharpened these skills to perfection, and although his current skill level remained at a fraction of his previous level, it would still stack up heavily against any adversary Sanderson might throw at him.

The lobby door slid open, and he was greeted by muggy, slightly polluted mid-Atlantic air. He noticed a few couples seated in the courtyard, at tables scattered around the patio area, enjoying a temperate evening. The clear sky still held some light on the western horizon, casting a deep blue ribbon that faded into stars above the hotel, competing with the orange artificial illumination cast by the decorative sodium vapor street lamps surrounding the courtyard.

A stocky man dressed in dark pants and a short-sleeved green polo shirt sat alone on one of the granite stone benches at the far edge of the courtyard, near the walkway leading to a large parking garage that probably served the University of Maryland College Park campus. Daniel shifted his duffel bag over to his left hand, freeing his most capable side for action. From what he could tell, the man had a briefcase open next to him on the bench and was concentrating on some paperwork inside. He thought it was a little late, and a little dark, for glancing at papers.

Petrovich wandered to the right, away from the man on the bench and toward the parking lot where he had parked the rental car. He didn't look back to see if the man was following him. There was plenty of time to do that without attracting attention.

**

Jeremy Cummings, ex-Navy SEAL, flipped his cell phone closed and focused on the green picture cast by a powerful third generation night vision spotting scope. He grabbed a radio handset sitting on the dashboard in front of him and gave brief instructions to his man keeping watch in the courtyard.

"Garrity, our man might be on the move. Keep a tight watch around you," he said.

"Stand by," echoed inside the black Suburban, and there was a pause.

"Did he already exit the hotel?" crackled Garrity over the radio.

"How the fuck am I supposed to know. This guy is killing me," Cummings said to the two other men in the SUV, who all chuckled softly as Cummings transmitted his official answer.

"All we know is that he could be on the move. Do you have something?"

"Affirmative. Male fitting general characteristics carrying a black duffel bag. Headed your way, but his hair is blond, not black. You should have him in a few seconds. He's walking down the stairs to the lot."

"Got him. We need a positive ID before we move. Garrity, start walking toward the parking lot. Stay out of his line of vision," Cummings said.

"Roger," they all heard through the radio.

Ben Sanchez, former Green Beret, lowered his tinted window far enough to push a thick, tubular camera lens through to start snapping pictures. The camera was connected to a laptop that sat jammed against the steering wheel, in Doug Porter's lap. Cummings heard the camera taking pictures and focused all of his attention on the night vision scope. His 5X magnification couldn't make a positive ID until the target moved deeper into the parking lot.

The team's black Suburban was parked four rows back from the entrance, buried far enough into the lot to blend with the other cars, but keeping an unobstructed view of the walkway leading down from the hotel's courtyard. Once the ID was made, they would slip out of the car and take Petrovich down as he walked through the quiet parking area.

The car was silent for several seconds, while Cummings watched the man cross a small street and enter the parking lot. He could see Garrity's head emerge over the top of the walkway stair and hoped it wasn't visible to their target. Garrity hadn't been his first choice for this operation, but Mr. Jackson wanted two full teams on the road immediately, and he had run out of experienced faces at the compound.

Garrity had joined Brown River's Special Missions Group (SMG) two months ago after leaving the Rangers, where he had seen heavy combat with the 3rd Ranger Battalion, 75th Ranger Regiment, in both Afghanistan and Iraq. Still, Cummings didn't think Sergeant Nathan Garrity belonged with his guys in the SMG.

Regardless of the 75th Ranger Regiment's classification as a special operations unit, Cummings never saw the Rangers as anything but better trained infantry. They jumped out of planes, fast roped down from helicopters and pulled tough missions, but they weren't "operators." He reserved that term for SEALs, Force Recon, Green Berets and Delta Force. Membership in this club wasn't open to Rangers. He started to mumble about Garrity, when he was interrupted.

"It's him. Confirmed," the driver said, slamming the laptop shut in an overly excited manner and tossing it in the back seat.

"Let's go. Move fast and stay low. Ben, you hit him with the non-lethal first. Doug bags him. I'll cover you both and keep Garrity from accidentally killing any of us," he said.

His last command went to Garrity, telling him to stay up in the courtyard until he received the signal. Cummings quickly attached his radio set to a cord protruding from his black tactical vest. They were now all linked together through voice-activated throat microphone headsets, to keep their hands free. Garrity monitored the situation through a small transparent earpiece hidden in his left ear.

The entire team exited the Suburban on the driver's side, forcing Cummings to climb over the center console and slide out onto the parking lot's warm pavement. They quickly stacked themselves along the side of the Suburban, and Cummings reacquired Petrovich through the tinted glass, watching as Petrovich approached the first row of cars in the lot.

Cummings leaned back. "If he stays in the center, we'll fan out simultaneously and take him down. If he turns, we'll weave low through the cars. Hit him quick," he whispered to his team.

Once the team sprang into action, they would be on Petrovich with enough electrical current to drop a gorilla. If they couldn't make that happen, then Cummings would cut him down with his suppressed MP-9 submachine gun. Dead or alive, Petrovich would leave in the back of their Suburban.

Cummings glanced through the large tinted window again and saw that Petrovich had turned in front of the first row and was now opening a sedan parked in one of the handicapped spaces.

"Son of a bitch. Back into the vehicle," Cummings snapped.

The team scrambled back into their seats, as a Dodge Charger drifted slowly out of the parking lot and took a left out of the parking lot.

"Get us moving, Doug. We can't lose him. We'll have to take him down when he stops," Cummings said, as the Suburban lurched backwards into the lot toward the exit.

"What about Garrity?" Doug asked.

"We don't have time for him," Cummings said, just as Garrity appeared running at the top of the stairs.

"He should be here any—"

"Step on it!" Cummings interrupted, and Doug Porter pressed the accelerator, leaving Garrity behind.

Cummings saw a sedan cross Adelphi Road, merging onto Route 193 West, which headed toward Silver Spring, Maryland. He pulled out his cell phone and made a call to his second team, which was positioned to keep an eye on 8800 Lanier Drive in Silver Spring. He wanted the second team ready to pounce when Petrovich arrived. As far as the team could tell, the target at Lanier Drive was still inside the apartment, which is where Cummings wanted to keep him. As long as he stayed inside, there was no way he could react in time to help Petrovich.

**

Daniel ripped the stolen handicap sign off the rearview mirror and accelerated the over-powered Dodge Charger onto Route 193. He glanced into the rearview mirror, just in time to see the Suburban pass through a red light at the Adelphi Road intersection. He could barely believe anyone had found him this quickly, but took some solace in the fact that these were not law enforcement types. If the FBI had discovered that he was staying at the Marriott, they would have probably sealed off the entire building, until they figured out that Scott Barber had checked in late in the afternoon and had rented a car between College Park and BWI. He could have expected a heavily armed SWAT team lined up in the hallway outside of his room.

Another thing was certain; the team following him in the Suburban was not comprised of clandestine intelligence professionals. The guy sitting in the courtyard would not have piqued Daniel's interest under normal circumstances, but given the very abnormal nature of his visit to D.C., a stocky guy with a tight military haircut raised an alarm. Even if he hadn't been spooked by the guy in the courtyard, the team in the Suburban would have been impossible to miss, even for a trainee. He had identified the oversized black vehicle as suspicious from the top of the stairs, which was confirmed moments later. While he descended the stairs from the courtyard, the rear passenger window lowered several inches, exposing a camera lens.

Regardless of their espionage skills, he had no doubt that the team was lethal. The guy in the courtyard looked formidable. Definitely ex-military. He needed to warn Parker immediately. If someone could find Daniel this easily, he didn't have high hopes for Sanderson's assistant. Parker might be ex-special forces, but he was worse than the guys in the Suburban when it came to sneaking around.

He pulled the cellphone out of his front jacket pocket, lowered the driver's window and tossed it out onto the road. He had no idea how they had tracked him, but couldn't help suspect that someone had worked some serious magic intercepting his cell phone calls. He unzipped a pocket on the outside of the duffel bag sitting on the front passenger seat and took out another cellphone to call Parker.

Parker answered on the first ring.

"Parker, shut up and listen carefully. I'm being tracked by a black Suburban filled with guys that look like you. They were waiting for me outside of my hotel, and I think they were planning to take me down right there. I'd be shocked if this was the only black Suburban filled with commandos on the streets around here. I'm on 193 headed in your direction."

"Understood. I'll hit the streets with our gear and wait for you to shake the Suburban. We should meet at a different safe house," Parker said.

"Parker, I don't think you're fully appreciating the situation. If they found me, there is a solid chance that you have the same problem. Frankly, I don't care if you get stuffed into the trunk of a car, but I have a feeling that General Sanderson might feel differently. Stay put until I can draw them away from you," Petrovich said.

"What's your plan?" Parker asked.

"I might stop for some groceries. Any suggestions?"

"There's a nice Natural Foods on the way through town. Find Wayne Avenue from 193. You'll see it as you approach the downtown avenue," Parker said.

"What the fuck is a Natural Foods?" Petrovich said.

"Organic grocery store. Good coffee. You'll like it."

"Will it be busy?"

"Busy enough. The aisles are crowded. Shit jammed everywhere. You should be able to disappear in the store," Parker said.

"I don't have any intention of vanishing. Just evening the odds a bit. Be ready to move with our gear when I call. We'll need to leave Silver Spring immediately. You need to let Sanderson know that the situation in D.C. has changed," Petrovich said and ended the call.

**

"What the fuck is this guy doing?" Cummings said.

The Charger cruised into a parking lot off Wayne Avenue, and Cummings saw a large green-illuminated Natural Foods sign appear between the trees. He wondered exactly how dangerous Petrovich could be, if he was stopping in the middle of a terrorist operation to chase down healthy snacks. Maybe he planned to stock the safe house with food. It didn't matter now. Cummings had new orders. He had called Berg to report their missed opportunity at the Marriott, and Berg changed the rules of engagement significantly. He told Cummings that Petrovich was too much of national security danger to take any more risks, and ordered them to terminate Petrovich with extreme prejudice at the next given opportunity. This might well be that opportunity.

"Slow down, and stay back, Goddamn it. We'll follow him into the lot and set up around his car. Ben, you'll pick him up in the store and call us when he's coming out. We have orders to kill this guy on the spot," he hissed.

"Jesus," Doug whispered, turning the wheel of the car to follow Petrovich.

The parking lot was half full, and Petrovich picked the first open handicapped space, about two cars back from the storefront, and two rows to the right of the entrance. Cummings was surprised by how quickly Petrovich was out of the car and moving toward the grocery store. Ben Sanchez spoke up from the back seat.

"Jer? What if we lose him in the store? He could walk out on Fenton Street and disappear. There's a street entrance on the other side, and it leads right down to the train station. We're screwed if he hops the Metro."

Cummings thought about the situation while the Suburban settled into a parking spot several spaces back from the store, providing them with a perfect line of sight toward the entrance and the target's car. He could still see Petrovich walking toward the store. Two more seconds passed, and Cummings made a decision. They would follow the terrorist into Natural

Foods and kill him. They were at war with Al Qaeda, and this traitorous son of a bitch was helping them bring the war back onto U.S. soil. Petrovich would die in that store.

"New plan, Ben. Strip down to street clothes. Suppressed pistols only. Let's go!"

Cummings and Sanchez got out of the Suburban and hastily removed all of their tactical gear. Comms gear, vests and pistol rigs piled up on their seats within seconds, as each man hurried to shed all visual cues that would normally cause civilian panic. Cummings screwed a four-inch suppressor onto the threaded barrel of his .40 USP Tactical Compact and tucked the pistol into the rear waistline of his faded jeans, barely covering it with the bottom of his tight fitting dark blue sweatshirt. The pistol's suppressor made it nearly impossible to jam the gun far enough down his pants to stay in place. He would have to keep a hand on it the whole time. Sanchez was having the same problem.

"Don't worry about it, just keep the gun out of sight for now," Cummings advised, walking rapidly toward the Natural Foods entrance.

He turned around and yelled to Doug, "Get the other team over here now!"

**

Daniel walked through the store's automatic doors, and was treated to a blanket of cold, lavender-scented air punctuated by the rich smell of cooked food. He was also greeted by a layout that presented him with a challenge. He had never been inside a Natural Foods store, and though it felt infinitely more comfortable than the standard fluorescent-lit food mausoleums they normally frequented—he needed familiarity more than anything right now. Grimacing, he grabbed a green plastic hand basket from a pile just inside of the sliding glass doors and walked into the produce section, which appeared to be the only section of the store located where Daniel expected.

Moving briskly through the crowded section, he tried to put as much distance between himself and the door without drawing attention. He really wanted to get them into one of the long aisles, where he would be able to execute a few of his better tricks. Daniel nearly broke into a jog when he exited the maze-like produce area and still saw no aisles. Glancing back at the entrance, he didn't see anyone that looked suspicious.

A tall, precariously stacked dry foods display loomed ahead, and beyond that—Daniel saw at least a dozen aisles. *Finally.* As he walked toward them, two men, dressed in simple, dark clothing, entered the store side by side. They moved with a purpose, and Daniel was pretty sure their purpose wasn't surveillance.

He stopped at the beginning of the third aisle, pretending to check out the items on the end cap. Daniel wanted them to see him, so he could lure them down one of the aisles. Out of his peripheral vision, he saw them round the produce section corner and slow down, as they spilled into the store's center connecting aisle. He placed a bag of organic tortilla chips and a jar of salsa into his basket and waited for the two men to make a move.

They approached slowly, pretending to examine items, and Daniel waited until they reached the first aisle before disappearing down the aisle to his left. He needed to see how they operated. If they both came down the same aisle, then he was in business. If they separated, then his chance of success in the store would be minimal, and he would have to quickly find another exit.

He stopped two-thirds of the way down the aisle, about sixty feet, and placed three cans of tuna in his basket, waiting for one of them to either peek around the corner or enter the aisle. Filling his peripheral vision, they both stepped into the aisle and walked toward him. Daniel turned and opened the distance between them, moving briskly toward the back of the store. He turned the corner and started the transformation, oblivious to the fact that the two men had almost broken into a full run.

As soon as was he out of their sight, he slid the shopping basket as far as he could across the aisles, landing it two aisles over. Turning down the adjacent aisle, Daniel deftly removed the golf jacket and pulled it inside out to reveal a brown and blue patterned flannel interior. He donned the jacket and pulled out several flaps surrounding the bottom, turning the jacket into what looked like an oversized, unbuttoned flannel shirt. The final touch, pulled out of one of the pockets, was a worn blue Cubs hat, with fake brown hair protruding from the bottom.

In a practiced manner, he placed this on his head and tucked the hair on the sides with his fingers. A pair of thick-rimmed fake designer eyeglasses and a non-functioning cell phone from one of the exterior flannel pockets completed the look. He had just pushed the glasses up his nose and turned his head down to examine the cell phone in his left hand, when two serious, dark-haired men rushed around the corner, each with a hand behind his back.

Daniel glanced up at the first man, hoping all he processed for the next few seconds was a slightly disheveled, slack-looking graduate student in a worn flannel shirt fumbling with a cell phone. He just needed them off guard for a few seconds. Apparently, the quick change satisfied the first man, and he continued toward the next aisle without breaking pace.

Daniel slipped his right hand down to the four-inch folded knife in his back pocket, as the next man, slightly shorter and stockier, barreled into the opening, glancing at Daniel and continuing toward his partner. He took a few steps and suddenly swung his body to face Petrovich, bringing his pistol around as he turned. Petrovich had seen this coming. The fake cell phone struck the floor, leaving Daniel's hands free.

He bolted inside of the man's striking radius and gripped the man's shooting arm at the wrist with his left hand, while viciously slashing the knife blade across the commando's throat with a powerful reverse grip. A hot spray pulsed across the back of his head and neck, and bright red arterial splash hit several yellow boxes of spaghetti in front of him. Before the killer could react, Daniel jammed the blade back into his throat, causing the man to go slack. He hated knife work.

Daniel quickly slid his left hand forward along the guy's wrist and removed the pistol from his non-existent grip. He kept the pistol aimed at the corner of the next aisle, right at head level. Within a fraction of a second, Daniel saw the black cylindrical shape of a suppressor appear, followed by the second killer's head. They fired at the same time.

A snap passed by Daniel's right ear, as the shooter's first bullet missed his head by less than an inch. The bullet continued through the store, striking a decorative glass frame above a large serving station filled with barbequed meats. Glass rained down into the simmering bins and a brown carton held by a woman standing next to the station. The second bullet went wider and higher than the first, striking a suspended light. A cascade of sparks blanked a young couple standing in front of the meat counter.

Daniel's first and only bullet didn't miss. It punctured the commando's left eye, spraying the store's macaroni and cheese selection with brains and blood. Momentum carried the man's useless body forward into a large, square column of twenty-six-ounce tomato cans beyond the aisles end cap. The heavy aluminum cans tumbled over his body, spreading hundreds of cylinders into the open aisles around them. Several cans rolled through the thick, spreading pool of blood around the first killer's body, leaving bright red trails in every direction.

Petrovich picked up the second pistol and removed his blood-splattered, reversible jacket. He used it to conceal the identical semi-automatic pistols, wrapping the jacket in a way to keep one of the pistols secure, while gripping the second pistol under the thick material. Satisfied that he could use the pistol quickly if needed, he took off the fake glasses and threw them onto the second killer's corpse.

Glancing around, he carefully stepped over the cans and moved to the next aisle, before turning toward the front of the store. He didn't see anyone headed in his direction yet, which meant he should have enough time to escape before mayhem descended on the store. Petrovich moved briskly down the aisle, passing an Indian woman wearing a headscarf. The woman stared at him, and he realized that he must have a considerable amount of the first man's blood on the side of his neck.

Daniel ignored the woman's stunned look and pressed forward to the checkout area. Only four of the dozen cashier lanes were open, all toward the entrance, which might it easier for him to exit unnoticed. In total, he counted about thirty people, including employees, crowded around the bustling area. It was a large group to pass without attracting attention, but everyone looked extremely busy, as he continued toward one of the empty lanes a few registers away from the commotion. He continued to scan the group for any signs of alarm, painfully aware that the back of his neck and shirt were stained red.

Instinctively, he focused on a woman closing her purse near the closest open lane and decided to use her to get out of the store undetected. She had short, cropped, dark hair and was dressed in a gray suit—a sensible woman, he hoped. Daniel walked through one of the empty lanes and turned toward the busy exit, which kept his blood-splattered right side partially hidden from view.

He passed the group unnoticed and concentrated on his target. The woman put her purse in the shopping basket's empty child's seat and started to push the loaded metal cage toward the entrance. Daniel counted at least five brown paper bags stacked in the cart. Timing his pace, he arrived behind her in an area devoid of windows and shopper traffic—just before the exit. She stopped to look at the community bulletin board, which made it easy for him to nestle behind her.

The sliding glass door opened in front of them, and a young woman wearing a yoga outfit walked through, glancing briefly in their direction. His target waited for yoga-lady to cross into the produce section and tried to push the cart forward, which didn't budge. Daniel held the cart in place with his left hand and pushed the barrel of the pistol into the small of her back.

He whispered closely into her left ear, "I'm holding a silenced pistol at the base of your spine right now. If you make a sound, you'll never walk again. I need your cart. You can keep your purse. Can you give me your cart?"

He pressed the pistol into her back again, and she nodded.

"Let's get moving. When we get into the vestibule, you'll let go of the cart and go left, out of the door. Keep walking until you find a coffee shop. Relax with an iced drink, and don't worry about your groceries. The parking lot is not safe for you right now," he said, as the cart moved forward through the sliding doors and into the vestibule.

"Take your purse and go," he said, removing the gun from her back.

She carefully lifted her purse out of the cart and walked through the door, never looking back at him. Daniel was impressed by her ability to remain calm. He had given her a fifty percent chance of screaming as soon as he pushed the gun into her back and had resigned himself to hitting her over the head with the pistol.

Just as she passed a small potted plant display along the outside wall of the store, he heard a muffled scream from inside the store. Knowing he had little time left before a call went out to the police, he unwrapped his jacket and placed both pistols into the shopping cart seat, hidden by the groceries. He slipped the jacket on; flannel side out, very aware that the collar was soaked with cold, thickening blood.

**

Douglass Porter, former Army Special Operations staff sergeant, sat impatiently behind the wheel of the running Suburban. The team had been in the store long enough for him to start feeling nervous, and he kept his eyes glued to the store's entrance vestibule. The vestibule didn't empty directly into the parking lot; instead, it contained a front wall, with doors on both sides, which had disgorged nearly two-dozen shoppers since Cummings and Sanchez had disappeared from sight. Parking the truck diagonally to the left of the front wall, he was able to see the automatic doors slide open, but had no clear view of those exiting from the right side.

A woman in a business suit had just walked out of the right side and kept walking toward the far end of the building. He caught some motion and returned his eyes to see a full shopping cart emerge from the left side doors. A grungy-looking guy in a baseball cap followed the cart and pushed it down his parking lot aisle. Doug made a quick assessment of the guy and returned his attention to Natural Foods. The man with the cart drifted over to the other side of the parking lane, and in the flash of a brain synapse, Doug Porter sensed that something was wrong. His next set of synapses told him to think about the MP-9 submachine gun that Cummings had left on the passenger seat, but his hands remained on the wheel, scanning the doors. When the police scanner nestled into one of the Suburban's center console drink holders crackled to life, he quickly turned his head toward the man with the cart. He didn't have much time to process his mistake.

**

Daniel gripped a silenced pistol in each hand and rapidly turned away from the shopping cart, extending both weapons at the driver's side of the Suburban's windshield. He registered the look of surprise on the man's face and alternated trigger pulls. The first two bullets struck the safety glass a few inches apart, right where he saw the driver's upper torso and head, followed by another closely grouped pair just below the first. The entire front windshield transformed into an opaque, blue-tinted mosaic of tightly packed glass particles, as the safety glass shattered, but held in place.

With his view obscured by the safety glass, Daniel walked slowly toward the vehicle, concentrating the pistol fire on the milky white glass surrounding the driver's seat. Bullets ripped through the windshield, tearing into the upper dashboard and the driver beyond, confirmed by bright red splotches on the broken glass. A few bullets hit the metal frame of the Suburban, causing the only noise that might attract anyone's attention in the parking lot.

He approached the driver's door, still firing methodically, as the door window's red-stained glass particles fell to the parking lot surface, directly exposing the driver to Daniel's deadly aim. At point-blank range, he fired a few bullets into the driver's head, having noticed the man's bulletproof tactical vest at the outset of the engagement.

Daniel considered firing the remaining rounds into the back seat, but decided to keep some ammunition in the pistols for immediate use. He had only seen one silhouette in the vehicle on his approach, which led him to believe they'd left the guy from the hotel courtyard behind in their haste to follow his car, but he could always be wrong. Glancing around the parking lot, he didn't see any unwanted attention directed at the Suburban and didn't detect anyone lurking nearby.

Deciding he was temporarily safe from any immediate parking lot threats, he de-cocked one of the pistols and slipped it into the back of his pant's waistband. With the remaining pistol in his right hand, he yanked open the rear passenger door of the Suburban with his left and aimed inside.

The interior of the truck resembled a slaughterhouse. A small armory of gear sat covered in blood and skull fragments on the rear passenger seat. He spotted a laptop computer buried underneath the gear, which piqued his interest, so he closed the door and ran around to the other side, where he wouldn't be as exposed to shoppers leaving the store.

Daniel opened the door and tossed his pistol onto the floor, reaching for the short-barreled M-4 assault rifle leaned against the back of the seat. He swung the blood-slicked rifle over his shoulder, securing it in place with its tactical sling. A quick examination of the blood and brain showered tactical vest convinced him to leave it behind. He'd undoubtedly be back on foot soon. The blood and brain soaked vest would draw more attention that it was worth on the street.

Shoving the heavy vest to the middle of the long bench seat, he uncovered the partially hidden laptop. When he pulled the computer through the door, a digital camera attached by a USB cable nearly fell to the parking lot pavement. Daniel grabbed the camera, along with the laptop, and shut the door quietly, before opening to the front passenger door.

Unable to see through the blood stained windows, he stood on the Suburban's running board to scan the parking lot in front of the store. Two people had just exited the store; a woman pushing a cart away from the Suburban's aisle and a tall man carrying a single grocery bag—headed in his direction.

He ducked into the front passenger seat and sifted through the gear piled on the seat. He took the tactical vest first, checking for blood and only finding a small dime-sized splatter. The vest contained ammunition magazines for the M-4 and a submachine gun. The magazines were too long and thick for a pistol. Daniel dug through the front passenger foot well, until he found a silenced MP-9 jammed up against the center console. He considered leaving the M-4 rifle for the smaller, more concealable submachine gun, but the heavy screeching of tires nearby put any thoughts of ditching the rifle on temporary hold.

Juggling the rifle and gear, he donned the vest and slung the MP-9 submachine gun over his other shoulder. He reached back into the truck and grabbed the police scanner, which squawked excitedly. It was about to get very busy in this parking lot. With all of the gear in place, he sprinted toward his car, which was located several parking spaces toward the store entrance.

A few cars down the aisle, he passed the tall man, who turned his attention from the bullet-riddled Suburban to Daniel and muttered a prayer before backing up against the hood of a white minivan. Daniel focused on getting to the car, which he had left unlocked, with the key partially inserted into the ignition. A power truck engine roared somewhere near the back of the lot, as he reached the driver's door and pulled it open.

He started to duck into the car, but caught rapid movement in his side vision. A figure filled the gap between the two cars parked directly ahead of Daniel's Dodge Charger, running toward him. His brain registered a pistol in one hand, which was all he needed to respond. The compact MP-9 submachine gun spit an extended burst through the driver's door window, shattering the glass and slamming his target to the pavement with a sickening thud.

Daniel heard a pistol clatter underneath one of the cars and caught a glimpse of a police badge gripped in a bloody hand jammed up against the front tire. He recognized the woman's gray business suit and froze for a second, staring at her lifeless body. She should have walked away from this, but understood why she hadn't. Duty. He swallowed hard, wondering how many more people, innocent or guilty, would die tonight because of Sanderson's lethal agenda.

Tires squealed at the edge of the parking lot, jarring him out of the daze. He tossed all of the gear into the front passenger seat and started the car, drowning the distant sirens with the Charger's powerful engine.

Daniel pulled the car out into the lane and accelerated toward the back of the parking lot, reaching the end as the black Suburban careened into the same lane on the other side of the parking lot. Behind the Suburban, large groups of people piled out of the store as he jammed the accelerator and turned toward Pershing Drive. The car lurched forward toward the quiet suburbs of Silver Spring, where Daniel hoped to reduce the odds even further in his favor. His plan was simple, he'd race ahead, opening some distance as they entered the twisting, crowded streets, where he'd pull the same trick he used in the grocery store.

The Suburban gained some ground as he sped past Cedar Street. Wind poured through the open window, and Daniel drove a few blocks before he realized that Pershing Drive was a one-way street. Approaching headlights confirmed this, as a car's high beams flashed. The car quickly swerved to the left, as Daniel's car approached rapidly with no intention of moving. He would need to get off this road before someone didn't react quickly enough to his approach. Another street passed his car before he could make a decision, and the GPS indicated that Springvale Road was no longer an option.

The next street was a one-way that emptied onto Pershing Drive, so he pushed the pedal to the floor and rocketed past it toward Mayfair Place. He took the right onto Mayfair at an incredible speed, hoping the sound of squealing tires would warn any pedestrians out for a walk. The neighborhood was about to turn into a war zone.

Daniel's car screeched through a left turn onto Greenbrier Drive, just as the Suburban's lights emptied onto the far end of road. He decelerated the car and turned into the first driveway, bringing the Charger to a stop next to a Toyota 4Runner. After killing the lights, he jumped out of the car with the assault rifle and sprinted for a thick tree just to the right of the driveway entrance.

The street sat oddly quiet for a moment, only broken by the frantic radio transmissions from the police scanner deep inside of Daniel's car. Distant sirens competed with the radio transmissions for a few seconds, until unmistakable drumming of the Suburban's engine echoed off the houses surrounding him. He reached the tree and checked the rifle's EOTech Holographic sight, as the intersection filled with a rapidly expanding light.

The truck burned through the turn, screeching its tires as it swung onto Greenbrier Drive. When it started to straighten from the turn, Daniel fired a sustained burst from his rifle, keeping the green holographic bull's-eye centered on the driver's side windshield. A dozen bullets simultaneously perforated the glass, instantly causing the truck to accelerate and swerve in Daniel's direction. As the Suburban barreled past, he raked the side exposed to him with automatic fire.

The disabled Suburban cut diagonally across the driveway and collided squarely with a solid maple tree in the middle of the front yard. The truck's back end lifted a few feet off the grass and slammed down with a deep crunch. Daniel reloaded the rifle with a spare magazine from his vest and approached the back of the truck, crouching low to present a small silhouette to anyone still capable of a fight. The truck's engine continued to roar and whine, which surprised him, considering the speed of the vehicle upon impact.

A rhythmic thumping on the opposite side of the truck drew his attention, and he risked a peek. The truck door opened several inches, and Daniel saw a bloody fist pull back into the vehicle. Whoever had survived was using his fist to pound the door open, which probably meant that their legs were pinned inside the truck. Daniel assessed the risk of approaching the target and decided it wasn't worth the gamble.

Before he pulled his head back, a face briefly appeared in the Suburban's side mirror, followed by a seemingly endless, fully automatic fusillade down the side of the truck. Daniel lurched behind the SUV, feeling the supersonic hiss of several near misses, before the deafening roar reached his eardrums.

Daniel knew the submachine gun's magazine had been expended by the driver's last-ditch effort to defend himself. Firing at a cyclic rate of eight hundred rounds per minute, the gun would expend an entire magazine in roughly two seconds. He didn't time the burst, but he knew from experience that the shooter had gambled everything on the maelstrom of bullets. Daniel decided to take a chance.

He sprinted around the corner of the truck, staying low, and pointed the green holographic sighting image at the open crack of the door. The engine continued to scream as frantic movement inside the truck confirmed his suspicion that the shooter had expended the entire magazine. Daniel edged a little further until a head came into view.

"Stop reloading the weapon. If I sense any movement inside the vehicle, you're dead!" he yelled.

The movement stopped.

"Just tell me who sent you, and I'll leave. Otherwise, you get to join the rest of the team. I just want to know who sent you out into the field on a suicide mission. Who do you work for?"

"You murdered my friends," the man spat.

"Nothing personal, I guarantee you. Someone fucked you over big time today. You need to talk to *them* about why your friends are dead. You look like contract military types. Who do you work for?"

Daniel listened to the approaching sirens for a few seconds. "Last chance. Trust me, it would be pointless for you to die in that seat. I guarantee that your operation is illegal and under the table. If you die here, you'll be swept under the rug like dust. Who sent you?"

"We work for Brown River Security. I wasn't told who pulled the trigger on this, just that you were an immediate threat to national security. Black flagged," the man said.

"You were specifically told I was black flagged?" Daniel asked.

"Yes."

Use of the term "black flagged" meant one thing: CIA. And if the CIA was involved, then someone other than General Sanderson had stumbled onto his secret.

"Throw me your laptop," Daniel said.

"I can't turn around to reach it," the voice coughed, "my legs are pinned."

Daniel rushed forward and opened the rear door. A blood-soaked body tumbled halfway out of the truck, stopped by the waist restraint of the seatbelt. He saw the laptop at the dead man's feet on the floor and snatched it, taking off for his car as the sirens grew louder. Daniel stopped a few feet from the Charger, amazed to see a dark-haired, middle-aged woman standing at the top of the driveway with a butcher knife.

"Where the fuck do you think you're going?" she yelled.

"To get a grocery bag for your head," he said, staring at her until she dropped the knife to the driveway.

Leaving the woman in shock, he hopped in his rental car and backed it onto Greenbrier. He decided to risk exposing the car to the surviving Brown River contractor and gunned the engine, sending the car north on the road. He planned to work his way back to the downtown area, avoiding the closest point of approach from Natural Foods. Any police officers in the vicinity of Natural Foods would have heard the distant rattle of automatic weapons fire, which would have been immediately followed by several calls from this neighborhood. Half of the Silver Spring police force was probably en route to this address. He just hoped they hadn't found the dead detective yet. Once word spread that he was a cop killer, every available unit in the entire Montgomery County police force would descend on Silver Spring. He didn't have much time to get to a Metro Station before his only hope of escaping would involve more dead police—which was the last thing he wanted at this point.

He took a quick left onto Woodside Parkway and drove at a reasonable pace to Colesville Road, where he took another left and cruised out of the tree-lined streets into the crowded, downtown area. From the chatter on the police scanner, he could tell that they had not discovered the detective, but he didn't expect the calm to last much longer.

He could see the blue and red reflections of flashing police strobes as he approached Fenton Street, but didn't see any police cars. He kept the car on Colesville Road until he saw signs for the Metro station, which led him to a massive public parking garage. He took the handicapped placard off the dashboard and hooked it onto the rearview mirror, easily finding an open spot close to the walkway leading to the Metro. He tossed the gear he had collected from the Suburbans over the front seat and quickly got out of the car to move into the rear driver's side passenger seat. He needed to clean up and get out of here immediately.

First, he removed the Cubs hat, business shirt and jacket, jamming them under the seat with his feet. He opened the black nylon bag and removed the dark green backpack, placing it on the seat next to him. He dug through the pack until he found a large Ziploc bag containing a black hairpiece. He set this aside and removed a small plastic container of baby wipes next, which he used to thoroughly wipe his neck and head of any traces of blood. From there, he continued to transform himself, emerging within three minutes looking starkly different than before. He was now Michael Hinshaw from Annapolis, Maryland.

He wore dark blue designer jeans, expensive black leather shoes, and an untucked, crisply-pressed, white button down shirt with the sleeves rolled halfway between the wrist and elbow. His hair was jet black, hanging a half-inch over his ears, and his matching eyebrows were neatly trimmed. He'd planned the look carefully, mimicking the recent "metrosexual" trend that gave most straight men an uncomfortable feeling. The vast majority of the cops were men, and none of them wanted to get caught staring too long at a possible homosexual. Locker room humor could be brutal, especially in the macho world of law enforcement.

With the car's remote, he popped open the trunk and placed the duffle bag inside, followed by the tactical vest and assault rifle. With one smashed window, it wouldn't be long before someone studied the car more closely. Finding a military-grade rifle or a tactical body armor vest in plain view would certainly result in a call to the police. At this point, Daniel wanted to put as much distance between this car and himself as possible. He knew they'd find it eventually, but there was no need to make it too easy for them.

He studied his reflection in the rear passenger window of the car and slung the heavily burdened backpack over his left shoulder. Inside the backpack, he carried $30,000 in cash, six prepaid cell phones, several maps, his two remaining ID packets, two additional disguise kits, a bloodstained knife, hair dye, a GPS receiver, police scanner, and the MP-9 submachine gun. He had to remove the gun's bulky suppressor to fit the weapon by itself into the middle compartment, where it could be removed within seconds. The assortment of laptop computers and digital cameras stuffed into the main compartment added to the bulkiness and weight of the backpack.

He approached the north side Metro entrance, pulled his prepaid Metro card from his front jeans pocket and swiped it through the turnstile access point. He would take the next southbound train into D.C. and figure out where to meet Parker, or even better, General Sanderson. The outdoor platform was large and still busy with commuters, which was good for blending. According to the digital sign hanging above the tracks, the next train was scheduled to arrive in two minutes. He pulled a cell phone out of a small compartment in his backpack and dialed General Sanderson, who answered on the first ring.

"You're all right?"

"For now. I'm waiting to get the fuck out of Silver Spring on the Metro. Headed into the city. Did Parker get out?" he said, in a low enough voice not to attract unnecessary attention around him.

"Yes. Apparently the team waiting for him left right after you called him," General Sanderson said.

"I'm surprised Parker could pick them out," Daniel said.

"Don't underestimate Parker. He's better trained than you think. He just doesn't have the same real-world experience."

"He doesn't have the edge needed for this work. I just ran into some Brown River contractors with a similar problem."

"Brown River? Are you sure?"

"I had a little chat with one of them. Are you ready for this? He was under the distinct impression that I was an immediate terrorist risk to national security. Black flagged by whoever hired them," Daniel said.

"He used those terms?"

"Yes. I specifically asked about that."

"Daniel, this changes things drastically. I need to accelerate our timetable. Keep this phone on at all times. Parker will call you shortly with a rendezvous location. What the hell happened out there?"

Daniel didn't care to hear the word "timetable."

"They tried to kill me, and I responded," Daniel said, looking around the crowded platform for any sign of law enforcement.

"Jesus, Daniel, it sounds like you did more than just respond. I'm picking up cross-county chatter on all police bands," Sanderson said.

"My train's coming. I'll be waiting for that call," he said, wondering if Sanderson would abandon him if the heat intensified.

Nobody gave him a second glance as he boarded the train headed for the city.

Chapter Twenty-Seven

Special Agent Frank Mendoza shut the office door and locked it before approaching Sharpe's cluttered desk.

"Grab a seat, Frank, and tell me about Black Flag. Based on your fax, I can only imagine the worst," Sharpe said.

Glancing out of his office window onto 9th Street, he imagined some of the nation's preeminent powerbrokers sipping a few too many drinks over dinner in the Caucus Room and telling jokes about dead Arabs—oblivious to the implications of the day's events, He looked back at Frank, who appeared equally troubled.

"It's not good. I think we may have found our next investigation."

"Black Flag isn't our mess to unscrew. I just want to unravel enough of it to figure out what happened today," Sharpe said.

"We'll need to nab a few more of them. Munoz is useless to us at this point. He's covered by a nice immunity agreement," Mendoza said.

"We'll see about that. I'm not ready to release my only link to Black Flag. I've given Boston orders to transport Munoz here. Olson will lead the prisoner transport convoy. We should have Munoz at HQ early in the morning."

Mendoza failed to hide a disapproving glance.

"We can't let him walk free until we've determined exactly what happened today. For all we know, Munoz and his friends might be part of an Islamic conspiracy, or worse. We don't know anything right now, and people are getting nervous. Very nervous. We should have some new leads within the hour. I've mobilized SWAT and FBI field teams to take every operative on the list. I'm just waiting for word that all of the teams are in place, ready to go, and we'll hit them all at once. I want a coordinated move against Black Flag. I don't know if they're all talking to each other, but I'm not taking any chances," Sharpe said.

"Well, sir. I wouldn't get your hopes up too high. Munoz took his sweet time spilling information. Probably long enough to miss a few pre-assigned check-ins. I'd be surprised if any of these guys were still around," Mendoza said.

"Yeah, the thought wasn't lost on me, but we might get lucky one more time today. So, what are we really dealing with here?" Sharpe said.

"From what I've been allowed to see by this mysterious Mr. McKie gentleman, Black Flag was a highly-specialized program designed to create undercover operatives for our military. McKie said the program training lasted approximately four years, which is a long time for any training program. Hell, the CIA doesn't even train field agents for that long."

"CIA agents are usually assigned to legitimate jobs as cover. This sounds dramatically different," Sharpe interrupted.

"Right. Black Flag operatives are trained as small teams, according to their assigned area of operation. They are selected for the area of operation first, then brought into the program. Daniel Petrovich was assigned to Serbia, which makes sense given his background. Father Serbian, mother Polish. Not sure if he spoke Serbian before the program, but it's fair to make that assumption. McKie said the selection process was the key to Black Flag's success."

"Success?" Sharpe said.

"I asked. McKie wasn't willing to share any operational details. Like my fax implied, this group is extremely dangerous. They have the skills to survive and escape nearly any situation, backed by extensive experience putting these skills through the wringer. I assume the takedown teams know what they're facing?"

"They've been thoroughly briefed. I could read between the lines of your fax. It must really burn Munoz to have been caught like this. He turned his back on Sanderson pretty quick," Sharpe said.

"Maybe they were all dragged back into this against their will. The Black Flag program was run exclusively by Sanderson. I didn't get the impression there was any oversight. These rogue programs always have problems. Who knows? But Munoz wasn't exactly living like some disgruntled, mentally-scarred burnout. He left one of his coffee shops in the middle of the afternoon yesterday, for an appointment that wasn't on the books, and wound up unconscious in Newport. Hell, maybe we'll find a few more of these guys sitting around, waiting to chat about General Sanderson,"

Mendoza said, and they both sat quietly for a few moments, contemplating Mendoza's comment.

"I wonder if Petrovich falls into this category," Sharpe muttered, just above his breath.

"Why the focus on Petrovich?"

"Something about him didn't fit from the start. He only lives a few miles from the murder scene, which seemed a little close to home…"

"Convenient. Knows the landscape, traffic patterns, can dress like a local. I think it's perfect. Shit, if Munoz hadn't slipped, we would never have found Petrovich," Mendoza said.

"I know," Sharpe whispered, "but none of the other suspects live closer than sixty miles. Most live even further away. And then there's the operative in Concord, New Hampshire. Steven Gedman. Our team just discovered some interesting news about him."

Mendoza shrugged.

"A National Crime Information Center database search," Sharpe continued, "turned up a quick hit. Mr. Gedman was recently picked up by police for a domestic incident. We called the Concord police and learned that he's an involuntary guest at Concord Hospital's inpatient psychiatric ward. His wife said he had a breakdown and started running around the house packing suitcases, yelling…are you ready for this?"

Mendoza nodded.

"He kept screaming, 'They're trying to drag me back in!' and all kinds of stuff that made no sense to her."

"No kidding. Are you thinking—"

"Yes. That Gedman was supposed to be the one to kill Mohammed Ghani, but he crumbled under the pressure. I can't imagine any of these guys can remain stable for the long run. Especially if their main mission was undercover work."

"Still, Sanderson had other choices. A guy in upstate New York could have made the trip," Mendoza countered.

"I don't know. Gedman was hospitalized one night before the murders. Petrovich was right there. I think he's their weak link. We find him, we find Sanderson. At the end of the day, I just want confirmation that this isn't the beginning of a bigger attack. I'll need Sanderson for that. The FBI and White House can figure out what to do with his pet project later."

Sharpe's desk phone punctuated the conversation with a shrill ring tone, causing the agent to quickly sweep it out of its cradle.

"Special Agent Sharpe," he said and listened.

"Give all locations a ten-minute warning. I want a coordinated strike at 2100 hours, Eastern Time. We'll be right there," Sharpe said and hung up the phone. "All of the teams are ready."

"Let's go fishing, sir," Mendoza said, rising from his chair.

Chapter Twenty-Eight

Special Agent Justin Edwards felt like a second-class citizen. He sat in the front passenger seat of a rented Chevy Impala, parked deep inside the Longfellow Elementary School parking lot. Underneath his navy blue, nylon FBI parka, he wore a stripped-down tactical vest loaned to him by the Portland Police Department. His service pistol, a boxy Glock 23, was jammed uncomfortably between his waist and seat, causing him to fidget like a child on a long car trip. The Impala, supposedly the best car available on the FBI's budget, smelled like stale cigarette smoke and cherry air freshener. The car's windows had been open since they drove it off the rental lot at the Portland Jetport, but the nasty odor continued to permeate the car, itching his lungs.

Nearly a dozen police vehicles crowded the southern corner of the lot, casting long shadows across the parking lot from the orange security light glowing over the gymnasium entrance door. Five black and white Suburbans formed a row, extending from an industrial dumpster near the kitchen delivery dock to the edge of the ancient, three-story school—positioned for a quick exit onto Stevens Avenue toward their target. Several fully equipped SWAT officers stood in a loose circle around the second SUV in line, and he could see at least a dozen more heavily armed officers scattered throughout the rest of the vehicles.

The other cars were unmarked sedans, like Edward's car, filled with at least twenty additional plain-clothed and uniformed law enforcement officers. They had arrived at the parking lot two hours earlier through a back entrance to the lot, waiting for the sun to disappear below the trees. He was accustomed to long, boring stakeouts, but the situation was different in this parking lot, and he detested the dynamic that had developed.

Every time he approached the SWAT huddle up near the half dozen Portland Police Department SUVs, he got cold looks from the heavily armed, black-clad men. So he sat back with the rest of the FBI team, crammed into a crappy, American-made sedan that he wouldn't be caught dead in on the weekend. At least he wasn't in the minivan with the forensics equipment and the real geeks. One of the younger agents, whose name he didn't care enough to remember, suggested that the minivan should be his command post. He just shook his head at the kid.

Technically, Justin Edwards was in charge of this entire operation. The investigation fell under federal jurisdiction, and he was the senior agent on scene. Unfortunately, the FBI had no organic assets in Maine or New Hampshire, and nobody cared enough to send Boston SWAT assets up Interstate 95 to give him some semblance of authority here. Instead, he had been forced to grovel with the Portland Police Department to assemble their SWAT team for the takedown at 18 Lawn Avenue. After placing an uncomfortable call to FBI headquarters, right in front of Edwards, the Portland Police liaison officer got the ball rolling for him.

Within an hour, he had Portland and Maine State Police SWAT teams at his disposal. He briefed the teams about the threat level and rules of engagement (ROE), and that was when he lost control of the operation. Once the SWAT teams had their target and ROE, it became frustratingly clear to Edwards that they didn't need or want his input. They started planning the operation and scouting the location without seeking his input, or keeping him informed. He knew they had a few cars on Lawn Avenue, keeping an eye on the house, but beyond that, he didn't know very much about their planned raid.

At this point, Special Agent Edwards had been relegated to relaying information from headquarters, and several times over the past few hours, he would reluctantly get out of the car to let them know that the other teams were still assembling. They never said it, but he could read their faces, which clearly broadcast, "Stay in your car unless you have something useful to tell us."

Edwards stretched his body, purposefully hitting the driver, Special Agent Derek Ravenell, jarring the agent out of a light sleep. He had worked with Ravenell on a few bank robbery cases in Boston and found him to be competent, but more importantly, obedient. He understood the importance of the rank structure and the subtleties of loyalty, although the look he flashed Edwards didn't exactly comport with this assessment.

"Stay sharp. You don't see those guys napping out here," Edwards said, examining the agents in the back seat.

Of course, Special Agent Olson had assigned him the ugliest female special agent on the East Coast, Special Agent Sara Velasquez. So, now he had the dream team sitting in his car, including Special Agent Paul Adams, who was about as exciting as his name. No wonder the SWAT guys wouldn't deal with him. He didn't say a word to the agents in the back of the car, who both nodded apathetically.

Edwards' cell phone mercifully rang and delivered some good news. He listened intently and acknowledged the call from Task Force HYDRA's operations center. He turned around and nearly yelled into the back seat, startling Velasquez and Adams.

"Ten minute warning. We hit the house at 2100 hours!" he said and jumped out of the car to alert the SWAT team.

"Douche bag," Special Agent Sara Velasquez uttered, and everyone in the car mumbled agreement.

Chapter Twenty-Nine

Special Agents Sharpe and Mendoza entered the task force's operations center, which scrambled to pass the word to FBI teams in a dozen cities across the East Coast. The coordinated raid was a major undertaking, and every workstation was occupied. Agents ran from one workstation to another, shouting information, and Sharpe could see that one of the plasma screens served as a status board for live information from each site. Sharpe knew the clamorous activity would fall deathly quiet at the prescribed time, as everyone waited for word from the tactical teams.

Mixed SWAT units sat ready to pounce on nearly two dozen residential locations and commercial establishments in the hope of capturing another Black Flag operative. Since his task force received the list of Black Flag operatives, law enforcement agents had been quietly investigating the most probable after work locations for the suspects. So far, the team had no confirmed sightings, which didn't leave Sharpe with a hopeful feeling for the operation, but he just needed to get lucky in one of the locations.

Sharpe walked over to Special Agent O'Reilly, who worked at a computer station powered to access several national and international criminal databases. Special Agent O'Reilly scratched her head, staring between two widescreen monitors as Sharpe approached. She had put together comprehensive information packages for each of the SWAT teams and didn't appear to be resting like several other agents. She didn't notice him kneel down next to her chair until his face broke her peripheral vision. She turned her head slowly, still examining the data on the screen, until she noticed who was next to her.

"Oh...sorry, sir. You know, I have a hard time believing that none of these guys have any kind of criminal record. Not even a speeding ticket," she said and leaned in a little to whisper. "I mean, we can all read between

146

the lines here. Right, sir? Eight murders, an organized list of suspects, strict ROE to the SWAT teams. This is a dangerous group of individuals, probably professional assassins, yet I'm getting nothing. I've worked organized crime, and their enforcers always had the worst records. Mafia, Russians, cartel groups. Without exception, they'd all done hard time, or had at least been arrested on murder charges. This group is too clean."

"Dana, you've always been one of the most perceptive agents on the task force, and you're right about this group. They're different. I need you to check a different source. Have you run this through INTERPOL yet?"

"Yes. The potential for an international connection was too strong to ignore, but I got the same result," she said, typing at the keyboard and bringing up the INTERPOL search results.

Sharpe stared at the data on the screen, deciding to skirt the boundaries of his information security arrangement with the Pentagon. Agent O'Reilly was not authorized for CIS Category One information, and he didn't plan to directly pass her any information. She had already thought to conduct an INTERPOL search, which was not a violation. Still, by nudging her further, Sharpe was probably crossing a line that could heat things up for him.

"Dana, did you submit a photo identification match request through INTERPOL's database?" he said, and that was all it took for her to run with it.

"No, sir. Not through INTERPOL. National NCIC does it automatically for us. Same with VICAP. Do you think they're foreign operatives? They all have pretty solid histories here in the U.S.," she said.

"No assumptions," he said and leaned in closer to whisper, "Start with Petrovich...and let's keep this between the two of us for now."

"All right, I'll start working on this," she said and started typing.

As Sharpe stood up to walk over to Special Agent Mendoza near the front of the operations center, he saw pictures from Daniel Petrovich's current Maine driver's license and former Department of Defense military ID flash onto her screen. She looked back at him, and he nodded before turning away.

Chapter Thirty

The Chevy Impala crept down Lawn Avenue, preceded by two Portland Police Department Suburbans. Beyond the vehicles, invisible to Edwards on the dimly lit street, two additional Suburbans approached from the opposite direction. From the front seat of the Impala, Edwards secretly admired the heavily armed men standing on the running boards of the trucks, clinging with one hand to the roof bars. Though technically a two-way street, Edwards watched uncomfortably as the thick Suburbans squeezed through cars, and the men tucked their bodies tightly against the truck.

He had voiced his desire to ride on one of the trucks with the SWAT team, but his request was shot down immediately. The SWAT commander wanted Edward's entourage to wait in the parking lot, with the other non-tactical units, until the house was secured, but Edwards finally put his foot down. He wasn't about to sit back like some loser, waiting for the "all safe" signal. He'd rushed through plenty of doors into dangerous situations before, and this situation was no different. They agreed on a compromise. Edwards would follow the SWAT team into the house, while the rest of his FBI team secured the front of the house.

Edwards felt a flutter of adrenaline when the Suburban's brake lights bathed his car in red light, illuminating its occupants and momentarily blinding him. Out of the corner of his eye, he saw movement, which he tracked in the side view mirror. Two figures darted across the back of his car, causing Edwards to go wide-eyed. He quickly assumed this was the surveillance team that had been stationed across the street from Petrovich's house.

He turned his head back to the front and caught a glimpse of another

148

figure positioned behind a tree ahead of the Suburbans. He could see the outline of a tactical helmet, so he knew it was one of theirs, but it still unnerved him to see someone emerge from the darkness so quickly. The figure braced a scoped assault rifle against the tree, pointing toward the front of Petrovich's house. He felt a little better knowing that they had someone covering the assault run on the house. A few more feet and they should be in position. His headset crackled to life.

"Standby. Standby...Go. All teams. Go!"

The team attached to the Suburban in front of him jumped to the pavement and sprinted toward the front door of Petrovich's house. Edwards scrambled out of the door, drawing his service pistol for the first time in two years. It had been a while since Special Agent Edwards had participated in a raid, and he found himself a little disoriented on the street. He ran around the front of the Impala, noticing that the passenger compartment light grossly illuminated his entire team. That stupid ass Ravenell had forgotten to turn off the interior lights, and now he'd probably have to endure some kind of a lecture from the SWAT guys.

He raced between two parked cars and sprinted through the shattered white picket fence gate, slowing as he approached the team. None of them acknowledged his approach. They were focused on their objective, which was a highly trained, extremely dangerous terrorist operative. The SWAT team finished stacking up on the front door, and Edwards just hoped they didn't kill Petrovich on sight.

Another team, just out of his sight behind a large evergreen bush to his right, swarmed around the mudroom door. He wasn't one hundred percent sure, since he had been excluded from the assault-planning phase, but he thought there was another team around back doing the same thing. As soon as everyone at the front door stopped moving, he heard more reports on the radio, as each team reported that they were ready. The final round of reports unnerved him, and he felt his bladder loosen just slightly.

"All teams be advised, there is movement in the kitchen. Rear team. Take this suspect upon entry. Stand by. Stand by. Breach. All teams. Breach."

The second SWAT member in line rushed the door carrying a portable battering ram, which resembled a thick metal cylinder with two handles on top. He swung the solid metal ram at a spot on the door just above the handle, and the door slammed inward, releasing the acoustic guitar sounds of the Gypsy Kings into the neighborhood. The ram had barely receded from the open doorway before seven heavily-armed men disappeared into the house.

Special Agent Edwards moved forward with the team onto the porch, but stopped when he heard crashing glass and female screaming. He decided to stay out of the house until things calmed down, and he wasn't altogether convinced that the SWAT guys wouldn't try to knock him flat. He didn't like the way they looked at him.

Less than a minute passed before Edwards heard "all clear." He holstered his weapon and entered the house, which had a warm, but purposefully constructed Pottery Barn feel. The Petrovich couple clearly hadn't held back spending money on decorating their house. He noted a few expensively framed local prints set against the deep rust-colored paint in the hallway. A string of harsh obscenities drew him toward the kitchen.

One of the pendant lights swung over kitchen island; the deep blue glass casing of the light lay scattered on the dark brown granite. To his left, shattered glass covered the small pine table and hardwood flooring in the small nook area right off the kitchen. A SWAT team member stood in the middle of an opening that used to be a sliding glass door; his assault rifle pointed downward at the deck.

Shards of broken glass crackled under Special Agent Edwards' expensive leather shoes as he rounded the brown granite kitchen island to get a better view of what was causing all of the commotion. He was immediately turned on by what he saw.

"Careful. She moves quick," said one of the black-clad officers near the mudroom door.

An athletic woman, dressed in black running shorts and a jog bra, lay pressed to the hardwood floor by two men in full body armor and tactical gear. The woman's face, covered by her luxurious brown hair, was jammed against the dark pine planks by one of the men's thick, gloved hands. He really wanted to the see the face attached to this woman's body. He saw a few shards of blue glass from the pendant light near one of the officer's boots and hoped they hadn't jammed her face down on any glass. If they did, she was taking the pain pretty well. He suddenly liked the possibility of her taking pain. Another agent kneeled on her lower back, struggling to tighten the black zip tie surrounding her wrists. She struggled against the men and almost turned over onto her side.

"Will someone fucking sit on her legs!" the officer attempting to cuff her shouted, and another SWAT officer edged past the refrigerator and jumped down on her legs.

The woman cried out in pain and gave it one more try, nearly toppling the guy working on her hands. She was strong, and Edwards felt strangely aroused. He wanted to be on top of her and had to use every ounce of self-restraint he possessed to keep himself from making the suggestion. They'd laugh him out of the house, and frankly, he was better off where he stood. Right now, she looked like she could snap him in half.

"Hit her with the stun gun!" the officer on her back yelled, then mumbled, "Calm this bitch down."

"Sergeant! We need to hit her with the zapper!" another officer yelled through the house.

Sergeant Jimmy Haldron ran into the kitchen from the family room, pushed Edwards aside, and quickly assessed the situation. He leaned down toward the woman's head to speak to her.

"Ma'am, I need you to calm down. This is over. There's nothing you can do about your situation right now, except calm down. We don't want to hurt you, but we need you to take it easy. We're not here for you, and if you calm down, you'll be released once we finish our job here. Can you help me with this?" he said, in a calm, authoritative voice.

The woman stopped twisting and seemed to melt into the flooring. The officer on her back pressed down harder, yanking the twist ties deeply into her wrists, causing her to gasp.

"Donnelly! Take it easy," Sergeant Haldron said and gave him a pissed off look.

"We'll get those off you soon. Everyone is a little amped up here," he said.

Edwards decided he would step in at this point and take charge of the situation, now that SWAT was no longer needed. He couldn't wait to dismiss these idiots from the scene.

"Sergeant, have your men move her over into the family room, on the couch. I assume Petrovich isn't here?" Edwards said.

"No. His car is gone, and the house is clear. My teams are checking for hidden compartments," he said and directed orders to his men, "Get her up, and bring her over here."

"Have your men start working the neighborhood for leads. I'll deal with her," Edwards said, excited about starting his interrogation of Jessica Petrovich.

"My men aren't going door to door. We've got detectives and patrol officers for that. You want a couple of my guys to stand by while you talk to her?" Haldron said, looking him square in the eye.

"Probably not a bad idea. She seems a little feisty," Edwards admitted.

"Feisty? She came at me with some kind of judo chop," the officer pinning her head to the floor said.

"This Nazi stormtrooper tried to butt stroke me with his rifle. I was just standing there," the woman hissed.

"She came at me with a weapon," the officer said.

"I was about to have some yogurt when you crashed through the glass. Sorry if I couldn't react fast enough to drop the spoon in my hand," she said, in a voice muffled by her squished face.

Edwards glanced at the wet floor between her waist and the counter cabinets, and spotted a small spoon protruding from under her body. He chuckled and turned to Sergeant Haldron.

"I'll have my techs bag up the spoon she used against your officers," he said, pointing at the silverware next to her body.

Nobody laughed, and he heard a few mumbled "fuck you's," but he didn't care. They would never respect him, and he would always resent their type. He had better things to do with his time, and one of those things was Daniel Petrovich's wife. When they lifted her off the kitchen floor, he got really excited. She was beautiful, almost exotic, possibly Middle Eastern. Their eyes locked for a moment, and he would have sworn her murderous glare softened. He couldn't wait to break the news to her that her husband was wanted by the FBI for murder and terrorism. He'd watch her world crumble and her self-esteem evaporate, then he'd offer her a shoulder to cry on, and maybe a drink down in that crummy little downtown area they call the Old Port. Maybe this trip wouldn't be such a waste of time after all.

"We're not here for her. Take it easy," Edwards said.

One of the officers holding her hissed in her ear, "Just make a move and I'll bust up that pretty face."

"Sergeant Haldron!" Edwards yelled, and Haldron walked over to intervene.

"What do you need?" Haldron said, clearly sick of Edwards.

"I just need some professionalism. And I need you to control your men. Now sit her down on the couch and remove her restraints," Edwards said, staring at one of the officers holding her.

"Are you fucking kidding me? We just busted our asses getting this one under control," the same officer said.

"I don't think that would be a good idea," Sergeant Haldron said, and a few other officers chimed in from the kitchen.

Edwards walked briskly past the officers, pushing his way through to the back of the kitchen. At this point, he had experienced enough of their insubordination. They were undermining his authority with the witness and sabotaging his carefully laid plans to coax information out of her. These goons had no idea that nothing else mattered at this point. Only Jessica Petrovich held the key to finding her husband, and if he didn't play the situation right, she'd shut down for good. He grabbed a pair of kitchen shears from the knife rack and walked up to Jessica, who was still in the grips of two very large, heavily geared officers.

"Move out of the way," he said, and the two officers let go of Jessica.

Edwards cut her plastic restraints and tossed the scissors to the floor behind him. He lingered close to her—she smelled intoxicating.

"Sorry about this. Why don't you grab a seat on the couch," he said softly, before turning to Haldron.

"I don't want any of these guys in here. Understood?"

"You want to be in here alone with this one?" Haldron asked.

Edwards considered Haldron's comment and decided that it held no double entendre. He wanted to be alone with this woman more than anyone could possibly know, but that's not what Haldron meant. Couldn't be. They thought she was dangerous.

"I think she'll be fine without someone trying to smash her skull in," Edwards said.

"She was holding a weapon!" an officer from the kitchen yelled.

"She was holding a spoon, dummy," Edwards said.

"Hey. Take it easy on my men. They don't have the luxury of walking into a cleared structure. They go in first and have no idea what they'll find. I didn't notice you rushing in behind them," Haldron said.

"I didn't want to get shot...by them," Edwards said, and Haldron looked like he might lose his composure.

Standing peacefully in front of the couch, Jessica regarded them both, showing a small sign of smiling at Edwards.

"I'll give you some privacy here, but as long as Portland police officers are required on the scene, I'll keep some of my guys posted to keep an eye on her."

"That's fine, Sergeant," Edwards said and turned to Jessica.

"Please. Have a seat. Are you all right? I saw some glass on the floor," he said, walking over to her.

"I think I'm okay. I just haven't had any time to process what's happening. Someone said something about my husband being a murderer. What's going on here? Who's going to pay for everything they've broken? Look, I…"

"Take it easy, Mrs. Petrovich. You need to take a few moments to sit back and relax…"

"Is my husband okay? Did something happen to him?" she said, rubbing her face with her hands.

Her eyes were red, and he could see that she was starting to tear up. Fortunately for Edwards, she wore no make up to ruin the face with running streaks. God, she was stunning. Angular face, dark exotic skin, or she tanned a lot. Either way, he didn't care. He didn't care how she got there. The dark skin, killer looks and kick boxer physique was all he needed. He was glad to know that Petrovich wouldn't be fucking her anymore. He couldn't stand the thought of someone else entangled in those legs. He had his work cut out for him, but he was starting to feel confident about his chances of seeing her naked tonight.

"Ms. Petrovich…"

"Jess. Please call me Jess. What's going on with my husband?"

"It's complicated," Edwards said, taking a seat on the leather chair next to the couch.

He could move over to the couch if she started crying, but didn't want to seem eager to get close to her.

"Is he safe? What were these guys expecting to find?" she pressed.

"I don't know how to put this, but your husband is the prime suspect in a federal murder investigation," he said.

"That doesn't make any sense, Agent…?"

"Edwards. But just call me Justin."

"Justin, none of this makes any sense. I think you all have the wrong house, or something isn't right," she said, looking around the room, frightened.

At this point, though only a few officers lingered in the family room with them, dozens of officers had poured into the house over the past few minutes and more were entering. Since the house wasn't considered a crime scene, the Portland police wouldn't tiptoe through her house. This would only get worse as they tore the place apart looking for hidden compartments or clues linking Daniel Petrovich to the murders and the past life he had hidden from his wife. He might need to get her out of here soon. She would find it hard to concentrate on him once his team started taking photos out of the frames for scanning.

"Jessica, how long have you and your husband been married?" Edwards asked, though he knew the answer would somehow eat away at something inside of him.

He glanced at a wedding photo sitting on a dark wood side table next to the couch. The picture had been taken with the ocean in the background. He thought it looked like the East Coast, somewhere north. Possibly right here in Maine.

"What do you...we've been married for four years," she said.

"Have you known each other for a long time?"

"Long enough to know that you guys have made a serious mistake. This is ridiculous. We're talking about having kids, and...does my husband have a lawyer yet? Maybe I shouldn't be talking to you right now. I need to see my husband," she said, stringing each sentence together one after the other quickly.

Edwards needed to diffuse the lawyer talk quick. She wasn't a suspect and technically didn't need one, but if she shut down on him and contacted a lawyer, he knew exactly what kind of advice the lawyer will give her: Shut up. He had limited time to work on this one and hoped to wrap things up tonight, in more ways than one. He didn't need some lawyer cooling things off.

"Jess, Jess," he soothed, "I know this is a lot to take in, and I'm sorry you got roughed up here tonight, but we don't have much time to help your husband."

"What do you mean help him? Where is he?" she said, confused.

"That's the problem. Nobody knows where he is. Can you help us with this? When did you see him last?" he said and shifted a little closer to her.

"This morning before work. He left me a message in the morning saying he had to fly to D.C. to meet with one of his company's clients. Something last minute. I was supposed to meet some friends out for drinks after work, but he always calls me, so I got a little worried. I went for a run instead. He must have something big going on at work. He didn't sound like himself," Jessica admitted.

Edwards thought this might be easier than he had expected. She had already given him information that could narrow their search for Petrovich, which surprised him. He had expected her to hold stuff like this from him, but for some reason she didn't hesitate. Maybe their marriage wasn't as solid as all of the pictures might indicate. She was clearly a little pissed that he had taken off without calling and was willing to give up some general details. When she found out the true scope of his betrayal, he wondered if she might give him up completely. He didn't believe for one second that she didn't know exactly where they could find Petrovich, and now he was willing to bet she would cough him up given the right information about her husband.

"Did he give you any more details?" he said, hoping he might get lucky.

"No. He just said he had to fly unexpectedly to D.C. to meet with..." she said and stopped cold. "What exactly is he suspected of?" she snapped.

"Jess, he's a prime suspect in the murder of Mohammed Ghani. He was killed last night just a few miles from here in Cape Elizabeth. I was at the scene earlier today, and it wasn't pretty. Whoever killed him knew exactly what they were doing," Edwards said.

"I must be missing something here. How the fuck is my husband a suspect in that?" she said, raising her voice to the point that a few black helmets leaned into the room.

"I wish I could go into that more, but the details are classified for now. I'll say this though," he said and leaned in close enough to smell her, "and you need to keep it to yourself for now," he whispered.

She nodded quizzically and leaned in further, which drove his senses crazy. He felt a wave of raw physical energy pass through him and nearly shuddered. Blood started to immediately flow to his groin, and he felt a tingling in his legs as he grew erect. He had to stop this, but he didn't want to move away from her. He couldn't imagine what it would be like to strip her down in bed. He moved back slightly, afraid he might lose control, and regained enough of his senses to continue talking to her. Only a few women had affected him like this before, and he'd enjoyed dominating them in bed. This one would be no exception to Justin's conquests, but first he had some work to do.

"Your husband's name came up on a list of former covert military operatives connected to the murders. Have you seen the news today? Eight prominent Arab businessmen were killed last night," he said and let this sink in, studying her face for a reaction.

She looked confused for a few seconds, but this changed when she started to speak. "This is crazy. I know my husband, and I can assure you this is a major fuck up. I want everyone out of my house right now!" she yelled and stood up from the couch.

The two SWAT officers stepped into the room, and Edwards gently placed a hand on her left shoulder.

"Please, Jess. I don't think you fully understand the situation here. We have a warrant for your husband's arrest and to search this house," he said, and she hesitated to sit back down on the couch, looking at him with distrust.

"Special Agent Adams!" he yelled and heard a muffled acknowledgement.

A few seconds later, a middle-aged Caucasian man wearing a blue windbreaker with the letters "FBI" printed across the front in bright yellow letters, appeared from the kitchen area.

"I need the warrant," Edwards said, and Adams stepped into the room with a black nylon document bag.

He pulled the warrant out and handed it to Edwards, who dismissed him with his hand. One of the SWAT officers saw the dismissal and mumbled something just loud enough to be heard by the agent in charge.

"I'm sorry. What was that? Officer...?"

"Officer 'none of your motherfucking business,'" said the serious-looking police officer, completely unimpressed with Edwards.

He looked at Jess and shook his head. "I'm glad my team was here for this. These guys are animals," he said loud enough for the officer to hear him, and she nodded her head slightly, which was a good sign for Edwards.

"Here. Take a few minutes to read through this. I'm afraid there is no mistake."

He sat there fidgeting while she took her time reading the warrant. He glanced nervously at the two openings to the room, looking specifically for the SWAT officers. His hatred for these arrogant animals penetrated his core. They were the same in the FBI. A bunch of gun-crazy bullies dressed up in scary body armor, carrying enough weaponry to level a small building. And when they couldn't level doors and buildings, they pushed everyone else around, including the "regular" agents. Edwards had done the research and discovered that the advent of FBI and local SWAT teams had had no impact on public or law enforcement safety. From what he could tell, the teams just ate up funding and delayed every single investigation involving a possible dangerous suspect. He hated them.

Jessica took close to five minutes to read through the warrant, which seemed like an eternity to Edwards. She handed it back, and he could see tears forming in her exotic brown eyes.

"There has to be a serious mistake. Danny served in the navy, but not on some kind of special squad, or anything like that," she said, wiping her eyes.

"I really can't go into details about the source of our information, but I can assure you it is reliable. Look, we're not saying he killed this guy, but his name is closely linked to a group that is most definitely involved in these killings. He needs to come out of hiding and clear his name..."

"He's not hiding. He's on a business trip," she said, and Edwards sensed that her faith in the statement regarding the business trip might be fading.

"What hotel is he staying in?" Edwards asked.

"I don't know. He hasn't called...and I can't get a hold of him on his cell phone," she muttered.

"Is that normal? Can we try his number?" he said.

"Yes. No. I mean...it's not normal, and sure, you can try his number. It just goes right to voicemail."

"Doesn't that strike you as odd? I'm sorry, Jess, but it's too much of a coincidence for either me or you to ignore. I hope you're right that he's not involved, but frankly, something's up, and we need to get to the bottom of it. This investigation is a matter of national security, and if he can clear some things up for us, I know I can help him out."

She stared at him in shock, and he could see the gravity of the situation weighing down on her. She alternated between despair and courage, but he sensed a shift downward. The spunky Jessica Petrovich he met on the kitchen floor would soon be replaced by a deflated, betrayed woman, ripe for his picking. He needed to get her out of here soon, before these local idiots ruined it for him.

"I'm really confused here. What do I have to do? Do I have to leave my house? How long are these people going to be here?"

"Probably all night..." he started, and his phone buzzed in his front suit pant pocket.

"Give me a second. Sorry about this," he said and stepped away toward the back window of the house, making sure the SWAT guy kept his distance.

"Special Agent Edwards," he said and listened.

"Negative. The house is clean. I was about to call operations," he said and found himself listening again.

"When? Are you sure it's him? All right. I'll be in touch if we find anything," he said and replaced the phone in his pocket.

"Jess, your husband is in a serious situation. A man fitting his description just killed several people in D.C., including an off-duty police officer," he said and realized then that he had spoken too loudly.

He heard a commotion in the kitchen and knew he needed to get her out of here immediately.

"What? This isn't Danny. He's not capable of this," she said and stood up.

She looked panicked, and Edwards needed to keep her away from the police officers. He heard the words "cop killer's wife," and knew this could spiral out of control quickly, especially with the lack of control and professionalism displayed by local police already.

"Jess, I think it would be in our best interest to get you out of here and into a federal office where," he leaned in to whisper, "these idiots have no jurisdiction. They take the cop killing thing very seriously, and I don't know if I can control the situation with you here. We'll head to our satellite office and figure things out there. Sound fair?"

She nodded her head to indicate yes, but he could tell she was in a daze.

"I need to change," she offered weakly.

"I'll escort you upstairs, and you can pick out an outfit. You can change at the office. I don't think these guys will let you out of their sight, and they may become hostile when they figure out we're leaving," he whispered.

"All right," she said and tried to stand up, but she looked like she might pass out.

"Forget it. I have a better idea," he said.

"Special Agent Velasquez! Someone get Special Agent Velasquez," he said, and the SWAT officer surprisingly relayed his request.

He heard footsteps descend the stairs, and Velasquez appeared at the front of the room. She looked even uglier contrasted with Jessica Petrovich. Round face, poorly-styled, light brown hair. Non-existent figure. He was pretty sure she was a lesbian, which made sense to him. He couldn't imagine she'd have any luck with men. She approached the back of the couch, and he loathed the idea of getting close enough to her to whisper.

"Agent Velasquez, I need you to go back upstairs, and as discreetly as possible, find Mrs. Petrovich an outfit to wear. Nothing fancy…"

"I have one hanging up on my closet door. It'll be fine," Jessica said with a catatonic look on her face.

Velasquez looked confused.

"Word just got out that her husband killed an off-duty cop in D.C. I need to get her out of here before things get out of hand, and she shuts down on us completely," he whispered, hoping Jessica couldn't hear what he said.

Agent Velasquez glanced past Edwards at Jessica, who was staring at the wall with a blank expression.

"Might be too late for that," she said.

"Just get the outfit."

"Got it. I'll have Ravenell bring the outfit and the keys to the car. All of our gear is offloaded, so you won't have to stick around," she said and turned to leave.

"My purse too, please. It's in the kitchen. I have some makeup in there," Jessica said.

"Uh...sure, hon," the agent said.

"Let's give them a minute, and we'll walk you out of here," he whispered to Jessica.

"Thank you," she said, lightly touching his knee with her hand.

He felt a surge of adrenaline pour through his body with the touch. Electric energy tingled throughout, stimulating all of his senses at once. He worried that he might ejaculate in his pants on the couch if she moved her hand closer to his groin. He didn't want her to remove her hand, but he would need to stand up in a minute, and he was worried that everyone would see his growing erection. He couldn't imagine the sensation he'd feel if she touched his manhood. She'd have to help him with this later, and he had a plan to make this happen. But first, he had to regain control of himself and get her out of here without completely embarrassing himself.

He stood up and turned away from her, breaking the connection, pretending to check on the police progress in the kitchen. He saw Agent Ravenell grab her purse, and they shared a knowing glance. Once Ravenell began walking toward the front door, Edwards took Jessica's hand, almost stopping dead in his tracks from the sheer ecstasy of her touch, and took her to the front door. The SWAT officer at the doorway leading out of the family room accosted them.

"Where are you headed with her?"

Instead of insulting the officer, he went with a different approach, which required all of the restraint Edwards could muster. "I'm taking her outside to get some fresh air. She doesn't look so good. Excuse us," he said and edged past the officer.

They got to the door before the officer spoke into his headset, obviously no longer under Edward's spell. He heard some commotion in the kitchen just as Agent Ravenell met them and handed Jessica the purse.

"Outfit's in the car. Car keys are in the purse," he whispered to Edwards.

Ravenell turned back toward the hallway, just as a tall man dressed in a navy blue suit appeared in the kitchen and started his way toward them. He cleverly positioned himself in the man's way, pretending to be confused, trying to buy Edwards some time. The agent's quick reaction allowed Edwards to move Jessica halfway across the lawn before he heard footsteps closing in.

"Excuse me," an insistent voice said, and Edwards turned toward the source of his newest level of harassment and potential embarrassment.

He found himself standing several feet from an incredibly tall, stocky man in a dark blue suit, who had placed both hands on his hips and cocked his head slightly to one side. Blue and red strobe lights bathed the seasoned police officer's face, and his grayish hair absorbed each color that passed over the tight haircut. He looked deadly serious and had a commanding presence that made Edwards nervous. The man's face betrayed no emotion, regarding Edwards with disinterest. He was suddenly very aware of the several civilians, probably neighbors, who were standing about thirty feet away in an adjacent yard, perfectly situated to watch the brewing showdown. He wouldn't back down. Not for these bullies.

"Yes?"

"Where are you going with her?" the man said, and Edwards caught a glimpse of a silver badge under his suit coat, at waist level.

"I'm sorry, we haven't met. I'm Special Agent Justin Edwards. I'm in charge of this entire investigation. And you?"

"Lieutenant Ken Moody. Portland Police Department. This entire operation is under my control, and I can't let you take a key witness away from the scene," he said, taking a step forward.

Edwards was accustomed to this game and stood his ground.

"And it was a well-executed high risk warrant operation, but I need to move the witness to a more secure location for questioning," Edwards said.

"I can't imagine a more secure location. Every SWAT officer within fifty miles is on scene," Moody said.

"I'm looking for something lower profile, with fewer distractions. She had a rough go of it in there, and I don't think she'll be much of a help to the investigation while half of Maine's police force tears her house apart," he said.

"Look, if she has information about her husband, she's not leaving my sight. We have a cop down because of her husband," Moody said.

"She's not a suspect in any local crime, right?" he said and waited two seconds before continuing through Moody's icy stare.

"Right. I'll pass any relevant information regarding Daniel Petrovich through your office. I have the liaison's number. If any of your men attempt to stop me, or Mrs. Petrovich, I'll make sure you're cutting bait on one of those lobster boats out there by the end of the month," Edwards said, and he turned around.

"I'm filing an official complaint with your office, Special Agent Edwards. Your colleague at the local field office warned us about you. This is ridiculous," he said.

"File away, Lieutenant. I'm pretty sure nobody in D.C. will give a shit about your whining. This investigation is a matter of national security. It's for the big boys and girls, not crybabies," he said and walked to the car with Jessica, fully expecting to get punched in the back of the neck.

Always the gentleman, he opened the front passenger door for Jessica, avoiding the burning stare from Moody as he crossed back over to his own door. After he was seated behind the wheel of the distasteful rental car, he opened the purse in her lap without her permission, digging around inside it. She protested his invasion of privacy, but he pulled out the car keys before it got serious and started the car.

He glanced around, checking for any of the local idiots that might decide to take matters into their own hands. Lieutenant Moody just stared at the car shaking his head, then spoke into a radio. An officer hopped into the Suburban immediately forward of Edward's car and moved it out of his way onto the Petrovich's driveway. Edwards edged his own car forward and squeezed by the second Suburban. By the time he picked up speed, a few more police vehicles had moved to let him pass.

So that's it, he thought. *Show a little balls and get a little respect.* He despised the low level of functioning that embodied their bullying world. None of this was tolerated in the FBI, where competence and intelligence was valued more than your ability to "square off" against another colleague. Then again, he had to remind himself there was a reason he investigated national security level crimes and these guys sniffed around dumpsters all day.

"You all right?" he said, as the car cleared the maze of flashing red and blue police lights.

"I think so. I just want to talk to my husband. Something is wrong here, and I don't know how to help him," she said.

"The best thing you can do to help him is to convince him to come out of hiding. To turn himself in to us. He's in serious danger from the types of guys you saw back at the house. They don't care if there was a mix up. His name and face went out on a national alert. They'll kill him if they find him before we do."

"Why would he be hiding?" she said.

He really hoped it was the shock of the situation that was causing her to fail to grasp the implications of her husband's predicament. If she was just plain stupid, it would detract from the overall experience. Then again, what did he care? He'd fucked plenty of stupid women before, but he'd never taken any of those relationships beyond the bedroom. He had thought this one might be different.

"I think we both know he's hiding, Jessica. Let's get somewhere quiet, and figure this out."

"Where are you taking me?"

"To our satellite office on Middle Street. We have a conference room and a few spare offices. Nice and quiet," he said and savored the idea of being alone with her in that office, though he suspected the resident agent would insist on being present.

He'd let the comment made by Lieutenant Moody about the resident agent slide for now. He needed as much cooperation as possible from the locals, and Special Agent D'Angelo seemed to be on good footing with the Portland Police Department. He'd pay her back later for the comment Moody mentioned. He had a few like-minded connections in the right places, and he'd do whatever he could to make sure she continued to draw shitty assignments like Portland, Maine. The fewer uppity women in the major field offices, the better.

"Can we grab something to eat on the way? I haven't eaten since lunch," she said, confirming his earlier observation in the kitchen.

Now he would be able to work his magic. He had always been better at the interrogation side of the business and had no intention of caving in to her needs so quickly. Like a hostage negotiation, Edwards needed to get something from Jessica before he indulged her in any comforts. This was shaping up to be a perfect evening.

"Let's get settled in at the office, and come up with a plan to help your husband, then we can take a walk to one of the restaurants in the Old Port. My treat. I just want to get the ball rolling here. He may not have a lot of time."

She nodded absently at his comment, and he could feel that this would turn out to be a very productive night for him. He pulled out his cell phone and placed a call to Special Agent D'Angelo.

Chapter Thirty-One

Special Agent Sharpe stood in the middle of his operations center, listening intently to the multiple streams of chatter emanating from his agents. He kept a constant eye on the screens mounted to the wall at the front of the room and occasionally glanced at his assistant, Special Agent Mendoza, who just shook his head every time their eyes met. None of the raids had yielded a suspect, and most of the teams had reported. If they came up empty tonight, he had no idea where they could turn.

He still had Munoz, but that would quickly become a sticky situation once the lawyers figured out that he had been transferred to FBI headquarters. According to the immunity agreement signed by the Justice Department, Munoz should be back in Hartford, closing up his coffee shops. Instead, Munoz was hopefully sitting handcuffed in the back of a van, surrounded by Boston's FBI SWAT contingent, heading across Connecticut along Interstate 95. Sharpe wasn't about to lose his only lead so quickly, especially if they come up with nothing from the raids.

As he scanned the room again, he caught Special Agent O'Reilly's eye, and she nodded discreetly, maintaining eye contact for a few seconds. Intrigued, Sharpe made his way over to her workstation. Mendoza saw the furtive transaction and started to drift in the same direction, but Sharpe cautiously shook his head. Mendoza gave him a quick nod of acknowledgement and returned to his previous position at the communications desk. Sharpe didn't want to draw any unwarranted attention to Special Agent O'Reilly's research, and having both of them at one workstation, huddled over a screen, wouldn't help matters. The fewer people involved, the better, and if it became necessary, he could make an argument to have O'Reilly's CIS agreement augmented to Level One.

"Did you find anything?" Sharpe said.

"Something rather interesting, but I'm not sure it's going to help. I got a hit on the INTERPOL database for Daniel Petrovich. Take a look," she said, typing furiously at her keyboard, as one of her screens split into two similar images.

One contained Daniel Petrovich's driver's license image, with statistics and basic information listed below; the other screen showed a grainier image, most likely taken from a camera using a zoom lens, but there was little doubt that the two images showed the same man. INTERPOL's own system gave the match a 96% accuracy rating, and he was sure that the FBI's own facial matching software would agree.

He studied the sparse details on the INTERPOL wanted poster.

A Warrant for the Arrest of Marko Resja, suspected of war-crimes-related murder, is issued on behalf of The International Criminal Tribunal for the former Yugoslavia.

He glanced at Agent O'Reilly, who turned her head slightly and raised an eyebrow. At this point, the sooner she signed a new CIS agreement, the better. This information could ignite a firestorm if it fell into the wrong hands. Daniel Petrovich was listed on active duty in the navy during the period of time covered by the warrant. He couldn't imagine the fallout this could create. An active duty United States service member somehow connected with Serbian war crimes? What in God's name had General Sanderson done with this group?

"Anything on the other operatives?" Sharpe said, eyes still fixed on Petrovich's image, or whoever he claimed to be.

"Nothing yet. The INTERPOL system has finished with two-thirds of the list. They have a pretty efficient setup. I wouldn't be surprised if we receive a phone call from INTERPOL at some point tonight," O'Reilly said.

"Can you pull the details of this warrant from the INTERPOL system? I need to know everything possible about this guy. Actually, pull everything we can get on Petrovich, and make it available under my access code," Sharpe said, who drifted toward Mendoza.

"If you give me a second, I can pull the detailed warrant right now," she said, and Sharpe pulled back toward the screen.

The warrant came up on the second screen, and Sharpe read the details.

He had expected a laundry list of crimes, but found himself staring at one charge, and it was enough to turn his stomach. Marko Resja was wanted for the brutal torture, mutilation and murder of Zorana Zekulic, a Serbian national. He continued to absorb the details, shocked by the excerpts of testimony included with the warrant. Multiple beheadings? He couldn't believe this guy was loose on American soil, and that he was a product of a rogue U.S. military program. No wonder the Pentagon had put an end to Sanderson's career and sealed the evidence.

Now he understood why the Pentagon had assigned a special handler to the file. The mysterious Mr. McKie carefully parceled out information, keeping the potentially explosive information sealed away forever. He would need to double the task force's efforts to crack open the day's conspiracy, and it would start with Munoz.

Based on his knowledge of the forces at work today, he highly doubted anyone would have a problem with keeping Munoz in FBI custody for the moment. The Pentagon obviously felt that the need to unravel today's conspiracy was worth the risk of unearthing the Black Flag file and potentially exposing its toxic contents. He'd start with Munoz, but he had another idea brewing, and he'd have to be extremely careful if he turned in this direction.

"Jesus, this just gets worse. Dana, I'm going to need to upgrade your CIS agreement," he said.

"I kinda figured that when Petrovich popped up under an alias on an INTERPOL wanted poster," she said.

"Consider yourself under this agreement now. You know the deal. Only Mendoza and myself are cleared for CIS Category One information, and our CIA liaison, Keller. I'm going to need to relocate you to one of the private workstations near the front of the room," he said.

"I'll get the tech's working on that immediately," she said.

"Perfect," he said, but his mind was already miles away.

He wondered what Petrovich's current wife would think about the details of Marko Resja's activities in Serbia? As he moved away from Agent O'Reilly's station, Agent Mendoza rushed over and intercepted him.

"You need to hear this. Something big is going on up in Montgomery County, in Silver Spring. Comms says every law enforcement channel up there is going crazy. It's like world war three broke out. Every available unit within the area is responding," he said.

"Did the raid in Portland turn up anything on Petrovich?" Sharpe interrupted.

"Nothing so far, but I have a strange feeling he might be here. Wait until you hear this," Mendoza said, and Sharpe stopped in his tracks.

Something on a gut level scared Sharpe. Just the thought of this guy roaming the D.C. area made his skin crawl. Glancing at the communications section, Sharpe saw Special Agent Keith Weber talking on a phone, nodding excitedly and taking notes. As they approached this chaotic part of the operations center, he could hear Weber's conversation.

"...two trucks, and...hold on, did you just say a taxi? The guy is in custody. All right. Detective, I assure you this is not an FBI operation...Yes. Thank you. Keep an open line for us, this might be related to an ongoing investigation. Thanks again," Weber said and hung up the phone. He turned to the two senior agents and said, "Wow. They have a serious situation up in Silver Spring."

"Give me the short version," Sharpe said.

"Right. Silver Spring police have two dead bodies inside of a Natural Foods store. One with his throat cut, the other shot in the face. Nobody inside heard any shooting. They're reviewing the surveillance videos as we speak. Out in the parking lot, they found an off-duty detective between two parked cars, dead from multiple gunshot wounds. They also found a shot up Suburban with one guy in the driver's seat. Dead. The guy I just talked to said the Suburban looked like a portable armory. Tactical vests, night vision, radio equipment, two assault rifles and a shotgun. All high end, U.S. issue stuff..."

"Do they have anyone in custody?" Sharpe said.

"Not from Natural Foods. They nabbed two guys down the street, but they don't think either is the shooter," Weber stated. "A few minutes after the first units arrived on scene, officers in the parking lot heard automatic weapons fire and received reports from a nearby neighborhood that a gun battle had erupted on their street. Responding units found another SUV, loaded to the gills with weapons and dead guys dressed like commandos. They pulled one survivor from the truck and rushed him to Holy Cross Hospital. He was unconscious with massive external bleeding."

"You said they grabbed two guys?"

"It gets better. They caught another guy who showed up in a taxi just as the police converged on the scene. Apparently, the cab driver jumped out of the cab and ran screaming to the police. He told them that the guy in the cab had put a gun to his head and told him to run the police roadblock. They have this guy in custody, and he swears that his team is part of an official counterterrorism operation. He's a Brown River employee."

"Oh shit," Mendoza muttered.

"Get this. One of the neighbors ran into the suspect on her driveway before the police arrived, and she said he threatened to cut her head off," Weber said, muffling a laugh.

"Got a good look at the suspect before he took off. Car and everything. Said he was dressed like some kind of hippie. They're mobilizing everything to find this guy," Weber added, but Sharpe's mind was somewhere else.

"Frank, we need to sit down in my office. Agent O'Reilly is now cleared for CIS Category One, and she's putting together a complete workup for Petrovich. Help her out with this. I want to sit down and analyze his file. We have nothing from any of the other raids?" he asked.

A young female agent at another station answered the question. "Last units just reported. Nothing, sir. It looks like all of the suspects have gone underground."

Sharpe looked at Mendoza. "Apparently all but one," he said, "and we're not the only ones interested in finding him. I want agents talking to this Brown River guy immediately, and I want to see the surveillance tapes from that Natural Foods. Tell the team up in Portland to tear Petrovich's house apart. Start by scanning every picture of Petrovich in that house for our new facial recognition software database. We can create a composite picture that won't be fooled by anything short of plastic surgery. Let's get this rolling immediately. Meet me in ten minutes. I need to make some phone calls."

"Yes, sir," Mendoza said, who immediately walked over to Agent O'Reilly.

Sharpe didn't like the sound of this at all. He briefly considered calling home and checking on his family, but he knew it didn't make any sense. Something about Petrovich sent a visceral signal through Sharpe, activating a strong instinct to protect his wife and two teenage daughters. He knew what bothered him. Sanderson had apparently created a highly trained serial killer. He wondered how many people Petrovich had beheaded under the guise of military service and if he had stopped after Serbia.

Chapter Thirty-Two

9:17 p.m.
Washington, D.C.

Daniel Petrovich emerged from the New York Avenue Metro station and studied the area around the exit structure. The street looked well-lit and relatively uncrowded, which suited him well. He merged with a small group of young adults headed toward N Street and followed them at a close, but unintimidating distance. He had chosen to get off the Metro before hitting one of the transfer hubs deeper in the city, figuring that the police presence at one of D.C.'s major Metro stops would be elevated. The Metro Police kiosk at the New York Avenue station contained two extremely vigilant-looking officers, who tried to scan the emerging passengers without being blatantly obvious. They did a decent job, but he could tell they weren't trained for this type of work.

Petrovich drew a few conclusions from the Metro Police officers' behavior. He decided that a wide-scale alert had been issued to all D.C. area law enforcement agencies, which didn't surprise him. He had killed a police officer, and the police would turn the city and surrounding counties inside out trying to find him. He also concluded that the police were being cautious. They knew what they were up against, and he could tell that the two officers at the station didn't feel very confident about their situation. They had made a good assessment, which ensured that they would return safely to their families tonight. Neither of them had any idea how close to death they had come, as Daniel walked within ten feet of them, his new disguise not even attracting a second glance.

Daniel just wanted to get through the rest of the day to see Jessica again. They had more than earned the right to be together, and he would show little mercy for anyone standing in their way. He hadn't asked for any of this and had thought he had sent a clear enough message, several years ago, that he was done. He had topped that message with more than a hundred million dollars, which apparently hadn't been enough. It was never enough for General Sanderson, but none of that really mattered now. He had to figure out how to move forward and start over. This was how he had been trained to think. Two steps ahead, and never look back.

Just as he turned onto N Street, a D.C. police car pulled up to the Metro station and parked right in front of the exit. Two officers emerged from the patrol car and hurried toward the Metro entrance, neither of them glancing around at any of the emerging Metro passengers. One of them carried the patrol car's shotgun. He was glad he chose to get off the Metro before Union Station. A few more minutes on the train, and he would have been forced to walk through a chokepoint of police officers emboldened by reinforcements and heavy weaponry.

Daniel planned to work his way toward the Mall area, sticking close to other groups of people on heavily commercialized streets. It was still early for D.C., and he didn't see this as a problem. He liked the idea of the Mall area, since it was always filled with tourists and locals of every type. He'd have no trouble blending in with the crowd there, while waiting for Parker to pick him up. The Mall was roughly one mile away.

Chapter Thirty-Three

Berg sank back into the deep leather chair and called Jeremy Cummings' cell phone again. The phone abruptly went to voicemail. He had lost contact with Cummings just over thirty minutes ago, after his team had pulled into a Natural Foods parking lot in Silver Spring, Maryland. He'd given Cummings the order to terminate Petrovich and had expected to hear back from him within ten minutes. Despite a burning desire to personally avenge Nicole's murder, he forced himself to acknowledge the bigger picture. The man was a trained intelligence operative, on the run from the authorities, and it was only a matter of time before he spotted the teams trailing him. He didn't have any more favors to use at Fort Meade, and if he ditched the Brown River teams, they might never find him again. When Cummings reported that Petrovich was headed into a grocery store, he knew this would be their best opportunity, so he gave the order.

He knew something wasn't right and decided to call CIA headquarters' communications desk. He placed the burner phone on the table next to his chair and pulled out his personal cell phone. An automated system answered, and Berg spoke several passwords to authenticate himself.

"Good evening, Mr. Berg, how can we assist you?" a calm voice said.

"Thank you. A friend of mine from Silver Spring called asking if something big was going on up there. He thinks I'm some bigwig over at the FBI, so I always get calls from him about stuff like this. Most of the time it's his imagination, but he insists that the Metro station down there is swarming with cops," he lied and wondered if his voice was being analyzed by any electronic equipment.

"Stand by, sir. Looks like your friend is not imagining things today. I'm showing a D.C. Metro Area APB for a suspect in the murder of a police officer," the voice said.

"Well, I guess that would explain the activity," Berg said, wondering if maybe Cummings' cell phone had died.

"The same suspect is sought in connection with multiple homicides. This all happened in the same area, at the same time. The police officer was found shot to death in a Natural Foods parking lot, and several other bodies were found at the same scene. More bodies were recovered a few blocks away, in a residential neighborhood. Yeah, your friend was not imagining this. Sounds like a small battle took place in Silver Spring. Every law enforcement agency in and around the beltway is looking for the shooter."

"Sounds like a bad night to be on the streets up there. I'll give him a call, and tell him to stay inside until the police figure this out," Berg said.

"I think that's probably a good call. Is there anything else we can help you with?"

"No. Thank you very much. Sorry to bother you guys with something like this," he said.

"No trouble at all, it's been an unusually quiet night," the voice said, and Berg heard a click.

Berg decided he would take a walk and destroy the cell phone used to contact the Brown River team, but first he needed to make one more call. He used a third, separate cell phone, reserved solely for the purpose of calling this number. The phone rang for what seemed an eternity to Berg, but was finally answered by a familiar voice.

"I assume the team took care of your business," Darryl Jackson said.

"I think we have a problem," Berg said.

"You mean I have a problem," Jackson stated.

"I talked with the team leader right before they followed him into a grocery store. I lost contact with them after that, and now every cop in the D.C. area is converging on that same area. Multiple homicides, dead cop...I just wanted to give you the heads up. It won't be long before you get a call," Berg said.

"Fuck. I thought two teams would be enough," Jackson said.

"Sounds like he took them both out. There is a report of multiple homicides in two different locations. I know these are your guys, and I'm sorry, but...did you cushion yourself from this operation?"

"Shit. As much as I could. Nothing in writing. Cummings assembled the team. I gave him complete authority on this one. I didn't want a big trail," Jackson said.

"This is going to sound bad, and I apologize, but if Cummings was killed, would any of the other team members know who issued the orders?"

"Not likely...are you suggesting that Cummings take the fall for this?" Jackson said.

"I'm just suggesting that if Cummings is dead, why expose anyone else?"

"All right. I don't like it, but reality is reality. I can tell from your voice that this wasn't exactly a legit mission on your end, so that leaves a lot of asses hanging in the breeze."

"Precisely," Berg said, relieved that his friend could see the big picture.

"So here's what I need from you. A large sum of money," Jackson said.

"I don't understand," Berg said, hesitantly.

"Not for me, you jack ass. For Cummings. Let's just say that it's possible for some of our team leaders to have undisclosed accounts, into which money is sometimes deposited for extra work. Work that nobody wants to acknowledge here at Brown River, or perhaps at the Pentagon. I might have access to some of these accounts, and a large, untraceable payment to the right account, very fucking soon, might give me all of the plausible deniability I need to steer this thing well clear of Brown River...and you. Do you know anyone that might be able to do us...you, a favor like this, and deposit some cash into the right account?"

"I think I can figure something out. I'll call you back when I'm ready," Berg said.

"Perfect. The larger the sum, the better. Six figure range. I'm willing to personally stake this cash to keep my ass out of jail, so don't be shy...and don't hesitate to throw some money into the pot yourself. I know you're not used to throwing your own money around, but this would probably be the right time to make an investment," Jackson said.

"I agree," Berg said.

"And make sure you toss the cell phone you used to call Cummings."

"Now you're giving operational security advice to a CIA operative?" Berg joked.

"Well, I'd like to continue to have the opportunity to sit around and sip fine Scotch with that operative, and I don't think they allow alcohol in prison...so don't take offense," Jackson said.

"Get me the account information, and I'll call you as soon as I have something. Sorry about the mess," Berg said.

"It's not your fault, really, and regardless of what happens today, I still owe you. I'll be waiting for your call, but please don't ponder this for too long. With a dead cop involved, things might move quicker than either of us expects," Jackson said, and the line went dead.

Berg thought about their situation for a few minutes. He was utterly disappointed that this opportunity had slipped through his fingers, but he might still get another shot at it. Petrovich would have a difficult time snaking his way out of this one. Everyone was looking for him at this point. He was now the key figure in both a federal and local manhunt. He had few doubts that Petrovich was capable of eluding everyone, but he liked the odds, and if Petrovich surfaced again, Berg would kill the murderer himself.

Chapter Thirty-Four

Colonel Farrington received the "green light" from General Sanderson earlier than he had anticipated. Frankly, he thought early tomorrow morning would be the best time to take possession of the file. He would attract little attention leaving in the morning, amidst the thousands of Pentagon personnel pouring into the building. At this point in the evening, the security staff would have very little to do at their station, and he might be searched. The search would likely be limited to his briefcase, which would be empty of anything suspicious. All of the file's contents would be strapped to an ingenious vest system under his uniform. If they decided to pat him down, Sanderson's extraction team had better be ready for a hot pickup.

He looked around his deserted section and thought about the six individuals inside the Sanctum. Neutralizing six people in rapid succession would be a challenge, but he had some equipment to help him with the task. Slowly, over the course of several months, he had managed to smuggle the pieces of two non-lethal devices into the Pentagon. He would be glad to get it over with. He faced a wide spectrum of capabilities in that room, and he wasn't looking forward to the encounter, for various reasons.

Two senior enlisted staff personnel, neither with any specialized hand-to-hand combat training, but resourceful nonetheless, would be the most dangerous to underestimate. One CIA agent with a photographic memory. Probably trained as a field agent, but not recently active in a dangerous assignment. His reaction would not be instinctual, but still dangerous. The two FBI agents would be armed, but they would be the least of his challenges.

The most dangerous man in the room was McKie. He was a former

176

Black Flag operative, and the only traitor to the program known to General Sanderson. He'd actively brought Black Flag's questionable activities to the attention of General William Tierney, who sparked a Congressional investigation into Sanderson's program. The Congressional inquiry effectively killed the program, burying it along with both of the generals' careers. Nobody wanted the details of this program to become public knowledge, which is why the file had been kept in its original form and sent to the military's most secure tomb. Sanderson's orders regarding McKie were explicit and had only been revealed to Colonel Farrington minutes ago. The orders actually made his job inside the room easier.

He wondered why they hadn't just burned the file, if it could be so damning to the country. In his opinion, this was the curse of intelligence gathering. Even the most toxic information had its value, and in an important room somewhere in this city, someone wasn't willing to forsake that value to make the right decision. Sanderson's plan would rectify this situation, and he needed to get moving. According to the general, his ride would be here shortly.

He opened the lower drawer of a three-level file cabinet to the left of his workstation and moved a stack of manila files onto his desk. Under the files sat a gray metal box, which he quickly unlocked. The box was filled with an exotic array of non-lethal weapons, and one long black commando knife. Alone in the Pentagon's Special Information Section, Colonel Farrington started to assemble the various devices.

**

Julio Mendez retreated to the back of the custodial closet and lowered himself onto the folding chair he called home. He'd found that metal box one day, while snooping through the file cabinets after hours, and thought it was suspicious. Buried under a bunch of files, hidden from view, he'd seen Colonel Shifty open it before, early in the morning, and place something inside. The box is what put the colonel onto Julio's watch list from the start. He'd felt bad about poking into desk drawers and unlocked cabinets, right up until the day he found the colonel's secret box. Then, a few days ago, the colonel started taking secret calls on a cell phone he kept hidden in his briefcase, which was a complete violation of the Special Information Section's security policy.

He had to take immediate action. He could sense that something important was going on in the Sanctum, and that the colonel was up to no good. It was a bad combination in his mind, and even if nothing big was going down, it was still his duty to report the cell phone. Colonel Farrington should know better, especially in this section. He decided to call security on the cell phone he had hidden inside his thermos. He finished unscrewing the lid, when the door suddenly swung open. Colonel Farrington stood in the doorway pointing something black at him. The metal leads from the Taser reached Julio before his brain really processed what was happening. He didn't remember much after that.

**

Colonel Farrington locked and shut the door to Julio's custodial closet, confident that the nosy janitor wouldn't be found until tomorrow morning. He liked Julio and was glad that the confrontation hadn't turned deadly. He hadn't suffered a heart attack and didn't show any abnormal vital signs. He would wake up in a few hours, hog-tied to the floor, unable to make a sound. Beyond a little panic, he'd be fine.

Farrington had been onto Mendez from the beginning. The slightly cracked open closet door was so obvious to him, he had found it next to impossible to ignore over the past few months, and when the telltales left in the lower cabinet had been disturbed, he knew Mendez was up to something.

Once the authorities tore the tape off his mouth, he'd be able to tell them how close he had come to foiling the colonel's plan by staying late to keep an eye on him. This had been the final tip-off for Farrington today. He had checked the assigned work schedule for the Compartmentalized Information Section, and Mendez' shift ended at 4 p.m. The man never worked a minute past his assigned shift and had said goodbye on his way out every day for the two years Farrington had worked in the section.

He went back to his desk and reloaded the Taser, rechecking his equipment one more time. Everything was in place. He took a deep breath and walked over to the Sanctum's access panel, shifting the long, thin commando knife to his left hand in order to press the fingers on his right hand onto the fingerprint recognition scanner. Once this was completed, he entered numbers on a keypad and shifted the knife back to his right hand, placing it in a concealed grip, with the flat part of blade pressed against his wrist and lower arm. The door's locking mechanisms clanged, and the door slowly opened. At this point there was no turning back, so he stepped inside.

He passed through a small entry vestibule containing several coat hooks filled with suit jackets and entered the main room. He assessed the situation quickly, as he walked purposefully toward Derren McKie, who was seated at a gray, metallic table in the middle of the room, with the open Black Flag briefcase in front of him. Keller looked up at him from an office chair on the other side of the table. Only one of the FBI agents, Calhoun, sat at the table against the wall on the right side of the room, studying several sheets of paper. The other agent was out of sight, presumably taking a nap or using the bathroom.

Technical Sergeant D'Onofrie and Staff Sergeant Brodin were located exactly where he expected to find them, on the left side of the room at the secured communications workstation. D'Onofrie sat in front of the fax machine, feeding a few sheets of paper cleared by McKie through to the FBI, while Brodin observed. The marine staff sergeant looked up at him with a slightly surprised look. He usually called her before re-entering the Sanctum, and his presence always meant that the accessed file had been closed.

"The file's closed, sir?" she asked, and McKie turned his head lazily toward Keller and Calhoun.

"Gentlemen, that's it for the file," McKie uttered, and these were the last words anyone would hear him speak.

Colonel Farrington lunged past the table and grabbed McKie's thick, brown hair, yanking his head backward. McKie managed to get a hand up to grab Farrington's arm, but it was a futile effort. Farrington plunged the seven-inch blade downward through the right side of McKie's neck, just above the collarbone, instantly severing the carotid artery and slicing through the spinal cord. Farrington felt the man's body slacken and knew he didn't need to waste any more time on McKie. He left the knife buried in his neck and wheeled the dying man's chair toward the secured communications station, which averted a potential disaster. Staff Sergeant Brodin had already cleared half the distance between the station and the colonel when she collided with the chair, giving Farrington the time he needed to properly react.

Farrington drew two Tasers from holsters that were attached to his uniform belt behind his back and aimed one in each direction. His first priority was Brodin, who was now covered in bright red arterial spray from

McKie's neck. She pushed the chair out of the way and hesitated, unsure of how to proceed against Farrington. He fired the Taser leads into her chest, and she dropped to the blood-slicked floor, convulsing.

He had set the Taser to deliver an incapacitating initial shock, followed by a continuous stream of lower voltage "reminders" that would keep her down until he deactivated the device. Through the pulsing spray of blood, he caught an image of Technical Sergeant D'Onofrie, frozen in horror with a blood-splattered sheet of paper in his hands. He wouldn't be a problem anytime soon.

With Brodin out of the picture, he fired the second Taser at Keller, who had at this point only managed to back his chair a few feet from the table and look at Special Agent Calhoun, who was having serious trouble extracting his service pistol. The effect was immediate, and Keller stiffened in his seat, unable to move. Farrington dropped both Tasers to the ground and grabbed two shiny metallic cylinders from his front trouser pockets.

Each device looked like a retractable toilet paper holder and held several darts fired by compressed air. The device was a one shot deal, firing all of the darts at once in a tight circle. At a range of twenty feet, most of the darts should hit within the radius of a regulation basketball and would strike with enough force to penetrate a business suit. Beyond twenty feet, the darts had a tendency to wander and lost too much kinetic energy to reliably punch through clothing. Each dart delivered a specialized neurotoxin that instantaneously disrupted the primary signal pathway required to voluntarily operate the body's musculoskeletal system, while leaving the body's smooth muscle and cardiac muscle unhindered.

At a distance of fifteen feet, all six darts hit Calhoun in the upper right shoulder and chest, just as he cleared his pistol from the holster. The effects were immediate, and Calhoun's pistol dropped to the floor. Farrington could see the agent's lips quivering, which was a telltale sign that the neurotoxin had completely disabled him. Frozen like a statue, he fell over onto the white linoleum tiled floor a few seconds later, his muscles no longer receiving the signals needed to maintain balance.

The colonel heard a toilet flush toward the back of the room and picked up Calhoun's semi-automatic pistol. He pointed it at D'Onofrie and shook his head, waiting for Special Agent Harris to emerge. The door to the bathroom swung open.

"I can't believe the bathroom doesn't have a fan. I wouldn't recommend anyone..." He froze when he saw Farrington.

The second cylinder hissed, and Harris didn't react. He couldn't. All six darts had delivered their neurotoxin through the agent's white dress shirt, in a noticeable concentric circle on his chest. As the agent teetered and fell, Colonel Farrington returned his attention to Technical Sergeant D'Onofrie, who continued to stare in shock at McKie's lifeless form, which had tumbled partway out of the chair and jammed against the rear door leading to the break area. The former Black Flag operative's body weakly pumped the last remains of its crimson reservoir onto the lower half of the gray metal door.

D'Onofrie tried to speak. "Why...what did...?"

"Tech Sergeant, I don't have time to explain this, but I need your help. The FBI agents were hit by a neurotoxin delivered by small darts. They'll be fine in a few hours. Brodin and Keller were hit by Tasers, which are still active. I need you to zip tie their hands for me, as soon as I deactivate the Tasers, and drag them into that room," he said, pointing at the bloodstained door behind McKie's body.

The air force sergeant, still dazed, glanced toward the carnage at the door and dropped the sheets of paper in his hand.

"D'Onofrie, I need you to pull yourself together, and get this done immediately. Pull the two FBI agents into the room, and we'll work on the other two. If you want to leave this room alive, you must do what I ask," Farrington said.

The sergeant looked back at the door again and hesitated. Farrington walked over to McKie's body and grabbed the dead man's blood-soaked shirt collar, yanking him back into the chair and wheeling him away from the door. He removed the knife from McKie's neck and tossed it onto the table next to the Black Flag files. Staring intently at D'Onofrie, he opened the door to the break room and jammed several thick plastic zip tie handcuffs into one of the sergeant's hands.

"You need to get to work before I decide it would be easier to kill the rest of you. Start with that one," Farrington said and pointed at Agent Calhoun with the agent's own pistol.

As the sergeant started to move Calhoun into the back room, Farrington removed Harris's service pistol and tucked it into his pants, purposefully locking eyes with D'Onofrie as he stepped over Calhoun's frozen body on his way across the room. The sergeant looked relieved to have the last gun taken out of play. Still watching D'Onofrie, the colonel ripped the fax's connection from the wall and threw the fax machine onto the floor. He stomped on it a few times to make sure it was permanently disabled. The fax machine was the only device capable of communicating beyond the Sanctum and the Pentagon.

The single phone at the communications desk was hardwired directly to Colonel Farrington's desk, which he would deactivate before he left the building. Security patrols through this section were rare, and the patrol wouldn't hear anything through the fireproof metal walls of the Sanctum. The fire alarm would be their most likely way to attract attention, and there was little Farrington could do about this, beyond confiscating any lighters and making sure they were all incapacitated. He had a few more doses of the neurotoxin for that.

He wanted to be out of the Sanctum in a few minutes, which didn't leave him with much time. He still needed to collect all of the pieces of the Black Flag file and secure it under a new uniform. McKie's blood covered most of his right shoulder, and looking down, he could see some dark spots on his collar around his silver colonel insignia. Although most of the blood would be covered by his uniform jacket, he didn't want to take any unnecessary chances leaving the building. In thirty minutes he'd walk straight out of one life and into another. A life not hampered by bureaucrats and politicians. He would finally be on the path he had chosen when he accepted an appointment to West Point, twenty-one years ago. He'd be a warrior, unhindered.

**

Wearing a black windbreaker-style uniform jacket over a brand new uniform, Colonel Farrington greeted the security guards at the main exit with the blank, zombified expression of someone who worked an excessively long day.

"Late night, Colonel?" commented one of the guards that Farrington recognized well.

"Yeah. We're receiving guests tomorrow. The kind that like to inspect everything, so it's been a long day," he said, feigning a tired smile.

"Pain in the ass for sure, Colonel. I'll be here tomorrow morning. We could pull them aside for the special treatment," the guard said, motioning to one of the private rooms reserved for random, detailed searches.

Farrington faked a laugh and scanned his name badge. "It's tempting, Ray, but I don't think it'll be necessary. Then again, we'll see how the inspection goes. You gonna be here in the late morning?"

All of the guards laughed, especially Ray, who said, "Nah, Colonel. I'm on all night, then off at 10. I could do you a solid when they arrive. Just give us a call."

"I'll keep it in mind," Farrington said and placed his briefcase on the long inspection table in front of the guards.

"Go ahead, Colonel. You're good," Ray said.

"Thanks, Ray. I'll let you know if I change my mind," he said and picked up his briefcase.

"I'll be here. Have a good night," he said.

"Yep. Keep the peace," Farrington said and turned toward the exit.

He kept walking and reached the massive bank of automated doors that led to the South parking lot. The closest door opened, and Farrington felt the warm, humid air pour over him as he stepped out of the Pentagon for the last time. He glanced back through the opening, watching as it closed. He could see the guards searching through another officer's backpack.

In the distance ahead of him, he saw a car pull up. Instinctively, he knew this was his ride. Farrington picked up the pace, nearly jogging through the empty handicapped lot and arriving at the access road on the other side of the lot. He saw Parker sitting behind the wheel of a Honda Accord and crossed behind the car to get in the front passenger seat.

"What happened to the Cherokee?" Farrington said, getting in the car.

"Ditched it. We were compromised earlier tonight. Badly. I assume you have the file?" Parker said, driving the car out of the parking lot.

"Strapped to my body. Everything went without a hitch," he said.

"McKie?"

"Dead. I assumed something happened, but the general didn't elaborate."

"Someone sent a Brown River assassination team to kill one of our operatives. They were temporarily tracking me as well," Parker said.

"Had to be CIA. I'm surprised the general didn't want Keller eliminated. Aside from the limited information sent to the FBI, Keller's photographic memory is all that's left of the Black Flag file," Farrington said.

"We still don't know the motivation behind the Brown River fiasco. They were sent on a specific mission against one of our guys, but in the context of today's events, the reason appears to be unrelated. The general wants to close the loop on this," Parker said, taking the car onto Interstate 395 heading into the heart of D.C.

"Where are we headed next?" Farrington asked, unconsciously touching his chest and the thick stack of papers hidden underneath his jacket.

"First, we need to make a pickup at the Mall. Then, we'll go underground and wait for the next mission," Parker said.

"Any idea what the next mission is?"

"None. I've been flying by the seat of my pants since yesterday. It sounds like Sanderson's plan is mostly intact. The Brown River thing has been the only deviation so far, but they're out of the picture at this point," said Parker.

"How do we know they're out of the picture?" Farrington said, glancing nervously behind them through the rear windshield.

"Because most of the team is dead, and the rest are in custody," Parker said, scanning the street ahead for Independence Avenue.

"I didn't think we had a team in place here," the colonel said. "It sounded like we would be mostly on our own until the rendezvous."

"We don't have a team here. The only active team available is waiting in Stamford," he said.

"Then who took out the hit team?"

Parker's cell phone beeped, and he flipped it open to read the screen. He pushed it back into the center console and turned left a few seconds later at an empty green light on Seventh Street Southwest.

"Hold that thought a second," Parker said and cruised slowly up to the intersection of Seventh and Jefferson, just as the light turned yellow.

The car kept moving at an even pace and cleared the light before Farrington saw any red at the top of the front windshield. The car slowed for a pedestrian walkway as it entered the tree-lined Henry Park area of the Mall. The area was poorly lit by a single streetlamp set several feet back along the pedestrian path cutting across the street. Though darker than Farrington had expected, the background illumination from the immense Smithsonian buildings cast enough ambient light to feel relatively safe, as evidenced by the large number of people present on the walkway.

Farrington saw Parker flash the left turn signal, then the right signal, sliding the car into a parking spot on the right side of the street. A man wearing a backpack broke off from a small group passing their car along the sidewalk and opened the back door, sliding into the back seat.

"Colonel Farrington, meet Daniel Petrovich. He managed to single-handedly solve our problem with Brown River tonight," Parker said, putting the car back into gear as soon as the rear door shut.

"What the fuck took you so long? Pleased to meet you, Colonel."

"The general moved up the colonel's timetable significantly. I had to pick the colonel up from the Pentagon immediately. You're not the only one busy here tonight," Parker said.

"Generals, colonels...this sounds like a game of Stratego. When do I get a rank? And please tell me we are leaving the city. Every law enforcement officer within fifty miles is looking for me," Petrovich said.

"We're moving to a safe house in Alexandria, to meet up with General Sanderson. We need to take a look at the laptops you pulled from the Suburbans. See how much they know about us," he said.

"He's gonna be there?" Petrovich asked.

"He was there when I talked to him twenty minutes ago," Parker said.

"You better let him know we're on the way. He might not want to be there when I arrive," Petrovich said.

"What's up with him?" Farrington said, addressing Parker.

Petrovich cut off Parker's response.

"I'll tell you what's up. About thirty-one hours ago, I was living a pretty normal life. Married to the woman I love, working a decent job and spreading mulch around my garden beds...then this guy shows up, and here I am. Wanted for murder and God knows what else. I have General Sanderson to thank for all of this. Just remember, Colonel, once Sanderson sinks his hooks into you, there's no escape. He'll squeeze the last bit of usefulness out of you and discard your carcass with the rest of the human compost he's created."

They rode in silence for several minutes before Petrovich interrupted the quiet.

"We're going to need someplace further than Alexandria. It's only four miles from here. Jesus, get us outside the Beltway at least."

"We'll stop in Alexandria, grab some gear, and figure out what we're doing next. We're almost there anyway," Parker said, pointing at the signs for Alexandria and Interstate 495.

"Sanderson better have a good plan worked out. You guys really fucked me on this one," Petrovich said.

"We're all fucked. None of us will be able to call this place home again," Farrington said.

"Yeah? What did *you* do that'll keep you on the run for the rest of your life?" Petrovich asked sarcastically.

"I stole the only remaining copy of the Black Flag file, which is by all counts, a treasonous offense, punishable by life imprisonment. In the process, I killed a Pentagon employee and assaulted agents from the FBI and CIA. Don't lecture me about being screwed," Farrington said.

"When are you going to rack up a body count, Parker? I'd feel better if I knew you were just as fucked as the good colonel and I," Petrovich said.

"Don't worry. I believe I'm an accessory to every murder today," Parker said.

"Good point. I'll be sure to offer that up for a deal if I get caught. Though it appears someone beat me to it today. Who ratted us out?" Petrovich said.

"We're working on that. The general doesn't like to leave loose ends," Parker said.

"That's good to know, as long as you're never classified as a loose end. I'd hold onto that file for a while, Colonel," Petrovich said.

"Nice. I don't think you understand what's going on here today," Farrington said.

"I really don't. Anytime someone would like to open up and share, don't hesitate," Petrovich said.

Farrington turned his head back to Petrovich, but Parker shook his head.

"General Sanderson plans to explain everything to you. You're part of something bigger than you can imagine," Parker said.

"I have a big imagination."

"I think you'll be pleasantly surprised," Parker said, and Farrington nodded.

"Gentlemen, I'm intrigued. Let's find Sanderson because now I have to hear him explain how ruining my life yields a pleasant surprise. I hope he's in Alexandria."

"We'll soon find out," said Colonel Farrington.

Chapter Thirty-Five

Special Agent Heather Olson sat in the front passenger seat of an unmarked FBI Chevy Tahoe, carefully studying the multiple brake lights appearing ahead of them. The driver, dressed in full SWAT gear, without helmet, slowed the Tahoe as Olson radioed the Connecticut state police. They were entering the outer limits of Stamford, Connecticut, and traffic had been relatively light, until now. They had left Boston a few minutes before seven and had avoided most traffic, only running into a slight backup on the 91 in Hartford. Every time the Tahoe decelerated, Olson tensed. She didn't feel comfortable transporting Munoz by car, but Sharpe thought an air transfer would be even riskier. Too many predictable points of passage for an assassin to take out Munoz.

She didn't agree, but she kept her concerns quiet. The assignment to handle Munoz was a significant opportunity for Olson, and she didn't want to sour her spotless performance right at the end. They had managed to break Munoz and provide headquarters with information that kept the investigation moving forward. It was the FBI's only win today, and she had spearheaded the entire effort with Gregory Carlisle's help. His team had performed brilliantly throughout the interrogation phase, and she appreciated the opportunity to work with such an FBI legend.

She received word from the state police that there had been an accident just past exit ten, on the westbound side, which involved several vehicles. He stated that the accident involved a few minor injuries and mostly superficial damage to the vehicles, but that the westbound lanes were closed. They were diverting all traffic through off ramp, which emptied onto Ledge Road and reemerged on the other side of the accident, about a half-mile down from the exit. Olson notified the state police that they were transporting a federal prisoner and requested that they clear the stretch of

Ledge Road for their three-vehicle convoy. The state troopers said they would stop all further traffic from exiting the highway until they arrived.

Olson picked up a different radio and spoke with the tactical teams in each vehicle, relaying standard operating instructions and warning them to stay vigilant. Her own SUV carried three SWAT agents from the Boston field office, including the driver, and the rear SUV carried four additional SWAT agents. The prisoner transport vehicle, a windowless Ford Econoline van on loan from the Suffolk County Sheriff's Department, carried a mix of six FBI and Suffolk County Sheriff's Department SWAT personnel and a Suffolk County driver. They had sufficient firepower to repel any attempt to free Munoz, but what she feared most was an assassination attempt. Munoz had blown the lid on a major clandestine operation involving some nasty people, and a retribution strike was highly likely. They would be defenseless against an improvised explosive device, or any similar massive attempt to destroy one of their vehicles. None of the trucks were armored.

The vehicles tightened their column formation and veered onto the shoulder of the road, speeding past the slowing traffic. Agent Olson could see the state trooper's red and blue strobes in the distance, which meant she had a clear shot at reaching the exit. She told the driver to accelerate.

They arrived at the top of the exit, and the state troopers executed their plan flawlessly. One of the two police cars moved to block the exit, and the other moved far enough into the exit roadway to allow the FBI convoy to roll past. The strobe lights bathed the Tahoe's interior as they rumbled through the gravel past the two police cars.

The road ahead of them was not empty, and Olson became annoyed. She had specifically requested that the road be emptied of all civilian traffic, but she could see several cars stopped at an intersection below the Interstate overpass. Her dashboard mounted GPS receiver indicated that this was Noroton Avenue, and for some reason, the police officers in the intersection were letting traffic onto their road, flowing in the opposite direction.

Olson radioed the state police as their convoy slowed to an uncomfortable stop next to a busy diner parking lot, and the cars in front of them attempted to move to the side of the road. Olson could tell that they wouldn't have enough room to maneuver down the middle of the one-lane road, unless the oncoming traffic was stopped. Several cars passed, until she received word that the officers at the intersection were halting all Noroton

Avenue traffic. Once the last car cleared the convoy, they pulled around the line of waiting cars and sped toward the intersection. Nobody in the van or the lead SUV noticed that the rear SUV failed to follow.

As they sped past Noroton Avenue onto the highway ramp, Olson saw the highway lights emerge beyond the road ahead. She started to loosen up and took a deep breath. What she heard next nearly sent her into cardiac arrest. Her intra-vehicle radio crackled to life.

"I've lost the rear van."

"Shit. Stop the vehicle," she ordered, drawing her pistol from a hip holster jammed up against the door.

A second later, she heard someone in the back seat say, "Oh shit," right before the front of their Tahoe was T-boned from the left by a gigantic pickup truck, grinding both vehicles to a halt in the middle of the on-ramp. Agent Olson's head and pistol slammed against the passenger window, shattering the glass. The prisoner van barely screeched to a stop just behind the tangled heap of American-built trucks. Shadowy figures emerged from the tree line several meters away to the right, wearing gas masks and carrying assault weapons. They broke up into two teams of three, each team carrying a large metal canister connected to portable compression gear. They nestled in low on each of the convoy vehicles.

**

Munoz sat facing two SWAT agents in the middle of the van. The transport van was an aging ten-passenger Econoline monster, reconfigured for correctional system use. The first two rows of seating faced each other, so a sheriff, or in this case, two SWAT officers, could accompany prisoners. The third row behind Munoz was occupied by two more heavily breathing SWAT guys, one of whom kept jamming his knee into Munoz's back.

He was secured by his ankles and wrists to the solid metal structure buried underneath the seat's thin plastic cushioning and couldn't budge. A metal cage wall separated the driver and another black-clad commando from the transport compartment. All of the rear windows were tinted and covered with a thick metal screen, and the passengers had to enter from the rear doors, which represented a tactical disadvantage if the van was attacked. The van's sliding doors had been welded shut for security, and he didn't think the agents could effectively shoot out of the side windows.

Overall, he assessed the vehicle as low security. He'd escaped from

189

much more difficult situations, under much worse conditions, but that wasn't his job today. He'd already accomplished his mission, and would, for the first time in his career, let himself be rescued. The van came to a sudden unexpected stop; he took a deep breath and held it. Panic overtook the van. One of the SWAT agents jammed Munoz's head down, and the officers scrambled to take positions covering three hundred and sixty degrees.

A high-pitched mechanical drilling sound filled the van, and someone screamed, "Back us the fuck out of here now!"

"Does anyone have anything?" yelled the SWAT agent in the front passenger seat.

"Contact right side, low! No shot!" one of the agents screamed.

With his head jammed down, he saw two holes penetrate the lower right side of the van compartment. One second later, compressed air instantly filled the van with a cloudy vapor, and he felt the hand pressing down on his head ease up a little. He continued to hold his breath, and the hand completely slackened, replaced by 250 pounds of body weight and tactical gear. Munoz lost some of his breath, but managed to roll the agent onto the floor. He sat upright and glanced around at the slumped figures filling the van.

A small explosive charge rocked the back of the van, and two armed men wearing gas masks pulled the door open and hopped in. One of them had to yank a slumbering FBI agent down out of the van, so they could proceed through the opening between the benches and the side. Munoz's lungs burned as he tried to hold his breath long enough to receive the empty mask in one of the men's hands. The mask was pushed over his face, and he felt a cool rush of air as the man gave him a thumbs up sign right in front of the eye piece. Munoz took a shallow breath of fresh air, then gulped massive breaths while the team worked on freeing him from the van. He had held his breath for over a minute, something he had practiced for several weeks.

The men ditched all of their gear in place, except for the weapons, and took off toward the highway. Munoz sprinted with the men past the wrecked trucks, as three slightly-damaged SUVs rolled across the flat grass and met them halfway to the top of the on-ramp. The vehicles were full when they sped away down Interstate 95 toward Stamford. Five minutes later, they had just exited the Interstate at East Putnam Road, close to seven miles down the highway, when the police scanner exploded with activity. Fifteen minutes after that, they were speeding through Cos Cob Harbor on two powerful cruising boats, just a few buoy markers away from emptying into the Long Island Sound.

Chapter Thirty-Six

10:10 p.m.
FBI Headquarters, Washington, D.C.

Special Agent Sharpe examined the contents of the sealed folder at a workstation borrowed from Special Agent Weber's communications team. The fax contained two sheets of paper, which gave them sparse, additional information regarding Petrovich and Munoz. The second page ended abruptly, stopping in the middle of a sentence:

Munoz not assigned to permanent undercover operation in Central/South America. His specialty skill utilized for focused penetration of drug cartel detainees

Sharpe stared at the last sentence, but without the rest of the words, the implication of Munoz's talent didn't sink in. The third page of the fax lay on the floor of the Sanctum, in the middle of a massive, thickening pool of blood. It was barely readable at this point, but the information contained in the single remaining paragraph contained on the page would have raised an immediate alarm for Sharpe. Munoz had been trained to extract information from prisoners by posing as one, in most cases without indigenous law enforcement collusion or knowledge.

"Weber, this fax is incomplete. Would you request the third page for me?"

"Not a problem, sir. We have a full team on duty in the communications hub," Weber replied, reaching for a phone.

"And Weber?"

The agent stopped and looked up at Sharpe.

"You've been here for over thirty-six hours at this point and look like death warmed over. I think you've earned a little break. Things will settle down tonight, but we'll need to be focused again tomorrow. Why don't you head out and report back at zero four thirty," Sharpe said.

"Thanks, sir. How about I grab one of the couches in the comms lounge? I'll make sure everyone here has my cell. I appreciate it...I'm about to fall over," Weber said.

"You look like it. Request the rest of the fax, and go get some rest. We'll see you in the morning, and I know where to find you. Thanks for the hard work today, Weber. I appreciate it," Sharpe said and signaled for Agent O'Reilly to join him.

The two agents walked back to Sharpe's office, where Mendoza was waiting. Instead of the institutional fluorescent overhead lighting common throughout the building, Sharpe's office was softly lit by two standing floor lamps and a green banker's lamp on his desk. At this juncture in his career, Sharpe was accustomed to late nights and took efforts to make the time as comfortable as possible. Mendoza sat in Sharpe's usual late night working spot, a custom leather armchair illuminated by one of the standing lamps. Sharpe appreciated Mendoza's ability to make himself feel comfortable in any surrounding. Mendoza always seemed laid back and at ease, even under duress.

It was one of the key traits that convinced Sharpe to ask Mendoza to postpone his next assignment, a promotional move to Investigations, until Task Force HYDRA finished the next phase in its anticipated life cycle. His prospective supervisor within Investigations signed off on the delay, and Mendoza appeared more than happy to stay on for another six months, especially since they were making such rapid gains unraveling Al Qaeda's U.S.-based financial support network. He expected Mendoza to appear deflated at some point during the day, as the bad news piled onto them, but the man either kept it to himself, or truly remained unshaken. Sharpe admired either possibility, considering what could be at stake for both of their careers.

Mendoza got up from the chair, with an open file in his hands.

"Don't get up for me, Frank. Seriously, we all need some time in that chair today. Plus, I guarantee I'll just have to get up and answer that phone as soon as my ass is firmly planted. Dana, grab any seat, just don't steal Frank's."

Sharpe moved around to his government-supplied desk chair as Mendoza sank back into the leather chair.

"Dana's CIS papers are on your desk. She just needs to sign on the highlighted lines," Mendoza said, and Agent O'Reilly stopped her descent into one of the office chairs to the left of Sharpe's desk.

"Take a few minutes to review the agreement, and sign your life away. I don't mean to insult your intelligence, but I just want to make sure you understand the importance of this agreement. It's simple. You can only discuss CIS Category One information with myself, Agent Mendoza and the CIA liaison, Randy Keller. At this point, these are the only people that aren't locked in a room at the Pentagon with the Black Flag files," Sharpe said.

"Black Flag?" O'Reilly asked.

"Yes. To bring you up to speed in under thirty seconds...the list of names you've worked on all day belong to a group of operatives trained under a clandestine program called Black Flag. It no longer exists, having been shut down by Congress and buried by the Pentagon for several years. However, as you saw today, someone reactivated former members of this group to assassinate every one of this task force's Al Qaeda financing suspects. I don't need to reinforce the fact that the task force's investigation was effectively destroyed today.

"At this point, we are simply trying to figure out why they were assassinated. Is this a rogue anti-terrorist-focused group taking their own fight to Al Qaeda? Is this sponsored by Al Qaeda? Did they discover that we were close to fully unraveling their financial network? Is this the prelude to another major attack, and they're just cleaning up any loose ends? I'm having a hard time believing that this group is working for Al Qaeda, but maybe the individual operatives don't ask questions, and their leader, General Terrence Sanderson, took a huge payoff to mislead them."

"Sanderson. That's a familiar name," O'Reilly said, signing the paperwork without reading it.

"Yeah, a few years ago, he was all over the news. He retired under suspicious circumstances that were never fully disclosed. Now we know why. I can't stress the importance of information security in this case. This is a guaranteed prison sentence for screwing up. You'll continue working in the operations center, but one of us will need to approve any work you are conducting, just to make sure it's not a CIS One spin off. All discussions of the restricted material need to take place in person and away from other personnel. Are you good with this?" Sharpe said.

"Absolutely. I assume the INTERPOL digging probably falls under CIS One?" O'Reilly said.

"Yes, and you conducted the search after signing these papers. Right?"

"Of course," O'Reilly said.

"So, this information sheds some light on Petrovich, and all of the Black Flag operatives," Sharpe said, handing the newest Sanctum information to Agent Mendoza.

"I'm not at all surprised he was able to do so much damage up in Silver Spring. Petrovich's assigned area of operation was Serbia, and he spent two years operating there, starting in early '97 and ending at some point in '99."

"His military service record indicates an honorable discharge in September '99," Mendoza added.

"All right. So this was his last tour of duty, so to speak. Prior to that, he received training in all of the areas listed on our first fax, with a specialty focus in skills. Sniper operations, urban combat survival, and oddly enough, computer networking/security," Sharpe said.

"That's odd, especially for Serbia," O'Reilly commented.

"Why do you say that?' Mendoza asked.

"Well, I can't imagine a need for that skill, especially in that region in the late nineties. There was barely a need for it here. I mean, the systems were still pretty basic in the U.S. at that point. But in war-torn Serbia? Does the sheet mention the specifics of his assignment there?"

"His job was to penetrate one of the ultra-nationalist paramilitary groups," Sharpe said.

"And do what?" Mendoza asked.

"The Pentagon didn't feel the need to convey that information," Sharpe said.

"Great. Well, whatever he did, or still does, he's highly dangerous. He murdered a cop without hesitation and killed six ex-special forces guys with ease..." Mendoza said, whose comment was interrupted by Sharpe's desk phone.

"Hold that thought," Sharpe said and picked up the handset, "Special Agent Ryan Sharpe."

"Sir, it's Weber. No luck getting through to the Sanctum. The line appears to be dead. I called Pentagon security and asked them to notify whoever was in charge of the Sanctum that the line was busted."

"Thanks, Weber. Now get some rest," Sharpe said, then hung up the phone and turned back to the others. "Some snafu over at the Pentagon. What have we come up with for Petrovich?"

"Agent O'Reilly put together a chronology with details. Here's the short version: born and raised in Crystal Lake, Illinois, by parents who are still living in that town. No brothers or sisters. Went to undergrad at

Northwestern, not too far away in Evanston, Illinois, right on Lake Michigan. Graduated in '91 with a degree in economics/finance and received a commission as a naval officer through the NROTC program at Northwestern. Minored in Russian language. He attended the Surface Warfare School in Coronado, California, during the summer of '91 and reported to a frigate stationed in Japan later that year. Transferred to Naval Post Graduate School in Monterey in '93..."

"Is that normal?" Sharpe asked. "I know a lot of former military officers, and that seems pretty quick to go from ship to shore."

"It is unusual. As a marine officer, you do two tours, roughly two years each, then a B Billet, the navy's equivalent to a shore tour. It's pretty standard across the board from service to service. Post-grad school would definitely be a post junior officer tour. Not something you'd do after your first sea tour...and a short sea tour at that. He reported to the *USS Rodney M. Davis* in November of '91 and left in the spring of '93. That's also unusual, and it gets better. After grad school, he reports to a joint command attached to NORAD. How much do you want to bet nobody ever ran into him at either one of these stations? Finally, in early '97 he transfers overseas to SACEUR's Maritime headquarters in London, where he stays through discharge in '99."

"And we all know he damn well didn't spend a minute in London. Four years of training? '93 to '97?" Sharpe asked.

"It would appear that way. That's a long training program," Mendoza said.

"Makes sense for an undercover operation. This program must have been extremely successful," O'Reilly said.

"But old habits die hard, and it doesn't look like this group skipped a beat. Petrovich is the perfect example. I don't believe for one second that Petrovich was the original choice for the Maine hit. They tried to recruit Steven Gedman for this operation, and he had a complete mental breakdown a few days ago. Petrovich literally walked right in off the street and accomplished the mission, in a particularly nasty fashion. No sniper rifles for this guy. He likes using a knife and cutting off heads," Sharpe said, looking at O'Reilly while Mendoza shook his head.

"We have to find this guy. We won't be able to play musical chairs with Munoz for much longer. Keep digging through his file for anything valuable. I'll have Special Agent Edwards turn up the heat on his wife..."

O'Reilly chuckled, then apologized. "Sorry, sir."

"You might want to be careful how you word that to Edwards. He might take it literally," Mendoza said, smiling at O'Reilly.

"And we'll tap every phone he could think of calling, pull phone records, start staking out friends. Everything. He can't leave the country at this point. Every law enforcement agency in the country is looking for him," Sharpe finished.

Sharpe's phone rang again, and he snapped it off the receiver. "Special Agent Sharpe."

"It's Weber again…"

"Weber. Why are you on the phone talking to me? You should be lying down on some very uncomfortable couch right now. Seriously, you need some rest," Sharpe said, and he could hear O'Reilly and Mendoza laughing.

"Sir, I have Special Agent Dan Bernstein on the line. He's the New Haven SAC. Olson's convoy got hit," Weber said, and Sharpe shot up from his chair.

"Put him through," he said, covering the mouthpiece. "Olson's convoy was hit," he said to Mendoza and O'Reilly, who stood up from their seats and moved toward the desk. Sharpe heard a few clicks and then Weber's voice.

"You're connected, Agent Bernstein."

"Ryan, it's Dan Bernstein. I have a situation here. State troopers contacted my office and said they have three disabled vehicles filled with FBI agents off exit ten, just on the outskirts of Stamford."

"What about the agents? Are they…"

"They're fine. Vitals are strong. The agents in the rear SUV and the van were disabled by some kind of gas. One of the troopers passed out entering the van. The front SUV was hit by a massive pickup truck, and the four agents inside were banged up pretty bad, but they should be fine. The driver and Olson took it the worst. I guess the trucks collided engine block to engine block, crunching the two of them pretty badly. They're en route to the hospital now, in stable condition."

"I assume the prisoner is dead," Sharpe said.

"There was no sign of a prisoner. They could tell he was cut free of his restraints, but other than that, nothing. State police say the whole thing was over in less than a minute," Bernstein said.

"Does anyone have any idea why they were off the highway?" Sharpe said.

"All part of the takedown. State troopers had a dozen or so scraped up cars between the southbound ramps at exit 10. Minor accident about twenty minutes before the FBI arrived. They were diverting traffic through the off ramp…and right back onto the highway on the other side of the accident. Troopers said that as soon as the FBI convoy left the highway, some of the people started getting back into their vehicles. They had no idea what to make of it. A large pickup truck takes off, and they all hear the collision. The rest of the vehicles speed over to the on ramp and take off down the interstate ten seconds later. This was a highly-organized strike, Ryan, and they simply disappeared."

"Nobody's in pursuit? How many state troopers did they have on scene?" said Sharpe.

"It took them a few minutes to realize what happened. They radioed ahead, but unfortunately, every state trooper on duty along that stretch of the Interstate was sitting at that accident site," Bernstein said.

"This is unbelievable. I can't stress to you how important it is that we find this crew. Even just one of them. It's critical," Sharpe said.

"I fully understand the situation, and every law enforcement officer along the Interstate 95 corridor is looking for them. So far they have nothing. They also have a possible police impersonator, and this is throwing everyone for a loop. Local cops at the intersection below the highway were told by a state trooper to switch radio frequencies a few minutes before the FBI convoy arrived at the off ramp. They then got orders to let traffic from one of the local roads pass, effectively blocking Olson's group at the intersection. The rear SUV was hit with the gas while they were stopped at the intersection. State police swear that nobody told them to switch frequencies or walk down to the intersection after the locals established their roadblock."

"What happened to the state trooper?" Sharpe asked.

"Local police say he walked up the off ramp. They assumed he rejoined the troopers," Bernstein said.

"Shit, this is a mess. Thanks, Dan. I need to make some calls really quick. Call me immediately if you hear anything else," he said and hung up the phone.

"Frank, I need you over at the Pentagon ASAP. Weber said the fax line was dead. I think we have more than one problem on our hands right now. Munoz was our last link," Sharpe said, closing his eyes and leaning his head back.

"Did Olson make it?" O'Reilly asked.

"Uh...shit. Sorry. Yes. Yes. Everyone is fine. Olson and the agents in the first car were hit by another vehicle and injured, but they'll be fine. The others were knocked out by some kind of gas. Munoz is gone."

"Dead?" Mendoza asked.

"No. Gone. Get over to the Pentagon, Frank. I want to know why the line to the Sanctum is down," Sharpe said. "O'Reilly, make sure the team up in Portland starts downloading every picture of Petrovich available. If we can create a composite impression for the new National Surveillance Network, we might be able to start scanning surveillance and traffic cams registered with this system for a match. It's a long shot, but we might get lucky."

"They should already be doing this, but I'll make sure they understand the priority. I'll start the process for creating the required NSN composite. I'll need you to call the NSA to get me one of the templates necessary to build it," she said.

"That'll be my first call," he said, as agent Mendoza opened the door to leave.

Mendoza checked his watch. "NSA's gonna love this. I'll call your cell as soon as I figure out what's going on over there."

"Hopefully I'm being paranoid," Sharpe said.

Chapter Thirty-Seven

The first thing Daniel noticed when he walked through the safe house door was the familiar smell of Sanderson's strongly brewed coffee. Bolivian coffee. The odor brought back unpleasant memories of Sanderson's office complex at The Ranch. The second thing he noticed was that Colonel Farrington drifted behind him in the hallway, just before Parker stopped at the apartment door. He was sure that neither man fully trusted Daniel in the presence of the general, nor would Sanderson himself. What none of them knew was that Daniel Petrovich had no idea how he would react when he walked through the safe house door.

He wanted to kill Sanderson for dragging him back into this hellish life and potentially destroying what he had struggled to build with Jessica, but the practical side of him knew he might need to rely on Sanderson to fully elude the authorities and land on distant shores. They could always start another life. He shifted his backpack and thought of the submachine gun inside. He was pretty sure Colonel Farrington wouldn't let him get to that. The knife hidden in his front pants pocket might be another story, but for now, he didn't want to open that book. He'd listen to the general and decide the best course of action.

Sanderson's voice filled the room as soon as the door shut behind Petrovich.

"Danny, it's really good to see you again," he said and walked toward him for a hug that was surely meant as more of a pat down than a display of emotion.

He barely embraced the hug, and the general backed away. Sanderson was a physically impressive man, even in his late fifties, and hadn't aged a year as far as Daniel could tell. Like most Black Flag operatives, his face was forgettable. Not overly handsome, or unattractive, but a face that could blend, if it wasn't perched on a body more appropriate for someone half his age.

Sanderson was dressed in a light blue oxford shirt, stretched tightly over his muscled body, and similarly strained khaki pants. He had always been an exercise fanatic, and even when his recruits at The Ranch were finally in peak physical condition, he kept pace and often ran circles around everyone. He was the product of nearly two decades of special forces training and experience, combined with nearly a decade of his own fanatical "off the books" program. He was also one of the most cunningly intelligent human beings Petrovich had ever encountered.

"Is this place even safe?" Daniel said, and Sanderson smirked, clearly not expecting a warm welcome.

"I wouldn't be here if it wasn't. The team that tracked you down today was a fluke. We're investigating it," Sanderson said.

"Didn't seem like a fluke to me. Seemed like more of a leak," he said and glanced around the sterile room at Parker and Farrington.

"I guarantee you we've had no leaks today. Everything has proceeded according to plan, except for the team sent to intercept you. Everyone, please have a seat," he said and motioned toward the couch and chairs arranged around an empty coffee table.

Daniel glanced at the dining room table, which was covered with three laptop computers and a mess of power cords and wires. He saw the hallway outside of the apartment on one of the monitors, which gave him some reassurance that they might be safe here.

"Intercept is certainly one way to describe it. It felt more like a Black Flag mission. There was no hesitation to kill me," Daniel said, while he placed his green backpack in the middle of the bare coffee table and opened it.

Parker and Farrington tensed, but they didn't move. General Sanderson kept the same indifferent expression on his face while Daniel reached into the pack and took out one of the laptops.

"Excellent work. Parker, I want you to take a look at the files on this computer. There are two of them, right?"

Daniel didn't answer, but instead pulled the second one out of the main compartment. He felt the heavy weight of the MP-9 through the thin nylon and dismissed the thought that formed from the contact.

"I pulled some cameras from the trucks, too," he said and spilled these out onto the table over the computers.

Sanderson opened one of the laptops and shook his head.

"Now this is very interesting," he said, turning the computer around for Daniel.

He found himself facing a recent driver's license photo and a ghost from his past, Marko Resja.

"Shit," Petrovich uttered.

"Shit is right. You were brought into this at the last minute, so I think this might be related to the little problem we discussed, Colonel," he said, and Colonel Farrington nodded.

"Something else that fell through the cracks today?" Petrovich said, glaring at the general.

"Something we couldn't have foreseen, but we can certainly handle. I'll need your help with this. Probably later tonight. Maybe tomorrow. When do you think they'll figure out what happened at the Sanctum?" Sanderson said, addressing Colonel Farrington.

"Impossible to say. They might know already...or if it's a relatively quiet night for the FBI, it might not become apparent until morning," he said.

"It won't be a quiet night for the FBI. Our team in the northeast just took down the FBI convoy transporting Munoz," Sanderson said.

"Then they probably know something is wrong. The only line in and out of the Sanctum has been cut, and one of my staff was holding a fax sheet in his hands. I couldn't tell if this was incoming or outgoing. It fell into a pool of blood," the colonel said.

"Let's assume they know. Our problem should be out on the streets tonight. Right?"

"The toxin I gave him lasts a little under an hour and has no known side effects aside from dizziness. If he can clear the FBI's red tape, he should be back on the streets pretty quickly," Farrington said.

"Who is this problem you're talking about? I think we're all far enough along in this to cut the need-to-know bullshit," Petrovich interrupted, tired of the semantics game they were playing.

"The CIA liaison at the FBI has an eidetic memory," Sanderson said. "That means he has a..."

"I know what it means, General. So, you want me kill a CIA employee now? Fine. Who else knows about me, or Black Flag, or whatever the fuck else you're going after today? I'll kill them all if it puts an end to this," he said, glaring at Sanderson.

Sanderson didn't speak right away, and Parker looked uncomfortable.

He couldn't get a read from Farrington, and for a fleeting moment, Daniel thought he might have to shoot his way out of the apartment. His mind started calculating the process, and within the flash of a second, he envisioned it all. The MP-9 was loaded with a round in the chamber, and all he'd have to do was get his hand into the backpack. The top was unzipped roughly four inches to allow him quick access. He wouldn't have time to remove the weapon, so he'd fire it from inside the backpack.

"Danny, there won't be any need for you to shoot your way out of here. You're part of the team. We just need you to tie up a loose end, and our work is done here. We're all free to start over," Sanderson said.

"There's more than one loose end. Someone on your *team* talked to the feds. Have you heard from the man you assigned to the Newport killing?" Petrovich said.

"You caught that? The story was up for a total of thirty-three minutes before the feds pulled the plug on the article," Sanderson said.

"Not exactly what I wanted to see when I woke up this morning. How much of today's operation was compromised because of that? Or did you have a contingency plan, as usual?" Petrovich said.

"I didn't need one. His capture was a critical part of my plan. Without his flawless performance, all we'd have to show for our efforts are eight dead Al Qaeda financiers. You met him during your initial training, before we split you up for area-specific indoctrination," Sanderson said.

Petrovich didn't know what to ask next. For the first time, in as long as he could remember, he was thoroughly confused. He let the general's statement settle for a few seconds, before responding. "You purposely put one of our guys in FBI custody?"

"I had to," Sanderson said, studying Daniel's response.

"I didn't leave him hanging out to dry, if that's what you're thinking. You know me better than that, Daniel. I may be a shitty son-of-a-bitch to work for, but I have never put one of my people into a situation that they were not adequately prepared to handle, or without the best possible plan to help them achieve the mission. The convoy we just hit was transporting him to FBI headquarters here in D.C. Right now, Munoz is on a boat slicing through the waters of Long Island Sound, headed for a quiet rendezvous and a secure transit to our training compound."

"And the rest of the operatives? If the CIA somehow connected the dots to me, then parts of the file are out. Right, Colonel?" Daniel said.

"Very limited information. Roughly a dozen names along the East Coast were provided to the FBI from the Black Flag file, which is what we counted on. I destroyed those faxes on the way out. I saw some detailed information from your file on the last fax sent to the FBI. McKie tightly controlled the flow of information on behalf of the Pentagon. Nobody wanted the contents of this file to go widespread," Farrington said.

"McKie? I figured he'd be in hiding with General Tierney," Daniel said.

"McKie stuck around the Pentagon and landed himself a cushy job doing nothing, except managing the flow of our military's best kept secrets. That's how our country rewards traitors," Sanderson said.

"I assume he's dead," Daniel said, looking to Farrington.

"Very dead," the colonel confirmed.

Daniel sat back into the couch, processing everything he had been told, but he still couldn't make any sense of the day's events. He had assumed that the entire day had been some version of a revenge play orchestrated to cripple Al Qaeda's operations within the U.S. Sanderson could be almost childlike in his need to seek revenge, but beyond last evening's assassinations and the death of McKie, nothing else he had just heard from Sanderson fit this assumption.

"This isn't about taking Al Qaeda down, is it?" Petrovich said.

"Cutting off funds to Al Qaeda's growing U.S. presence is my gift to the U.S. government. They would have watched and waited until it was too late. But you're right, this wasn't the main event," Sanderson said.

"Then why exactly has my life been turned upside down today?" Petrovich said.

"Colonel?"

At his prompt, Colonel Farrington removed his jacket and started unbuttoning his uniform shirt. Daniel thought he was wearing a bulletproof vest, which would be a nice addition to his own equipment list given the circumstances.

"There's gotta be an easier way to set me up for a striptease act," Daniel said, and Parker laughed.

"Always quick with a joke, even under extreme duress. You know, this was one of the key indicators that you were a good match for my program. My staff psychologists spent more time than you can imagine examining your reactions to stress. You were by far their favorite," Sanderson said.

"Glad I could amuse someone. My wife finds it annoying," he said, and his mind flashed to Jessica, but was jarred out of the thought by Farrington.

"The entire Black Flag file," he said, handing the light tan colored nylon vest to General Sanderson.

"Thank you, Richard. Excellent work. Simply flawless execution on your part," he said and looked at Daniel while he ripped open the velcro straps to expose the contents of the vest.

Daniel started to sink into himself and felt his focus narrow. If the entire day's events had been orchestrated to steal top-secret information for Sanderson's benefit, he would kill all three of them in their seats without hesitation and take his chances on the outside. He had all of the money and papers he'd need to disappear with Jessica forever, even with the U.S. government and Sanderson's people on his trail. Money bought security and anonymity in warmer climates.

He watched Sanderson and Parker closely, as Farrington announced he would change into civilian clothes. This would be his best opportunity. With the colonel out of the room, and the other two preoccupied with the papers in the vest, he could put the MP-9 into action within a second. He desperately wanted to cut the general's strings for good and was convinced that the only way he could ever disentangle himself permanently from Sanderson was to kill him. Five years on his own, and the man walked right back in to unravel everything. All for this file? None of this made any sense.

"Still thinking about killing me? I don't blame you," Sanderson said, and Daniel lunged for the backpack.

His hand grasped the submachine gun's pistol grip and flipped the safety off before anyone reacted, but he didn't start firing. Instead, he rushed around the table and placed the gun next to Parker's head, aiming at the general. Parker and Sanderson remained motionless and silent, which kept them alive.

"What's in the file?" Daniel said, mentally giving Sanderson three seconds to respond before putting a bullet through Parker's head.

"I've never seen someone move that fast. Amazing," Sanderson said.

Daniel's expression never changed as he reached three seconds and committed to killing all of them. He could read the file for himself. His grip tensed on the gun still covered by the backpack.

"It's all that remains of the original Black Flag file, Daniel," he said, and this statement bought them some more time.

"You don't need the Black Flag file," Daniel said, as he slid the compact, black weapon out of the backpack and shifted to a position behind Sanderson's chair.

"You're right. I don't need it. I need to destroy it."

"General, you know how my mind works better than anyone…"

"Better than you," Sanderson interrupted.

"Then you know I'm not seeing a reason to keep any of you alive right now," Petrovich said.

"I needed to remove all remaining traces of Black Flag from the official archives, Daniel. Destroy any link to the dozens of graduates still out there. The ones not already reactivated," he said and turned his body around in the chair to face Daniel. "I'm restarting the program."

The words hit him like shockwave, quickly followed by General Sanderson's iron grip to a pressure point located on Daniel's wrist. Sanderson squeezed the pressure point with brutal force, causing Petrovich's trigger hand to reflexively open and lose its hold. Parker swung around the chair at the same moment, aiming a martial arts kick at his throat, which forced Daniel to abandon his remaining grip on the weapon to parry the potentially devastating attack. He felt the weapon slip away and knew he was essentially screwed. Oddly, the general released the pressure point, giving him a chance.

He backed out of Parker's immediate hand-to-hand combat range, but the former SEAL pressed the attack, while General Sanderson removed the ammunition from the submachine gun. Petrovich didn't have much time to process why Sanderson was doing this, while blocking a series of judo-style hand chops and launching his own retaliatory strikes. His forearms burned from each blocked chop, but he managed to get inside of Parker's balance line and swept the commando's legs. Parker toppled back, nearly falling over the table laden with computer equipment. In a flash, Petrovich retrieved the knife hidden in his front pocket and flicked it open.

"That's enough! Put the knife away!" General Sanderson yelled, and Daniel glanced in his direction long enough to see Farrington emerge from one of the bedrooms aiming a suppressed pistol at him.

"That won't be necessary either, Colonel," Sanderson announced, and Farrington reluctantly lowered the weapon.

Sensing no immediate danger from anyone in the room, Petrovich closed the blade and focused on one of the computer screens.

"That's my house. What the fuck is going on here?" said Daniel, staring at a screen filled with nearly a dozen camera feeds.

"Every location was raided about an hour ago. Simultaneously. Of course, nobody was home," he said.

"My wife was home," Daniel said.

"She'll be fine. She can take care of herself," Sanderson said.

Daniel stared at the screens for a few seconds and walked back over to the group standing near the couch. He had a little more respect now for Parker's skills. The former navy commando's hand-to-hand skills were impressive, but lacked the depth that could only be acquired by applying these skills in real situations, where your life depended on the outcome. Schoolhouse skills, but pretty damn good.

"You're already training new operatives?" Daniel asked.

"And recruiting old ones," Sanderson replied.

"I'm not interested."

"Suit yourself, but I'll still require your help with our CIA problem."

"And then I'm finished."

General Sanderson nodded and walked over to the table next to Daniel.

"You know, none of them hesitated to come back," he said and looked directly into Daniel's eyes. "And most of them were leading successful lives. Families, businesses, solid jobs…bright futures by American standards. Every one of them looked relieved when I asked them to join the new program. Their lives were covert missions, and they were waiting, praying to get out. You can't tell me you don't feel the same way, Danny. At least somewhat. You were one of the best to come out of the program," Sanderson said.

"I haven't had much time to think it over. My life has been pretty much gutted over the past twenty-four hours thanks to you."

"Well, if it makes you feel any better, I didn't have any confidence that you would take part in this voluntarily. The Ghani job had been assigned to another operative, but a problem developed at the last minute," Sanderson said.

"I don't believe you for a second," Petrovich said, and Parker interjected.

"He's telling the truth. The operative assigned to the Ghani job had a mental breakdown two days ago."

Petrovich started laughing, taking several seconds to regain control of himself. "Imagine that. Another one of your willing participants, General? And for the record, Parker, your glorious leader may be telling the truth about the last minute assignment, but his truths can be slippery. One way or the other, my life in Portland, Maine, was scheduled to come to an end today. It didn't matter who killed Ghani. Once the list of operatives surfaced, I was burned. Having that assassination shoved down my throat gave me a little more time to prepare for the inevitable," Daniel said.

"Nice work by the way. Parker should have provided you with a knife," Sanderson said.

"I keep a few around the house for the occasional murder," Daniel replied, wondering how much the general really knew about what happened the night of Ghani's murder.

"Parker, what do you think?" Sanderson asked.

"Based on the profile workup I'm seeing in this laptop, and Brown River's involvement, I'm pretty sure we have two problems at the CIA. Keller's memory is one, and that needs to be erased, but I think we have a bigger problem out there. Someone moved pretty quickly to take you out, and they didn't hire a few ghetto thugs to do the job. Keller took the information back to the CIA, and within a few hours, they found you. That's both impressive and frightening, and suggests the work of someone highly placed within the CIA, with NSA contacts..."

"Or a leak within your group," Daniel interjected.

"There's no leak here. Parker's the only one other than myself that knew about you, and I trust him completely. Whoever activated the Brown River team has a personal grudge against something you did while assigned to the Black Flag program. I can only think of one possibility."

Daniel tensed at the thought that someone at the CIA had made the connection to a secret he had taken every precaution to keep buried. Secrets like Daniel's died hard, and Sanderson's supernatural efforts to resurrect Black Flag might have raised a few other unintended specters from their burial sites. He had no choice but to finish this day's work for Sanderson. Black Flag would rise from the ashes, but Daniel's connection to Zorana Zekulic had to be put back under the ground, for good.

"Do you have anyone working in Langley?" Daniel said.

General Sanderson smiled, which gave Petrovich little satisfaction.

"We have a few people in the CIA, but not at Langley."

"I guess it doesn't matter. Colonel, what is Keller's status? Will he need to be hospitalized?" Daniel asked.

"No, I hit him with a Taser and gave him a specialized neurotoxin. He might be coming around right now. The toxin is harmless, as far as we know," Farrington said.

"They'll still take him to the hospital, or FBI headquarters for questioning. The FBI is going to shut everything down, I assume," Petrovich said.

"They'll be in a panic. As of thirty minutes ago, they lost every link to Black Flag and any hope of figuring out what happened today. The trail went cold for them," Sanderson said.

"We need to take care of the CIA problem immediately. I can breach hospital security. Might get messy, but they probably wouldn't expect it, especially since Keller was left unharmed at the Pentagon. I assume Farrington left him alive so we could find the bigger fish?" Petrovich said.

"Precisely. Brown River's involvement suggested a bigger issue. Pictures of you in this laptop confirm it. I doubt Keller will consent to hospitalization. He'll want to report immediately to his supervising agent. I'm not the only one who will suggest the Brown River CIA connection. He'll most likely report in person, and I have an idea where they might meet. If my instincts prove correct, we'll be able to take them both out at once."

"I don't think we have the resources available to breach Langley," Daniel said.

General Sanderson gave him a quizzical look and shook his head.

"You were always fucking crazy, and I mean that in a good way," Sanderson said.

"I didn't take it any other way."

"People talk in this town. Rumors fly…it's hard to keep a secret. There's a wonderful, quiet little street in Georgetown that I'd like you and the colonel to visit."

Chapter Thirty-Eight

9:45 p.m.
FBI Satellite Office, Portland, Maine

Special Agent D'Angelo led Edwards and Jessica Petrovich through a small maze of hallways and offices shared by several federal law enforcement agencies on the fourth floor of the building. The FBI officially occupied two rooms toward the back. One was Special Agent D'Angelo's office, and the other served as an administrative support center, with room for an assistant, several file cabinets, and a large all-in-one copy/fax machine. The different agencies shared a conference room past the DEA's offices, several doors down, and this was their destination. As team leader, Edwards had been given one of the spare offices used by agents on assignment to Maine, but hadn't felt the need to leave anything there. Everyone else processed the information he needed and reported to him, so there was little need for a briefcase or files.

While he walked the key piece of the FBI's puzzle to the conference room, his team was busy at her house with local police detectives, searching for evidence and clues linking her husband to the murder in Cape Elizabeth. He didn't think they would find anything relevant at the house. The Cape Elizabeth murder scene had been sterile and yielded nothing useful to the investigation. Still, he couldn't voice this opinion openly.

He had received a call from Special Agent Frank Mendoza stressing the importance of finding information that might help them locate Petrovich, so he put his relatively useless team to work processing the house. Address books with friends' information, computer contact lists, bank information, and the pictures. They seemed really focused on scanning and downloading every picture of Petrovich in the house. It sounded like another waste of time, but he could tell it was important to someone back in D.C. Hopefully D'Angelo would join his team back at the house. So far she had proved useful dealing with the locals, and he had made a mistake by keeping her out of the raid on Petrovich's house.

"Here you go, Mrs. Petrovich. Would you like some coffee, water, or a soda?" D'Angelo said, standing at the door to the conference room.

"I'm fine right now, thank you. Is there a bathroom I can use to change?"

"You can use one of the spare offices right across the hall. Do you have any shoes?" D'Angelo said.

"We sort of left in a hurry," she said.

"It was a hostile environment. They'll be lucky if she doesn't press charges," Edwards said, and D'Angelo shot him a concerned look.

"I've already heard," she said and added, "I keep a pair of running shoes in my office. You can use those for now."

"That would be great, Agent D'Angelo. I can't thank you enough. My head is still swimming," Jess said and walked across the hall to an empty office with her outfit.

Once the door to the spare office shut, D'Angelo turned to Edwards.

"What happened at the house? I get a call from Lieutenant Moody, and he's pissed. Pissed at you. Pissed at the FBI. Said you treated his officers like shit. Justin, I have to deal with these guys when you leave. Can you take it easy on them?"

"You should have seen what was going on over there. If we treated anyone like that, we'd have a lawsuit on our hands and agents would be fired," Edwards said.

"Unfortunately, I wasn't there," she said and paused. "Moody said she pulled a weapon on his men?"

"She had a spoon. I saw it on the floor next to her. That's the level of professionalism we're dealing with here. They're just looking to crack some skulls, and they're not about to let a spoon get in the way. I don't know how you deal with this level of incompetence on a daily basis," Edwards said.

"They're fine. I should have been there to run interference," she stated.

"They're not fine, but you're right. You should have been there. I think you should head over and make sure everyone is getting along with my agents," he said.

D'Angelo stared at him for a few seconds, and he couldn't get a read from her.

"Are you sure it's a good idea for me to leave the two of you alone here?"

"I can handle her...what are you saying, D'Angelo?"

"Nothing. I'm just not sure it's safe for the two of you. I'd feel more comfortable if you brought her to the police station across the street. I'll smooth things out for you," she said.

"No way. Her husband killed a cop in D.C. You didn't see the looks she was getting at the house. No way I'm marching her into that building," he said, pointing across the street at the Portland Police Department headquarters building.

"When did you learn this? This is the kind of thing I need to know," she said, irritated.

"I got a call from my task force ops center while we were in the house. Your local boys got the news right about the same time, and it started to get ugly," he said.

D'Angelo stood her ground, shaking her head and grimacing.

"You didn't see it," he insisted.

"That's the point. I wasn't there. I know you don't like dealing with the locals, me included, but this is the real world. These guys don't give a shit where you went to college, or what field offices you've been assigned to in the past. They judge you right on the spot, and you don't get many second chances to make an impression. I'll head over to the house to make sure things are running smoothly. I'd recommend staying here until I get back."

"We might step out to grab some dinner. She hasn't eaten since lunch," Edwards said.

"I'd order pizza. There are sodas in the fridge. You don't want her out on the streets if her husband is wrapped up into whatever happened today. I still think you should be over in the other building," she said.

"We'll be fine here," he replied, and the door to the office slowly opened.

"I hope so. Let me get you those shoes," she said to Jessica, who appeared in the hallway from the spare office.

She wore a pair of dark jeans and an untucked, white-patterned, long-sleeve blouse. She had pulled her hair back tight into a ponytail. Edwards thought she looked incredible and caught himself staring. If he could have seen D'Angelo's face, he would have known that Jessica's security situation wasn't her only concern. He had no idea that his reputation as a misogynistic womanizer preceded him everywhere in the FBI.

"Is everything all right?" Jessica said.

"Absolutely. Why don't you grab a seat at the table," Edwards said, leading her inside the small conference room.

D'Angelo returned a few minutes later with a pair of white running shoes and socks.

"These will look a little clunky with that outfit," she said.

"They'll be fine for getting around in here. I hate walking around in bare feet, especially in an office. At least this office is clean. You should see mine…junk all over the floors. It's really quite disgusting," Jessica said, and Edwards thought she sounded a little less shell-shocked.

"Sounds good. I'll be over at the house. Stay in touch," she said to Edwards.

"Make sure they don't tear the place apart. They did a lot of damage breaking in," Edwards said, figuring the place was already destroyed, but wanting to score points with Jessica.

"I'm sure they won't do any more damage," D'Angelo said and left the office.

As soon as she was gone, Edwards walked back into the conference room with a legal pad and a few pens, which he tossed on the table in front of Jessica.

"Can we get something to eat? I don't know if I'll be able to concentrate. I could use a strong drink, too, if that's allowed," she said, smiling demurely.

Edward couldn't have been happier. The whole evening was shaping up nicely. Jessica had no food in her stomach and didn't appear to have any hang-ups about alcohol. He would delay her request long enough to plant the seed of fear and distrust about her husband in her, then loosen her up enough with alcohol to spill the information needed to track down her husband. A few more drinks after that, and he could offer her some kind of deal to help her husband, for a price. He'd administer a few chemicals at some point later in the evening to remove that memory and leave her in a confused state of exhaustive guilt.

"Let's go over some basic questions, and we can take a walk down into the Old Port to grab a late dinner. My treat."

"Thank you. I know a nice Italian place that stays open late. It's not very far from here," she said.

"Sounds like a plan. So, tell me, did your husband come home later than usual last night, or run any last minute errands that seemed odd?" he said, hoping to catch her off guard with a direct question.

"I don't think…" she said, pausing, "he had soccer practice, but they practice all the time…last night was an extra practice. They haven't been winning many games lately, so it seemed normal, I guess. He was home by eight."

"Can you provide me with some contact information for his soccer team? I'll need to check into this," he said and grabbed the yellow legal pad and a pen.

"Sure. His league plays at the big indoor field near Westbrook. I think it's the Portland Sports Complex. I can give you the numbers of some of the guys on his team when we get back to my house. Was the murder before eight?"

"I can't really disclose any of the details regarding the investigation, but the information you provide is critical to figuring it out," Edwards said.

"Danny wouldn't shoot anyone," she said.

"Mr. Ghani wasn't shot."

"What happened?" she asked.

"I suppose the details will become public knowledge soon enough," he said, leaning in a little for effect.

"It was brutal and efficient. The work of a professional killer. Single stab wound through the neck and into the chest cavity. I've never seen that much blood before at a murder scene. I really hope it wasn't your husband. How familiar are you with Daniel's military background?" he said and looked up into her terrified eyes.

"Danny's not capable of doing something like that. He barely touches knives in the kitchen. He's sort of clumsy with them..." she said, and her voice trailed off.

"What about his military training?" he pressed.

"He was in the navy for eight years or so, but he wasn't like a SEAL or anything. He was on a ship. He'd been stationed in Europe for a few years before we met in business school at BU," she said.

"Have you ever met any of his navy friends?"

"I think so. I don't really know. He doesn't really talk about it much."

"Eight years is a long time not to make friends," Edwards said.

"I guess, but...he got to live in Europe, and..."

"Have you noticed anything strange about him lately?"

"No."

"Calls coming into his phone at odd times?"

"No. Not that I can remember," she said.

Edwards studied her closely. She had emerged from the office reenergized in a fresh outfit, peppy and uplifted, but now she looked glum again. He would continue to pepper her with meaningless questions for another twenty or thirty minutes, occasionally casting a few well-crafted questions designed to raise serious doubts about the man she married and ultimately break down her natural instinct to protect him. A few drinks should seal the deal on Daniel Petrovich…a few more drinks would ensure that the hotel room he reserved in the Old Port wouldn't go to waste.

Chapter Thirty-Nine

10:50 p.m.
FBI Headquarters, Washington, D.C.

A dull murmur had blanketed the operations center for nearly twenty minutes, as agents simply ran their last assigned tasks into the ground. Little to no evidence was found throughout the day at any of the eight murder sites along the East Coast, aside from the fortuitous and purely accidental acquisition of one of their murder suspects, who was no longer in custody.

Of the two Brown River contractors captured in Silver Spring, only one was conscious, and he swore up and down that their operation was a legally sanctioned counterterrorist operation. Of course, he had no evidence to back this claim, other than his insistence that the group's team leader had specifically briefed them prior to departing Brown River's headquarters in Fredericksburg, Virginia. Jeremy Cummings, apparent team leader for the eight men, lay dead in the Natural Foods, surrounded by forensics specialists and police officers.

The FBI raids didn't look promising either. The data processing and analysis team, led by Special Agent O'Reilly, had been busy processing images from over a dozen raid locations, and Sharpe considered shifting other agents in an effort to assist them. So far, nothing immediately useful had been recovered at any of the raid sites, and the trail had gone cold for every one of the operatives on the supplied Black Flag list, except for Petrovich.

His wife had been home when Special Agent Edwards' team hit the house, and Daniel Petrovich had reported to his job earlier that day, which further supported his loose theory that Petrovich was a last minute replacement for the mental patient guy in New Hampshire. The rest of the Black Flag suspects had gone underground over a week before, taking family with them.

Sharpe flipped open his cell phone again and tried to call Mendoza. He knew that cell phones wouldn't be allowed in the Compartmentalized Information Section, especially if they discovered a problem, but he could barely stand the suspense. Mendoza had left nearly thirty minutes earlier and should have arrived at the Sanctum by now. He had a terrible feeling about what they would find.

Special Agent Weber called out from the communication section, one of the few busy areas in the operations center.

"Sir, it's Mendoza," he said, and Sharpe ran across the room.

"Frank, give me some good news. The trail on Munoz has gone cold. Eight heavily-armed men just vanished into thin air," he said.

"Ryan, it's bad over here. The Sanctum was breached, and the file is gone."

"Be careful what you say over the phone, Frank."

"I understand. The only one missing is the colonel in charge. Farrington. He departed the Pentagon at exactly 9:52. Looked like Hannibal Lecter got loose in that room, Ryan."

"What about Harris and Calhoun?" Sharpe said, praying they weren't dead.

"They're fine, as far as we can tell. They were each hit with about a dozen small darts that we assume were coated with something that took them down. Keller and the Pentagon personnel are starting to come around. They weren't hit with any darts, but it's clear that something happened to them. McKie was slaughtered. Same cut we saw in Cape Elizabeth, Maine. One knife wound down through the neck, right above the collar bone," Mendoza said.

"Jesus Christ. We need to see some video. This could be Petrovich," Sharpe hissed.

"No video inside the Sanctum. Prohibited for obvious reasons. No video within the section either. Security says Farrington departed alone and did not log any visitors into the building."

Sharpe could hear yelling beyond Agent Mendoza's voice.

"Hold on, sir...they found something," Mendoza said, and Sharpe's mind entertained any possibility.

He wouldn't be surprised if they found Farrington's unconscious body stuffed in a closet. The Black Flag file said these operatives were trained experts in disguise. His mind was spinning with possibilities when Mendoza broke the spell.

"They just found a janitor tied up in one of the closets. He was coherent enough to confirm that Farrington put him there," Mendoza said.

"This isn't good, Frank, and now we have no way of expanding the search for these operatives. Are they sure the file is gone?" Sharpe said, looking around at his own task force's agents.

"Positive. They didn't seem overly concerned about any of the personnel, until they established what happened to the file. Some kind of special response team from deep inside the Pentagon. I didn't see anyone below the rank of full colonel...hold on, Ryan...shit, I'm being told by some very serious-looking gentlemen that I need to wrap this up. They've locked down the building, and that will soon include all outgoing unsecured communications," Mendoza said.

"Stay with Harris and Calhoun, and contact me when you can. I'm gonna play the last card I have right now and pray it gives us something," Sharpe said.

"Petrovich's wife?"

"It's all we have. Good luck over there," Sharpe said and closed the phone.

He looked up again and saw that O'Reilly was standing near him, waiting for him to finish. Everyone had been waiting. One of the FBI's top agents was injured in the convoy hit, and the status of two agents that had worked in this task force for over a year was unknown. He needed to address Task Force HYDRA and redistribute priorities.

"Hold on, Dana. I'll be with you in a second," he said.

"I found something interesting," she said, and he nodded.

"Everyone! I need everyone's attention for a minute!" he said and walked toward the front of the operations center.

Normally, it could take several minutes to quiet an active operations center, but nearly every agent had been waiting for word about Harris and Calhoun. The rumors started spreading quickly once Mendoza scrambled for the Pentagon, and when Weber uttered Mendoza's name, the place went still.

"Thank you. A couple things. First, Harris and Calhoun are fine. Nobody's sure exactly what happened to them. They were rendered unconscious, but their vitals are strong. Very similar to the convoy hit," he said, and the room broke into scattered conversation expressing relief.

"Second, the source of information used to obtain the list of suspects is gone. For now, this is it. We have to spin something out of what we already have. Suspect bank account information, phone records, scraps of paper in the bathroom trash bin. We need to be creative at every site connected with today's murders because it is unlikely we'll be given anything beyond what we have. Because of this, I'm going to assign some of you to help process data associated with each of the raid sites. Others will be diverted to scour financial records, phone records, everything. This is what we do best. This is how we unraveled Al Qaeda's domestic financial network. We can do it again. Unfortunately, we don't have months to put this together. We need to turn something up by tomorrow."

More mumbling among the ranks, which sounded more positive than negative to Sharpe. This was a dedicated crew that essentially had the rug pulled out from under them this morning. They had built a legacy over the past three years, and he was confident they were in this for the long haul.

"Lastly, I want to thank all of you for your hard work in the face of this morning's disaster. It's been a long, frustrating day, and I wish I could tell you it's going to end sometime soon, but I can't. If you need a break, coordinate with your team and grab some rest. Just stay out of my office," he said, and several agents broke into tired laughter.

"I'll pass word to your section chiefs, and we'll redirect those that need redirecting," he said and turned to O'Reilly. "What's up?"

"Nothing substantial, but it might be something that can help Edwards put some pressure on Petrovich's wife," she said, and he immediately moved her away from a group of agents standing nearby.

"Let's keep talk like that between the two of us. What did you find?" he whispered.

"Sorry, sir. I've been running the pictures from Petrovich's house through our facial recognition software, trying to get a three-dimensional composite prepared for widespread distribution. INTERPOL provided us with more images of Marko Resja."

"You didn't request that, did you?"

"Not really. Sort of. I made up some bullshit about some international war criminal database maintenance on our end, and they sent me electronic files for over a hundred suspected war criminals. I can't imagine this will raise any alarms anywhere," she said.

"All right...nice work. Is that it?"

"I found a few pictures of Petrovich, as Marko...with Zekulic," she whispered.

"Really? I see where you're going with this, and I'd love to send those off to Edwards, but—"

"It gets better. I ran some images of Jessica Petrovich through the system, to compare with Zekulic, and I'm getting a 62% match average over several photographs," she said.

"That sick son-of-a-bitch cut his girlfriend's head off in Serbia, then replaced her when he got back to the states. I bet if you showed her one of these photos and told her the story...she'd cough him up pretty quick. Throw in the need for our Witness Protection Program and it'll be a slam dunk," she said softly enough to avoid being overheard.

"Can you send these pictures to my computer? I don't think we should talk about this again. It's a nice idea, but it would completely violate our CIS agreements. This is the fruit of a very poisonous tree. Good work," he said and turned toward the door leading out of the center.

A pit rose in Sharpe's stomach, as he walked down the hallway to his office. He had very few options at this point and wasn't hopeful that his task force could turn anything up at this point. His pep talk was a mandatory push. He knew they'd have to dig enthusiastically through this haystack, for at least forty-eight hours, before dialing down the intensity. Tomorrow he'd have every high-profile FBI and Justice Department VIP rolling through the operations center, and they'd be watching his task force closely. Unless he could break this open tonight.

He reached his desk and gave the situation one more spin through his head, weighing the positives and negatives of the course he was considering. His heart race each time he flipped open his cellphone. He counted far more negatives, but there was no other way.

An email message from O'Reilly hit his computer inbox, which provided a brief distraction. He opened one of the attachments and saw a black and white picture of Marko Resja and Zorana Zekulic, walking arm in arm down a crowded street somewhere in Serbia. The next one was a color photo of the couple in a barren park. Zorana was laughing in the photo, which sealed it for Sharpe. What kind of psycho butchers his girlfriend like that? He pressed send on his cellphone. *Screw the rules.*

Chapter Forty

Special Agent Edwards glanced around the office, about to shut the door and lock it behind him, when his cell phone rang. He kept the door open and fished the phone out of his front pocket. The caller ID read "Sharpe," and he immediately answered the call.

"Special Agent Edwards."

"Edwards, this is Sharpe. Where are you right now?"

"I'm at the satellite office with Jessica Petrovich. We just finished an initial battery of questions, and we're taking a break to get her some food," he said and whispered to her, "Just a minute."

"Who's in charge at her house?" Sharpe said.

"My team's processing the house, and D'Angelo is coordinating with the Portland police. I needed to get her out of there," he replied.

"Can you go somewhere private? I have some information to relay that is sensitive," Sharpe said.

"Sure, hold on one second, sir," he said.

"I need you to wait in the reception area here while I take this call," he said to Jessica, and she frowned.

"I'm starting to lose my patience with this. I'm starving," she said, not budging from the hallway.

"Please. He might have information about your husband. It won't be long," he said and motioned for her to come back inside, which she reluctantly did.

Edwards walked over to the nearest office and closed the door.

"All right, I'm alone."

"Justin, we've had a few major setbacks within the past hour..."

"I heard about the shootout outside of D.C., and so did every cop in

221

Mrs. Petrovich's house. That's why I had to get her out of there. Mendoza stressed the importance of getting some useful information out of her, and nothing was coming out while they tore her house apart in front of her."

"We've had bigger problems than that. Munoz escaped. Olson's prisoner transport convoy was hit outside of Stamford, and the Pentagon was hit from the inside. We've been mining information from a classified source, and that source was stolen less than an hour ago."

"Jesus, sir. Is everyone okay?" he said, not really caring if Special Agent Olson survived the attack.

"Everyone's fine, but we lost everything moving our investigation forward. Jessica Petrovich is all we have right now," Sharpe said.

"I'm getting close with her," Edwards said.

"Do you think she knows how to find him?" Sharpe asked.

"She has to know something. Two calls originating from D.C. cell towers were placed to her house this evening. Each from a different cell phone. She's changed her story once. Now she remembers that her husband checked in with her about an hour before we hit the house, but he didn't give her any details about where he was staying or when he'd be back. She told me in the house that he hadn't called. She knows more than she's telling us," he said.

"All right. I need to trust you with something delicate..."

"You can count on my discretion, sir," Edwards said.

"Can you log into a computer in that office?" Sharpe asked.

"Uhhh...yeah. I have an access code. I just need to grab one of the empty offices."

"Here's what I need you to do. I'm going to send a few images to your bureau account. I want you to show these images to her. Let me give you a little background on this. Nothing I say to you is to ever be repeated. Are we clear on that? I can't stress how important this is," Sharpe said.

"I understand. You can trust me implicitly," Edwards said.

"Daniel Petrovich lived a very different life less than a decade ago. A life that gave him the skills to pull off what you saw today at Mr. Ghani's house and vanish without a trace. A background that allowed him to cut through two teams of ex-special forces security contractors without skipping a beat. I'm sending you a picture of Petrovich from his former life, and the picture shows him with a woman he is accused of brutally murdering. Hacked her head off to be precise. This is one hundred percent confirmed. No mistake.

"Our facial recognition software match Jessica's and the former girlfriend's face at sixty-two percent. There should be enough similarity between the two of them to seriously scare the shit out of her. I need you to convince her that she is in danger, that her husband is a murderer and that we can protect her, if she helps us bring him in. Can you do that?"

"I'm already more than halfway there. I'm going to feed her a few drinks and a nice dinner. She's physically tough, but mentally, she's on the verge of a collapse. I'll have this wrapped up quickly. I'll let you know as soon as I have a lead on Petrovich."

"The pictures were taken in Serbia, sometime in the very late nineties. And keep this between the two of us. You pull this off, and I'll take care of you," Sharpe said, though Edwards wasn't exactly sure how much clout Sharpe would have within the FBI when the fallout settled.

"Send me the file, and I'll get started," he said.

"It's waiting in your inbox. Keep me posted," Sharpe said.

Edwards left the office and found Jessica reading a copy of Smithsonian magazine in the tiny reception area. She had a white paper cup of water on the small, rectangular black table in front of her.

"Finally," she said.

"I have to show you something important. I think you might be in serious danger," he said and proceeded to give her the watered-down version of what happened outside of Stamford and inside the Pentagon.

He didn't want to hit her with the big punch before she had a chance to see the pictures of her husband embracing another woman. A little female anger and jealousy to start would guarantee the result he was after. A few minutes later, he had logged onto the guest computer station and accessed his email. The first image of her husband flashed onto the screen, and Edwards watched her face closely. She didn't react at first, and he was worried that she might pass out, but her face slowly contorted into a controlled look of anger. Her lips pressed together and tightened. He imagined how much fun she would be in bed later, trying to fuck the memory of this woman out of her head.

"What is this? Why are you showing me this?" she said, turning to look at him.

He let the moment intensify.

"Hey, I'm talking to you. Who the fuck is this?" she demanded, and he finally broke his intentional silence.

"Your husband hacked this woman's head off about five years ago in Serbia," he said, and she inhaled sharply.

"I always knew something wasn't right," she whispered and added, "I really need a drink."

"I'm really sorry to have shown you this, but something went really wrong today with your husband's associates…and they're cleaning house. I don't think you're safe on the streets. We'll have a quick dinner as promised, but then we're putting you into protective custody," he said.

"Danny would never hurt me," she protested weakly.

"I wonder how many other women thought the same thing. The best way for you to keep yourself safe is to help us find him. He can't hurt you if we have him in custody. Until then, we need to keep you hidden. Come on, let's get you that drink. God knows you've earned it," he said, and escorted her out of the office.

Chapter Forty-One

11:51 p.m.
FBI Headquarters, Washington, D.C.

"Agent Sharpe!"

The words startled him. The day had been full of surprises and chaos, filling the room with an insurmountable level of noise at times, but Agent O'Reilly's voice sounded distressed. He turned in her direction.

"Sir, you have to see this. Now," she urged, and he hurried over to her station.

"I was reviewing the photos of Petrovich when I came back across this one. It was an anomaly from the original batch. A picture of Daniel and Jessica together. 100% match between Jessica Petrovich and Zorana Zekulic," she said hurriedly.

"This system always gives us outliers. That's why we enter as many pictures as possible," he said.

"I understand that, sir, but I thought these two first met at grad school in Boston. This is a picture of the two of them together at Navy Pier in Chicago. She's wearing a Loyola sweatshirt. That's a school in Chicago. Daniel Petrovich attended Northwestern. They look really young in this picture. I think they've known each other for more than just five years," she stated.

"I don't know. We have to trust the system. How many photos of Jessica did you enter?"

"Almost thirty…"

"Shit, that's a lot of pictures."

"Hold on, sir. I'm running a search on another computer. There!" she yelled, and Sharpe stared at the screen with a sinking feeling.

The screen displayed a 1990 Loyola College student ID picture of Nicole Erak, a young woman vaguely resembling the current Jessica Petrovich, but not close enough to justify a match, even after factoring in a fifteen-year age difference. Unless she had undergone plastic surgery. Now he was getting ridiculous. He considered calling Edwards, but shelved the idea for the moment. He wondered if Nicole Erak had been found decapitated in Chicago.

A hundred ideas ran wild through his head as O'Reilly finished typing another analysis request through the computer system. The system immediately gave them the results, and Special Agent Sharpe fired his hand into his pocket to retrieve his cell phone. The student ID picture of Nicole Erak matched Zorana Zekulic. 100%.

"Call the Portland police immediately! Get them everything we have on this woman! They're somewhere eating dinner in the Old Port!" he yelled, auto-dialing Edwards.

Chapter Forty-Two

The elevator hummed as Special Agent Justin Edwards stood next to Jessica, who was rambling on about nearly anything at this point. He could tell she was tired, drunk and emotionally spent. She wasn't stumbling, but her speech was slurred, and he couldn't shut her up. Three straight martinis in one hour would do that to anyone, especially a slim woman who had gone without food for nearly twelve hours. The first drink was finished before the bread arrived, and the second drink vanished as their entrées appeared. He had enjoyed an expensive glass of Cabernet, which he sipped over the course of the dinner, though he desperately wanted to match her drink for drink.

He got a little buzzed from the wine, but it wasn't enough. Their chemistry was a little off throughout the meal, as she steamed ahead with the martinis, and he didn't get the information he desperately sought during dinner. Still, he managed to convince her that she needed FBI protection until they figured out what was going on with her husband. She stopped denying that her husband might be involved, but stubbornly kept insisting that her husband would never hurt her, which was fine for now. He had made enough progress to get her into the hotel room, which he told her was the FBI's idea of a security precaution.

The elevator stopped on the fourth floor.

"What, we're not hiding out in one of the suites? The FBI must be going through some budget cuts," she said, in a silly manner that grated on Edward's nerves.

"We like to keep this as low profile as possible. If it were me travelling with someone like you, I'd go for the suite," he said, eager to gauge her response.

"Are you supposed to flirt with protected witnesses?" she said, and for a second Edwards saw a look that suggested he would be in business once they got comfortable in the hotel room.

"Not usually, but in your case, it's hard to resist. Ladies first," he said, motioning to the open door.

"Why, thank you," she said, and he was pretty sure she glanced down at his bulge forming in his pants.

He led her down the hallway to room 438, hoping for a discreet moment to adjust the awkwardly protruding erection stuck in his underwear. Maybe she'd just rip his pants down as soon as they were in the room, and it wouldn't matter. He felt like exploding as he put the key card into the door slot. The door opened, and his phone rang, which was a real buzz kill. He let it ring, showing her into the room, which already contained his personal belongings.

A spare suit hung in the closet, above an extra pair of dress shoes and a pair of running shoes. He could see his toiletry kit neatly arranged in the bathroom as he passed. He wondered what she thought of his stuff being here, but didn't think she'd notice anything beyond the chilled bottle of white wine in a silver bucket on the desk. She'd begged him for another drink at the restaurant, but he didn't want her to become incoherent and legless yet. Instead, he'd stepped outside of the restaurant, pretending to take a call, and ordered the wine. He watched as she took the bait.

"Very nice. Is this how you treat all of your protectees?" she said, slurring her speech a little more than before.

"Only our VIPs," he said. He removed his jacket, still ignoring the cell phone. When he hung the jacket in the foyer closet, he briefly considered answering his phone.

"You gonna answer that?" Jessica said, pouring herself a glass of wine.

"Not right now. We have more important things to do," he said.

The phone finally stopped ringing.

"I guess we do," she said, pouring a second glass.

He started to walk toward her when his phone rang again.

"God damn it," he muttered. "Hold on, let me get this over with."

He needed to make this quick. It looked like things were progressing quicker than he'd expected.

"Special Agent Edwards," he said.

"Justin. This is Special Agent Ryan Sharpe. Whatever you do, do not interrupt me, or say a word unless I tell you to. Are you with Jessica

Petrovich? Answer yes or no, and do not look at her."

**

Jessica watched Edwards from the desk as she poured a glass of wine intended for Edwards. Actually, both glasses were for the FBI agent, along with the rest of the bottle, which she planned to force him to chug. Edwards examined the phone and appeared to debate whether to answer it. She placed the bottle back in the cooling bucket, which distracted Edwards and caused him to turn his head in the direction of the icy sound. She listened carefully as he answered the phone and could sense a shift in his posture. When he stiffly answered, "Yes," and didn't say another word, her hand flashed under her blouse and pulled a sleek knife from the front pocket of her jeans. She pounced as Agent Edwards tried to draw his gun.

Jessica crossed the ten foot divide before Edwards cleared the pistol from his holster, and put him in a chokehold, squeezing the inside of her forearm harshly against his neck. She pulled his head back and pressed the tip of the knife against the right side of his throat.

"I think you know what could happen next," she whispered into his ear, "drop your gun and cell phone."

He hesitated, and Jessica pushed the razor sharp blade a millimeter further and anchored her grip across the top of his throat, under his chin. She heard both items hit the carpeted floor a few seconds later and detected a faint ammonia smell. The cell phone continued to squawk from the floor, and she could hear someone repeating Edward's name. She turned his body ninety degrees to the left and stomped on the cell phone repeatedly, until she was sure it was completely destroyed.

Jessica glanced into the mirror and saw a dark stain spreading down Edward's pants, originating from his groin, which was a welcome sight compared to the numerous erections she had been forced to ignore most of the night. She barely noticed the steady trickle of blood flowing down his neck and saturating the collar of his blue dress shirt. She yanked him out of the mirror's view and turned him to face the chilled bottle of wine.

"Try anything, and I'll cut you open so badly they'll have no choice but to bury you in a closed coffin. Understood?" Jessica said.

"Please don't kill me. I won't say a..."

She pulled hard against his neck, right under his chin, and he choked on the words. His hands uselessly grabbed at her rock-solid grip, and she pushed the knife another millimeter into his neck. His hands went still.

"Do not resist, and do not say a word unless I ask. Understood?" she hissed and loosened her grip.

"Yes."

"That's better," she replied and loosened her grip a little further.

"Did you think you were going to fuck me all night on that bed?"

Silence. She moved the knife against his neck, but not enough to draw blood.

"I...I don't know what I was..."

"You like to take advantage of women? Degrade them, make them feel vulnerable, wrecked...then fuck them like trash? Is that what you like?" she whispered in his ear.

"No. No. I really..."

"Are you a rapist?" she whispered and ran the blade up and down his neck, catching his stubble.

"No," he pleaded.

"Date rapist? Bet we find some Gamma in your piss-soaked pockets," she said.

"Who are you?" he asked weakly, as if he knew this question would cost him.

"Didn't they tell you?"

"No," he said.

"What exactly *did* they tell you?" she asked, and he didn't answer.

She removed the knife from his neck, which caused Edwards to tense. At this point, any movement near his neck caused him to flinch. She quickly placed the knife as far as she could between his legs and pushed upward through the wet fabric of his pants against his testicles, which appeared to have retracted as far as possible into his abdomen.

"I'm going to slash this knife upward and back if you don't start talking. I imagine that crime scene photo would end up in every Power Point lecture, given by every crime scene investigator across the country. Might go international. Are you looking to get famous tonight?" she said, adding a little more pressure to the knife against his crotch.

Edwards sucked small, careful breaths through his teeth. "They...they just told me that you were highly dangerous...and..." he hesitated.

"And what," she breathed into his neck.

"That...that I was to hold you here at gunpoint and use lethal force if you tried to escape," he admitted.

"Do they know about this room?"

"Yes. You don't have much time before—"

She pulled back on her left forearm and stepped back, pulling Edwards further off balance and angling the knife forward, where a backward slash would cut deep into his now completely limp manhood.

"I'll give you one shot at this, and I'm going to help you out. I know your team is staying at the Econo Lodge by the mall. I figured a pretentious little prick like yourself would not be content with shitty government-authorized lodging, so I think this room is off the books. Am I right?" she said.

"Yes, but they'll trace the cell pho—"

"We both know that's not happening. Your phone is dead, and if you don't follow my explicit directions, you'll be dead too. I'll need the password to the laptop in your briefcase," she said. Edwards didn't respond.

"Password, please. Don't make me ask again," she said.

He whispered something that she heard, but needed to hear again for her own amusement.

"I'm sorry, I didn't catch that," she said.

"Ladykiller69," he grunted.

"No shit. Are you wearing a backup piece?" she barked.

"No."

She used her right foot to feel around his ankles for a holster. In a swift motion, she withdrew the knife, leaving his undercarriage intact, and released him, following with a solid kick in the lower back. Edwards hit the bed and crumpled over the corner, still in shock. He laid there, his chest pressed against the down comforter and his legs dangling uselessly over the side onto the floor. Jessica picked up his service pistol and pointed it at him.

"No time for a nap, Justin, dear. We have some partying to do. Stand up and strip," she said, emphasizing the point by aiming the pistol at his groin.

"What?" He slowly stood.

She delivered a sharp kick to his kidneys, which caused his back to arch and straightened him up quickly.

"I don't have all night. You wanted to get naked with me, right? Now's your chance. We have some partying to do," she said.

She could see tears welling up in his eyes as he unbuttoned his shirt.

"You didn't have enough to drink?"

"I don't drink on the job unless I have to. I do love martinis though," she said, watching him remove his blue dress shirt, along with his undershirt.

Edwards took good care of himself. He had a slightly chiseled body, with little body fat, clearly the product of endless high repetition, low weight circuit training, combined with a daily thirty-minute fat-burning stint on a treadmill. He avoided her piercing stare, occasionally meeting her glance with a combination of humiliation and anger.

"I told the bartender that a late dinner was your idea of a job interview for a promotion. He substituted water for vodka and refused to take a nice tip for helping a poor lady out. Now that was a true gentleman. I'd say you could take a few lessons from him, but I think your hatred of women runs too deep. Time for the pants," she said.

"Why do you want me naked?" he asked.

"Because we're going to party, Justin. I don't like to waste good wine, and I must admit, a 2003 St. Francis Chardonnay is a nice choice," she said and pointed at the bottle with the gun.

He glanced at her, barely meeting her eyes as he dropped his pants and boxer shorts.

"Now what?" he said.

"Drink both of those glasses, and chug the rest of the bottle," she said, emphasizing her request with the pistol aimed at his head.

"What?"

"Drink up. The clock is ticking," she said and watched with satisfaction as he downed one of the drug-laced glasses of wine.

Justin Edwards is going to have a rough morning, she thought and cracked a thin smile.

Chapter Forty-Three

Special Agent Sharpe listened to the phone and finally spoke with a dejected voice.

"Thank you, D'Angelo. Let's keep each other posted," he said and closed his phone.

He turned to O'Reilly's workstation. She shook her head.

"Nothing from his cell phone, and his GPS signal is dead," she said.

"D'Angelo said all of the FBI hotel rooms were empty, and her office is clear. She's coordinating a search of hotels near the satellite office. He has to be in the Old Port section of Portland," he said.

"Why would he have a hotel room in the downtown area?" she asked.

"Who knows," he said.

He didn't plan to bring her up to speed on the nature of his phone conversations with Edwards. It had been a bad idea to share information with him in the first place, but Sharpe was desperate, and it sounded like Edwards might be able to extract some useful information out of her. Now Edwards was missing, and he had a bad feeling that the agent was dead. Sharpe had never cared for Edwards personally, but he had been a reasonably competent investigative agent and knew how to play the game within the Beltway.

Deep down inside, a part of him hoped Edwards was dead. Sharpe would have enough explaining to do tomorrow morning, without the added complication of why he unofficially sanctioned Edwards to press Jessica Petrovich, or whoever she was, with information that skirted the border of his CIS agreement. In the hands of a skillful prosecutor, he could wind up behind bars.

"This has turned into a complete disaster, and I'm starting to get the sinking feeling that we've been played. Played since last night. Nothing is what it seems to be, or should be," he said. His phone rang again.

"Mendoza. Any word from our agents? How are they doing?" Sharpe said.

"They're fine, sir. It was definitely the colonel. Calhoun and Harris said he walked in like everything was normal and just stabbed McKie in the neck. Then all hell broke loose. Forced Sergeant D'Onofrie at gunpoint to drag everyone into the back room, then hit him with the same neurotoxin. Farrington worked closely with D'Onofrie and Staff Sergeant Brodin for over two years. Turned on them like a viper."

"Was anything else taken?" Sharpe asked.

"The archives section wasn't breached, so it looks like all he took was the file. We found the last page of the fax in a pool of McKie's blood. Care to guess what it says?"

"That Munoz's specialty has something to do with infiltrating jails and police custody?"

"That pretty much sums it up," Mendoza said.

"Played."

"What was that, sir?"

"Played. We've been played all along, Mendoza. The murders, Munoz's capture, the Sanctum. Everything. And now Edwards is missing. I can't go into details on the phone, but he was with Jessica Petrovich."

"Jesus Christ," Mendoza whispered.

"Exactly. What's the CIA's angle on what happened?" Sharpe said.

"I wouldn't know. Keller bolted as soon as he regained consciousness."

"What! This is a federal investigation. How the fuck did he get out of the Pentagon?" he said, and several heads throughout the silent room looked in his direction.

"Someone high up at Langley convinced Pentagon security that Keller needed to make an immediate report, in person," Mendoza said.

"And you didn't stop him?"

"I have no authority to stop him. As a matter of fact, I have no authority in this building at all. This place is under lockdown, and I have been relieved of my weapon. Someone pulled serious strings to get Keller out of here," Mendoza said.

"And that reeks of bullshit. When did he leave?"

"Fifteen minutes ago," Mendoza said.

"All right. I need to take care of something. Keep me posted, Frank," Sharpe said.

"Will do, sir."

Sharpe set his phone down on a nearby desk and ran his hands through his matted brown hair, pausing to think for a moment. He briefly laughed at himself and turned to a young agent sitting at a desk in the communications section.

"Agent Fayad?" he said.

"Sir?" the agent said, swiveling his chair to face Sharpe.

"I need a cell phone GPS trace immediately," he said.

"Send me the number, and we'll activate the system. Should have it in a few minutes," he said.

"We already have the number on file. Randy Keller."

"Our CIA liaison?" Fayad said, with a skeptical look.

"That's it. We don't have time to notify Langley. Wake up Weber if you need help."

"I can take care of it, sir."

"Thanks, Fayad. Let me know as soon as you have a signal. O'Reilly, scramble a team of agents. Four from the task force, including yourself. Two cars. I have a surveillance job for you," he said.

O'Reilly's face perked up for the first time in several hours, despite the fact that she was rapidly approaching twenty-four hours on her feet.

Chapter Forty-Four

12:25 a.m.
Georgetown, Washington, D.C.

Keller got off the Metro at the Rosslyn Station and walked a few blocks over to North Lynn Avenue. He hailed a taxi, which drove him north over the Key Bridge and deposited him in front of a random bar along M Street in Georgetown. Still slightly disoriented, Keller paid his fare, leaving the cab driver surprised by the generous tip. To the driver and anyone on the street, Keller might have appeared slightly inebriated, which didn't draw any unwarranted attention on a Thursday night along M Street. Keller focused on his surroundings and took deep, slow breaths.

He was starting to feel better in the fresh air, despite the occasional wafts of tobacco and stale beer. He had fled the Pentagon in a hurry, not wanting to get caught in a bureaucratic prison for the next several hours. Berg's call had been convincing enough to get him out, and Keller was grateful for the favor. He had more data stored in his head and needed a brief respite to flush it out. He didn't have a headache or sore muscles, just a vague feeling that the gravity around his body had been slightly increased.

Keller spotted the street sign that would lead him deep into the quiet neighborhoods of Georgetown and to the safe house. He glanced at the traffic and found a break between cars large enough for him to cross safely.

**

Daniel Petrovich crouched, concealed in a long clump of bushes behind a white picket fence located diagonally across the street from the address provided by General Sanderson. He carried night vision equipment in his backpack, but the ambient lighting provided by the randomly placed streetlamps and the occasional porch light allowed him to see well enough with the naked eye through the well-trimmed bushes. Colonel Farrington sat in a similarly hidden position, behind a shoulder-height red brick wall topped with greenery, on the same side of the street, covering the approach from 33rd Street. Daniel kept his eye toward 34th.

The safe house was an unremarkable dark red brownstone, set between a white-painted brownstone to the right, and a brilliant yellow wooden building to the left. The two brownstones appeared to be attached, sharing a black wrought iron fence along the front and separated by a similar fence running inward through the short front yard. Petrovich could see a small sign next to the target entrance, but couldn't read it from this distance. Neither of the men passed close enough on their approach to get a good look at the sign.

They had arrived on O Street at 11:30, to begin what could potentially be a long evening for both of them. One at a time, they walked onto O Street from opposite ends and slipped into their concealed locations without a sound. Satisfied that neither of them had tripped an alarm or raised any attention, they settled in to observe the street, which had been nearly devoid of passenger traffic since their arrival. They watched a drunken couple stumble off 34th Street and stop to grope each other for several minutes within ten feet of Petrovich, until the college students decided to take their activities indoors just a few houses down from the target house. They would wait until Keller arrived, if he showed, which Farrington estimated could happen at any time after midnight, based on the neurotoxin profile.

Parker sat in General Sanderson's Toyota 4Runner a few blocks away, in one of the few legal parking spaces he could find at this time of night big enough to accommodate the SUV. He would spring into action once their quarry entered the safe house. A few blocks closer to M Street, his area contained more activity, and he had settled into one of the back seats behind tinted glass to avoid unwanted attention by police patrols or concerned citizens. He closely monitored General Sanderson's direct frequency on one of his radios. The general would provide them early warning of law enforcement activity when O Street exploded and coordinate the sensitive timing of their mission. Petrovich would have less than two minutes to eliminate Keller and his handler. Anything beyond that would draw unacceptable law enforcement complications.

Petrovich shifted to his left knee and checked his weapon. He had opted to keep the MP-9 submachine gun, due to its easy concealment and effective suppressor. He had five spare magazines for the MP-9, each holding thirty rounds, attached to a light utility vest hidden under his dark blue nylon windbreaker. A compact semi-automatic pistol rested in a concealed holster near the small of his back, with three spare magazines stuffed into the front pockets of his jeans.

Earlier, he removed a pouch carrying several grenades of different varieties from his backpack and attached it to the front right side of his belt. Daniel felt confident that he carried enough firepower to overcome any resistance offered by two CIA desk types. He loosened his throat microphone slightly, bothered by the constrictive feeling of the communications rig, but impressed by its sleek design and technological advantage. He would not have to fumble with a microphone headset, which tended to be a problem in the heat of battle.

Chapter Forty-Five

"We're tracking him, sir. He's moving slowly…probably on foot, down 33rd St, NW, between N and O," Agent Fayad said.

"I knew it. I bet there's a CIA safe house down there. Keep tracking him," he said and whipped out his phone to make a call.

"O'Reilly, where are you?" he spoke into the cell.

"Sir, we're on our way down to the parking garage. We grabbed some surveillance gear. We should be on the road in five to ten minutes," she said.

"Head to Georgetown. 34th Street off of M. I'll give you instructions when you get there."

"Understood, sir."

Petrovich's earpiece came to life.

"Movement. One pedestrian from the south, exiting 33rd. Caucasian male. Stand by, I can't make an ID yet."

Petrovich acquired the man with his own eyes and squinted for details. The area was still too dark for a positive identification. It didn't really matter. If the man turned into the target building, they would pounce.

"Can you ID him?" Petrovich said into the microphone attached to his head set.

"Negative. Not enough light. Switching to night vision," Farrington said.

"Don't bother. We'll wait and see what he does," Petrovich said, readying himself to hop through the bushes and over the waist-high fence.

The figure moved briskly down the opposite side of the street and pulled out what looked like a cell phone to Petrovich. Then everything moved too quickly. The man sped toward the gate and was at the front door before Farrington hissed something over the radio circuit. Daniel heard the gate squeak on its hinges and made a split second calculation. They would never make it across in time to grab Keller. He had expected more of a delay entering the safe house. A new plan formed in the same span of time, and he told Farrington to hold his position. Farrington had to ease himself back down the brick wall he had just scaled like a cat, careful not to make a sound.

Petrovich's instincts were right, and Keller entered the brownstone's vestibule as soon as he arrived at the door. Someone had opened it for him, which meant that a camera monitored the front door. If they had made a run to grab Keller, they would have failed, giving the building's occupants enough warning to fortify against an assault. They would have to do this the hard way, which was Petrovich's specialty.

Daniel removed a black ski mask from his backpack and pulled it tight over his head, adjusting the eye holes. He issued orders for a forced entry and set his watch to chronograph. They would have a very limited amount of time once the explosive charges detonated, turning this quiet neighborhood into downtown Fallujah. Farrington would cover the street from the brownstone's entrance and serve as backup if Petrovich needed help inside. Parker would position his car one block over, ready to pick them up on whichever entrance to O Street wasn't blocked by police.

He waited roughly one minute, then gave the signal to move. He saw Farrington sprinting across the street ahead of him and briefly gave the man credit for his physical capabilities. Petrovich just hoped the colonel would hold up under the stress of the next few minutes. He reached the iron gate first and swung it open for Farrington, who entered and took a position on the steps, away from the door and out of Daniel's way.

**

Claire McHatten was a light sleeper, especially when agents occupied her "house" after hours. She never asked questions and never expressed her opinion about certain senior CIA officials' specific "use" of the house late in the evening, but she was glad that the wall separating her brownstone from the safe house was both sound and blast proof. She didn't care to hear the noises that might emanate from some of the female "guests" that frequented the location.

Tonight she didn't have to worry about women of questionable repute entering her house, but she still slept uneasily with Berg next door. Langley wasn't that far away, and she was convinced that he was up to something. Or maybe not. Spies were spies, and even when they no longer served in the field, they liked to play the game. She could certainly understand how they felt, though most of this emotion had been washed out of her system over the past twenty years, sitting behind her desk next door.

She had served with her husband, Frederick, in Eastern Europe for eight years at the height of the Cold War, stationed for most of it at the U.S. Embassy in Warsaw, Poland. They ran a highly successful husband and wife operation until Frederick was brutally murdered in 1985, on a train destined for Czechoslovakia. He had left Poland to meet with CIA operatives in Prague, who had just begun to foster and support a grassroots solidarity movement. Claire and her husband were at least a year ahead of their CIA counterparts in Czechoslovakia, and they had planned to discuss ways to accelerate the Czech movement. One of the countries' governments, if not both, didn't want the meeting to take place. Her husband was killed during a prolonged stop at the Czech/Polish border, and neither country accepted responsibility for investigating the murder.

Devastated, Claire returned to the U.S., unsure of how to proceed with her life. She accepted what was supposed to be a temporary position at the safe house, but settled into a quiet life and never left. After ten years on the job, the CIA signed an open-ended lease to have her live in the attached brownstone. Ten years after that, she was an enigma to most agents who crossed the safe house's threshold. Most agents figured she was a stuffy, miserable wife for some aging member of the wealthy Georgetown elite. Few would ever suspect that she was the building's guardian and keeper twenty-four hours a day, 365 days a year.

She was specially attuned to her "house," and when the gate squeaked the first time, she figured it was Keller and eased back to sleep. When the gate squeaked again, a few minutes later, Claire became a little more alert. In fact, she found her arms covered in goosebumps. Something wasn't right. She glanced at the digital clock on her nightstand. 12:35. She never saw 12:36. A low-pitched alarm sounded throughout her home, and she sprang into action.

**

Petrovich focused on the door as thermite charges burned through the locks and hinges at 2,500 Celsius.. Thermite was overkill for this door, but he didn't want to waste any time. The charges burned for five seconds, turning any solid metal components in their path into molten liquid. Daniel kicked the solid wood into the vestibule and started the chronometer on his watch.

He immediately set to work on the second door, placing small plastic explosive charges where he would logically expect to find hinges. He set a larger charge around the door handle and attached wires to each package. The wires led to a small black device that he dug out of the backpack, which lay open at his feet. He grabbed the backpack and evacuated the porch.

"Move," he whispered and pushed Farrington off the porch.

Huddled against the front of the house with Farrington, Daniel rapidly squeezed the "clacker," catapulting the serene, multi-million dollar neighborhood into a war zone. The simultaneous detonation of four compact charges blew wood and brick fragments onto the parked cars in front of the house and activated every car alarm within a one-block radius. It also removed the door cleanly. Daniel mounted the stairs and rushed through the dust and floating debris, and saw that the twisted door had simply fallen inward.

Petrovich sprinted through the heated smoke, searching for the front desk. He found it at the back of the room. His attention was drawn to a single burning stack of yellow Post-Its in the center of the desk. Everything else had been knocked clear by the concussion wave generated by the C-4, scattered in disarray on the floor behind the desk. Petrovich noticed several other small fires throughout the room, but they didn't concern him. He should be out of this structure before any of the fires become consequential. He methodically searched the back of the desk and found what he was seeking. A bank of three hidden buttons. Now he was really in business.

Daniel reached into the black military style pouch attached to his belt and removed a "special." He didn't need to visually confirm what he held. He knew the feel of the three types of grenades in the pouch and hoped he wouldn't have to search for the round, smooth type. He pulled the pin on the grenade and released the trigger handle. In one expertly timed motion, he pressed all three buttons and sprinted to the staircase, casually tossing the grenade with his left hand, in an arch toward the door at the top of the stairs. His timing was perfect.

**

Berg slowly got up from one of the dining room chairs when the alarm sounded. Keller had just arrived and was drinking a glass of water across from him at the dining table. He thought Keller would need more than a glass of water after the attack on the Pentagon, but didn't want to risk an interaction with the toxin that was likely still present in his body. He couldn't believe the raw nerve of the Black Flag group.

Keller stared off at an original piece of Revolutionary War art hanging on the wall, as Berg glanced at him, slightly annoyed. Keller must have left one of the doors ajar. He couldn't really blame the agent, but now he'd probably have to listen to one of Ms. Claire's lectures about security. He begrudgingly walked toward the hallway door when the entire building seemed to shake on its foundation and the lights flickered, causing both of them to sprint into the hallway. Neither of them was armed.

"Keller, check the front windows. I'll call—"

"First priority is securing this door!" a female voice screamed from the front of the hallway.

Claire appeared from the conference room doorway holding two weapons, a semi-automatic shotgun fitted with an ammunition drum and an MP-5 submachine gun. She tossed the MP-5 and two spare magazines at Keller, who was already sprinting toward the door leading to the stairway. The door buzzed before Berg could move.

"Help me with the door!" she screamed, just as Berg was knocked off his feet by another blast.

**

The grenade sailed up the staircase in a perfect trajectory and detonated less than one foot from the door. The "special" was a unique device used to achieve maximum distraction and confusion during a hostage rescue operation. It would first send a concussive shockwave in every direction, followed immediately by a two-millisecond-delayed flash of blinding light. All of this was topped off by a controversial third stage. A small white phosphorous charge simultaneously exploded with the flash, sending specks of smoldering material in a spectacular shower throughout a fifteen-foot radius. The pieces of white phosphorous were no larger than a grain of rice, but they ignited whatever they touched, and even the most steadfast opponent couldn't ignore the fact that they were on fire.

In this case, the shock wave created by the initial blast flung the door wide open, knocking Keller flat on his back and saving him from a direct shower of white phosphorus. Still, his clothes caught fire in several places. Blinded by the flash, he was temporarily unaware that his custom fit suit had ignited.

Claire was jammed back against the conference room doorframe, but was spared the effects of the flash and white phosphorous that had been funneled straight through the open door. She quickly regained her senses and leveled the shotgun at the opening, preparing herself to fire down the staircase at the slightest sound.

Berg remained lying on the floor, stunned by the blinding flash and concussion. Still far enough away from the door when the grenade exploded, he didn't get hit with any of the burning fragments. Hazy vision returned, and he saw the open doorway to the stairwell, which caused him to panic and scramble out of sight into the kitchen doorway.

**

A shower of smoking fragments hit the bottom of the staircase a few feet from Daniel Petrovich. Some bounced off the walls and bannister, hissing, while others immediately adhered to whatever they first struck. Regardless of how the pieces of white phosphorous behaved in those first few seconds, without fail, they all ignited their final resting place. Daniel rounded the corner of the burning bannister, leveling the MP-9 toward the open door at the top of the staircase, aiming down the sight as he took the stairs in a rapid, controlled manner. He kept his focus on the hazy opening. If he had glanced around, or expanded his field of vision, he might have been slightly unnerved to realize that the entire staircase was tightly sprinkled with over a hundred tiny, dancing fires. Growing fires. For now, all he registered was a growing sensation of heat.

He'd reached a point halfway up the stairs when he heard a female voice yell a command.

"Get Keller out of there! I'll cover the staircase."

He processed the possibilities and continued up the stairs. Anyone who appeared at the top of the stairs would be killed immediately. Barely a second after he heard the brusque voice, he saw a shotgun barrel appear from the right side of the door. By the orientation of the gun, he could tell that it was braced straight against someone's shoulder and that his or her head should appear...now. Through the thickening smoke, he saw the faintest trace of a head appear at the door frame and fired a quick, tightly-aimed burst where he knew the rest of the head would emerge within a fraction of a second.

**

Claire watched Berg sprint over to Keller and decided it was time to earn the paycheck she had been collecting for nearly twenty years. She wasn't afraid to face down the enemy at the bottom of the stairs, but she did have some concern that another grenade like the last one might explode in her face. She could see Keller's clothes starting to catch fire and could not imagine the horror of taking a burst of those fragments to her face. Because of this trepidation, and the fact that she didn't move as fast as she did as a field agent in her thirties, she hesitated at the doorway.

She heard a sudden snap as she started to move into the opening, and the wooden frame directly in front of her face splintered. She knew what had happened before the bullets' sonic trail changed the air pressure around her eye cavities. One of the bullets had missed hitting the far side of her face by millimeters. Though the threat of these bullets had long passed, Claire reacted instinctively and pulled her body back. Still, she persisted in her mission and forced the shotgun around the corner, squeezing the trigger until she thought her hand might break. Eight deafening blasts roared into the opening.

**

Daniel knew he had miscalculated the burst as soon as he pulled the trigger. If the head had followed at the same speed of the shotgun, he would be able to charge the top of the stairs unopposed. Instead, two hands jammed the shotgun into the doorway opening, which meant immediate trouble. He lurched backward and managed to throw himself through the burning bannister, crashing down on top of a smoldering antique table and chair—

chased by shotgun blasts.

A sharp, spiking pain struck his lower ribcage, when his body crushed the table. In complete agony, Daniel rolled onto his back, checking his chest for blood. Finding nothing, he concluded that he'd probably broken several ribs in the fall. He could deal with that—fore now. He gripped the MP-9 and pushed off the floor; his knee nearly failing as he stood. If his knee was trashed, they were out of business. He put some more weight on the knee, relieved to find that it supported him without too much protest.

Farrington crouched in the vestibule and assessed the situation. He was dressed in dark blue jeans and black turtleneck sweater, holding a shortened M-4 assault carbine fitted with a red-dot sighting system. He looked deadly serious and well practiced in this type of work, though Daniel doubted the man had ever kicked a door down in his life.

"Need help?" Farrington said, aiming his rifle up the stairs.

"Negative. Keep an eye outside," he replied.

"Out in sixty seconds," Farrington said, and Daniel realized he would have to escalate his use of force to get the job done.

He took two grenades out of his pouch and walked over to the staircase. One was a "special" and the other had a smooth, round surface. Daniel was done fucking around with this situation. He laid the submachine gun on the first step and pulled the pin on both grenades. The M67 frag grenade sailed through the now impenetrable smoke and hit the floor somewhere beyond the door, followed by panicked screams. He'd add the "special" to their misery, as soon as the frag detonated.

**

Claire's shotgun heroics bought the CIA agents fifteen seconds to regroup and get Keller out of the hallway. Berg pulled Keller back to the kitchen entrance and started to rip the burning pants from his body, but Keller had regained his senses enough to take care of himself. Berg turned his attention back to the burning doorway and braced the German made MP-5 submachine gun against the kitchen doorframe, tucking his exposed elbow tight against his body and shifting his head as far behind the frame as possible while still sighting down the barrel of the gun. He presented little for his attacker to hit and braced himself for the inevitable assault. Just as he settled into the frame, a grenade hit the hardwood floor in the hallway and rolled toward Berg.

"Grenade!" he screamed and stumbled backward into Keller, knocking them both across the small kitchen floor.

The grenade exploded several feet from the kitchen entrance, cratering the floor and dislodging drywall, instantly filling the hallway with smoke and fine dust. Small pieces of the grenade's metallic outer shell splintered wood, shredded light fixtures and ripped through the walls.

Berg crawled desperately over Keller to get back into position in the doorway, which had been shattered by the direct blast. He could see damage from several fragments embedded in the stainless steel refrigerator standing next to the doorway and realized that his jumbled panic had been justified. Some of the fragments had traveled through two sets of drywall to reach the refrigerator and would have likely instead found a home in Berg's body if he had stayed.

Just as Berg slammed himself against the loose doorframe to stare down the sights of his weapon, he heard another metallic object strike the floor somewhere in the thick haze ahead of him. He didn't have time to retreat, but luckily for him, the sharp concussion of the "special" didn't send steel fragments through his internal organs. Instead, it showered the entire hallway with more white phosphorous and blinded him for several seconds. Out of desperation and panic, he blindly fired two quick bursts in the direction of the doorway, which almost hit Claire as she sprinted down the hallway for a better position.

**

Daniel mounted the stairs quickly, and his eyes caught rapid movement as his weapon's barrel cleared the top of the stairs. He fired a quick burst at a fast-moving shadow and heard a scream, but couldn't concentrate fire on the target. Several small-caliber bullets snapped overhead, causing him to take cover behind the top of the staircase. His knee buckle as he crouched, but he pushed forward knowing that he would catch fire if he remained in place. Taking a massive risk, he sprinted up the stairs and threw himself into the first room to his right, fully expecting to collide with one of the CIA agents.

He rolled and swept the room, finding it clear of threats. Oddly, a small doorway in the back wall of the room appeared to extend into the adjacent townhouse. The opening would normally be concealed behind a massive dark wooden china cabinet, which now swung to the side on reinforced hinges. It made sense. The whole building would be owned by the CIA. He hated turning his back on the secret door, but didn't really have any choice. Instead, he yanked the pin on another fragmentation grenade and hurled it through the opening. The explosion rocked the townhouse, belching dust and wood fragments into the room.

Satisfied that nobody would surprise him from behind, he inched toward the hallway, pulling another fragmentation grenade out of the pouch. The area around the hallway door splintered from the impact of several shotgun shells and 9mm bullets, forcing Daniel back into the room.

He couldn't believe the woman with the shotgun was still fighting. He had definitely hit her from the top of the stairs, and she was still working the shotgun like a professional. He couldn't advance with that kind of accurate firepower bearing down on him, and he'd already been in the house for more than a minute. His earpiece remained silent, which was a good sign, but he couldn't imagine the good fortune lasting much longer.

He pulled the pin on his last frag and tossed it toward the end of the hallway, where it detonated amidst a bloodcurdling scream. Satisfied that the threat was neutralized, he emerged from the room into the dimly lit, smoke-filled hallway, aiming right down the wall toward the nearest doorframe. He could see something moving in there, and if it moved another inch into the hallway, he'd be in business.

A sudden movement toward the back of the hallway caught his attention, as the words "cover me!" reached his ears. He pulled the MP-9 far enough away from the nearby doorframe to fire at the target sprinting across the obscured passage. The figure tumbled into an open doorway on the other side of the hallway, leaving Daniel unsure if his bullets struck home. He shifted his submachine gun back to the nearest doorway, just in time to see the front sight of an MP-5 emerge—rapidly spitting bullets.

Daniel pressed himself against the burning wall and fired a hastily aimed burst at the barely visible target in front of him. He considered moving forward, but the MP-5 continued to rattle, forcing him back into the conference room. The shooter didn't expose his head far enough to fire accurately, but Daniel couldn't risk the chance that this might change. He was once again stuck in place, running out of time.

A few seconds later, the shotgun rejoined the fight, pounding the conference room doorway with "double ought" buckshot, removing all hope of advancing down the hallway. One of the other agents had taken over the shotgun. He glanced at the opening in the wall and wondered who had run through there to join the fight. Whoever it was deserved a medal.

His earpiece crackled with Parker's voice. "Status report."

"Send updated timeline," Petrovich replied.

"Thirty seconds. Police en route. Can you still accomplish the mission?"

Daniel processed all of his options within the span of a millisecond and realized that he needed more time, unless…he was willing to endure a shower of white phosphorous. He could probably land one of the grenades in the closer opening and send the submachine gunner running, followed by another grenade toward the shooter at the end of the hallway. When they scrambled to shield themselves, he would charge forward and take his chances with the firestorm of burning fragments. His other option was to abandon the mission and retreat through the passage in the conference room wall. He could be out on the street in less than fifteen seconds. If he could make it to the staircase next to him, he would be out of the house even faster.

The concept of retreat didn't sit well with Petrovich. He had to put an end to this tonight. Jessica was waiting and had already endured enough over the last twenty-four hours. They desperately needed a fresh start, and failing one of Sanderson's missions wouldn't help. Apparently, everyone had succeeded in their role over the past few days, except for him.

"Affirmative," he said and pulled one of the "special" grenades from his bag.

He had just placed his index finger through the firing pin, when Parker's voice broke through his focus again.

"Change of plans. The general wants you to throw your cell phone to one of the agents. Someone named Karl Berg. Do it immediately."

"What?"

"Just do it. We're out of time."

"Understood."

He took his cellphone out of a pouch on his nylon vest, edged his head out of the conference room doorway, and examined the scene. The upstairs hallway had taken on a surreal hellish look, with several dozen small fires burning on every surface, including the ceiling. The fires burned a dark orange color through the smoke and drywall dust, illuminating the darkened area with dancing, flickering light. He found it strangely beautiful, but didn't linger to admire it. He tossed the cellphone right into the kitchen doorway opening, hearing it clatter on the floor, followed by the sound of furniture crashing, as someone scrambled in fear. Strangely, the shotgun did not erupt. Instead, his cellphone rang, and Daniel yelled into the haze.

"Answer the phone! I have enough C-4 here to take out this entire floor. Do it now!"

He heard some shuffling from the kitchen, and the doorway exploded from the force of several shotgun blasts. He pulled out the last "special" grenade and prepared to execute his final, desperate plan. His watch showed the total elapsed time in the house to be one minute and fifty-two seconds.

**

Berg shifted the submachine gun into his left hand and kept it trained on the smoking inferno past the open doorway. With his right arm extended, he snatched the ringing phone from the floor, half expecting to be shot through the wall. Retreating into the relative safety of the kitchen, he placed the phone to his ear.

"Hello?" he said, fully prepared for the possibility that the call was a distraction.

A female voice answered. "Karl? Is that you?"

"Who is this?" Berg said, the voice triggering hazy memories.

"Karl, this is Seraph. I need you to listen closely."

"Nicole? How is this…"

"I don't have time to explain, but right now you must listen. I have General Sanderson on the line, and he has a proposition for you."

"I don't need a deal to save my life."

"Yes, you do. Daniel Petrovich, my husband, is in your safe house."

"What? Jesus, Nicole. What did you do?"

"I'll explain later. The general has a mutual proposition. There's very little time."

"Put him on," Berg said and listened to the general's proposal.

Fifteen seconds later, Berg disconnected the call and called out to Keller, "Keller! Hold your fire!" He received no response.

**

Petrovich heard Berg order Keller to stop firing, followed by Parker in his headset.

"Withdraw from the house immediately. The agents are no longer a threat. Move fast. Police units are ten seconds out."

"Understood. On my way," he said and dashed through the conflagration in the hallway.

He nearly took the entire staircase in a single leap that sent a shockwave of pain up his leg from the damaged knee and caused one of his fractured ribs to fully break. For a brief moment, he thought he might have been shot leaving the room. Farrington burst into the house from his position in the shattered vestibule and pulled him to his feet.

"We need to get the fuck off this street," he said, yanking Daniel through the door and into the fresh air.

Just as they cleared the vestibule, police cars screeched to a halt on 34th Street, blocking their exit from O Street on that side.

"Coming up on 33rd Street intersection. Police units just passed N Street on 34th. You need to be there now. I see police lights," Parker said.

Chapter Forty-Six

12:35 a.m.
Georgetown, Washington, D.C.

Special Agent O'Reilly's small caravan of agents drove down 33rd Street, passing Prospect and approaching N Street. Sharpe had given her the suspected address on O Street, and they were to approach cautiously, verify the location, and set up car surveillance to confirm Keller's presence. Sharpe had confided in O'Reilly. He didn't put the CIA past being involved in today's fiasco and found it oddly suspicious that Keller had fled the Pentagon to hide in some undisclosed location hidden deep in the heart of Georgetown. To him, it didn't add up to anything but trouble for the FBI, and Sharpe wasn't taking any chances. Tomorrow, he would have to explain a lot of things to his superiors, and he might need to draw a little attention away from the task force. A possible CIA mole in his group was a great distraction.

As her car passed N Street, she noticed several things out of place at once. First, she saw a dark SUV stopped in the middle of the next intersection, and then police lights suddenly appeared in her rearview mirror, but no sirens sounded. Strangely, she also saw police lights dancing on the sides of some of the structures deeper into O Street, which couldn't be cast by the cars behind her. As her car approached the SUV, more of O Street came into focus, and she grabbed her car's radio to contact task force headquarters. She dropped the radio when she saw two masked men running toward the black SUV. One of them was limping, and they were both carrying military-style weapons.

"Stop the car!" she screamed, and the tires immediately screeched to a halt.

She bailed out of the car and ran toward the vehicles behind her, holding her FBI badge extended in one hand and her pistol in the other. Police cars skidded and stopped, as confused officers jumped out.

"FBI! Take cover!"

O'Reilly didn't want to take a bullet from a Washington, D.C., police weapon, so she held the badge high with her left hand. Instead, she caught a 5.56mm round from Farrington's rifle, which tore through her forearm muscle and skipped off the bone, passing straight through her raised arm. She stood there in shock, with the arm still raised, as her badge toppled down the length of her arm, and twenty-nine more 5.56mm bullets poured over the vehicles, miraculously failing to hit any of the agents or police officers. O'Reilly, still on her feet, whirled around with her Glock and fired on the men nearing the SUV. A few of the agents' service pistols joined her own weapon, and she saw the effects of their bullets shatter the back window of the 4Runner before a D.C. police officer tackled her to the ground.

Another burst of automatic weapons fire tore into their cars, shattering windows, puncturing metal and connecting with flesh. Screams punctuated the echoes of gunfire, and O'Reilly leaned her head back to see one of her agents sitting with his back against the side of a car holding his right shoulder. Blood spurted through his fingers onto his bulletproof vest. Under the car, she saw another agent hit the street pavement with a sick thud. A police officer dashed past her and started to pull the bleeding agent back when the next fusillade erupted.

**

Parker yelled at them through the open driver's side door, but Daniel couldn't hear over the gunfire. Farrington's first warning burst at the nearby police cars stirred up a hornet's nest of return fire, and bullets continued to crack past Petrovich, as he limped toward the SUV. From a position along the rear driver's side of the 4Runner, Farrington calmly fired a second, well-aimed burst of fire into the gaggle of police vehicles bottlenecked on 33rd Street. His second, shorter burst connected with at least two of the officers and dropped them to the pavement.

As the truck window next to him shattered, Farrington shifted his rifle toward the police officers advancing through the O Street neighborhood and emptied the rest of his magazine in controlled bursts, firing above the lead officers. Empty shells from Farrington's rifle pelted Daniel as he reached the SUV, causing him to stop and fire his freshly reloaded MP-9 in the direction of the officers on 33rd, who appeared to be regrouping in the absence of Farrington's automatic fusillade. Aiming high above their heads, Daniel fired with the hope of discouraging any further bravery and avoiding police casualties.

The volume of fire from police officers on 33rd Street nearly stopped altogether, and Petrovich jumped into the back seat of the car, moving to the far side of the rear bench seat. Farrington followed, reloading his weapon and immediately began firing out of the missing rear window. Parker accelerated the SUV down 33rd, and Petrovich jammed his way into the front passenger seat to provide firepower forward of the vehicle if necessary. Pain fired through his entire chest when he climbed over the seat and jammed the headrest into his ribs. He settled into the seat, taking a few seconds to recover from the blinding agony that brought him close to a blackout. He reloaded the MP-9 with a new magazine from his vest and lowered his window. They drove in silence for several seconds, surprised to meet no resistance as they approached Wisconsin Avenue.

"Fuck!" Parker yelled, as the intersection of Q Street and 33rd filled with police cars and flashing blue lights.

Parker didn't have much time to react, and most drivers would instinctively slam on the brakes, effectively disabling their own vehicle for the police. To Daniel's surprise, Parker yanked the car left without slowing and somehow squeezed it between a signal light post and a small tree. Daniel was showered with small pieces of plastic and glass when the passenger side mirror disintegrated upon impact with the signal post. Parker's side of the vehicle slid along a red brick property wall, exploding the side mirror and catching the rear bumper of the SUV.

The 4Runner was thrown out into the street, sideswiping the rearmost police car and knocking the cruiser into a parked car on the other side of Q Street, where it blocked the cramped Georgetown street. Daniel heard several gunshots as Parker steadied the SUV, which accelerated down Q Street, structurally undamaged after miraculously sailing through a cramped city corner at over 50 miles per hour. Farrington fired three extended bursts with his assault rifle down the street at the maneuvering police cars, showering the SUV's cab with spent brass.

Petrovich had been tossed around the front seat like a rag doll, but beyond a few additional bruises and the growing pain around his lower ribcage, he was fine. He turned in his seat immediately, aiming his gun toward the rapidly shrinking police cars at the intersection. He knew it would take them time to bypass the disabled police vehicle blocking the road. Farrington remained braced against the center of the second row bench seat, his assault rifle steadied against the middle headrest, aiming back toward the receding blue lights.

Colonel Farrington glanced back at Daniel with an impassionate face. "The mission failed," he uttered.

"We're fine," Parker said.

"The general said he made an arrangement that far exceeded his expectations for the day. He called your raid a success, and he doesn't say that kind of shit unless he means it." Parker turned right onto 35th Street, heading north.

He kept the SUV on the road for a few seconds, then killed the lights and turned left, departing the road and driving across a Georgetown University soccer field. He continued straight across the field as police cars turned right at the intersection, following their path, but continued past the soccer field, heading north on 35th Street.

"This should buy us a few minutes," Parker said.

"Let me guess. Your specialty is getaway car driver?" Daniel said.

"Aggressive Mobile Escape and Evasion," Parker replied.

"Things have changed since you graduated from the program. It's a little more sophisticated," Farrington said, still turned toward the back of the vehicle.

"Barely," Petrovich said and turned forward in his seat, putting on his seatbelt.

The 4Runner reached a small parking lot on the other side of the field, and more police cars raced north on 35th. Parker stopped momentarily, and they listened to the city's emergency services mobilize. Fire engine and police car sirens filled the late evening quiet with a sense of urgency.

"So, now what?" Petrovich asked.

"First priority is finding a new ride," Parker commented.

"I assume one of you knows how to hotwire a car?" Petrovich said.

"That's why we brought you along," Parker said.

"You're kidding me. Neither of you can jump a car? I'm going to have talk to Sanderson about his curriculum."

"I think he had something like that in mind. Full time," Parker said.

"I bet," Petrovich said.

They stepped out of the battered 4Runner into a humid, but temperate night on the Georgetown campus.

"You might want to take off that ski mask," Farrington said, grinning at him over the hood.

"Right. Probably not the best way to fit in on campus," Daniel replied, tossing the mask back into the truck through the open window.

They sanitized the SUV, taking all communications gear and armament. Farrington hefted a black backpack filled with spare ammunition magazines and explosives over his shoulder, while Parker stuffed Daniel's backpack with the remaining loose radios. Each of them removed their communications rig, detaching their throat microphones and earpieces, and stuffed them in Daniel's pack. They considered torching the SUV, which was standard operating procedure, but decided against drawing the unnecessary attention. The police wouldn't find anything useful in the vehicle beyond some DNA, which at this point didn't really matter.

Petrovich and Farrington would soon find themselves on the FBI's most wanted list, and Parker would join them in a specialized subcategory of known associates to General Terrence Sanderson. All of them would be permanently out of the country as soon as practical.

"I went to school here. We should cut south and head toward student housing. We can find a suitable vehicle down there," Farrington said, and they headed down the center of the parking lot toward some of the taller buildings.

"Georgetown? Not bad. Northwestern. What about you, Parker?"

"Cornell. Rich, you might want to tuck that M-4 away better."

Farrington did his best to conceal the assault rifle under a short brown jacket. The barrel still protruded a few inches from the bottom, but to the untrained eye, it would likely go unnoticed. Unfortunately, three serious-looking men in their mid to late thirties, strolling through an undergraduate college campus at one in the morning would likely result in a 911 call. They would need to find a new vehicle fast.

They walked among the trees between a large two-story gray building and tennis courts, headed toward a sparsely populated parking lot. Daniel did his best to keep up with the two men, despite a throbbing knee and the sidesplitting pain of two broken ribs. He would need medical attention soon, to make sure he had no internal bleeding from the fractured ribs. Right now, he focused on finding a car.

So far, they hadn't seen anyone on campus. A five-story residence hall loomed over the parking lot, and Daniel began to wonder if the campus might be an unlikely place to find a car this late in the spring. Most of the students would be finished with classes, and the campus should be relatively deserted. He didn't want to head back out onto the streets of Georgetown at the moment. The college campus felt insulated, though it wouldn't take the police long to discover their deception.

"Georgetown and Cornell? I feel like the underachiever. How did three smart guys get mixed up in this kind of shit?"

"Are you always this chatty?" Farrington said.

"Usually."

"Great, and we have a three-hour car ride ahead of us."

"Where to?" Daniel asked and stopped, bringing the rest of his entourage to a halt.

"South. We don't have time to stop and discuss this. We need to keep moving," Parker replied.

"I'll be headed in the opposite direction," Petrovich said, scanning the trees and benches around them.

"Sanderson wants to keep us all in one place and debrief us together. We still have a long way to go before we're in the clear," Parker said.

Daniel weighed his options and decided that he'd been through enough today on behalf of General Sanderson. He could join up with Sanderson's crew a little later, after he had time to discuss their predicament with Jessica. He had no idea where the rest of the day might lead them. He and Jessica might decide to follow a path separate from Sanderson. One thing was certain: he needed to get out of Sanderson's gravitational field to think straight. He'd been attached to invisible strings for the past two days and needed a chance to move around on his own. Mostly, he needed to see Jessica.

"I think this is where we part ways, for now. I need to take care of something a lot more important than Sanderson's timeline. I'll be in touch," he said and continued down the small hill along a red brick walkway toward the parking lot, keeping his eye on both of the general's operatives.

"Sanderson's orders were specific," Parker said, casting a furtive glance at Farrington.

Petrovich stopped and turned around to face them. "Did his orders include killing me?"

"No. Quite the opposite."

"Then the last thing either of you would want to do is point a gun at me. My orders don't include a restriction on killing either of you."

Petrovich turned around to continue down the path, talking over his shoulder. "Gentlemen, I'd be happy to help you jump a car, but after…"

Farrington never reached inside of his jacket for the M-4 rifle, an action that would have gotten him killed very quickly. He had, however, retrieved an item from his coat pocket as soon as Petrovich showed resistance to the general's rendezvous plan. The item resembled a small cylinder and spit a tight pattern of darts in Daniel's direction. Daniel heard an angry hiss and felt the darts strike his upper back, but couldn't react. He tried to grip the MP-9, but his hand didn't respond. Nothing did. He remained upright for a brief second before toppling forward, his head still over his shoulder. His sight dimmed, while his hearing faded. He heard Parker say something that enraged him.

"Daniel, don't worry about Jessica. Sanderson said she was safe and already on her way to meet us."

Everything faded for Daniel.

FADE TO BLACK

May 26, 2005

Chapter Forty-Seven

Jessica jogged through Central Parking toward the row and section Daniel had indicated in his first phone call. She held a key fob in her right hand and pressed the unlock button. After several tries, a dark sedan answered the call, flashing its rear brake lights in response to the fob's signal. At least getting out of Portland and finding the car hadn't been a problem for her. The rest of the day hadn't exactly gone as planned, but she improvised, and as always, she came out on top.

She had expected the FBI to come to her office, but as the day dragged onward, with no sign of the police or FBI, she began to worry that Daniel might have already been taken into custody. Two phone calls, one late in the afternoon and one in the early evening, assured her that Daniel was fine, but did little to relieve her anxiety.

General Sanderson had contacted her at her office before she left work to prepare her for the inevitable raid on her house. He also asked her to do him a favor, stressing that it would be in Daniel's best interest if she didn't mention his call. He spoke in nebulous terms and answered few of her detailed questions about Daniel, but his favor mirrored Daniel's suggested course of action, so Jessica played along.

Before Daniel left for D.C., they had worked out a rough plan for the day, which was the only reason she remained in town. Daniel had assured her earlier that within twenty-four hours, they would vanish from the grid together and start over. She trusted his assessment of the situation, and her own skills. One way or the other, she could get out of Portland, even if placed in full police custody.

Daniel called her as soon as she left work, on one of her untraceable cell phones, and convinced her that he was fine. He was waiting at a Marriott Hotel for further instructions and told her to follow her regular routine. She went for a run after that and spotted the police trucks behind the elementary school. She added an extra mile to her run in order to give the two stakeout cars on her street the impression that she hadn't been near the elementary school. She waited for what seemed like an eternity in the house, playing music and pretending to be busy.

The Portland Police Department's SWAT officers did an amazingly professional job moving in on the house undetected. The team's sudden entry truly startled her, and she reacted instinctively, almost putting her entire plan in jeopardy. Luckily for her, she had only been holding a spoon, preparing to pull a yogurt from the refrigerator. A knife or fork might have resulted in a bullet to the head. Agent Edwards arrived in time to break things up and keep her out of police custody, which was a blessing. She could tell by his first glance at her on the floor that he would be an easy target for later. She softened one of her looks in his direction, and Edwards did the rest. She didn't even have to suggest they leave the house. He was already forming that plan while she lay on the floor.

Once her job with Edwards was finished at the hotel, she grabbed the first taxi she could find and called Daniel, but the phone he had been using went to voicemail immediately. She tried the next number in the sequence she had been given, and it did the same thing. Her next call went to Sanderson, but he didn't answer either. She tried the same combination of numbers several times on the way to Logan Airport, with the same result. She wondered if it was possible that Sanderson's entire crew had been rolled up by the FBI. She doubted it.

At this point, she didn't see any option other than to proceed west on the Massachusetts Turnpike, toward West Virginia. Sanderson had given her a rendezvous point where he claimed Daniel would be waiting, and they could organize their departure from the United States. Sanderson promised to help them in any way possible. Daniel had wanted her to head south toward D.C., but given her complete inability to make contact with either of them, she decided to head in a safer direction.

She opened the trunk of the Toyota Camry and removed a black nylon gym bag, taking it into the car with her. She placed it on the passenger seat and zipped it open. At the top, a pistol sat under an envelope. She opened it and read Daniel's note:

"Sorry this caught up to us so quickly. We've both been through hell and back, so this is nothing. A small bump in the road. We'll be fine. If for some reason you lose

contact with me for more than twenty-four hours, find Sanderson. I don't completely trust him, but he will be your best option for setting up the arrangements to leave the country. Sunset drinks at the Santa Isabel. Love you always, Danny."

"Damn it," she whispered and leaned her head back against the headrest.

Jessica took a moment to clear her head, which didn't work. Her thoughts kept returning to their house and the pictures. She had to walk around the house for hours and wait for the inevitable, staring at the memories she couldn't take with her. This was almost more than she could endure, and she considered putting together a package to mail…somewhere. She didn't know where, but she wanted to save something. Anything. Daniel had warned her against doing this, and he had been right. Anything she did could have tipped off the police or FBI…though she doubted Edwards would have figured it out. She could have pulled a small framed picture out of her purse in the hotel room, and he wouldn't have put it together. His mind had strayed about as far as possible from the investigation at that point.

She wondered if they'd ever be safe in one place again. Maybe it didn't matter. Maybe it was a ridiculous dream to invest so much energy into creating a "normal" life. Nothing about either of them was normal, and this next time around, they wouldn't fall into the same mental trap. Still, a deep part of her yearned for everything in that house, and it comforted her in a way. It reminded her that she hadn't been completely ruined.

She folded the letter and stuffed it between the bag and the back of the seat. She removed the pistol, with suppressor already attached, and pulled the slide back far enough to check the chamber. She saw the brief reflection of brass and could tell that Danny had left the gun ready for immediate use. She tucked the pistol under the driver's seat for quick access, hoping she would never have to use it. She despised firearms. Dirty, unsophisticated instruments. She preferred the cold, razor-sharp blade of a knife, if circumstances allowed. She had taken to edged weapon training at The Farm like it was second nature, eventually pushing the CIA's best instructors to their limits.

Reaching into the bag again, she found several large Ziploc bags, each filled with a different style wig. She pushed through the bags, selecting a medium-length red one. Using the rearview mirror to adjust the hairpiece, she tied her own hair down in several tight knots and made a sudden transformation from black to dark red hair. A kit containing various contact lenses completed the one-minute change. Now she had red hair and green eyes. Once she located a suitable bathroom, she'd change clothing and get rid of Agent D'Angelo's hideous running shoes.

She had a lot of things to ditch along the way, including all of her current identification and credit cards. She felt around for the other object that would have to go, according to standard procedure. She wasn't sure if Daniel had already taken care of it for her and started to give up searching through the bag, until her hand bumped up against the familiar nylon scabbard. She pulled the Gerber commando knife out of the bag and stared at it for a moment. Less than thirty-six hours ago, this knife had sealed their involvement in Sanderson's plan. She promised herself that if the general had double-crossed them, she would plunge the same knife deep into his neck.

Satisfied that everything was ready, she started the car, bracing herself for a long drive. She wanted to get out of Massachusetts by sunrise. More importantly, she needed to put as much distance behind her as possible. She was used to running and didn't have any expectation that this aspect of her life would ever change. At least she had someone to run with.

Chapter Forty-Eight

5:42 a.m.
Portland, Maine

Justin Edwards' head pounded, and his mouth stuck together, completely lacking any recent, significant saliva production. He could barely separate his caked-together lips. His face felt a little numb, like he was drunk, but beyond this slight anesthesia, his entire body ached. What the fuck had happened?

He lifted his eyelids, but the effort required to keep them open was a near Herculean task for him, so he squinted for a few seconds, then closed them. He lay on his back, not wanting to turn his head, but he didn't recognize the room during the brief eyeball reconnaissance. He could tell it was a hotel, but his mind couldn't process any facts or data related to his presence in this room.

He opened his eyes a little further and could see the green glass of a wine bottle on the desk out of the corner of his eye. He managed to move his head far enough to examine the bottle through his hazy vision, evoking a splitting migraine. He could see two empty wine glasses on the desk next to the bottle, one stained around the rim with lipstick. He undertook the effort to move his hand across his body, which was no small task, and his hand dragged across his privates. He now realized that he was naked.

No memories of this room passed through his head, though he started to process other important aspects of his visit to Portland. Did he screw Jessica Petrovich, and let her go home? Shit, he was in trouble. How long had he been here? His thoughts were coming faster, but his body could not keep up. He glanced at his watch, which told him it was early, and at first this made him happy.

This sense of satisfaction faded within seconds, as the full scope of his situation started to sink in. He realized that his entire team had probably been at the house all night, while he had disappeared. What had he done?

He thought he remembered having dinner with Jessica Petrovich, but the memory was a fleeting blur. It was jarred out of his mind, along with every other rational thought, as a bright light flashed and the room exploded.

Several heavily armed black-clad men poured into the room, filling every corner. He could barely see them through the retinal image burn of the flash-bang grenade. The ringing cleared enough for him to hear what they were yelling.

"Clear! Clear! Room is clear! Agent Edwards appears unharmed! No sign of the suspect! Agent Edwards, are you all right?"

Edwards opened his mouth to answer, but decided against worsening his situation. Instead, he squinted his eyes, wishing he was dead as Sergeant Jimmy Haldron, Portland's SWAT commander, walked up and rested the butt of his rifle on the foot of the rumpled king-sized bed, a few inches from his bare leg. The impossibly tall Lieutenant Ken Moody followed, accompanied by Special Agent D'Angelo, who had a disgusted look on her face as she surveyed the room. Sergeant Haldron broke into a wide smile.

"Looks like party central in here. Let's get Agent Edwards a paramedic and some fluids. Lover boy had a rough night," he stated in a strong Maine accent.

Edwards sank back in despair. He had no idea what had happened to him the night before, but he was pretty sure it wouldn't help his career.

Chapter Forty-Nine

Audra Bauer, director of the Counterterrorism Center, contemplated Berg's proposal in her office. It represented a very interesting opportunity for the CIA, and he could have kept this to himself and possibly even run a sideline operation to support the whole idea.

"This was his idea? Nothing in return?"

"I wouldn't say nothing. We turn a blind eye to their operations throughout the world and provide resources where practical," Berg said, shifting in his seat.

"I don't know. Sanderson's crew killed two CIA employees this morning and burned down one of our safe houses. Not exactly a friendly act. What makes you think we can trust him?"

"Sanderson could have finished the job at the safe house, but he's extremely practical. He ran the Black Flag program right under our noses, in several countries, and his program closely resembled our Covert Operations Resident Program. In many ways it might be superior to our program. Regardless, if we play our cards right with Sanderson's new program, we stand to benefit. Deep intelligence and the ability to conduct sensitive operations at arm's length. Put a little more distance between the CIA and the dirty work."

Audra wasn't in love with the idea, but it truly wouldn't cost the CIA anything to try the relationship. They'd made deals with people far worse than General Sanderson, people with no sense of loyalty or honor. At least with Sanderson, they had a decorated soldier who had dedicated his life to defending America. Something was definitely wrong with him, and they'd have to keep that in mind, but there was very little downside, though they'd have to keep their distance until the FBI lost interest in Sanderson, which

267

could take a while. Based on yesterday's events, the Department of Justice's "number one son" took a beating on all fronts. Same with the Department of Defense, which worried her more than the FBI. The FBI was limited in its ability to reach overseas, but the Department of Defense didn't have this issue. They'd have to walk a fine line until the dust settled, but she agreed with Berg. Sanderson's new program represented a solid opportunity for the Counterterrorism Center.

"Tell me more about their Middle East program," she said.

"It supposedly extends beyond the Middle East. He calls it their Muslim Extremist branch. Operatives are trained specifically for placement in Afghanistan, Iraq, Germany, France, the Netherlands, the Russian Republics. A dozen Arab-descended operatives ready for deep immersion within one year."

"All right, I'm sold for now. I'd like to talk with General Sanderson," she said.

"He said he'd be in touch within a few weeks. I believe he has a national and international dragnet to evade," Berg said, and she nodded.

"This stays between us. I can't bring this up to the deputy, or anyone else," she said.

"Of course. We're good at keeping secrets," Berg replied.

"I'm really sorry about Keller," she said.

"I wish I could have dragged them both out of there, but Keller was dead, and I thought there might be a chance to save Claire," he lied and buried a few more secrets.

Chapter Fifty

Sharpe finished his presentation well aware that he had broken into a sweat. He hadn't slept in nearly thirty-six hours and had poured nearly all of his remaining energy into sounding coherent. Truthfully, he didn't care how he looked at this point. Immediately prior to the start of his performance, he had stared into the bathroom mirror at his puffy, bloodshot eyes and sallow face. He looked like shit, so a little sweat was just the icing on the cake for his unusual audience.

He had expected to brief his direct boss, Sandra Delgado, associate director for the National Security Branch, but the sensitive nature of Black Flag excluded her from this briefing. The director of the FBI, Frederick Shelby, sat in front of him, along with the deputy director, and they didn't want a watered-down briefing. Sandra's boss, Fred Carroll, executive director for National Security, sat toward the back of the room. Several individuals that remained unidentified filled in the gaps. He assumed they were from the White House, Justice Department and the Department of Defense. As the most junior person in the room, Special Agent Frank Mendoza stood near the door. Sharpe envied his position near the only escape route from this nightmare.

Frederick Shelby leaned back in his seat and pressed his hands together like he was about to start praying. He moved the joined hands to his nose and took in a deep breath. He exhaled deeply.

"Agent Sharpe, do you see any way to salvage HYDRA's investigation at this point?"

"Negative, sir. Each head of the HYDRA led my task force to a primary contact, and in some cases, a secondary contact within the Muslim community. We've been monitoring these contacts for several months, trying to penetrate one of the terrorist cells. As of yesterday, everything went cold. There was a flurry of electronic chatter yesterday morning, and now all of our sources are silent. The suspected cell in Cleveland disappeared yesterday afternoon. We had a full surveillance package in place, watching a group of three suspected Al Qaeda operatives. They vanished."

The director turned to Fred Carroll. "I want that group found and removed from U.S. soil immediately."

"Yes, sir," Carroll replied, who looked just as terrified as Sharpe felt.

"Well, this has been the worst couple of days for the FBI in my recent recollection, though it could have been worse, I suppose. I agree with Sharpe's assessment that we have been manipulated on an unprecedented scale. I can only imagine that General Sanderson hatched this plot years ago. Colonel Farrington's placement in the Pentagon twenty-six months ago was no coincidence," the director said, pausing for a few moments before continuing.

"Effective immediately, Special Agent Frank Mendoza will lead a much smaller Task Force HYDRA, in an attempt to salvage something from the task force's three years of hard work."

The words hit Sharpe like a sledgehammer. That was it for him. Summarily replaced by the director. Three years of backbreaking work, late nights, and an estranged family. Now he had nothing to show for it but a sidelined position somewhere unimportant and forgotten.

"Don't look so depressed, Agent Sharpe. You came into this room looking like a warmed-over pile of dog feces. Now you look worse," he said, and only the deputy director stifled a brief laugh, which drew a strained look from the normally deadpan serious director.

Sharpe didn't know what to say, or do at this moment. His career hung by a thread, or maybe it was already done. He had no idea. Director Shelby was feared by everyone within the FBI and was infamous for dismissing agents on the spot for failure or incompetence.

"I've heard good things about you from Agents Delgado and Carroll. Pretty much from everyone. Task Force HYDRA had great potential, and frankly, yesterday's events went beyond our control. General Sanderson is a grave national security threat. A dangerous rogue, who feels he is above our laws, and shows no hesitation to strike at the heart of the Pentagon, FBI…even the CIA. I don't believe for one second that the strike on that Georgetown safe house was conducted by Serbian Ultra-nationalists. That's a pile of crap higher than the Capitol Building. Sanderson is up to something big, and I want him stopped."

He paused and glared at Sharpe.

"Agent Sharpe, you are now in charge of a new task force dedicated to putting an end to General Sanderson's activities domestic and abroad. I want this man behind bars. Nobody tramples on the FBI without severe consequences. Not while I'm in charge. Work with Mendoza to keep the right people on HYDRA, and start working with your directors to form the new task force. ASAP. One of your first tasks will be to figure out who paid the Brown River contractor. The Serbians? I don't think so. We need to start making a few connections," the director said and stood up.

"Thank you, sir. We'll put Sanderson out of business," Sharpe said.

"That's my expectation. Sooner rather than later. All of your people are okay?" the director asked.

"Some of my best agents got banged up pretty bad, but they'll be fine, sir."

"Good. Nothing better than a bunch of talented, pissed off agents on a task force. Make sure you keep those people close," the director said and walked toward the door, which Mendoza had opened.

"Mendoza."

"Yes, sir," Agent Mendoza replied.

"Don't you have something more important to do than hold the door?" Director Shelby asked.

"Yes, sir. Thank you for the assignment," Mendoza said.

"Don't thank me, thank Sharpe. He went to bat for everyone on the task force, except himself. For the life of me, I don't understand why my agents can't recognize their own success. Get out of here," he said, and Agent Mendoza met Sharpe's eyes briefly before he scrambled out of the conference room ahead of the director.

Chapter Fifty-One

Daniel rested on a rocking chair and stared out at a vast sea of spruces and firs, which was occasionally interrupted by a cluster of red maples and beech. An unimproved dirt road exited the thick forest and ended in a large field next to an old, gray two-story barn. The field held a dozen cars, with license plates from several different states. He had only seen one car arrive since he had parked himself on the covered porch of the main house, a restored farmhouse. The man who got out of the car looked Hispanic, and Daniel figured he was a former operative assigned to Central or South America. The man had walked behind the main house to a new structure connected by a breezeway.

Daniel had been treated for his injuries by a doctor in the new building and had been fed a hot meal. He still felt dizzy from whatever neurotoxin Farrington had used to disable him. Sanderson had been smart to keep them separated while at this compound. He had seen neither Parker nor Farrington since he had arrived. He had awoken in a stolen car halfway to West Virginia and rode in dead silence with the two of them for the remainder of the trip. Only Parker broke the silence during the initial few minutes. He informed Daniel that Jessica was safely on her way to the compound.

Petrovich wondered how long this place had been in operation. From what he could tell, it hadn't served as a farm in at least two decades. The barn showed signs of permanent neglect, and the majority of the house's restoration efforts had been focused on the inside. Driving up the dirt road, his first impression was that Sanderson had somehow mismanaged Srecko Hadzic's involuntary donation of nearly one hundred million dollars. But upon further inspection, he could tell that the shabby initial appearance was intentional. Subtle camouflage for anyone that wandered down the wrong road and then somehow managed to turn down three more unmarked roads to stumble upon the farm. The compound was secluded, and at the moment, well guarded by patrols and a hidden security checkpoint along the dirt road, far from the house.

He heard the screen door open and glanced lazily in the direction of the front door. General Sanderson pushed the squeaky door further out and stepped down onto the wide planked porch. Out of instinct, Daniel tensed in preparation to stand respectfully for his commanding officer, but that was as far as it went. Still, it shot a blinding pain through his ribcage. His knee throbbed sympathetically as the muscles in his leg also tightened. He might reconsider the offer of pain medications once Jessica arrived, but until then, he wasn't about to dull his senses any further.

The general was dressed in old blue jeans and a flannel shirt, tucked in of course, his tan work boots planted firmly on the deck. He stared off at the dirt road, waiting for his flock to arrive. Without looking at Daniel, he began to talk.

"Feeling better?"

"About what?"

"Moping around doesn't suit you, Daniel. I've built you up as a legend around here, so I suggest you ditch the 'poor me' act and start showing your true colors," he said, burning a serious look into him.

"You're really a piece of work," Daniel said, shaking his head.

"Do you know the first trait I look for in my operatives?" Sanderson asked, leaning up against the weathered porch railing with both hands.

Daniel remained silent.

"Unhampered pragmatism. The test you took while rotting away on that tin can in the navy? It was designed by a team of psychologists to gauge this trait. On paper at least. When I saw your results, I thought there had been a mistake. Your score was off the charts, and I was skeptical. I thought you would turn out to be some disgruntled, sarcastic junior officer messing with the test...but you lived up to the results in person. Exceeded them, even. Others might call you a sociopath, however, I like the term unhampered pragmatist."

"Maybe you should patent it," Daniel said.

"Not a bad idea. I know you're pathologically practical, and you've already moved on. This is how your brain works. Now it's just a matter of figuring out exactly how we can work together moving forward. I need instructors, and you need a safe place to stay off the radar for a while. I have a nice warm weather location in mind, a new training site already built. You and Jessica can start a new life in a familiar setting. Not that phony suburban existence the two of you have suffered through for the past five years."

"Our so-called existence worked pretty well."

"Barely. I know all about your trips into the woods of Maine, with a trunk full of rifles, ammunition and survival gear. Vast tracts of land purchased in the middle of nowhere, so you could return to your natural state for a few weeks at a time and keep from killing everyone in your cubicle block. You kept your skills intact, which is not the behavior of someone who has abandoned their past. You still embrace the true nature we unlocked. I sense the same with Jessica."

"Who are you, Darth Vader?"

General Sanderson laughed. "Give my proposal some serious thought. Did you know that your graduating batch was the most successful in the program's history? One hundred percent survival rate, and they all volunteered to come back. I don't need staff psychologists to tell me that the success stemmed from your influence during training. I need this in the new program."

"I think your concept of the word 'volunteer' is different than mine."

"I know you don't want to believe it, but everyone else did volunteer to join the new program when asked."

"Except for the guy in New Hampshire. How many other nervous breakdowns do you have on your hands?"

"One exception to the rule. An outlier. We need you back, Daniel. I'm asking you to volunteer."

"We'll ask Jessica. If she shows," Daniel said.

"She's less than two hours away."

"Is she?" Daniel asked, and Sanderson shot him a strange look. "I am, after all, the most practical person you've ever met."

For the first time ever, Daniel sensed a momentary lapse of confidence in General Sanderson's face as he processed Daniel's last comment. He saw the general's eyes involuntarily dart to several locations along the tree line.

"In order to truly walk away from all of this," Daniel continued, "I would have to offer up a pretty big fish. A fish big enough to buy me the biggest immunity deal in history."

"You might be pathologically practical, but you're also one of the most loyal soldiers I have ever worked with," Sanderson said.

"You don't sound so confident," Daniel said, leaning back in his rocker.

General Sanderson glared at him for a few seconds and broke into another laugh.

"You're fucking relentless, Petrovich. I look forward to meeting Jessica in person. We have women in the program now, and I lack an experienced edged weapons instructor. Someone with recent real world experience," Sanderson said.

Petrovich stifled a laugh. "Was it that obvious?"

"To me it was. I only had one knife guy assigned to a target. You are not a knife guy, my friend. Far from it. I knew the two of you were onboard as soon as I saw the details in the news," Sanderson said.

"She was onboard. I tried to convince her that your mission had absolutely nothing to do with crippling Al Qaeda operations in the U.S., but she still believes what they sold her in Langley, even after the hell they put her through. I told her I had no intention of carrying out your plan, but she insisted that it needed to be done. That was my mistake…telling her about Parker's visit. I should have skipped town with her that afternoon. Sadly, she's desperately seeking some kind of redemption, and she still buys all of this nationalistic, Uncle Sam shit. A dangerous combination."

"We're all believers here, Daniel. We did the government a favor yesterday. The HYDRA investigation had been ongoing for nearly three years, and they had barely cracked the nut on Al Qaeda. This would have dragged on for another year or two, until it was too late, or somebody tipped off the terrorists. It was a sideshow, but a worthwhile production. I had to remove that file from government custody. We're rebuilding, and the file contained information that could immediately undermine the process. We're going to take the fight to the enemy in ways our government can't."

"And get rich in the process," Daniel replied.

"I never heard you complain about your 'finder's fee,' or whatever you called it to make yourself feel better. I didn't take a cut and walk away like you did. I reinvested every dime of that money into the program and kept it going for an entire year after government funding vanished. Anyway, we won't need to skim off the top anymore. We have the guaranteed backing of some very powerful and wealthy individuals."

"What do you get when you combine my unhampered pragmatism with your undying patriotism?" Petrovich asked.

"A damn effective team," Sanderson said.

"I was thinking more along the lines of body bags and unnecessary funerals. Some innocent people fell yesterday," Daniel said.

"I regret putting you through that. We had some unexpected surprises that led to some unfortunate casualties."

"Unfortunate casualties? You've been pulling strings for too long."

"I feel terrible about the police officer. Not much you could have done about that."

"Really? I appreciate your supposed concern, but you're not the one who saw her shield fall to the pavement along with most of her guts. I don't blame myself at all. I blame you and whoever was pulling the assassination team's strings."

"I've been in your shoes, Daniel. I don't need a lecture," Sanderson said.

Daniel shook his head and stared out into the forest. There was no use arguing with Sanderson. He was a user and a fanatic, who had grown way too accustomed to calling the shots from a distance. Part of him wished Jessica had gone to the feds and cut a deal.

"Is that a helicopter I hear?" Daniel said, cupping his hand to one of his ears.

"Very funny. I'll be inside, working on our exfiltration from the States."

Daniel smiled, and General Sanderson opened the screen door, shaking his head.

Out of nowhere, Petrovich fired a question into the air. "What kind of deal did you make with the CIA?"

"The kind that will keep them off our backs and give us an early warning system. Maybe some new recruits."

"What are you giving them in return?" Petrovich said.

"Capabilities. Resources. All untraceable back to them."

"I'd love to know how you pulled that off in less than thirty seconds."

"Remember when I said there was no such thing as a coincidence?"

Daniel shrugged his shoulders to indicate he really didn't care what Sanderson planned to say next.

"Every once in a great while...I'm proven wrong."

"Any chance of drink service for the legendary Daniel Petrovich? Maybe one of the newbies?"

"I'll have Colonel Farrington get right on it. Welcome back, Daniel."

"Apparently, I never left," Daniel muttered as the screen door slammed shut.

Epilogue

One Month Later

7:55 p.m.
Havana, Cuba

Dario and Natalia Russo relaxed in comfortable chairs on the rooftop bar of the Santa Isabel Hotel in Old Havana, which overlooked the tree-lined Plaza de Armas. A small marble-topped wrought iron table sat between them, holding two recently emptied martini glasses. The napkins placed under each sweating glass were soaked to the table with condensation. A warm sea breeze passed lazily through the uncovered bar, compliments of the nearby Gulf of Mexico, providing a small respite from the heat and oppressive humidity. Still not accustomed to the warmer climate, Dario glistened from persistent beads of sweat. Natalia looked unaffected by the heat, but welcomed the breeze.

The couple had arrived at the hotel thirty minutes earlier, drawing envious stares all the way to the small table at the balcony's edge. They were the kind of couple that you would expect to find adorning the sun deck of a private luxury yacht docked in Cannes, France. Dario's tanned skin contrasted against a crisp, white, short-sleeved shirt tucked loosely into dark tailored pants. On his left wrist, an expensive watch shined in the fading sun when he ran his hand through his jet-black hair. Natalia sparkled from two silver cuff bracelets and a thick silver jeweled aquamarine necklace. The straps of her black dress hung loosely over the exotic dark skin of her well-toned shoulders. Her black hair was pulled back into a tight ponytail, accentuating her strong, angular face, and her eyes were dark brown to match her Argentinian passport.

The Russos were native Argentinians, descended from Italian and Irish immigrants, which on the surface didn't attract any attention. Nearly seventy percent of Argentina's population shared some degree of European descent, mostly Italian. The fact that neither of them spoke fluent Spanish or Italian was something they needed to correct, and they'd have plenty of time to work with Sanderson's linguistic experts once they were in place at the new training compound.

Dario, or Daniel, squinted as the sun slipped below the top of the two-story stone walls of the Palacio de los Capitanes Generales on the far side of the Plaza, casting a shadow across the rooftop terrace. The temperature dropped a few degrees, and a golden amber light poured through the Plaza over the mix of vendors and tourists straddling the sides of the cobblestone streets.

A waiter dressed in an impeccable white suit placed a single martini with two olives on the table between the two of them, removing the empty glasses. Daniel detected a hint of olive juice shaken into the clear, chilled vodka, by the slightly darkened blur swirling through the drink. He glanced up at their waiter, expecting to see another dirty vodka martini descend from his tray.

"Compliments of the gentleman," the waiter said, gesturing with his hand in the direction of the terrace's far side.

Dario and Natalia both glanced at the lone gentleman sitting at the far corner table. He was dressed in khaki pants and a white oxford shirt, wearing a light brown baseball cap. His shirt reflected the burnt orange color of the sun, which poured around the Palacio and still bathed the corner of the rooftop. The man nodded to them and removed his sunglasses. The man's face didn't register with Daniel, but when he glanced at Jessica, he saw an emotional response.

"Oh my God," she muttered under her breath.

"*Sabes lo?*" Daniel said, emphasizing their need to speak Spanish in order to avoid unnecessary suspicion.

"*Sí.* Give me a minute...and watch the door," she whispered.

"*Bien. Otro martini,,*" Daniel said.

Jessica picked up a black purse and her drink from the table. She kissed Daniel on the forehead before she walked over to meet the mystery guest. The man looked like he was in his early fifties, trim, and handsome. Daniel wondered if this man had been one of her professors in Boston, or possibly Loyola. Her warning to watch the doors suggested he was a ghost from a more distant past, which left him uncomfortable.

He didn't expect any trouble in Cuba, but underestimating situations wasn't a luxury he could afford, or a habit he wanted to start. He analyzed every object and angle within his view, running multiple scenarios through his head like a computer, still keeping an eye on Jessica. The man didn't get up to greet her; instead, he motioned for her to join him at the table. She placed both the purse and the drink on the table in front of him, which told Daniel everything he needed to know about the situation.

The purse contained the only knife they carried, and she would never have placed it within the man's reach if she didn't trust him. He felt a little better about the situation, but didn't relax. After a long ten minutes for Daniel, Jessica and the man stood up from the table. Poised for action, and wishing they had ordered an appetizer that would have placed a knife on the table, Daniel watched as they hugged. The interaction looked cordial, and the man patted her on the back right before they separated. He watched Jessica walk back to the table, along with every other man on the crowded terrace.

Daniel still wasn't accustomed to the strong machismo attitude found in South and Central America, which apparently allowed men to gawk at women in front of other women. Jessica certainly didn't help matters with her choice of expensive outfits, or the confident energy she exuded simply walking from one table to another. A subtle change had washed over her as they settled into their new lives. She was bolder. Happier. More in her element.

He couldn't help but think that maybe General Sanderson had been right about her. There was still so much that she wouldn't discuss about her time in Serbia, before they had rediscovered each other during a chance encounter in a Belgrade nightclub. Daniel avoided the club scene with regularity, preferring to spend time in the field staring through his sniper scope. On that fateful night, he had relented under pressure from his boss, Radovan Grahovac, agreeing to join him in a few shots of rakija to "ease the memories." As soon as he saw her in the cramped, smelly club, everything finally made sense to Daniel. CIA.

She had disappeared from his life after a casual pizza dinner near Wrigley Field, three days after college graduation. Stoically fighting back tears, she announced that they would not be able to see each other anymore. Daniel had barely noticed the uncomfortable waitress push the check between two empty pilsner glasses and scoot clear of the scene. He remained stunned and speechless as she kissed him lightly on the cheek and told him that she loved him…but they could never be together.

He didn't follow her or try to figure it out that night. He had ordered another beer and sat at the bar, wondering exactly what had gone wrong that day. He was accustomed to her wild mood swings, usually connected to something related to her parents, but this felt different. When he called early the next morning, her roommate told him that she had abruptly walked out of the apartment with her bags to a waiting taxi. She had left no forwarding address and never said goodbye. She just simply vanished.

He couldn't lose her again. They would give this new life a try and look for a way out along the way. Folding into Sanderson's new organization had been the path of least resistance for both of them. For now.

Jessica placed her empty drink and purse on the table and sat down, forcing a smile.

"Everything all right?" he said, stroking her bare arm.

"I think so."

"Who was that?"

She glanced around for the waiter, who was attending to a nearby table, and leaned in to whisper, "That was my former agency mentor." Then she leaned back to speak in a normal tone. "A very good, trusted friend."

Daniel turned his head to examine the man, but found the corner table empty, and no longer in the faded sunlight. He looked to the door that led into the hotel. Gone.

"In Cuba? Must have been important to him. Should we be concerned?"

"No. He was tipped off by our new employer. Sounds like they have an agreement," she said and reached into her purse.

Daniel started to wonder about Jessica's mentor, and if it was possible that...His thought was interrupted by something she placed on the table.

"He told me you left it with him in Georgetown," she said and slid it across to him.

He stared in disbelief at the same cell phone he had thrown into a burning doorway, a little over a month ago. He took a long sip of his martini, contemplating how close he had come to tossing a grenade into the doorway instead.

"You've never met him before, have you?" she said.

"Not really, but we talked briefly."

She grasped his hand, and they quietly watched the last rays of light creep back along the walls of the buildings lining the Plaza. Daniel kept an eye on the street below, until he saw the brown ball cap and white shirt. He tracked the man walking up Calle Obispo, past a small street side café, and into the last beam of sunlight to infiltrate the Plaza. He saw Karl Berg stop and look over his shoulder at the rooftop terrace. Daniel raised his right hand a few inches from the table and acknowledged him. Berg nodded and walked out of sight, chasing the sunlight deeper into Old Havana.

The End

To continue the Black Flagged saga, grab *Black Flagged Redux* on Amazon

To be among the first to learn about new releases, exclusive content, future discounts, visit Steven's blog at StevenKonkoly.com

Work by Steven Konkoly

Fractured State Series—Dystopian, near future thrillers
"2035. A land in ruin. A state on the verge of secession.
A man on the run with his family."
Fractured State (Book 1)

The Perseid Collapse Series—Post-apocalyptic/dystopian thrillers
"2019. Six years after the Jakarta Pandemic; life is back to normal
for Alex Fletcher and most Americans. Not for long."

The Jakarta Pandemic (Prequel)
The Perseid Collapse (Book 1)
Event Horizon (Book 2)
Point of Crisis (Book 3)
Dispatches (Book 4)

The Black Flagged Series—Black Ops/Political thrillers
"Daniel Petrovich, the most lethal operative created by the Department of Defense's
Black Flag Program, protects a secret buried in the deepest vaults of the Pentagon.
A secret that is about to unravel his life."

Black Flagged Alpha (Book 1)
Black Flagged Redux (Book 2)
Black Flagged Apex (Book 3)
Black Flagged Vektor (Book 4)
JET BLACK (Novella)

Wayward Pines Kindle World:
GENESIS (Compilation of novellas set in Blake Crouch's Wayward Pines story)

About the Author

Steven graduated from the United States Naval Academy in 1993, receiving a bachelor of science in English literature. He served the next eight years on active duty, traveling the world as a naval officer assigned to various Navy and Marine Corps units. His extensive journey spanned the globe, including a two-year tour of duty in Japan and travel to more than twenty countries throughout Asia and the Middle East.

From enforcing United Nations sanctions against Iraq as a maritime boarding officer in the Arabian Gulf, to directing aircraft bombing runs and naval gunfire strikes as a Forward Air Controller (FAC) assigned to a specialized Marine Corps unit, Steven's "in-house" experience with a wide range of regular and elite military units brings a unique authenticity to his thrillers.

He lives with his family in central Indiana, where he still wakes up at "zero dark thirty" to write for most of the day. When "off duty," he spends as much time as possible outdoors or travelling with his family—and dog.

Steven is the bestselling author of ten novels and several novellas, including a commissioned trilogy of novellas based on the popular Wayward Pines series. His canon of work includes the popular Black Flagged Series, a gritty, no-holds barred covert operations and espionage saga; The Perseid Collapse series, a post-apocalyptic thriller epic chronicling the events surrounding an inconceivable attack on the United States; and The Fractured State series, a near future, dystopian thriller trilogy set in the drought ravaged southwest.

He is an active member of the International Thriller Writers (ITW) and Science Fiction and Fantasy Writers of America (SFWA) organizations.

You can contact Steven directly by email (stevekonkoly@striblingmedia.com) or through his blog:

StevenKonkoly.com